I0613076

Aquatic Investigations

A GPSA Trilogy

Jodi Kendrick

SoulGate Publishing

Dragon Island

Dragon Heat

Enchanted Ardor

Wish

EveL Worlds : FUCN'A

Tough Nut
Diamond in the Ruff
Honeyed Nut
Gorilla in the Hiss
FUCN'A Collection One
Pedigree Collection

Finely Aged

Dragon Steel

Global Paranormal Security Agency

Awakened
Surfacing
Polestar
Aquatic Investigations
Prowler

The Kindred Chronicles

Healer
Mercenary

The Soaring Dragon Chronicles

Return Flight
Changeling

The Global Paranormal Security Agency

The Global Paranormal Security Agency is a hidden investigative group dedicated to bridging the paranormal and human worlds to keep everyone safe.

Protect. Defend. Seek Justice.

AWAKENED

GLOBAL PARANORMAL SECURITY AGENCY

JODI KENDRICK

AWAKENED

Ancient ocean legend, Lirikai of the Barra'kidai has awakened. She must discover if she is the last of her kind and if she can adapt to find her place in this new world.

Called in by the aquatic division, of the Global Paranormal Security Agency (GPSA), dragon shifter Carson Perenga investigates murder victims left on the beach, punctured with mysterious bite marks.

When Lirikai rolls out of the ocean surf asking after the Goddess in the ancient language, Carson questions whether she is connected to his case or if she was sent to him by his lost Goddess.

After centuries alone, how can Carson and Lirikai overcome their ingrained sense of duty and purpose to find common ground?

ONE

AT NINE A.M. AGENT Carson Parenga wandered into the Director's office, coffee in hand, greeting fellow agents he knew and politely acknowledging new faces. The red-eye flight from his little island had him jet-lagged and bleary eyed, but Maeda had been insistent over the phone when he called him to come in. His gaze drifted over his Global Paranormal Security Agency colleagues.

Jack Maeda handed Carson a beige file folder. "Agent Ortega called us, asked for you specifically. Two victims, their bodies mutilated and left on the beach. A local pawn shop owner and a spiritual leader of the downtrodden. Seems the good minister works with the vulnerable population."

"Mutilated how?" It was too damned early for this conversation. Carson sipped his coffee. From the corner of his eye, he caught Willow staring at his cup, longing clear on her face before she turned to talk to an unknown redhead. That must be Olivia, the new recruit.

"Bite marks from some large creature. But there's also a symbol carved into the back of the victim's heads. Locals can't decide between a cult or a rabid animal of the large kind."

Definitely too early. "Great."

"Next flight's at one."

Carson sighed.

Chase and Kai leaned in to peek at the crime scene photo half out of the folder. "Better you than us, man," Kai said.

"Thanks."

Carson's attention was drawn to Mike and Risa, at the mention of Back Water Bay and Ursanis. Risa was selling Willow on their mission to the arctic.

"Aww, damn, I'll trade you!" Carson grinned.

Willow quickly shot down the offer.

"I always get the messy cases. I'm considering retirement."

Director Maeda glanced up at Carson, "Not yet, old man, you still have plenty of work to do."

"Old man? What are you, thirty? Thirty-five?" Kai asked him.

"Something like that."

Maeda snorted.

CARSON STEPPED INTO THE sun-warmed water tumbling over his feet. The firm beach sand fell away as the surf sucked it back toward the ocean, luring him. Fiberglass board in hand, he tipped it forward and launched himself over the surface of the water, riding toward the ocean haze beyond the edge of the pier. As the sea paused and began its inward press, his powerful arms worked through it, keeping the surfboard from being pushed back, just until it shifted again, luring him farther out.

After several intense days reviewing the case, Ortega had suggested a swim, recommending this location for its waves. Driving from the precinct to the beach, the thirty second news break on the radio had recapped the day's progress. Journalist's wife wanted as a suspect in her husband's disappearance, police looking for the public's help in locating her. Second body found on beach, some locals fear large wild animal while others suspect a rise in local cult activities. Small congregation mourn the loss of their spiritual leader, a vigil will be held later in the evening. Still no word on the twelve young women and two young men gone missing from the community and surrounding areas along the coast. Politicians going head to head over funding cuts and gas prices again on the rise.

He needed the peace.

The farther the ocean pulled him out, the faster the responsibilities of the world rolled off his shoulders, until all he could hear was the roar of the surf and the cry of the seagulls riding the winds over head.

This case wasn't going to be a light beach walk. He floated for a long time beyond the end of the pier, the water tugging on the tether attaching the surf board to his ankle. It was the last irritant of the land world to be shed. Feeling secure that he was far enough out of sight of land to be forgotten by any beach bystander, he unfastened the ankle strap and instead tied it to a chain strung around one of the thick posts supporting the pier.

The seagull that had been keeping pace with him cried out, and he let himself drop down below the surface, ignoring the power of the surf rushing around the pier supports. Anchoring a foot against the post, he pushed himself farther out to sea, catching the current.

Then he shifted. The water around him rippled as his energy writhed through the ocean water. A moment later, Carson no longer existed. In his place floated a large, clawed, reptilian creature.

With a swish of his powerful tail, he was much farther out to sea than he could have ever paddled in human form. Muscles bunched and released in another surge out into the depths of the water, away from humanity and its complexities.

He needed to think.

Ana had been right to call him in.

His grief and frustration slid away with the fathoms. Faces of mangled victims dissipated as the ocean cleansed them from his memory—for a time. The simplicity of predator-prey cycled through him. Not the same as the predator-prey of humanity; doing evil things not for subsistence, but for self-pleasure and gain.

Nothing to do with survival, and everything to do with games of power and control.

Pushing hard through the water, diving deeper, seeking the silence of the deepest parts of the ocean.

Deeper still as the pressure encased him. Leveling out the dive, and sliding along, seeking.

Seeking what?

He stopped pushing through the water and floated. Thoughts drifted through his mind; he just let them tumble as he remained suspended in the cold darkness of the ocean. Letting the energy of the ocean work its way over his thick scale-covered skin, seeping into his pores, pushing the trauma and stress out of his being. An osmosis: Release the depravity of humanity, intake the simplicity of the sea, like tidal surges scrubbing him clean.

Goddess?

After a long moment, with nothing but silence shifting around him, he projected the question outward. Once, and then once more as a mental roar. Would she hear him, wherever she may be? She hadn't answered in a very long time.

He was tired after centuries of guardianship over the humans. Despite looking to be in his mid-thirties, the director referred to him as 'old man' and ribbed him about retirement for a reason. In the moment, the idea was very appealing.

He wanted to 'retire' as his director, Jack Maeda, would say.

He drifted over a region of underwater caves, 'listening' in barely suppressed desperation for the Goddess' energy signature.

He felt nothing.

Whether slumbering or awake, she was not anywhere near this aqua-territory.

After a few hours, he made his way back toward the surfboard attached to the pier, his mind clearer after the swim.

AN ELECTRIC SCENT DRIFTED past Lirikai's nostrils as the current eddied around her. Tugging, enticing her from the blackness of her cave.

The scent of power.

Curiosity encouraged awareness. Other scents had tried to pull her from her deep dormancy over the centuries but were never enough to awaken her. Not fully.

This scent wasn't the appetizing scent of prey that teased her hunger. For a long time, she ignored it. This was different, and yet familiar.

In her human form, it would have been like a deeply forgotten scent attached to a vital memory. A particular meadow or seaside location where a life changing event occurred.

It curled through the current sliding over her fins and scales, wrapping itself around her. Flexing the muscles of her body, the water slid under the edges of the razor-edged scales like silk over bared flesh, making it thrum.

Lured, her fins began working, her tail weaving through the water, propelling her toward the mouth of the cave.

She followed the trail, and more scents encircled her. Then the vibrations of the ocean worked their way through her layers. Slowly, she acclimated, moving as though tethered to the drifting scent of power that had captured her attention.

As sleep fell away, coherent thought filled the space despite the fog of deep ocean pressure.

What was calling her?

How much time had passed?

Had the Goddess also awakened from her slumber so much longer than her own?

Did any of her sisters still exist? Had they survived the centuries?

On emerging from the cave, she began to drift toward the lightness of the surface, tasting, smelling, feeling the ocean along the way.

She ignored the urge to sink back into the darkness of the cave.

Her senses were assaulted by alien scents and vibrations. The ocean felt wrong, tainted, sick.

Through it, the thread of that enticing scent tickled her dorsal fin, teasing, promising something worthwhile if she just followed along.

Curiosity drew her out and set her course.

Other, more familiar scents began to work their way through the ocean water, awakening the hunger.

Hunger, she knew. And a feast she could smell.

Her lithe body moved through the currents like a silver flash of lightening following a branch to its filament.

Curiosity and delicious hunger.

TWO

Lirikai followed the scent to shore. The power signature drifted in and out of massive pier posts. She was so close to shore, the power of the surf enticed her toward the beach.

Hunger overrode control and curiosity, especially now that the trail seemed to end here. Too many years without indulging in a hunt and she could feel the urge to frenzy creeping over her.

She drifted back and away beyond the catch of the pier, vying for control and coherent thought.

Enough!

She snapped her powerful jaws in irritation, and the protruding uneven spears of teeth vibrated from the impact and rippled back up into her skull.

She needed to feed on something before following the delicious scent that called to her. After a moment more, she turned back to deeper ocean to fill her belly.

And to figure out if she remembered her human form enough to reshape herself.

Her jaws closed over several unwary fish. She swallowed, oblivious to their frantic flipping and twisting to escape. Memory of the shape and feel of legs and arms formed in her mind. *Ah yes.*

Hair, ears, breasts, fingers and toes.

Another swallow of wriggling fish.

Clothing.

A memory of one of the last times she emerged and the frenzy of the villagers that followed. Half had thought her a water demon luring their men away for wanton endeavors. The other half dropped to her feet enthralled naming her their water goddess.

Not quite right on both accounts, but not too far off the mark on both accounts, either.

She was a servant of the Goddess and yet a demon to those inciting her wrath.

In the end, that last time, she had eaten a couple of humans from both camps. Work done, she returned to the ocean.

Showing up naked on shore never began the relationship with the right tone.

She floated a while longer, her fins and tail waving in the current.

There was no sign of the Goddess, no call, no signal, no trace. Only the tingle of power.

Power enough to awaken her from centuries of slumber. She still hadn't been able to recall what was familiar about the signature, but there was something. She hadn't found the right nerve yet. It was just at the edge of her skull, tickling the senses along her bones. She wriggled, trying to dispel the sensation and return her focus to the nearby beach.

Right now, she had to recall her human form, and do her duty hunting the delicious scent of predator-prey. The savoury taste of one that would inflict terrible deeds on another for no purpose but to find pleasure in it. They were the ones that tasted the best.

With a flick of her head, her jaw caught another cluster of passing fish from their school.

This was what the Goddess had created her for—created her, and her sisters, to do. The Goddess would answer the prayers of her followers, and the Barra'kidai would seek her vengeance, rewarded with the tastiest of villains.

If she were in her human form, she would be nigh on drooling.

With a surge, she threw herself into the wave rushing toward the beach, and with the right mental concentration, rolled out of the surf and over the pasty sand with shapely limbs, and soft flesh rosy with the glow of the setting sun.

The beach wasn't abandoned, but nearly so at this time of day. She remained as she was, collecting the muscle memory required to move the gangly limbs in the right way to get her up and moving away from the ocean.

The dimming light masked her nudity, as she found her footing and moved back toward the shelter of the pier to get a sense of what was around her, and the most effective source of clothing.

It didn't take long for a retreating family to drop a towel unnoticed. Once they were far enough away, she awkwardly ran out to grab it and returned to the shadows of the pier supports before one of the humans returned to the area realizing they'd left something behind.

Hidden, she observed the humans. Their clothes, their manner, the buildings along the road above the beach.

From this distance, she could see that the world had changed a great deal while she slept. Far more than it usually did.

Wrapping the thick linen securely around herself, she stepped out from the shelter of the pier, and moved purposefully toward the humanity at the other side of the beach shelf.

That power signature was out here somewhere.

And there would be plenty of food to sustain her between then and now. She could taste them in the air already.

Her mouth did indeed water.

CARSON PULLED THE LAST strap, securing his surfboard set in the back of his jeep. The wind was picking up, and he didn't want to lose his favourite board. He'd gone through the effort of checking it through 'oversized' luggage through two airports.

Parked in the sandy lot above the beach, he was tempted to go back out, for just a little longer. He stood a moment, feeling the tug, watching the waves, when he noticed a figure roll out of the surf and unsteadily make for the shelter of the pier supports.

Pulled back to the rolling ocean, he dropped his keys into the pocket of his cargo shorts, disengaged his feet from his flip-flops and let his feet dig into the sand one step at a time.

The call of a mother to her teenage son about a forgotten towel, and his reply that he couldn't find it, drifted over the rising wind and hush of each wave coming faster.

"... It isn't there, Ma."

The mother's disbelieving voice chattered about selective obliviousness and stomped over to where the family had been set up.

He smirked when she came away empty handed. One for the kid. A win for all kids around the globe, hearts rejoicing.

By now his toes were caked with wet sand, anticipating the flutter of water that would encase them. Once achieved, he turned and strolled in the direction of the pier. Maybe that elusive towel had been blown in that direction, although he didn't think the wind was quite strong enough for that yet.

Moving closer to the shadowy space, his pace slowed as he squinted into the shaded area. His instincts tugged at his skin and the hair on his arms and scalp rose.

He stopped as though taking a moment to watch the sea again and made a quick surveillance of the beach. By now, with the incoming storm, it was nearly abandoned.

Turning his attention back in the direction of the pier, his body jerked upon seeing a figure standing several dozen feet away. He blinked. It was a woman, wrapped in a beach towel. Her wet hair clung to her shoulders, and her eyes were glued to him.

His instincts sang louder, coursing the blood through his body faster.

The figure that rolled out of the surf?

Was she the one he'd been hunting?

They stared at each other across the distance. He drew in a breath and stepped forward, body taut. "May I be of assistance, Ma'am?"

Her head tilted back as she stepped toward him. She looked as though she were scenting the air.

His body tensed, ready in case she proved to be more of a threat than she appeared to be. As a non-human, he knew better.

She was close enough now he could see the smile spread on her lips. Clouds scudded across the sky, billowed by the storm winds. The rising moon illuminated her, and his breath fled.

The moon silvered her near-translucent flesh; ocean beads glimmered along her limbs and ends of her hair. Her curvy body seemed to be naked beneath the beach towel which covered her torso and hips, but left her lean legs visible for appreciation. She had full lips, a small nose, and incredibly pale eyes with unusual pupils that marked her as not truly human.

Her voice, when she spoke, was a soft rasp and the words were in a language he'd not heard in centuries.

She frowned when he failed to answer.

"Goddess?"

He remembered that word. Finding the mobility, he inclined his head, searching for the forgotten words to respond, letting her make the approach. He still didn't know what her intent was.

And if she was old enough to communicate in this language, Goddess on her lips, he couldn't predict anything. Except maybe trouble.

This wasn't how he'd envisioned ending his long, long week.

THREE

LIRIKAI STARED AT THE man, sensing his mind at work. She could smell the Goddess on him, and the sea. She was sure this was the scent that had awakened her from her dark cave.

She stepped closer. "Who are you?"

Why was he here?

Why had she been compelled to follow him?

She stepped closer still. He tensed.

She frowned at his wariness.

"Goddess?"

A thrill swept through her at his expression. He was adorable as confused recognition swept over him. She watched him struggle for words. He inclined his head.

"It's been so long since I have spoken to another soul, let alone another of the Goddess' blessings," she said with another step.

His hand came up, as though to hold her at bay. Haltingly, he said, "I struggle to recall the ancient language."

She nodded. She'd been asleep so long, she struggled to recall speech at all. It had been so long since she'd assumed human form.

His gaze studied her form. "You need clothing."

Looking more closely at what he was wearing, her hand moved to the thick linen she'd wrapped around herself. "Yes".

The wind gusted harder, flattening the linen against her body, teasing the edge from unraveling around her.

"Come?" he held a hand out to her. "My car is close."

She didn't take his hand, but smiled, and gestured for him to lead the way to wherever he was proposing they go.

On reaching the level ground above the beach, she hesitated.

He offered her the spare footwear he'd left in the sand, then rummaged for spare clothing in the back of a large metal cart of sorts. The clothing was like what he was wearing, and she donned them while he waited with his back turned.

He opened the door for her, let her step in and settle on the seat, then closed it and headed around to the driver's side.

Showing her the seatbelt, she mimicked him.

As soon as he started the engine, and pulled out onto the road, her right hand gripped the bar attached to the door beside her, but she remained otherwise impassive.

Inside, her mind was racing. She barely remembered the English she'd learned the last time she was awake in the world, and it certainly didn't sound like what little she heard now.

And this wagon! Incredible! She wondered if it could go faster than the light sailing ships she and her sisters used to race.

The roads were smooth, and they moved quickly through the city. She took it all in. The buildings, the shops, how people were dressed, snippets of exchange, music. Oh, the music! Everything had changed so much while she slept.

FOUR

CARSON LED THE WOMAN into the station. During the ride, he'd watched her from the corner of his eye. She took everything in. Flinched at nothing, following.

She said it had been a long time since she'd spoken to anyone. How long?

What was she? Not human.

He thought he knew what she was, or at least a strong suspicion. But he couldn't be sure.

Even now, she observed everything around her, taking it all in.

Was she somehow connected to the case he'd been called in for? He'd gone to the ocean to meditate, and this woman had mysteriously appeared on the beach.

He shot her another glance, ensuring she still followed him.

He knew looks meant nothing when it came to predators. Especially if she was a child of the Goddess.

He had to get her to Analiese Ortega's office for assessment and integration with the Global Paranormal Security Agency if it turned out to be necessary.

Wading through the press of noise and bodies in the bullpen toward the quiet of the office doors at the back of the room, he glanced again to check that she still cared to follow him, despite knowing nothing of where they were going or why.

She wasn't directly behind him.

She stood in the center of the room. His shirt and shorts hung loose on her, but she held herself as though she were a sea goddess. His mind conjured the image of her in a peplos. The noise dimmed somewhat as several men stopped talking to stare at her. Her eyes slid from person to person, body tense, nostrils twitching almost imperceptibly.

Something wasn't right, Carson moved toward her as her eyes silvered, pupils shifting to slits.

He reached for her. The expression on her face as he stepped into her sphere would have terrified a lesser being. He could feel his scales threatening to erupt over his skin in self-protection. Despite that, he stepped in close, blocking her view of the others in the room.

She blinked, nostrils flaring. Her eyes changed from wild and alien back to normal human eyes.

"Are you alright?" He asked in the old tongue.

She nodded, leaning toward him, inhaling. "They make me very hungry."

Hungry?

"I'll get you food."

She turned her head to the left, licking her lips. "That one smells tasty."

He followed her line of sight. "No, no, uhm, you don't want that one." He slipped his hand around hers and drew her back toward the office door. "Come this way, I'll get you food," he promised. He was going to have to call Jack. The director would want to hear all about this new discovery.

She resisted the tug of his hand, leaning toward another perp, "This one will do."

He pulled her, lightening fast, in through the door and slammed it shut. "You can't eat them." He said.

"Why not? They smell delicious, they're perfect."

"Excuse me?" a voice floated toward them from behind the large desk.

"Analiese, Hi, this is..." he turned his question to Lirikai, speaking in the old tongue, "What are you called?"

"Lirikai."

"She mentioned the Goddess," he said in English to Ana.

"Oh?"

He heard Ana's chair scrape the floor, her footsteps brought her close. "Lirikai?"

At the call of her name, she turned her attention to Ana, who smiled at her, but she remained mute.

"How may we help you, Lirikai?"

"Help?" Lirikai repeated, "Wake. Hungry... Now," she said in broken English.

Ana's eyes slid to Carson and back to Lirikai, "What do you eat?"

"Eat..." There was a long pause as Lirikai searched for words. "Human food, but bad people taste best." she turned her head back toward the door, licking her lips again with longing.

"I see, won't you sit?" Ana's hand swept toward the chairs placed in front of her desk, then walked around back toward her own seat, lifted the handset of the phone and poked a pre-set number "Freddie, grab the most palatable food from the cafeteria...ASAP," she added, her eyes lifted back to Lirikai, as she retrieved her seat and replaced the phone.

Carson waited for Lirikai to sit, then took the other chair, between her and the door, stretching out his long legs to fill the space. "I found her on the beach about half an hour ago."

Ana's brows shot up, "Fast work, Carson."

He shrugged, "She rolled out of the ocean, no clothes, speaking the ancient language and asking about the Goddess. Thought she might need your handy dandy 'Assessment and Integration' skills."

"You think she might be tied to your case?"

"Sometimes the Goddess delivers in strange ways. Most often not and it's just coincidence. In this case?" He shrugged again, "Gut says she is."

Ana reached into one of her desk drawers, and placed a digital recorder on her desk, switching it on.

"Lirikai," Ana said, drawing the woman's attention back to her.

Lirikai had been looking at the room decor, seemingly unengaged. At the sound of her name, her eyes snapped back to Ana.

"Are you comfortable communicating in English?"

"English different now."

"We can make do, the old language is coming back to me, ask what you want to know, and we'll sort it out," Carson said.

"Why did you bring me here?" Lirikai suddenly asked Carson in the old tongue.

"You indicated you'd been away a long time. I'm a member of the Global Paranormal Security Agency. We—Ana can help you adjust to the world. A lot has changed."

"I can go back to the sea."

"What brought you here?" he asked her, something pulled at him.

Carson could have asked her all this earlier, but his instinct had been to bring her in to see Ana, who listened without interruption, despite their conversing in the old language. He'd review the recording with her later.

"You did."

Carson's lips twitched."You came out of the ocean?"

She nodded."Why?"

"You."

This time he frowned. "Explain."

"I slept a very long time, in a cave along the ocean floor. Your scent drifted into my cave. You smell of the Goddess, and something else—I'm not sure what. I followed the trail."

Carson suppressed a thrill. Was she a mermaid? He considered his next questions. "When were you last awake?"

She didn't answer right away. A frown pulled at her forehead before she answered, "Centuries, I think. I can't be sure."

"Centuries!" he said in English, his gaze drifting to Ana. Quickly returning to the old language, "But why?"

Lirikai dropped her gaze to her hands. The moment dragged out. When she answered, her voice was tight, "I was alone. The Goddess was gone for a very long time. My sisters were disappearing. Some were finding mates and returning to life on land. Others were killed in battles. Too many killed." Her fingers clasped together. She looked up, her gaze steady on his face, despite the unexpressed sorrow in her eyes.

"I'm sorry," he whispered.

There was a brisk knock on the door before it jerked open. A young man stepped in carrying a tray of food that he dropped on Ana's desk with a clatter, then rushed back out of the room, jerking the door closed again.

Lirikai eyed the food. "Why won't you let me take one of them?" she jerked her head toward the door. "There are so many. I'll take him to the ocean, no mess."

Carson hastily grabbed the tray, depositing it on her thighs. "We don't eat perpetrators. At least not anymore." He said in English, then added "That's why you're here. So, we can integrate you into modern society."

"Or I could just return to the ocean and not bother," she lifted the plastic spoon frowning at the food that dropped from it, splattering back onto the plate. "This is edible?"

"Usually."

She sighed, took a bite and swallowed. She looked as though she were in pain. She dropped the spoon, "I'd rather eat more fish." She started to rise, but Carson extended his hand to take the tray back and quickly placed it back on the desk.

Ana reached out with a finger, pushing the tray as far to the edge of the desk as possible without it falling over. "Why do you want to eat the people in the other room?"

"That's what we do. The Goddess created us to devour the vilest among us." She answered in the old language, and Carson translated, the words coming more naturally now.

"How could you know who is who?" Ana asked her, reaching for her notepad and pen.

"I smell them. The viler their intentions and deeds, the more delicious they smell and taste."

Ana's face paled when Carson relayed Lirikai's response.

"Do you eat all of them? When was the last time you... ate someone?" Carson asked, rising from his chair and looking out of the office window into the bullpen.

"We don't eat the heads, they are for the Goddess. Not in a very long time," She sighed, they all heard her stomach growl as she licked her lips again.

"Not the heads." Carson's voice was low, he rubbed a hand over his face. He turned to look down at Lirikai. "Would you tell me if you had eaten someone recently?"

She shrugged, unconcerned with the question. "If I had, the scent drifting in from the other room would not be making me salivate so much. You did not tell me why eating the guilty is not permitted. It is my right to feed. The Goddess created me for this purpose."

"You said you went to sleep because the Goddess had gone away for a long time?" he waited for her nod. "I have been around a long time too, and have not felt the Goddess' presence since soon after I was created. Either she's gone or she is dormant, like you were. Her power no longer rules here. We now live by the rule of law—Human law, which does not permit cannibalism."

Lirikai got to her feet. "I am not a cannibal. I do not eat my own kind."

Carson's hands went up in a placating gesture, which didn't seem to calm her at all.

"Move, I wish to leave."

"You must understand, the world is different. You may not eat humans."

"I will eat whom I please," her voice rolled toward him.

Lowering his hands, he braced his feet, planting himself firmly between Lirikai and the door. He heard Ana's seat shift as she pushed herself back toward the wall.

"Just because your scent roused me from slumber, does not mean I will be subservient to your wishes, youngling."

Youngling? He nearly laughed but had enough self-preservation not to. She was indeed far more ancient than he was, but he still didn't know exactly what she was or how dangerous she could be. Given that she was created in the time before he was and had been dormant for who-knew how many centuries, he wouldn't push her too hard until he knew more about her. He wouldn't risk Ana's life, or the lives of those in the next room.

The longer he blocked her path, the angrier she became. The energy rippled toward him, and he could feel his scales forming. Her eyes had gone to slits again, and this time she opened her mouth, large teeth began to grow and elongate from the delicate perimeter of her lovely mouth.

The door jerked open again behind him, "Jesus!" Freddie squeaked, slamming the door closed again.

"Who?" Lirikai demanded.

Carson kept his eyes on Lirikai.

"Move."

He shook his head.

Lirikai growled, stepping forward.

Ana's phone rang, startling Lirikai. She snapped it up, "What?" After a moment, she put the phone down again. "Freddie said they found another one, Carson."

"Shit." He ran a hand over his forehead, eyes still glued to Lirikai's angry face. He thought quickly on what she'd told them, eyes lingering on her teeth. "You said about the heads, that 'they are for the Goddess'."

She didn't move.

"Would you help me?" He forced his body into a less defensive posture, gambling.

Curiosity flashed in her eyes as they returned to their human color.

He waited another moment.

Her teeth receded and she looked fully human again. Ana's sigh of relief spoke for both of them.

"I'm here to work on a murder case... it involves heads and unusual bite marks."

The corner of her mouth went up, "If I help you, do I get to-"

"No," he cut in quickly, "But I know a great steak place—steak is beef."

She pulled a face.

"Trust me. It's the best."

Suspicion warred with her earlier curiosity, though finally she nodded.

He glanced at Ana, who sagged in her chair. He blew out a breath. "Shall we go have a look at my work station?"

Lirikai picked up the abandoned tray and jammed several spoonfuls of the mystery food into her mouth, washing it all down with the entire cup of water. "Your cook should be eaten for that slop."

Her eyes twinkled and he laughed.

FIVE

LIRIKAI FOLLOWED CARSON BACK through the open area, doing her very best to ignore the aroma of the exploiters, rapists and murderers. They all smelled so good. But she had decided to help him, and it seemed eating the guilty was now forbidden.

Maybe later, she would hunt and lure one away. He would never know. There would be nothing left for anyone to find. As it should be.

So, with curiosity, she followed him into another room, smaller than the one belonging to his colleague Ana, but this one was far less clean. There were stacks of documents everywhere and images stuck to the walls and windows. Her hand reached for a stack, her fingers sliding over the surface of it. So smooth and fine.

"It's not that file," Carson said over his shoulder, then turned and handed her a similar one.

She held it across her upturned palms, unsure what to do with it. With care, she balanced the items on one hand, and lifted the top leaf. "What is this?"

He gave her a blank look, "It's a case file. Oh- Jesus, I forgot. Can you read?"

Lirikai looked down at the pages. The lines of script just that. She didn't recognize the characters. "Not this."

He ran a hand through his hair, snatched the folder up from her hands and smacked it down on top of the stack on his desk, "Here," he said, flipping it open. Her heart bounced up in to her throat at how carelessly he handled such precious materials.

Snapping several sheets over, he spread out several with images on them. She gasped. They were so lifelike! She looked up at him; he stared back at her expectantly. "Incredible," she breathed, hesitant to touch it.

Carson jabbed a blunt finger on the surface, "This— do you know this?"

Her eyes slid to where he pointed.

The image was of a mangled man, puncture parks on random parts of the headless body.

"Sloppy," she said.

"Sloppy?" he took a step back.

"Messy and wasteful, if he was a bad man."

"And if he wasn't?" Carson's voice took on an odd tone.

"Then unfortunate, and he should be mourned by his people."

"I see."

Lirikai squinted at the bite marks. "Why would you waste your vellum on such images? Wouldn't art be a better investment?"

"Vellum? The paper? It's easily made and cheap now," he said, pushing through several other sheets, "What of this one?"

She was taken aback by his dismissive attitude but turned her attention to the new image he pointed at.

There it was.

Her breath locked in her throat, and her stomach flipped.

The head, or rather the back of a very roughly detached head. It was inelegant. Whoever had done the detaching had struggled, but the lower part of the back of the head, where the skull meets the spine, had the hair shaved away to make room for a symbol carved into the flesh.

The door jerked open, the one called Freddie popped his head into the room, eyes widening when he saw Lirikai. His gaze shot to Carson, "Got a location on the new body, boss wants to know when you're going?"

"Now."

Freddie disappeared again.

"Does he always do that?" "Yep," he said, sliding his documents together again, and tucking the lot under his arm, then motioning her toward the door. "Let's go."

Carson snapped a colored paper from Freddie's extended hand as they made their way back through the crowded area toward the exit. "Car is this way," he said, walking through the open space of other cars of varying shapes and sizes. She climbed in while he tucked the sheets into a pocket attached to the back of his seat. While he situated himself, she looked around at the buildings, the lanterns, the sounds and smells of the air. Everything was so different. It truly was another world she had awakened to.

Could she adjust this time? Did she want to? There had always been changes to adapt to on awakening from a hibernation. But this one had been the longest in her lifetime.

She could always return to the sea. For now, Lirikai would make the most of this new era. She watched Carson closely as he made the car come alive and drove them out onto the road. Clearly, he'd adapted. She could too, if she chose to stay land-side.

If.

If she had a reason to. Her gaze swept Carson's profile, admiring his clean features, the nicely defined muscles under his shirt and his long legs. Away from the bustle of the crowded building, she could feel the undertone of his energy sweeping over her aura. She closed her eyes, reveling in the sensations of the wind on her face and hair, and his aura mingling with hers.

"What do you make of the pictures?"

She opened her eyes. "The body and head?" She shrugged, although he hadn't taken his gaze from the road ahead of them. "What happens to the person that did these things?"

"We will catch them. Then interrogate them to understand what happened and why, then imprison them."

"This is the human way?"

"For the most part, yes. But if this is one of our people - like you and me, as I suspect it is, then we must try to compromise between human law, and our own ways." They came to a stop and he turned his gaze on her. "The world is a very different place now, Lirikai. Our world, everything changed while you were sleeping." His expression was one of concern as he regarded her.

They were moving again, and he turned his eyes back to the road. Her stomach twisted at the loss of his attention.

The smell of the sea grew stronger. They turned onto a road that ran parallel to the ocean, traveling for what seemed to her to be a long distance. The landscape flew past them, as though she swam at her full speed. The moon illuminated the water rippling in the distance, hills and trees rolled past. Other cars intermittently blinded her with their lights, and they whipped past them. She closed her eyes, lulled by the motion of the car.

Her eyes snapped open when the car slowed and began bouncing over rough terrain. Sitting up from her slouched position, Carson smiled at her. "We're here. Maybe you'll solve this for us, and we can all go home, case closed."

They left the car on a rise overlooking a small bay, then picked their way down the rocky slope toward a brightly lit portion of rocky beach. It looked to her as though the sun had been stuffed into a large tent. People moved in and out of it, covered head to toe in white.

She glanced down at herself. Would Carson's borrowed clothing be acceptable for this ritual? He was dressed much like she was, and he seemed unconcerned.

She squinted against the square lanterns pointed at the tent. Someone broke from the group as they approached. Carson pulled something from his pocket, holding it up to the newcomer, who removed their head and face covering.

"Lana."

"Carson. Who's your friend?"

"Lirikai."

The woman's eyebrow raised.

Carson gestured toward the tent, "Same as the others?"

She nodded. "Suit up." She led the way to an area that had more white suits like her own.

Carson put one on, indicating that Lirikai should do the same.

She felt as though she were carefully wrapped in a shroud with almost nothing of herself exposed to the world. When it came time to pull the head and face coverings on, she hesitated, and only relented when the woman, Lana, insisted. Lirikai was constantly pulling at one section or another of the suit.

"You get used to it." Carson said as they were about to step into the illuminated tent. "Don't touch anything."

Inside, everything was too close. Lirikai focused on the sound of the ocean. It wasn't like her comfortable little cave where the sea flowed in and out. This tiny space didn't have a rhythm. It was a slice of the world blocked out.

What was she doing here? Just a few short hours ago, she'd been contentedly slumbering, oblivious to the world. But here she was, wrapped up in a tent to stare at someone's leavings.

The body itself had ragged crescents impressed into it, the skin broken and punctured. The head had been roughly detached. Hair and blood sprinkled the sand and the remains.

Despite the face covering, the scent of blood invaded her nostrils, and with it the underlying aroma of a guilty soul. It was nearly gone now, as the body had cooled after death. It was like staring at a fisherman's offal pile. And yet her gaze was glued to the corpse. The urge to bite made her mouth tingle, but it wasn't as overwhelming as it had been back at Carson's work building.

It looked like a poor example of Barra'kidai work - a sister? An impostor? She was sure that if someone turned the head over, there would be a shaved patch with a symbol carved into it too. Like in Carson's paper images. A token for the Goddess. But at the same time, this wasn't how it was supposed to be. None of this should be here. Justice was supposed to be exacted in the sea. The land wasn't the domain of the Barra'kidai. They were creatures of the sea goddess. The guilty were taken to their end in the ocean, to no longer be a blight on the world. The exposed bite marks read like frenzied desperation. The ritual was befouled.

She suddenly felt as though her shroud were constricting and crawling over her. The waves crashing in the surf called to her.

"Lirikai?" Carson called after her as she shoved her way outside, tearing the white barrier from her skin, eyes on the nearby ocean. She dropped the suit on the sand. Carson caught up to her, stripping off his own suit, leaving it with hers. He reached for her arm, "What do you know?"

She was forced to turn toward him when his strong grip halted her escape. Looking down at his hand encircling her arm, her anger rose sudden and hot. "Release me."

His fingers jerked open, but he remained insistent, leaning toward her as he spoke, "You know what happened to the victim."

"I am done here. I'm going back to the sea."

"I need to know what is happening here, Lirikai. If this killing is being done by one of ours, I must follow the law and handle it. My job is to protect the humans from those of our kind that can't co-exist." He dropped his voice so that it didn't carry back to the crew surrounding the tent.

The wind shifted, washing the scent of his power over her, enticing her toward him. The scent that had awakened and beckoned her from her hibernation.

His gaze was locked on her face, and the moment she relented, his intent expression relaxed, "Come on, let's get something to eat."

Her eyes drifted to the tent.

"Human food."

"I don't want more human food if the world now thinks that offal you gave me earlier is what is good."

Carson laughed, "Cafeteria food is always the worst. I promised you steak, but at this time of night, we'll have to settle for burgers instead."

She shrugged, falling in step next to him.

They climbed the rise to where his cart was parked. "What is cafeteria?"

Opening the door, he smiled, "The goddess' joke on us for straying too far out of the ocean and for too long."

SIX

CARSON COULD BARELY CONTAIN his excitement. She knew something.

Lirikai had knowledge that could help him stop the perpetrator, close the case, and return home.

He'd been called in on the case because of the unusual bite marks. The ritual marking might not have stood out as 'other' on its own, but both together did. The locals feared an out-of-control cult.

FBI had contacted GPSA, who disrupted his peaceful life on his little island. Peaceful, if not a little lonely. He'd agreed to work the case when the director called him, and had regretted it as soon as he read the case files during the flight west.

Glancing at the dash clock, he saw just how late it was getting. Lana had promised that her team liaison would send him the new data in the morning, and they still had a long drive back. His stomach rumbled, reminding him of his repeated promises of food for Lirikai.

He turned off the main highway, looking for an illuminated burger joint sign.

Once Carson ordered various items from the menu, they settled in at a large table farthest from the counter and door so they couldn't be overheard. Even at this hour, there were a few other patrons loitering, some biding time until they had to find a corner to sleep, others avoiding their spouses, and a couple were making deals. Making note of their positions, he settled in so that he could keep an eye on anyone that might take an interest and drift too close.

Spreading the food between them, he placed a wrapped burger in front of Lirikai and tucked into his own. Eating around a mouthful of food, he pointed at the condiments, "Sauces and seasonings."

She nodded, unwrapping her burger, glancing at how he was eating and took a tentative bite. "Much better than cafeteria offerings."

He chuckled at that, pulling some fries from another package.

He let her eat in peace, resisting interrogation mode, and observing instead. She was petite, with delicate features. If he hadn't seen it himself, he would never have believed anyone that had described the vicious teeth that erupted from her full lips earlier that evening. She looked like any number of women he'd met with surf boards in tow. Clearly a water baby, with the lean build to support the passion. He doubted she knew what a surf board was, never having needed one.

She sat back with a sigh.

"Tell me of yourself," Carson prompted.

When she looked at him, her expression turned wary, "There is nothing to tell. I live in the sea, I've been asleep."

His voice softened, "you said you had sisters— lost sisters."

Her finger poked at the condensation beading her cup. She nodded.

"Are they all," he hesitated, "dead? Are you the last?"

He watched her throat work before answering, "I don't know. I think so."

He considered this. "Are you a Mer-person?"

Her gaze met his, "No. I am Barra'kidai."

He blew a breath out as he sat back, a chill sweeping his spine. Barra'kidai!

He'd heard the legends, but in all his centuries, he'd never met one.

Fierce and terrible, the Barra'kidai were the weapons of the sea Goddess' justice.

Carson's kind was created to protect. Lirikai and her kin were avengers.

Despite all the questions tumbling through his head, none would form as he stared at her, her expression burning into his memory. She was fierce, but he could see the underlying loneliness in her. The loneliness that drove her into hibernation. When he was still enough, he could feel it pull at him.

She dropped her face into her hands, took a deep breath pushing her hands through her hair and sat back with a long exhale. "Ask what you want to know."

"Could one of your sisters be responsible for the victims being left on the beach - the one we saw tonight?"

"Maybe. Yes," she relented, "but it is all wrong."

"How do you mean?"

"No one should ever know about this man's death. The Barra'kidai lure their intended to the sea. The ritual is never for the public..." she hesitated, her hands fluttering in front of her, searching for the right words. "It's as though something isn't right. The natural process has been disrupted or broken."

He waited for her to continue.

"We mete out Justice. We track a target, one who has done terrible deeds, and make them disappear from the world. They deserve no memory, only obliteration. Once we have them in the water, we rip them to shreds with our teeth and devour them until there is nothing left."

"Except their head."

She nodded. "The offering. In our human form, we return to the land, shave the hair from the back and carve the Goddess' mark, so that only she will know the identity of the prosecuted; that we have fulfilled our duty to her. The victims of the guilty will no longer live under their exploitation. It is their prayers to the Goddess that activate our mission. The completion of this part on land brings it full circle."

"The legend I'd heard was that you were all once human women?"

"Most of us were women. Not all. We were people of the seas, living along the coastal waters, honoring the Goddess. Pirates and raiders targeted our settlements. Some of us were her priestesses. Taken from our temples and villages and used violently and then left to the seas. She breathed her magic into some of us. In the sea, she gave us the form of the Barracuda, fierce and terrifying, devouring the dredges of humanity so that the innocent of heart may flourish and live peacefully."

She gave a short laugh. "For a long time, we descended with vengeance on those that had destroyed our lives. There was some balance established, but it didn't last. The exploiters of the world continued on; our work was never ending."

She took a sip of her drink. "And then there came a time where there just weren't enough of us to continue, and by then the Goddess had gone away." She stifled a yawn.

"So, the question is, why is the body on the beach?"

"Yes."

"What do you think the answer is?

"I'm not sure. But it is very concerning. As much as I want to go back to the ocean, I should find out what is happening."

THE SPY HID AMONG the rocky dunes watching. Waiting, breath shuddering, hands trembling.

The scene below was on display under the harsh spot lights. First the beach joggers, out for their evening ritual, discovering the remains. Cell phones extracted, emergency number dialed. Sirens and lights, and then investigators swarming the area. It hadn't taken long before the yellow tape went around a wide perimeter and the tent and white suits appeared to protect the exposed area from further contamination.

Isn't this what they were looking for? The signs, the brutality, the evidence.

Crouched behind rocks and tall tufts of grass, the spy searched among the personnel for a familiar face. A familiar scent. Anything that would lead them to the one that started it all.

Two individuals in casual civilian clothing parked above the scene, picked their way down, and merged with the crowd. The tall male had been to some of the more recent crime scenes. The small female was new.

Piqued, the spy's attention homed in on the tent where the newcomer disappeared, to reappear some minutes later, nearly tearing the white suit from her body. The tall male followed close, stopped, pulled her aside, brought her closer to where the spy lurked. Turned as they were, the excess light from the spot lights illuminated the woman's features. Their short conversation couldn't be heard over the surf. But her face. The spy's heart soared.

Not the expected face, no—this face, the spy had expected never to see again.

She was leaving with the tall man, heading back toward the jeep parked on the rise.

With a last glance over the scene, the spy made the quick decision to leave their intended observational position and break cover, running low behind the rocks and dunes for their own vehicle, making it just in time to see which way the jeep had gone. They followed at a safe distance, hands drumming the steering wheel, excited.

SEVEN

BEFORE THEY GOT BACK into Carson's vehicle, he made a quick call to leave a message for Ana. He hadn't expected her to pick up, but he briefed her on the scene and Lirikai's intention to work with them.

"Be careful Carson. She's volatile.""Don't worry."

"And those teeth! Does nothing phase you? I think she could pierce even *your* hide, or do serious damage if you make the wrong move."

"Hey, you know me, I'm an island. I can handle whatever the sea throws at me."

"Funny."

He let his gaze wander to Lirikai belting herself into his car. "I can handle myself." He paused, "Hey, you're about the same height, aren't you? Do you think you'd have some clothes she could borrow for a few days?"

"Height, yeah. But she'd stretch my clothes out in places I enviably can't." He heard her sigh, then she relented, "I'll have a look. And before you ask, no she can't stay at my place. I live in a bachelor and Antony is here on leave. I'll see if the office will cover lodgings for her, but the new captain, he's pretty tight on the reins."

"Understood. Thanks, Ana."

"You owe me new clothes if she ruins mine." "Deal." He disconnected the call and dropped his phone into his pocket before sliding into the driver's seat. Once back on the road, he broached the subject of where she would stay. "Lirikai, I don't live around here. I'm contracted in to work on this case, then I get to go back home. But while I'm here, the locals put me up in a hotel."

She looked at him curiously.

"Like a traveler's hostel—a lodge."

She nodded.

"Humans are curious folk, and it would look odd if I were appearing from the sea every morning and disappearing every night. Might cause a stir."

She rolled her eyes at him. "I have noticed that we are no longer respected as we once were and now live hidden among them. That has become clear in my short time here."

He cleared his throat, feeling warmth creep up his neck, "You're welcome to share my hotel room for the time being. There is a sofa-bed I can sleep on." He cast her a glance. Her expression was curiously bemused. "Ana agreed to lend you some clothes," he nodded toward his t-shirt and shorts draping her lithe figure.

She looked down at herself, shrugged and said, "That is acceptable."

"I'll talk to the captain about adding you to the payroll too. You'll need money."

"Currency?"

He nodded.

"It would be easier if *I* was the one to come and go from the sea each day," she groaned.

"You'll be fine," he smiled at her.

THEY ARRIVED AT A large concrete building cut with evenly spaced rows of windows. "Well, here we are," he said with an unexcited sigh.

"Lacks elegance."

"That it does. Come on," he said, reaching to grab the file from the pocket behind his seat, then untie the surfboard from the back of the jeep. When he noticed her interested gaze on the board, he explained "It's a surfboard. People use them to float and ride the ocean waves standing up. It's fun," he insisted.

She smiled as she looked at him. They both knew how exhilarating it was to race the ocean, "Camouflage?"

He laughed, "Yes. But you should try it, it really is fun."

"Maybe."

They walked in through the lobby to the steel doors of the elevator banks. He drew the key card from his pocket and stepped in. After a moment's hesitation, she stepped in beside him, warily glancing around the interior of the confined space.

He remembered the first time he'd stepped into one, decades ago. He didn't care for the steel cages either. As soon as the doors opened again, she darted out.

"That was unpleasant."

"They're useful." He led her to a door toward the end of the long hall of identical doors, swiped the card and pushed the door open. She jumped when the heavy door slammed closed behind her. Her eyes were wide when he flicked the light switch on and gestured toward the large bed dominating the room. "You can sleep there."

Setting the surfboard out of the way, he dropped the file folder on the desk next to his laptop.

When he turned around, he saw her gaze considering the sofa.

"It opens into a bed," he moved forward to remove the cushions, and pulled the bed out. There was little space left in the small room.

After a moment, she looked up at him, "Thank you, Carson. I can sleep there, it is more than enough for me. You take your proper bed."

"I insist," he cleared his throat, turning the key card over between his fingers. "The lavatory is through that door if you wish to wash. Glancing at his watch, he said, "It's pretty late and I have to be back at the station early to go over the reports from tonight's scene."

Lirikai nodded and disappeared into the bathroom.

Carson dropped the car keys on the dresser and pulled a clean t-shirt and boxers from the top drawer. With a quick knock on the door, he reached his clothes in through the narrow opening.

"There's a spare hotel toothbrush still on the counter."

As soon as he pulled his hand back, the door shut.

With a sigh, he wandered to the desk, switched on the light and settled in to review the file he'd taken from his office and the emails on his laptop.

He heard the water running in the bathroom and did his best to block out the sound, and the random thoughts of Lirikai bathing that his imagination conjured. It was difficult, already having the image of her dripping wet in just a towel when he met her on the beach. All lithe limbs and silky skin.

He opened the file and began reviewing the case, which instantly scrubbed romantic images from his brain.

Opening his running word document on the case, he added notes about Lirikai, recording everything that had happened since he found her on the beach. He went over the events and information she'd given him, seeing how they fit into the case, trying to be as objective as possible.

He stared at the blinking cursor at the end of his last sentence. Objective. For all he really knew, *she* could be the one doing the killings. What did he *really* know of what she was? She could be spinning him a tale. He glanced at the bathroom door. The water was still running.

What had the Goddess of the Seas thrown at him this time?

He dropped his head with a groan, rubbing the back of his neck.

What was he getting himself into, here?

LIRIKAI NEARLY JUMPED OUT of her human skin, teeth erupting in self-defense, when a figure appeared from behind the lavatory door as she shut it.

It took a full moment for her senses to kick in enough to realize she was staring at her own image in the reflective glass set behind a counter. She stared at her Barra'kidai teeth projecting from her human face. How wonderfully monstrous she was! She jerked again at the rap on the lavatory door, followed by Carson's muffled voice. She opened the door just enough for his hand to appear bearing clothing. She snatched the fabric and snapped the door shut as soon as his hand disappeared.

Turning back to her own image, it dawned on her that she hadn't wanted Carson to see her as she was. Her appearance had never concerned her before, especially her Barra'kidai self. She was fiercely proud of the terror she instilled. This was what she was.

Did Carson find her teeth monstrous?

She turned away from the glass, instead assessing the white surfaces in the small room. It didn't take her long to figure out what they were for once she began twisting the silver knobs and levers. She surmised what the chair-like apparatus was for as she watched the water disappear then refill. Brilliant! From the large basin, the gush of water was a pleasant surprise and she was careful about the knobs that ejected pre-boiled water. The metallic overhanging flower imitated warm rain water. She dropped her borrowed clothing on the cold floor and stepped into it.

Some of these new experiences were worth awakening from the sea, at least for a little while. Gritty sand and bits of seaweed littered the basin by the time she turned off the water, and she wriggled her toes in it as it ran down into a small hole, then reached for a clean linen hanging from the wall, tucking it around herself.

Her thoughts returned to Carson, just beyond this small room. Just a few hours ago, she'd stepped out of the sea and into a completely new world. A world where she wasn't sure she belonged anymore. The Barra'kidai had ceased to serve their function before she went to sleep—it was the reason she'd gone into hibernation.

So, what now?

She'd somehow stumbled onto a beach where the God-dess-scented man had seemed to be waiting for her. Humans were being killed by someone that seemed to be a deranged Barra'kidai. Where was the Goddess pushing her toward? Her instinct told her she needed to see this through. Were it truly a Barra'kidai, only a Barra'kidai rightfully should handle it. If it were not, then who would besmirch the Barra'kidai in such as way? She wouldn't allow it to continue either way. It was her duty to discover what was happening and carry out justice. Perhaps the Goddess had pushed the ocean man into her path to awaken her to fulfill this duty.

She reached for the fresh clothes dropped on the counter. As she unfurled the new tunic, Carson's scent wafted under her nose. She brought it closer to her face. He smelled so good. He smelled like Goddess power, and...desire.

She jerked her feet into the other piece of clothing, hauling them up to cover her bottom. Catching her reflection again her eyes lingered on the plain fabric that was soft to the touch and smelled of him. These were his clothes. He wore them - over his naked flesh. She felt her cheeks tingle. As long as she'd been hibernating, it was even longer since she'd caressed a man. Retrieving the worn clothing from the floor, she didn't know what to do with them, so she folded and left the on the counter top. Opening the lavatory door, she headed straight for the bed Carson had indicated she should take, slid under the blanket, and turned toward the wall.

After a few moments, she heard Carson shuffle toward the lava-tory and close the door.

When she heard the hiss of water, her imagination got creative. She squeezed her eyes shut, determined to sleep.

EIGHT

AT SUNRISE, CARSON SHOWED Lirikai what to do with the toothbrush. They stood side by side in the bathroom, toothpaste foam rimming their mouths. Lirikai struggled not to gag on the stuff, as she stared at him awkwardly in the reflective glass. He smiled at her around the movement of his brush. He bent to spit, rinsed his mouth with water from the spout, "better?"

She copied his movements and nodded.

"Okay, lets grab a bite to eat, then get back to the station. You can change into some of Ana's clothes when we get there," he said, slipping straps over his shoulders to hold a pistol, and putting a leather folder into his pocket.

"That is acceptable," Lirikai mumbled, trying to scrub dribbled toothpaste from the front of Carson's borrowed t-shirt with a small cloth, leaving a wet patch.

He handed her a plastic key card, "you may need this if I'm not around. Keep it with you." He showed her how it opened the door.

She slipped her feet into the sandals Carson had loaned her the night before, and boarded his car. They collected food from a window in a brightly painted building and merged onto a road crammed with other cars like their own, moving slower than a sea slug.

Craning her neck to see over the cars ahead of them, she remarked, "Wouldn't it be faster to run there? It can't be so far?"

"It's a little farther than you would think. Be patient."

"Not my strongest characteristic."

"Clearly."

She narrowed her eyes at him, eliciting a deep chuckle. Giving up the scowl after a moment of appreciating the golden hue of his profile under the morning sun, she said, "tell me something of yourself."

He cast her a quick glance, apparently startled by the question. He made a lane change and passed several cars, and she thought he might not answer.

"Not much to tell. I lead a mostly mundane life among humans now, doing my duty to protect them when I can, but mostly from others like us—others that are more powerful than humans. Now, I mostly let humans protect themselves from other humans. I help where I can."

His shrug pulled at something in her. Humbleness.

"You know I am Barra'kidai. Who are your people?"

She watched the corner of his mouth and jaw tighten. His body lost its relaxed posture and he shifted himself more upright in his seat. The jeep accelerated, passing several more cars before darting back into slower traffic.

Lirikai turned her face away from Carson, watching the passing cars and greenery under the rising sun. Even at this hour, heat shimmered over the landscape.

"My people are the humans I watch over," he said after such a long time that the sound of his voice startled her from the reverie she'd drifted into.

She didn't press him.

On their return to the station, Lirikai was surprised to still see the main room full of criminals. There seemed to be an unending supply. As she followed Carson through the crowded space, her senses were as overloaded as they had been the night before. Mind you, not everyone in the room smelled tasty—not many at all, but some of them were overwhelming the room. By now, she observed who the 'cops' were and who Carson's 'perps' were, based on their demeanor and how some were dressed. The cops had pistols like Carson's. With others, the divisions weren't so clear. She felt drawn toward one or two so-called 'cops' that smelled more appealing than they should.

Was this the new world? To her instincts, it seemed that that deeply corrupt part of humanity hadn't abated over the centuries. It had merely adapted. As she passed among the men, some turned and smirked, giving her the up and down, others scowled, and yet others politely moved aside to let her pass with a 'Good morning'.

"Lirikai!" Ana's clear voice called to her over the din, cutting through the building haze of hunger.

She looked around, she didn't see Carson. Assuming he'd gone to his own small room, she headed toward Ana's door. It was a relief when the door closed on the noise.

"Here," Ana shoved a folded pile of fabric into Lirikai's hands. "These are the best hope I have of anything fitting your frame. There's more in that bag, and some shoes in the one on the floor."

"Thank you," Lirikai said in English, slipping the sandals from her feet while trying to peek through the clothes. "What is best for daytime?" she said gesturing at her the t-shirt and shorts she'd put on from the day before."

"Right, well, what you're wearing won't do, of course you know that. You'll want some work clothes, I suggest these, or these." Ana reached for the pile, separating and plopping the selections onto her neat desk. "There are undergarments in the other bag, although those I'm far less confident will fit you at all, but it was worth a try." She shrugged. "Oh! Oh, you're doing this right here, let me lock the door then." Ana bolted for the door, snapping the lock in place as Lirikai's t-shirt landed on one of the chairs in front of the desk, followed by the shorts.

Ana rushed across the windows, turning all the blinds before anyone noticed the naked woman in her office. She quickly retrieved the bag from the floor, ransacked the neatly folded underclothes and shoved a pair of panties in front of Lirikai, "like your shorts, but underneath."

Lirikai nodded in thanks and slipped into them.

Next, she pulled a bra free and Lirikai stared blankly at the thing, "That is clothes?" she said doubtful.

"Yes, uhm, here, I'll help you...?"

Again, Lirikai nodded, becoming rather bemused by Ana's awkward attempts to move around her without looking at or touching her.

Ana slid the thing over her arms, trying to position it properly without much success, "Uhm, those go in the cupped bits," she instructed waving her index finger at her exposed breasts. With Lirikai's help, Ana fastened the back.

"Why we need this?"

"Who knows," Ana muttered, "Customary to keep things in check."

They managed to get her into a skirt and blouse. Ana showed her how the top button worked, leaving her to the rest as she retrieved a couple pairs of shoes. "There are sneakers for walking and running in the bag, these are better for work."

Lirikai looked at the shoes, and stepped into the first pair, wobbled, tried the next, then abandoned both pairs for the sandals.

"Okay," Ana said with a nod. She stuffed the shoes back into the bag, then collected the rest of the clothing and put it in the other bag. "Well, everything almost fits," she tucked a lock of hair behind her ear, inspecting Lirikai. Now, with her model dressed, she freely tugged and shifted the fabric into place. "You definitely fill things out more than I do, so it may feel a little snug. The skirt is a bit shorter than appropriate, but I'm sure you'll be just fine." She bit her lip, looking Lirikai over. "Can you sit?"

Lirikai dropped into the cleared off chair, watching as Ana studied her with a frown, then pushed her knees together, encouraged her to sit straight, shoulders back, stomach in. "I go back to the sea," Lirikai huffed after several minutes. "These things are torture."

"No, you'll be fine. Honest." She fussed over Lirikai another minute, "Hair! May I?"

Lirikai looked at her dubiously, her eyes following her hand to a brush that had been placed on the desk. She nodded. She closed her eyes and relaxed after Ana's gentle touch moved the brush through her hair.

Tears stung her eyes and she sniffled a little.

"I'm sorry! Did I pull too hard?""No, no, you're fine. I—I just haven't—No one but my sisters has ever brushed my hair for me."

Ana's voice softened, "Shall I let you do it yourself?"

"No, please continue, if you would."

She continued in silence, Ana's hands gently fluttering about Lirikai's head. She began to hum as she lifted and shaped Lirikai's hair into a style fit for the work place. "All finished," she said with a final pat.

"Thank you, Ana."

Ana's body language had shifted drastically in those last moments. She no longer fluttered, but moved with more ease, letting her small hand rest a moment on Lirikai's shoulder. She smiled, and Lirikai smiled back at her.

The door jerked against the lock, there was a knock, "Ana? Is Lirikai with you?"

"Hold on," she rushed over to let him in, then moved aside to reopen the blinds.

Carson stepped in, his gaze turning immediately to Lirikai. She stood. His eyes followed her. He swallowed hard, clearing his throat, shifting a sheaf of papers from one hand to the other.

"Doesn't she look great?"

"Much more appropriate than my T-shirt and shorts."

"Listen, I have some work I need to do off-site. I'll put these bags in your jeep when I head out, but before I go, Captain Mack wanted a meeting with you, and yesterday's site crew will send their report over as soon as they can."

"I've already got some of it." he held up the pages.

"Good, if there's anything else you need, you have my cell number." She let her gaze shift between Carson and Lirikai. She touched

Lirikai's shoulder again and smiled, "I hope you don't return to the sea too soon." Ana picked up the bags and Carson closed the door behind her.

"Looks like you made a friend," he grinned.

Lirikai shrugged, "She is very likable."

He held up the folder, "Shall we?" He put it on the desk, and began flipping through the pages of solid text, passing a finger over some lines. "The first victim had a record, while the second didn't; he was a leader in his community. But this perp was known to the local police as an informant. Initially the other investigators thought these were random drug induced attacks, but now they're thinking it might be a little more organized."

Lirikai listened, not sure if this should mean anything to her.

Carson went on, "This escalation could mean more investigators working the cases from other departments who deal with gangs and drugs, potentially interfering with my work." He looked up from the file to Lirikai, "If one of your sisters is involved, this could get more difficult. I may lose my autonomy with these other departments around."

"I don't think they would figure out if she is involved, but what will happen to whomever they catch?"

"The killer will be taken into custody and go through a lengthy trial process and when found guilty, be imprisoned for the rest of their lives. If they catch someone and discover they aren't human, it would drastically change how they are treated. We need to avoid this at all costs." He stood and walked to the windows, looking into the inner bullpen where colleagues were processing perpetrators. "My job is to seek out individuals like us, and Ana helps me get them into the custody of our division. No one else here knows about us—that we're not human—and we need to keep it that way."

"I miss the old days when we were respected, but I know in the last centuries, humans' fear has begun to push them to hunt and kill us. If my sister is involved, I will handle it. If it is someone else, then it is up to you."

"Lirikai, even if this is your sister's doing, I have to take her in to my division. That's how it works."

She stared at him, anger tightening her chest muscles, "I don't work in your system."

"Everyone works in our system. It is the way the world works now." He frowned back at her.

"Not the Barra'kidai."

LIRIKAI'S BEST CHANCE TO find out if this was the work of one of her Barra'kidai sisters was by working with Carson and accessing the information he was being given.

A thrill shot down her spine. A sister!

The centuries had been so very long, especially with the absence of their Goddess. Lirikai thought herself to be the last of the Barra'kidai. She was among the first and had come to believe she was the last. If she had a sister walking the land, she needed to know. And if that sister was in need, she had to help her.

Her stomach dropped as she remembered the body on the beach. If this was her sister attacking these humans, there was something very wrong and she absolutely needed to find out what it was. If this wasn't her sister, then equally she needed to find out who was imitating a Barra'kidai.

She wasn't sure if she hoped it was a sister or not. Regardless, it wouldn't be an easy reunion.

No matter what the circumstances, something was very wrong. As she'd told Carson, the Barra'kidai didn't attack on land but far below the surface, away from any potential spectators, traces to be swept away. It meant whoever it was might not be able to fully shift into the sleek form of the Barracuda, with powerful jaws to rend and sever the guilty and deliver justice to the Goddess and her believers, those vulnerable humans that prayed to her for aid and vengeance when they could not achieve it for themselves. Or, *they* were the one being attacked and forced to defend themselves – to the death.

She had been one of those weak humans at one time. Despite the millennia, certain memories from her time as a human were seared into her consciousness. As a faithful priestess at the village temple, perched on an exposed cliff over-looking the seas, she was there daily making offerings and performing communal duties. Her husband tended the fields when he was not hunting, and together they took their turn tending the village children, providing respite for the elders who normally rounded them up and kept them in line.

A smile touched her lips, lost in her past. The crystal-clear memory of her husband before he was taken from her so long ago.

The raiding had begun. Again. They had enjoyed peace and free commerce for half a generation. The first whispers reached them when peddlers arrived for market day, bearing sad news of attacks along the coast in other places.

The elders immediately called on the village council to confer. They knew what was coming, they'd seen it before. The younger, like herself, had their childhood memories of the last attack, and while nervous, most didn't believe they'd really return to this village. They had no riches, there was nothing here of value for them. Their temple was modest and precious items were no longer prized offerings to the Goddess at this location. Instead, the priestesses devoted their time, heart and faith to her, and life had been good. Until now.

There was some resistance to extreme action, but in the end, it was decided that militia duty would double. Able bodied adults would assemble for practice as soon as they were finished their work in the fields. Those that could not fight would begin work on defenses.

But it was too late. Before anything could properly begin, the attack came in the night. The priestesses had also added to their temple duties by staying at the cliff top in long hours of prayers and offerings, pleading to the Goddess to save them from those that would harm them.

While assembled in meditation and prayer, the attack had come. The black sails were invisible on the dark waters. The natural crashing of surf and wind swallowed shouts and the clashing of weapons.

As soon as one of the priestesses realized what was happening, they grabbed their spears, running from the temple down the long winding path to the village. It was too late, the roofs of the mud-brick houses were ablaze, bodies strewn wherever they fell. Most held weapons of some kind in an attempt to defend themselves, but not all. Nearly all the elderly had been slain, and anyone that wasn't hale and whole of body lay dead and dying among them. The youngest of the children, unable to care for themselves, were littered among the elders who'd tried to save them.

Lirikai's infant niece lay in a pool of her aged father's blood, who'd died trying to protect his granddaughter. Her mind in a haze of grief and rage, she sought out her husband and young brothers, who had also been slain while protecting the village.

The priestesses rallied on the beach, fury and grief in their faces as the raiders corralled their booty to take on board their ships. There were no resources of trade value to be found in this village. Its people were its most valued commodity, and it seemed that was what the attackers had been seeking. Healthy, strong stock to trade into servitude, chained together, being pushed into the boats.

On seeing the priestesses gathered with their spears, they laughed and turned to engage them. They fought as hard as the militia had, to no avail. They too were captured and chained.

Aboard the ships, they were crowded into spaces meant for inanimate cargo, not people, and the sails turned them away from their burning village. By the time the shore line was lost in the haze of ocean mist mixed with smoke, the attackers turned their full attention on their goods.

They sought to defile and break the priestesses to gain their submission and that of their surviving villagers.

Every one of the Priestesses were terribly used and slain, their bodies dumped into the ocean.

Lirikai remembered every moment.

She remembered her death.

The seconds before her heart ceased to beat, she stood outside herself, still attached to the emotions, still feeling the agonizing pain throughout her body. One by one, beside her appeared her sisters outside their corporeal forms, watching as their white limbed bodies sank below the surface of the water, the cries of the grief-stricken villagers wailing around them. They had tried to defend what was left of their village, to save those that would be used and violated by these horrible raiders.

In the end, the villagers were not broken into submission, but called to the Goddess to vindicate their injustice in memory of their faithful priestesses. They made a last effort to attack their captors, fighting to their deaths.

Lirikai's next memory was of standing on the ocean floor before a formless being of energy which swirled before her and her slain sister-priestesses, their bodies drifting in the water above them.

Thought intruded into their minds collectively. This swirling mass of energy before them was their Goddess. The thoughts were overwhelming initially, emotions of tired fury rippled through the water. The Goddess' energy wavered and shifted from form to form—elegant blue scales and fins to graceful human limbs and hair, then back again.

Now when Lirikai recalled, as ancient and overwhelming as the Goddess felt even then, she now recognized the signs of a being that was beginning to fade.

She had made us before drifting away, even then.

Their bodies, floating above their ethereal heads, jerked in the current, and directed by the change in energy, gathered in a swirling collection, their pale lifeless selves were flashes of light in the darkness of the ocean floor in the darkest of the night.

"You shall be feared. You shall be the seekers of justice in this unjust world. Each individual has the gift of free will, and to abuse such a thing to violate another is an aberration."

Lirikai watched in fascination as the corpses twisted in the seawater, hair and limbs melding to their bodies, reforming into sleek silvered scales with razor sharp fins. She recognized the form of the barracuda; a creature feared among the villagers for its fierce teeth and its vicious and calculated attacks on its prey. The strong jaws and terrifying teeth able to sever limbs and snap bones.

She stared at the beautifully terrifying new form her body had become.

The goddess gave them their instruction. They may change into their human forms to complete their missions: To capture those that would exploit the innocent, drag them into the ocean and devour them until there was nothing left of their existence. Without a body to litter the land, humanity would forget those deemed unworthy to be remembered. Instead let the victims be the focus of memory. The guilty to fade and be forgotten. Their heads to be marked and remitted to the Goddess so that she may pass judgment on their souls.

Their new bodies ceased twisting in the currents above them, and their spirits were slammed back into them. Oh, the bliss of swimming as the newly formed Barra'kidai. The powerful sleek bodies. The power in their jaws.

Collectively, they twisted their bodies, and swam straight for the boats, following, plotting, luring, until every one of the attackers disappeared below the ocean surface, their heads piled at the Goddess' deep-sea cave.

These priestesses had fought and died together for their Goddess and for their families and village. Reborn, they only had each other, and remained so for centuries. In the early decades, the Goddess would periodically find another to add to their group.

Some of them were lost in battles, doing their duty. They fought to the death every time.

They secured their coast, and with legends of terrifying monsters in the waters of their home areas, raiding eventually stopped. Their original village had been destroyed, but their neighbors had come to bury the dead and perform the rites. Some of the nearby villages had daughters and sons who'd been born in Lirikai's village, and some returned to begin anew.

All this time later, she wondered if it still existed.

She'd not been back since long before she'd lost her sisters.

The last couple had reclaimed their humanity. They'd told her, that they had felt a shift in their hearts that they had finally achieved true justice for themselves. She couldn't fathom what that meant. She didn't believe she could ever feel that she would achieve justice for her husband, her aged father, her niece and siblings. She would never have justice for what was done to her village. It was too much. Her family could never be replaced in her heart. She had loved them with everything that she was. There was no heart left to offer to a human life. There was only the Goddess and her sisters now. How could justice be complete without the return of life? She had been given another life—without her family. This second life had a purpose and she meant to fulfill it. She would honor what had been gifted to her. She would fight to the death every time.

If she truly still had a sister left, then it was her duty to help her.

Even if, as she feared, that sister was locked in a state trapped between human and Barra'kidai, unable to control the instinct, overriding a body unable to fully shift to fulfill that instinct.

If Carson had the means to track her sister in this confusing modern world, then she would work with him.

Lirikai would never turn her back on a Barra'kidai, especially a sister that needed her.

NINE

CARSON DIDN'T TELL LIRIKAI that the legends of the Barra'kidai had faded. That only he remembered them because he himself was so old. Lirikai was the last of her kind, except of course the possible killer. From what he suspected, if this was indeed the work of a sister, something was very wrong in terms of ritual.

Aside from the fact that dead humans were turning up mutilated.

Now he stood before the station captain, Bruce Mack. "You wanted to see me, sir?" Carson struggled to control his breathing. The room was heavy with the scent of the man's aftershave. It smelled like a teenage boy had gotten hold of the bottle.

The stocky man looked up from his desk, a perma-frown carved into his brow. "Sit."

Carson ignored his bark and took the chair, easing himself back, propping an ankle over his knee. He let out a steady breath, forcing himself to relax, wishing he'd left the door open.

He stared back at the captain, waiting for him to state the reason for his summons. Despite what seemed to be the man's naturally furrowed brow, the rest of him was unreadable. "I understand you've brought someone into the department to work with you, a woman? I wasn't briefed on her presence."

"Yes. I will be responsible for her."

There was a quick knock and the door opened. Mack frowned at the intruder.

"Another missing person report, sir."

"Give it to Keenan, she's working those cases," he waved the person out and returned his scowl to Carson.

"You've done good work for us before, so I'll forgive this oversight. In the future, I want to know before-hand who is coming unvetted into my precinct." The eyes staring at Carson were inscrutable, but the overpowering scent of aftershave was distracting.

Carson frowned; as federal agents, they worked with whomever they wanted.

Ana was the west coast staff liaison and she usually dealt with the captain. Carson hated office politics. His thumb started tapping is knee. He just wanted to do the job. Ana handled the egos. She was good at it.

"Yes sir," he said, dropping his foot to the floor, sitting forward. "Anything else?"

"Any suspects yet? You need any help, see officer Keenan. She's my right hand 'round here."

"Not yet, but we're working on it."

The older man gave a sharp nod and waved his hand.

Carson gladly accepted the dismissal, taking a deep cleansing breath as soon as he had the office door open.

THEY SPENT HOURS REVIEWING the photos, reports and accompanying documents for each victim.

He had the sense that key information was missing. The witness and family interviews were sparse, and the background checks bordered on vague.

A shady pawnbroker with a rap sheet, a minister, and a known police informant. What was their connection?

Carson stood, scrubbed a hand over his face, stretched, yawned and looked at his watch. "Call it a day?"

"What day?" Lirikai asked absently as she leaned over the desk studying the victim photos lined up side by side, trying to determine and confirm the bite pattern.

He smiled, "End of the work day. Are you hungry?"

"Famished, just fetch someone from the next room for me." She looked up, a twinkle in her eye.

He glanced out his office door. *For her it must be like walking through a kitchen with several ovens roasting a feast.* That was the best way he could think of it to understand. He imagined himself the last time he'd been through a kitchen with a roast chicken, or turkey, or beef and the mouth-watering scents surrounding him. Is that what Lirikai experienced? He eyed a couple of the scruffy looking guys from his vantage point and shuddered. Definitely not to his taste, but hey, who was he to judge?

He turned back to her and admired her form leaning over the desk in thought. Especially for someone who looked like she did.

She had looked hot in his shorts and t-shirt. Now she was a wild woman confined to form-fitting formal work clothing—so much hotter. His eyes lingered on the curve of her breast and hips where the fabric strained, and the elegant lines of her toned legs. He curled his hands, resisting the urge to slide his fingers up the smooth skin of her thigh, or splay his hands round her hips and narrow waist. He wondered what the sensitive flesh just behind her knee would taste like. He closed his eyes, breaking the thoughts.

Opening his eyes, he smiled as his gaze landed on his flip flops which were far too large for her feet.

"Is something wrong with my feet?"

His eyes shot back up to her face, "No, not at all. Shall we go now?"

"Yes." She turned to gather together the papers and photos, sliding them into folders.

As they made their way to the parking lot, Carson watched which way Lirikai's head turned as she scented. He recognized that she usually picked up on the worst felons, not the petty thieves or drunken rabble, whom she ignored all together, but the worst of the worst. The ones intent on hurting others, or those willing to hurt others to get what they wanted.

He took the folders from her and tucked them into the usual pocket behind his seat while she went around to get into the jeep. Jumping in behind the wheel, he turned to check that she was in while he pulled his seat belt on, only to find that she was struggling to lift her leg, due to the unforgiving hem of the skirt. He was about to get out to help lift her in, when she yanked the skirt up, exposing the frill of her panties, and jumped in.

"Not practical," she murmured, trying to wriggle the fabric back down over her thighs.

Carson quickly turned his gaze away, swallowing hard, but the image of that little bit of lace on her silky skin was seared into his mind. His fists gripped the steering wheel as he struggled to focus. Where were they going? Right, food! But all he could think about was putting his mouth on that silky flesh where it met the lace trim.

"Carson?" Her voice was a question of concern. "Are you unwell? Your skin has gone pink."

He tossed her a smile, "I'm good, no worries. Where shall we go?"

She shrugged, "Since I have no money, I can always go to the sea and eat some fish."

"I recall I promised you a steak," relieved for that flash of memory, he latched on to it.

She nodded, "That is acceptable."

As he started the car and put it into gear, she reached into the back seat for the bags of clothing Ana had stowed there for her. "I wonder if there is something more comfortable," she said, rummaging through it. They hit a pothole, and she struggled to keep the clothing from being tossed around the jeep.

"Maybe look later when we have light and space." He said, upon seeing bras and panties spilling onto Lirikai's lap.

She huffed and stuffed everything back into the bag, tossing it into the backseat.

Moments later, they pulled into the parking lot of his favorite steak joint, overlooking the ocean. In an instant, he was around to Lirikai's door, opening and lifting her down out of the jeep. He smiled into her wide eyes as she gripped his shoulders in surprise. "Thought I'd save you the struggle."

She had flecks of silver and green in her eyes and tiny freckles across the bridge of her nose. She swayed, catching her balance as he set her on her feet, sending the heat and scent of her to encircle him. His nostrils flared as he inhaled, staring at her lips.

His hands flexed open, releasing her, and he stepped back.

Closing the jeep door, her gaze on his face was intent.

He gave her an awkward smile, "This way." He motioned toward the front door of the restaurant.

Inside, they were settled at a small table set into a window alcove for privacy. Carson explained what was on the menu.

"This is all new, I will try what you recommend."

He asked her several more questions about her preferences, gave the waiter their order, and asked for a bottle of wine.

"Wine!" she exclaimed, rubbing her hands together, "I recall I enjoy it."

He admired her broad smile, pleased that he had found something she liked. He struggled to find some topic to chat about other than the case. Most general modern cultural references or subjects would be meaningless to her. He wanted to keep the conversation light. "Tell me of where you've been."

"Everywhere warm."

"Favorite place?"

She thought a moment, a small frown marring her smooth forehead. "My home village."

The waiter returned with glasses of water, then brought glasses for their wine and opened the bottle, pouring the first glass for them. When he left, she told Carson of several places that she had been to that were beautiful. He'd been to a few of them himself.

"Have you ever traveled inland?"

She shook her head. "Always ocean and coastal lands."

By the time the steak arrived, their conversation had progressed, and Carson was enjoying learning more about some of the places she'd been to that he hadn't, and with those that he had, they compared experiences through their first glasses of wine.

"This is wonderful," Lirikai gushed, her mouth full of steak. "So much better than raw fish."

He winked at her, saluting her with his beef-laden fork as he chewed.

She asked him about his work, and he told her about some of his more interesting cases and colleagues with the Global Paranormal Security Agency.

Their plates cleared, wine bottle empty, they appeared to be having a wonderful evening, like any of the other companions in the dining space.

"It has been so long since I've had wine, I am not sure I can stand up now," Lirikai giggled.

"Let me help you, Lirikai" Carson stood, his hip bumped the table with less grace than he intended, drawing a giggle from Lirikai.

"Liri, my friends called me Liri."

He smiled, "Liri, then."

Outside, the ocean air immediately encircled them, enticing and fresh. Liri stood eyes closed inhaling deeply. "I will never tire of that smell."

"Shall we go down for a walk?"

Her face lit up and she immediately set off toward the path winding down to the beach. The wine and good food relaxed his body, allowing him to enjoy the evening more thoroughly. The case and his responsibilities were a foggy memory, better left for tomorrow. Tonight, he was going to enjoy a few leisurely hours in the company of this fascinating and beautiful woman.

Following her down the path, he smiled when she turned back to see if he was close behind, her own face aglow with moonlight, a satisfied belly, and a little too much wine. As soon as he was close enough, she grabbed his hand and pulled him toward the water. Once the ocean lapped at her feet, she stopped and turned toward him. Her face was so open he could see how at ease she was, too.

"I have not felt this wonderful in such a long time—I had forgotten it was possible."

"Me too." He smiled down into her face.

He was taken off guard when she grabbed his face, pulled him to her and kissed him, and just as quickly, before his arms could trap her, she released him again. "Thank you."

His chest tightened considering her joy, his groin tightened from the sensation of her mouth on his and the invasion of her scent burning into his memory.

"What?" Her words had come to him in a haze of confused happiness and desire.

"I said we should swim." She was already reaching for the buttons of her shirt.

"Wait," he managed before she could divest herself. "We can't let anyone see us."

"Oh, yes," she immediately turned, seeking some area of seclusion. In the distance there was a rocky outcrop. She laughed and started running, the flip flops kicking up sand behind her.

Pulling his shoes and socks off, he ran after her. She skidded to a halt and scrambled over the rocks. His heart was pounding in his ears when he caught up to her. The outcrop formed a small shielded 'U' open to the ocean. She was already down to her undergarments and he stood transfixed a moment. Shaking himself, he turned away and set his shoes into a safe place in the rocks, then pulled his pants off, ensuring his keys and wallet were safely tucked into the pockets and hoped someone didn't discover and take off with them. Next his shirt, and with a glance on seeing she was divested of her bra and panties, he tugged his shorts off and stuffed them in the rocks with her bundle of clothes.

She was gone in the space of time it required to secure the clothes. With a shrug, he set off for the water. He almost didn't care if there were others around. He too hadn't felt this free in a long time. Even when he shifted and swam the deepest parts of the ocean to rid himself of his worries, he wasn't so befuddled and clear all at once.

There was something about the last hours together that he felt had caused something in himself to shift. And she seemed to have been affected by it too.

A sense of abandon.

Maybe it was the wine.

Maybe it was Liri.

He moved into the water and she surfaced, drawing breath. Being in the ocean, he could feel the Goddess energy shimmering in her, calling to his own. It radiated between them.

He swam out to where she treaded water, her face pale against the darkness of the sea and sky.

"Do you know what I haven't done in a long time?"

He shook his head.

"Raced. I want to race!" She laughed.

He couldn't stop the grin spreading across his face if he'd wanted to. "We should move to deeper water." He turned to quickly scan the beach, ensuring there was no one around that might mistake them for drunken swimmers about to drown themselves. Drunken maybe, but as to the risk of drowning; there was none as long as they shifted. He couldn't see anyone.

Lirikai had already dropped below the surface. He drew in a deep breath and dove, swimming farther out from the beach toward where the land shelf dropped away. Silver flashed in the darkness. He shifted.

TEN

Lᴉʀɪᴋᴀɪ ᴇɴᴊᴏʏᴇᴅ ᴛʜᴇ ᴘʟᴇᴀsᴀɴᴛ buzz from the wine and the satisfaction of a full belly. As Carson had promised, the steak was delicious. It certainly stayed the annoying hunger that had been gnawing at her since entering the precinct.

As Carson checked for potential witnesses, she let herself sink below the surface. Floating, she closed her eyes and let the Barra'kidai take over her form, excited by the prospect of a race. Her scales caught the diffused moonlight as she circled, waiting for Carson to slip beneath the surface.

She observed his muscled human form as he dove and swam out to meet her. She admired the power of his limbs as he swam, then was entranced as she watched his shift. The area around him shimmered, blurring the lines of his body. Goddess energy surged and permeated the water. It was much like watching her sisters take their Barra'kidai form.

A thrill shuddered through her body as he emerged. He was magnificent! He must have been at least ten times her size, with pearlescent scales, spikes along his back and tail, webbed feet tipped with claws that would frighten the fiercest of polar bears. His head was broad and fierce with dangerous teeth and a powerful jaw.

She felt dwarfed in his presence and she knew she wasn't a small creature.

A wave of self-consciousness thrummed through her. Would he find her ugly? She knew he was interested in her human form, but her Barra'kidai was vastly different.

He drifted in front of her. The sensation of the Goddess enveloping them, causing her fins and tail to tingle, reminding her she had challenged him to a race.

She darted up over his head and arched down, sliding her belly along the side of his neck ensuring she had his attention. Given his size, he could easily out pace her. She gave him a little flick of her tail against his neck as she drew away and burst forward leaving him in a cloud of ocean algae.

The ocean rumbled and he was upon her. She darted again relying on the power of her body and slick scales to out distance him, determined to stay ahead of him. The thrill of the race pushed her on. They had no end point. She could choose the heading and see how far he would follow or take the lead. This motivated her to swim harder. But where to?

Thoughts of her cave invaded her mind. She sought ocean bed features to orient herself and corrected her direction. Seconds later he was with her again. She let herself twist and tumble, slicing through the sea water toward her goal, ever deeper until the surface was just a passing thought.

She slowed when the familiar darkened shape appeared. Carson curled around her, clearly curious by the direction she'd gone. Floating into the mouth of the cave, she looked around it. Had it been a full day since she'd awakened and left this place? Already, despite all the decades she'd slumbered here, it was now the place that felt distant. It wasn't a large cave, just large enough for Carson to enter and curl up in the blackness. In here, the vibration of the energy between them intensified as it reverberated off the rock walls, permeating every cell in her body.

Could he feel it too?

The space, which for centuries had been a comfortable haven to her, suddenly felt far too small.

She darted back out of the cave mouth. Carson emerged, his eyes on her. She had the impression he was concerned.

Mischievousness returned in a rush and she darted forward, letting the tip of her tail fin slap his snout and she was off again. She swam hard, not looking back. Any time she started to lag, she pushed harder to out-pace him in any direction she shifted toward. If she'd been in her human form, she'd have been laughing like a carefree child.

Eventually, growing weary, she rose toward the surface and banked toward the rising ocean floor that would bring them back to the shoreline.

Once within a reasonable distance of shore, she shifted, then broke the surface to look around. Carson's head appeared beside her.

"Where are we?"

Lirikai laughed, "I haven't any idea!"

They floated next to each other, treading water, Carson surveyed the landscape. "I can't tell, have to get closer."

They swam in, angling toward an area where the land rose up. The moon was much lower in the sky and the beach appeared to be deserted.

He laughed then, "Damn, I think we swam too far."

"No matter." Lirikai tossed over her shoulder as she headed toward the beach. "We can just swim back again."

"Lirikai, we have no clothes, we can't go up on the beach in the nude."

"So modest. I just want to get close enough to touch bottom."

They stood facing one another, sand drifting over their feet, the ocean swaying them gently. Carson stepped forward. "That cave, was that where you were before? Before we met on the beach?"

She nodded, looking up into his face, sharp angles and smooth planes under the moonlight. She could still feel the energy of the goddess between them, making her skin tingle.

He took another step closer to her, causing all her skin to turn to goosebumps.

His eyes were dark as he regarded her, she felt his fingers trail up her arm beneath the water, up over her shoulder to her jaw. "Seemed like a lonely little place."

She shrugged, "It was quiet and dark. What I wanted."

"Do you still want that? Quiet darkness? Solitude?" his thumb stroked over her cheek.

Her breath hitched. How long had it been since anyone, let alone a man, touched her with tenderness?

"Not at the moment." She tilted her head back to see his face more fully.

His eyes swept her face, lingering on her lips. He was closer now. Her tongue slipped over her lips, wanting to taste his.

Fingers reaching, they tentatively danced over his bare chest. His next step brought him so close his body warmed the sea water between them.

Lirikai closed the gap between them. His lips met hers as her body pressed to his. Her mind was divided between the press of his lips, and the thrill of his body against hers, chest to chest, hip to hip, his arousal caught between them.

Desire shot through her body. She slid the tip of her tongue over his bottom lip, then met his. He didn't hesitate once the invitation was made. His arms closed around her, his tongue and lips dominating her mouth.

The constant movement of the ocean kept their bodies sliding against one another. Her tight nipples grazed the taut muscles of his abdomen. Her hands trailed around the sensitive flesh of his ribs to slide over and up to his shoulder blades, then back down to his lower back and backside, eliciting a growl from deep in his chest. His hands were immediately on her hips, then her own backside, crushing her hard against him. His arousal pulsed between them, triggering her core to throb in response.

She wanted to climb him. Shifting so that her foot trailed up his calf, he grabbed her thigh, lifting it up to his hip. He stopped, looking down into her face, lips parted. The hunger in it matched her own. Her palms slid over his nipples as her hands found their way to his shoulders and neck, leaning into him. The ocean made her almost weightless as she locked her ankles behind him, her thighs gripping his hips, his member still between them, rubbing against her. His hands supported her bottom as he kissed her, working his way from her lips, along her jaw, down her throat and chest. Leaning back, she made room for his mouth to claim her breast, his tongue and teeth grazing over one taut nipple and then the other.

Reaching down between them, her hand gripped his shaft, making him growl again as she worked him. He sucked a little harder on her nipples and her grip on his shaft matched him. Until she could stand it no more and guided his tip to her entrance, trying to control her breathing.

Releasing her breasts, he looked up into her face as the grip of his hands on her bottom shifted to guide her down onto his shaft, filling her. They both groaned as they stared at each other, eye to eye.

This close to him, the moonlight illuminating his face, she could see something in his eyes that instinctively connected to that part of herself that knew what true solitude was, and that tentative desire to fill a longing which loneliness craved.

Since she'd been lured out of her lonely cave by the goddess energy, she'd reawakened to the shock of an alien world, been denied the temptation of her instincts, discovered she may yet still have a sister in a desperate state, and all of it was tied to this gorgeous man, who likely was the only one who had any sense of what she was in this world and what it meant. Her world had changed, and she no longer had a purpose in it. He was like her, and he was fully integrated into this world and had a role. Perhaps she could learn too. His strong hands supported her bottom as she leaned into him, her arms over his shoulders. One hand drifted to up his jaw and cheek as she looked into his eyes, her body slowly riding him.

She could see the hunger and tenderness as he looked into her face. She'd been with other men over the centuries, of course. A means to appease the body. Her primary companionship had been her sisters.

Carson elicited both possibilities. Would she eventually return to the cave? She kissed him, letting her tongue sweep his, moving faster, closing her eyes to blot out the thoughts and focus only on the feel of his body, the scent of him and the essence of his energy. She rode him, abandoning her concerns. She could sense the tension building in him and rode harder and faster. She could sense how close he was, the control he maintained over himself still. Her teeth grazed his shoulder, tongue tasting his flesh. She gripped him hard as her body exploded, rocking into him, denying herself the urge to claim.

As soon as her climax receded, Carson gripped her hips, thrusting into her swollen body, building to release. The second before he gave into orgasm, he claimed her mouth, withdrew from her body and gave his seed to the ocean. She kissed him thoroughly, but she felt a deep sense of loss at his sudden withdrawal. Once their bodies calmed, she unlinked her ankles and slid back to her feet.

Carson sighed, glancing at the angle of the moon. "It's late."

Her hands lingered on his shoulders and chest a moment longer. Stepping away from him, she turned and began to swim back to deeper water, Carson close by. She shifted, then felt the ripple of power envelope her as Carson shifted, causing her scales and fins to tingle.

AS THEY SWAM BACK to the rocky alcove where they'd left their clothes, Carson's thoughts were completely absorbed with Lirikai. Her barracuda form was lithe and powerful and impressively fierce. He had no doubt how she and her sisters had instilled terror in the guilty as they doled out the Goddess' judgment.

Their love making had been so unexpected, yet in the aftermath of the wine and the heady race through the ocean landscape, it felt right. As soon as she'd stepped into his embrace, it all felt right. She was incredible. So solid in her identity and purpose. She knew who she was and what she was meant to do.

What would happen if they did find one of her sisters was responsible for the murders? He was certain it wouldn't go well. The Barra'kidai sisterhood was legendary. She would fight for her sister, and it was his responsibility to bring killers to justice. Could he make Lirikai understand how things worked now? He doubted he could. She hadn't been part of the new world long enough.

He glanced at her silvered eyes and sharp teeth. He would have to convince her. Somehow. Could he lock a Barra'kidai in a human prison?

Could he put her in a prison with murdering, exploitive convicts? It would drive her to the madness. Is this what was happening to the killer? Was it another Barra'kidai after all? Given what he'd seen of Lirikai, and what little he knew of their legend, he tried to imagine what would happen to her if she were put into a position where her instincts to deliver justice were overwhelmed, but she was incapable of completing her purpose. Would it look something like what they were encountering?

He suddenly understood they were indeed tracking another Barra'kidai. He had to bring her in to the GPSA.

The landscape of the ocean floor became familiar. They shifted back to human form and surfaced, swimming to the rocks they'd launched their race from. Her human form was as lithe and powerful as her barracuda. She walked through the surf with a languid grace. Admiring her naked form in the moonlight, his body reacted. When she bent to retrieve the clothes from the nook, he'd stuffed them into, his shaft bucked. They were still secluded, but looking at the rocks and sand, he doubted either of them would appreciate the grit on exposed flesh. She turned, clothes in hand, and mischief curled her lips as she glanced at his groin, shoving his clothes into his chest. She dressed, careful to leave the sand on the beach, taking longer than necessary. He gritted his teeth, realizing she was doing it deliberately, then chuckled, stepping forward to help fasten her bra. He kissed her bare shoulder then pulled the blouse from her hand. Slipping her arms into the sleeves, he turned her so he could fasten the buttons. She watched his face closely as he admired her breasts. Thankfully he managed to ensure the buttons were all aligned properly.

He gestured toward the rise where the restaurant and parking lot were. "Shall we?" His voice was tight.

Her smile was blinding when she turned to scramble back over the rocks to the smoother sand of the beach. His jeep was the solitary vehicle in the lot next to the restaurant, now locked up for the night. Openly admiring her figure in the office clothes Ana had given her, he was lost in the sway of her hips when she reached for the jeep door. An instant later, his hands were on her hips as he lifted her to the seat—to spare the skirt, he told himself, knowing it was really to touch her again. She grinned up at him, slid a hand up his arm and squeezed his bicep, her hand lingering with appreciation.

Already leaning into the enclosed cab, inches from her mouth with his face close to hers, he closed the distance. Her tongue slipped over her lip, tagging his. His free hand moved to her face. It was as though now that he'd touched her, he needed to touch her more. His body agreed. Hands itching to roam over her, he withdrew with a soft peck on her lips and a sigh. He closed the door and rounded the jeep to his own side.

The drive back was peaceful and silent. The only sounds were the engine and the wind and night creatures overlaying the constant surge of the ocean along the length of the coastal highway.

Back at the hotel, with Ana's bags of clothing in hand, through the lobby and elevator ride Lirikai said little to nothing. Carson began to worry that she was having second thoughts about their evening. His gut dropped. And if she did? Then he would let her go. It wasn't a contract. But he couldn't deny, he didn't like the idea of parting.

He glanced at her again. What was he thinking? She'd only walked out of the sea the day before, she'd been a potential suspect, quickly turned investigative partner with her own agenda, and they'd ended the day with dinner and sex.

Through the door, she went into the washroom, turning on the tub faucet. Dropping his keys on the dresser, he scrubbed a hand over his face. When had he become so impulsive and careless? Probably right about the time Lirikai appeared on the beach in nothing but a stolen towel.

The water tumbled into the tub, then was cut by the sound as it shifted to the shower head. Lirikai emerged from the bathroom divested of the blouse and skirt. His eyes roamed all over the lace bra and panties as she leaned over the bag of clothes on the end of the bed. Dumping the bag, she rummaged through the fabric. "Which one is for sleeping?"

Helping her shuffle through the clothes, he cursed Ana's name under his breath. The closest thing to pajamas he could find in the pile was a very transparent negligee that dangled from his forefinger. "I have more t-shirts if you prefer."

She looked at the fabric dubiously, plucked it from his fingers held it up to her chest casting him a sidelong glance. "Decide later." The lingerie landed atop the pile as Lirikai grabbed Carson's hand, pulling him into the bathroom with her.

Well this is happening, again, already.

She was pulling his clothes from him, stitches tearing now and then. Propping her up on the counter, her breasts sprung free when he slipped the hooks of her bra, his mouth was quick to claim first one nipple then the other. He inhaled deeply the scent of ocean and their lovemaking that still clung to her skin, working his way down her tight stomach to the edge of her panties kissing her hip and the flesh along the edge of the lace. Pulling her off the counter, his fingers hooked the edges of the panties, pulling them down her legs so she could step out of them. His face drifted back up her legs and thighs, planting kisses along the way. She smelled so good, he couldn't resist. She gasped at the contact of his tongue, leaning back against the counter. Nudging her knees wider, his mouth fastened on her nub after a few tentative licks. Everything about her invaded his senses, the urge to devour her was strong.

By the time he was done with her, she was pliant in his care as he drew her toward the still running water of the shower, helping her step in. Picking up the soap, he lathered and bathed her flushed skin, then helped her wash the sea from her hair. As soon as she was clean, she took up the soap and returned the favor, carefully soaping every inch of him, paying special care to his perpetually erect shaft. It bucked with her every touch, when she knelt before him, he thought he was about to die. Her beautiful face was flushed with satisfaction, her lips, swollen from their kisses, opened and took him in. His hands shot out to brace himself against the shower walls as desire ripped through him hard and fast. It took everything he had to hold it back, reveling in her attentions. When he drew close, she licked his length, then worked her way up his abdomen and chest, claiming his mouth.

Then she turned around, braced her hands on the opposite wall and pushed her beautifully rounded bottom against his groin. His chest was tight. Slipping his fingers along the edge of her bottom he let them slide along her core, feeling how ready she was for him. He gave her hip a little squeeze, but instead of taking her against the shower wall, he turned off the water, and helped her out of the tub. Reaching for a towel, he wrapped it around her, ignoring the frown and confusion marring her lovely face. He kissed her nose and swept her up into his arms, putting her down on the bed, pushing the pile of clothing to the floor. He left her a moment to retrieve the condom from his wallet, letting it drop to the dresser top next to his keys.

Curiosity lit her face, her eyes on the package in his hands.

"Protection," he said, letting the wrapper drop to the bedside table as he quickly rolled the condom over his erection. "From what?"

"Children," he said, crawling up over her body.

"You don't need that."

He froze, his sheathed member hanging between them.

"I can't make children," she said.

He saw some emotion flutter across her face, but it was gone so quickly, he wasn't so sure. "That's alright, it's on now," he leaned in to kiss her as deeply as he could until her hands roamed and gripped and pulled at him.

"Carson," she whispered, her legs sliding up over his hips, her hands gripping his buttocks.

His tip at her entrance, he slid home and went still, his arms iron taut on either side of her as she groaned, her head rolled, lips parted. In effort to control his body, his tongue licked her parted lips and she reached up, locked onto him, seeking and delving the space of his mouth.

Goddess, she was passionate!

Her hands gripped harder, trying to push him deeper.

Wrapping his arms around her, he pulled her up as he sat back on his haunches and she sank down his length to the hilt. He nearly lost control as she moaned his name, her body going rigid in his embrace, her breath quick against his mouth. She gripped him. He remained very still, his hands locked her hips in place as she stared wide-eyed into his face, riding and grinding. His thumb grazed her nub and she exploded around him. A moment later he joined her, sparks flaring through his brain as he unloaded.

They remained as they were, skin slick, panting into each other's faces for a long moment. His lips touched hers slowly, softly, then he lay her back upon the pillow, slowly withdrawing. The cool air rushed between them, and he wanted nothing more than to have his body touching hers again.

Retreating to the bathroom, he discarded the spent condom, wiped himself down, then returned with a fresh cloth to clean Lirikai's sensitive flesh.

Her eyes widened in surprise as she watched him do this, trying to take the cloth from his hand to do it herself. Withholding it from her reach, he finished his task, kissed her thigh, and returned it to the bathroom before settling into the bed next to her. Pulling the sheet across their bodies, he pulled her close, tucked her hair into a safe crook and kissed the top of her head.

She said nothing, but entwined her fingers in his before relaxing into sleep. As soon as he heard her breathing shift, he let himself fall to darkness.

ELEVEN

LIRIKAI WOKE TO THE low sound of Carson's voice as he spoke to someone she couldn't see.

Every muscle was relaxed and alive at once. She rolled over, stretching every inch of herself.

She smiled, recalling the night before. Had it all been a wonderful dream? The lack of clothing and the feel of her muscles told her otherwise.

Seated on the arm of the sofa with his back to her and long legs stretched out before him, he held his cell phone device to his ear, listening. He had put shorts on but was otherwise unclothed. She admired his broad shoulders and the strong planes of his back that tapered to narrow hips. The sun was a golden spotlight illuminating his bronzed skin, making all the tiny hairs on his legs and arms glow, as were the tips of his hair, casting him with the halo around his head which she recalled artists favoring at one time.

He lowered his hand, pressing his thumb to the device, and placed it on the desk. Carson scrubbed a hand over his face, and his shoulders rose and fell with a deep sigh as he stood to look out the filmy window.

"What is it?" she asked, sitting up in the bed, chest tight.

He turned at the sound of her voice. "I didn't mean to wake you."

"The sun is up," she shrugged, "What has happened?"

"There's another body. A cop this time."

"A cop? Like... you?"

He nodded.

Her stomach dropped. "Was he a good man?"

It was his turn to shrug, "Woman. Couldn't say, I don't know the cops here very well. Ana might know her. But this changes things. A lot."

Pulling the sheet around herself, Lirikai moved across the room to stand next to Carson. The window was a mix of ocean and city. The sea and beach filled one side, bordered by the coastal highway holding the city back from the water on the opposite side. She looked up at him, waiting.

"With a cop dead, this will motivate the force to find the killer. That means everyone will be working the case, not just me and Ana—and you. That many more people with *hard* motivation."

She swallowed hard. Angry villagers made for brutal messy justice. And these weren't average villagers, they had power and weapons.

Lirikai crossed back to the bed, retrieving the spilled clothing from the floor, looking for something to wear.

"I will find her."

"Lirikai, when we find her, I have to bring her in."

She kept her back to him, lips pressed together.

"Lirikai?"

When she didn't answer, she heard him cross the carpet before his warm hands came to rest on her arms.

She stopped moving for a long moment finding comfort in the touch.

Her sister—she was sure these were the actions of a sister—was in trouble and she had to try to help her.

"I will find her," she said again.

"How?"

Stepping away from those strong hands, she resumed her search through the clothing, growled, and slammed the clothing back onto the bed, "Is there nothing reasonable in this pile?"

"I can take you shopping for new clothes," Carson said.

"There is no time for that," she snapped, snatching undergarments and a blouse.

Carson reached into the pile, "Try these jeans."

With a huff, she grabbed the clothing from his hand and went into the lavatory.

'How?' he'd asked her.

Indeed. The bodies barely had trace scents of anything on them. Normally, she would be able to detect at least a little bit, the scent of the killer, which would guide her in the direction she needed to go. She would not have been working alone to cover a village.

How?

Maybe this new body will lead her in the right direction. Barra'kidai didn't kill innocents or law enforcers. It was against the natural law for what they were created to do. Either this sister had fallen to madness or these victims were corrupt in some way. Abuse of power and position was as old as time. Surely Carson understood that? Or was he too ingrained in the modern world and ideas? Did they not believe such things could happen?

When she emerged from the bathroom, Carson had dressed and straightened the room.

She slid her feet into his flip flops. "I'm ready."

LIRIKAI WAS SILENT WHILE Carson drove them to the scene, which turned out to be close to the restaurant they'd dined at the night before. And now with the body this close to a location they'd just been to, Carson was on alert. It couldn't be a coincidence, could it?

The forensics tent was set up just beyond the rocky outcrop where they'd stashed their clothes. He glanced at Lirikai's face, her brow deeply furrowed and lips tight as she pulled on the white suit. Her nostrils twitched as she turned her head away from the tent scanning the landscape opposite the ocean. Still she didn't say anything but followed him inside.

The body was marked the same as the others, devoid of any identifiers including clothing. She'd been identified by the first responders as a known local officer. Preliminary report in hand, Carson leaned to see the victim's face. Dread clawed through his gut. He'd seen this cop in the bullpen every day. They hadn't been friendly, but she was still familiar.

"Has her family been notified?" he asked Lana O'Brien.

Lirikai crouched, removed her mask leaning to within inches of the body, inspecting the markings.

"Not yet," Lana's face was tight. "We're going to get the son of a bitch that's doing this. No one can take down a cop and get away with it. I've seen too many of these victims. This is someone with no humanity. They need to be put down like a rabid animal."

Lirikai rose from the body and left the tent.

"I need access to any cases she was working. Maybe it's connect-ed."

Lana gave him a sharp nod, "I'll see what I can do."

"We'll need to talk to everyone she worked closely with, and her family," he said, handing the report back to Lana. "Send it to my office as soon as possible."

Lost in thought, he pulled the suit off and discarded it with the others, then turned, expecting to find Lirikai by the shore waiting for him. Not seeing her, he turned again, his gaze sliding over the investigators and again not finding her. Not until he turned his attention up to the parking lot atop the rise did he see her talking to someone in a car.

It wasn't Ana's car. Who else would she be talking to? He called out, walking toward her.

She turned at the sound of his voice, and he could see a woman behind the wheel who spoke to Lirikai. His heart stopped when she darted around the vehicle and got in the passenger side. The car sped off with the door barely closed.

Carson launched into a run for his jeep, parked farther away.

Pulling his cell from his pocket as he ran, he called Ana, relaying what had just happened. Jumping into the jeep, he snapped the cell into its brace on his dash and tore out of the lot in pursuit. His knuckles were white on the wheel as he steered the jeep after the car. At the road, trying to see which direction it went, he listened for the sound of an accelerating vehicle. There was too much traffic on this Saturday afternoon, everyone out enjoying the day of beach and shopping. Far up the road he spotted what he thought was the unremarkable car he'd seen Liri get into and hit the gas, cutting several cars off as he went.

Ana was still on the line, shouting at him to be careful when horns sounded. "I need to get close enough for the plate," he snapped.

"Well don't kill yourself in the process, dammit!"

Carson snarled, "Not helpful." He veered in and out of traffic, eliciting more horns and angry shouts. He didn't have the benefit of a police car's light and sirens to alert people that he wasn't just a random maniac but was a man with a mission.

His heart was pounding in his ears, but it wasn't out of fear of the traffic.

What if Lirikai were hurt? What if he never saw her again? He had to get to her.

But she'd run to get into the car when she heard him. Surely, she wasn't in danger?

What if she was being coerced?

Who was the woman?

Was she a Barra'kidai? Was she *the* Barra'kidai?

Was she the killer?

And if she was? What would Liri do?

Would she stop her, or help her?

Would Liri help her sister complete her 'duty' by killing more people?

His foot pressed the gas pedal a little harder.

He had to stop both of them. Where the fuck was the car? He couldn't see it - wait! There it was! It made a right turn at a busy intersection. Carson sped up and darted around the cars blocking his way, thankful for the break in traffic, and continued to tear up the street in time to see it swerve through a narrow gap as the light turned red. He had no choice but to stop hard as a bus suddenly filled the space, lurching, then crawling. Hitting the horn and cursing, passengers peered down at him through the bus's windows confused by his urgency.

As soon as the rear of the bus cleared the front of his jeep, he edged forward but was again cut off by more encroaching traffic. He glanced ahead, frustrated to realize the car had disappeared. He had no idea which way it went. By the time he was able to get through the clogged intersection and up the road, they were long gone.

Ana was still on the line suffering through all the noise, his curses and extreme road rage. "Did you at least get a look at her?"

"Barely," he said as he accelerated up the road, hoping beyond hope to get a glimpse of something, a clue as to which way they'd gone only to discover absolutely nothing.

"Carson, just come to the station, maybe she'll turn up, you never know."

"I will, soon." He said, disconnecting the call.

Instead of turning back toward the office, he pulled over to recall the moments before Liri ran off. Reaching for the glove box, he pulled out a notebook and pen, bulleting the events.

Called to the scene, checked the body. Lirikai had looked at the body and left quickly. Then she was up at the parking lot.

She must have found something on the body to draw her outside. Had she seen something outside before going in? What was she doing before hand? She was looking at the ocean. Had there been someone there?

If this was a Barra'kidai, why would they be lurking around? What were they looking for? How could they know Liri would be there? Was it on purpose? What was going on?

Was Lirikai responsible in some way after all? Had he been wrong about her?

For a second, he thought maybe she had done it herself, but that was ridiculous. They'd been together nearly unbroken since he'd found her on the beach. She wouldn't have had the opportunity to do this last murder. But what of the others? Were they working together? Was her time with him a ruse to get information about the investigation from the inside? Was she playing him? Was she? All this time?

He thought back to their lovemaking. She'd led him away from the parking lot. She'd lured him into the ocean. Maybe it was all a ruse. All of it. She'd lured him out to see what manner of beast he was to see what she was working against.

He'd been so stupid. He'd brought her in on the investigation right away, without any thought as to whether she was involved. That wasn't entirely true, he'd had some thought, but had instantly brushed it a way. Now he had his doubts. He slammed his hands on the steering wheel. How fucking stupid could he be?

He'd never ever been so fucking careless in his life. He'd always been careful about who he let get close to him, and his work had always, always been performed with care.

He'd slipped and wasted time screwing someone who should be suspect. And now a cop was dead. A cop he saw every day was dead.

He thought back over the last day.

How had she found him? How had she known to target him?

"Goddess." She'd said to him when they met.

How could she have known?

She'd sensed it when he'd been swimming in the water. She must have. He could feel the Goddess energy coming from her too.

He dropped his head into his hands, scrubbing them over his face.

He'd instantly let his guard down because of the Goddess.

His natural suspicion had been overridden by his sense of loyalty to the goddess and excitement to meet someone else connected to her.

He'd thought that after all this time, the Goddess had sent someone to help him. Meeting anyone else of the Goddess in his entire long life had been rare occurrence and always had been meaningful. He'd trusted in that.

Had Lirikai helped him at all, or had he just stupidly fed her everything he knew, like a naive child?

He was so angry, he couldn't remember anything but her beautiful face and curvy body. It was all that had filled his mind and senses when they'd been anywhere near each other.

The sense of betrayal and his own stupidity were burrowing deeper and deeper.

This was why he was alone. This is exactly why he kept himself apart from any potential bonds. They either made him weak and got him killed, or they made him weak and got him stupid.

Goddessdammit. As soon as he was done this case, he was going home to his islands. He spent too much time working for the GPSA and needed a break to re-balance himself.

He drummed the steering wheel for a moment, then made his decision. He drew in a deep breath, trying to dispel his anger and find focus.

It had been such a long time since he'd lost himself to anger like that. It was entirely out of character for him to give into such deep and quick rage and doubt.

But as it abated, he felt as though some clarity were settling in its place. Like he'd been burned clean of something that had settled in him, stagnant and filmy. He didn't have a name for what it was just yet, but it would come.

He stared the jeep, made a U-turn on the quiet street and drove back to the scene at the beach.

He was going to go over everything. Everything. Very carefully.

LIRI'S EYES WERE GLUED to the driver's face, still disbelieving. She could not believe who she'd found out by the beach, in a car watching the scene. She had approached the car. Then Carson had shouted for her, and she hadn't thought anymore, just ran to get into the car before she disappeared, and she'd taken it as a cue to escape.

Now, the woman drove carefully, constantly checking the mirrors to see if they were still being followed.

"I can't see him anymore," Lirikai told her in the old language.

They drove on awhile longer. Lirikai's gut was tight over leaving Carson. She'd seen him run after her, then his jeep in the distance following them. She could only imagine what he was thinking right now.

The woman remained silent.

How long? How long had it been since they'd seen each other? But she knew her. She would never forget this face. She never forgot any of her sister's faces. Despite the sallowness of her skin, the sharp bones and haunted look around her eyes. She knew her.

"Milakai, what is happening?"

She steered the car into a diner parking lot that Lirikai recognized. She'd been here with Carson. A shiver slid up her neck.

Her voice was a hard whisper, "Liri, I need your help."

"How did you know I was here?"

"I saw you the other night. I've-I've been following."

"Why?"

"I don't know," her lips opened and closed, her eyes filled with tears. "I don't know," her voice broke.

Lirikai had never seen a sister like this. This was a stranger, not the woman she'd known before.

"Tell me what you've done," she said, her voice soft, her hand reaching out.

Milakai straightened at that, shoulders back, lips settling into a firm line. "I've been doing my duty." The haunted look vanished and her eyes burned with conviction.

Lirikai dropped her hand back to her lap. "What I have seen is not the way of the Barra'kidai, Mila."

"I am Barra'kidai."

"Are you?" she challenged. "The last time I saw you, you were happily waving those few of us left goodbye, while you sailed away with your mate to live a human life. Not a Barra'kidai life."

Mila's head snapped toward Liri, eyes narrowed. "Well, I can no longer live a human life. I need you and the other sisters to help me."

"Mila, there are no other sisters."

Liri watched the emotions play over Mila's face. Shock, pain, resolve. Her voice softened a little. "Then I need your help, Liri."

"What for?" She already knew the answer, but she asked anyway.

"To kill the last one."

"I will not commit murder, Mila, not even for you."

"It isn't murder, it's justice," she snapped.

Her gut flipped over. She'd seen the bodies. And she could see the pain and madness in Mila's eyes. Her instinct was what she always knew—the Barra'kidai were the Goddess' deliverers of justice. But Mila's countenance and surety wormed doubt and fear into her heart. Never before had she ever doubted a sister, or the purpose of the Barra'kidai. Never.

She hedged, "The last victim was a law enforcer."

"She was complicit," she hissed.

The sound slid up Lirikai's spine. The unnatural tenor and energy rolling off the woman struck her. She could feel the wrongness. The brokenness of her sister.

Was this what happened when the immortal lived too long among the humans?

Would this be her fate too? She'd gone into hibernation because she was tired of drifting alone in the world. The Barra'kidai either found their justice and lived out life as humans or died achieving it for others.

Clearly something had gone wrong for Mila. Centuries later, she was still living among the humans but now she was broken.

"Come to the sea with me."

Liri watched Mila crumble, "I can't! I can't, Liri. I want nothing more than to let the sea take my pain, but I can't."

Mila's grief flooded the small space of the car and Liri was consumed by it and for the first time in millennia was overwhelmed by raw emotion.

Not since the day she looked on the pale lifeless faces of her family did she feel such deep grief. It was Mila's, amplified by what little Goddess energy she had left in her, which Liri could feel. It was like a tsunami crashing uncontrolled through the car.

Liri understood this kind of loss. She grabbed Mila's hand. "You're not alone, sister."

Mila bent until her forehead rested on their hands as she cried. Liri waited, tears streaming down her own face unable to stem the flow.

"Tell me of your life since we last saw each other, Mila."

Mila sipped her coffee and Liri waited while she gathered centuries' worth of memories.

"Start with your mate," she prompted, "the reason you left us."

A pang of guilt and sadness fluttered across Mila's face.

"The bond is stronger than anything. It's stronger than what you had with your human family before the Barra'kidai. It's stronger than the Barra'kidai. It's your second chance at a life and it's your call to live that life as fully as possible."

"I thought you'd have died of old age long ago, how are you still here?"

Mila shrugged, "Well, we—John and I aren't sure, but we think it could be because we weren't able to conceive. My body didn't fully change back to human through the influx of hormones that having a child brings to complete the change. And John, well John is special in his own right. He isn't human and lives longer than most anyway." She sipped her coffee again, her eyes tearing up, "We were happy, for so long, Liri."

Liri reached out to squeeze her sister's hand, "What happened Mila?"

"John was investigating a story."

"He's a law enforcer?" Lirikai frowned.

Mila shook her head, "No, not quite. An investigative journalist. He finds out the truth of a situation and shares it with the public, so everyone knows what's going on."

"That sounds dangerous for someone that is not a law enforcer."

Mila shrugged, "He could handle himself. Most of the time, anyway."

"What was his story?"

"I didn't know at first. He was always working on something, and often it was dangerous. He usually did dangerous. Often, he shared his investigations with me, but I'd been swamped with my own work lately." Her hands tightened on her mug. She took a shaky breath and went on. "The day he disappeared, he gave me his sim card to hold on to because he was taking his phone in to repair a cracked screen. He didn't trust it wouldn't be copied. I had it in my purse when I went to work. He was going to a shady neighborhood where the guy works for cheap out of a pawn shop. When I came back from work the house was wrecked and his office was torn apart. He never came back."

"What happened next?"

Mila's thumb teased the rim of her mug, "I called the police about the break in, of course. They were familiar with him and questioned me about what he was working on. I didn't know what this case was about, but he was putting in a lot of hours. He didn't come back that night, I called the station again in the morning and they asked me to go in."

She paused to collect herself.

"John was supposed to meet me for dinner after he had his phone repaired. And I was trying not to worry about his absence—sometimes it happens when he's on a case. But by morning I was scared."

Lirikai waited in silence.

Mila looked up at her, "Do you remember the old days, when we'd be in a battle and a group of us would get separated? The waiting after the battle for the others to come swimming slowly back, likely wounded and recovering. And not knowing exactly how badly hurt the survivors were and who might have been lost?"

Liri nodded. She remembered.

"It was like that, but the waiting went on. When I went into the station, the officer that came to talk to me asked me a lot about John's work again, and then started asking about our relationship, pushing the questioning in a direction that didn't make sense. She started asking about affairs and maybe he'd just left me for another lover and elaborately tried to make it look like something else. Her dismissive attitude didn't make sense."

"Obviously you couldn't tell her that you and John had been mated for centuries and that your relationship didn't work that way."

Mila nodded. "But her attitude seemed like more was going on than her just being an asshole cop patronizing a jilted wife. My instincts, the Barra'kidai instincts, began to resurface in conjunction with my own natural instincts, I knew something was very wrong. Just like that, the Barra'kidai resurfaced under my skin, and I had to get out of there and out to my car before I lost control. It was happening so fast."

Lirikai knew the power of the instinct and how sometimes it was difficult to control. She couldn't imagine what it must have felt like to have had it buried for so long than suddenly break free like that. The utter loss of control would have been terrifying. She'd suspected something like this might have been happening, but now Mila was confirming it in her own words.

"I managed to calm down enough to drive to the beach front. I tried to do a controlled shift. I couldn't do it." Mila's eyes were full of tears. "I couldn't shift entirely, and I was barely controlling the instincts. I was shifting just enough to be dangerous, just a partial, and when it happened the Barra'kidai was in control."

Liri swallowed the horror in her heart. It was one thing to give in to the Barra'kidai in battle, it was another to be ruled by it when you didn't wish to be. A state of nightmare, a nightmare she feared for herself-being ruled by the beast rather than co-existence with it. "Do you think the Barra'kidai will fade once we find your John?"

"I don't know, Liri. If he hasn't come back to me by now, I don't think he will. I'm afraid what will happen when I know for sure he won't. I can't survive that again. Not again. Either I save him, or I die with him."

Liri blinked away her own tears. After all this time, she finally wasn't alone again, only to learn she might very well lose her sister, knowing she will never ever come back. Before, she had thought she might be the last of her kind, but there was still hope. This time, if Mila didn't find John alive, Liri knew she would be the last.

She took a deep breath, "How can I help you?"

The relief in Mila's face was palpable as tears dropping onto the paper covering the table. "When I remembered I had John's sim card in my purse, I put it in my phone and found his notes, which led me back along his investigative trail. I started at the pawn shop where he went to get his phone repaired. He was just the beginning."

Liri watched Mila's eyes turn silver as the Barra'kidai rose to the surface during the retelling of her own investigation to her mate's disappearance. She shivered. It was like the old days. The thrill of tracking and hunting, seeking justice. But Lirikai could also see something else in Mila, a burning that verged on frenzy. An imbalance. Danger.

She accounted for each of the victims in Carson's files. There was no longer any doubt that Mila was killing these individuals. But aside from her mate's disappearance, what were their crimes? Were their deaths warranted? If they weren't then Mila's actions were abominable, making her no better than the criminals the Barra'kidai executed. If she was destroying these people only to assuage the fear of losing her mate, and not because they were guilty of committing terrible crimes, then Mila would have to be destroyed and given over to the goddess.

She felt punched in the chest as she looked at the face of a sister, one she hadn't seen in half a millennia. Was there a chance all this could end well for all of them? What would Carson do if he caught Mila, now that Liri knew she had indeed killed these people.

He would lock her away. Liri couldn't imagine life locked away - especially in a place that housed criminals of the worst sort. She would lose completely to the Barra'kidai under such circumstances and exist in a place of madness.

She couldn't let that happen to Mila. They'd either find John alive and they would go away never to be found, or Mila would die.

TWELVE

ANA SAW CARSON IN his office staring at the files, with their key information displayed on the desktop, trying to piece together the victims' identities.

A cop, an informant, a local spiritual leader and a petty criminal.

A light tap on the door drew his attention. Ana stepped into the room and closed the door when he turned to her.

She approached, staring at the accumulation of photos, her gaze landing on the latest victim.

"I saw her everyday that I've been here," Carson said. "Did you know her?"

She frowned at the photo. "Dana Keenan. A little, but not really. I keep my distance from most of the cops here. I work from this post; I'm not one of them."

He turned toward her so he could see her face, "Why not? You've been here a long time."

She shrugged, "They know I'm not a cop. As a liaison for the federal bureau, they're leery of my presence. But this is the first case that has had us dealing directly. Usually I'm sending agents elsewhere up and down the coast, so I'm ignored." She paused for a moment, pushing the corner of Keenan's photo to straighten it. "I haven't interfered in their business before now. I'm no longer just occupying space, and the dynamic has shifted a bit."

Carson studied the photos a bit longer, not seeing anything new. Not seeing anything at all.

The door to Carson's office slammed open, the precinct captain stood framed in the doorway. Several officers stood behind him.

The bullpen was quiet. "You." He pointed at Carson. "Hand over all your work to my men, I want this killer found now."

"This is a federal investigation, captain."

"I don't give a shit. The bodies have been piling up while you're running around doing nothing. One of *my* cops is dead. We'll deal with the problem ourselves."

"It doesn't work that way." Carson turned toward the captain, his voice even.

The captain drew himself up, stomping toward Carson. "Who the hell do you think you are? This is my town, my cops, my territory. You know nothing about how things are run here. Hand over your files and go back to D.C."

Ana's skin prickled when Carson didn't move. The captain stepped to within inches of him. Her breath caught as the energy in the room shifted. Carson didn't move, but he seemed to grow larger, his presence filled the room. Still he didn't move.

The captain took a step back, perspiration sheening his temples, his face going pale.

"Agent Analiese Ortega and I will continue our investigation, Captain Mack. We thank you for your hospitality in your precinct and we will finish our job. We will find out who is responsible for all the tragedy. Then, and only then, will we think about returning to D.C."

Ana watched the captain struggle to contain himself, but after a moment he gave a curt nod, then turned on his heel and walked out. The other officers eventually turned away and the low usual din in the bullpen resumed.

She walked past Carson, closing the door with a soft click, then turned to him and let out a breath. His gaze was still on the doorway. She glanced behind her to see that he was still watching the captain, who was now talking to a couple of his subordinates, off to the side of the room. Every few seconds he'd glance at Carson's office door.

She shrugged, "Like I said, we're not one of them."

"No, we're not," he answered quietly.

"Come on, let's go over the victim's profiles again. Maybe something will pop."

Finally, he nodded and turned back to the task at hand. "I've read over everything, all of the interview reports. I think we'll have to go back and do them again ourselves."

Ana blew out a breath. "Okay." Shuffling through the folders, she pulled free the first one. "First victim, local petty thug, runs a pawn shop in the less desirable end of town. Cause of death blunt force trauma followed by blood loss from the bite marks. The symbol carved into his head was done post-mortem."

Carson nodded.

"Second victim was a spiritual leader of a small congregation in the community, third was an informant, and then Keenan."

"All same M.O."

Ana stepped back a moment, arms crossed, lower lip between her fingers as she considered what was before them. "What feedback has Lirikai given, if any?

"If we can rely on the idea that the killings have been done by a Barra'kidai, which are supposed to be all extinct, with the exception of Lirikai, then legends are that the Barra'kidai maul their victims to death because they are corrupted humans preying on others. They can sniff out the corrupt, which incites the instinct to devour and obliterate them at the behest of the Goddess."

"You know, it doesn't sound any better than the last time we discussed the details."

Carson laughed. "Yeah, no shit."

"So, if we're running with the legend, then every one of these victims is corrupt in some way... including Keenan." Ana said, her glance flickering toward the bullpen beyond the door. She repeated the list, "A cop, a church leader, an informant and a petty thug. Are they linked together, or are they just random?"

Carson turned back toward Ana, "Keenan's body was found very close to an area that Lirikai and I had been the night before.

"Shit." Ana turned back toward the bullpen now, the captain nowhere in sight. "Surveillance? If so, that might make you and Lirikai look suspicious depending on how many in the precinct were aware of this."

"I doubt they'd try to pin anything on me, but they might go after Lirikai."

"Where was she when she wasn't with you that night?"

"She was with me all night. We've been together constantly since she found me on the beach. Except when she was with you...."

"Well now," Ana grinned at him, watching the tips of his ears turn pink. "I guess all that lacy underwear did the trick."

He rolled his eyes at her, but turned away deliberately, focusing on tidying up the files. "Let's go knock on some doors already knocked on."

"Sure, let me get my jacket," Ana said, leaving him to clear up his desk. As she walked through the bullpen to her office, the usual din dropped, and she could feel eyes crawling over her. Suspicion rode high in the atmosphere. Something tugged at the back of her mind, feeling the urge to go and talk to the captain. Veering toward his door, she found him in conversation with the same few officers he'd been chatting with earlier on. He looked up at her approach and the hostility rolled toward her.

"Captain, I just wanted to express my condolences. I know Keenan worked here a long time. I'm sorry."

His jaw tightened, his eyes hard as he stared down at her. Underlying grief spiked the hostility, laced with guilt. "She was a good cop." His jaw worked, looking for proper, professional words to relay.

"I'm sorry I didn't know her better."

"Yeah, well...."

She sensed his impatience for her departure, so she left the group to get her jacket as intended. She found Carson by his jeep waiting for her to get in.

LIRIKAI AND MILA PULLED up to the bluffs overlooking the ocean. "Each of the guilty came out to the beaches for some reason. I tracked them to places relatively near here. John thought they were smuggling drugs to the caves to and from cargo ships."

The late evening winds buffeted their clothes and hair from where they stood looking down the cliff faces. They dropped at the sound of an engine, as a speed boat rounded the light-house point. Engine cut, it drifted, letting the water push it closer to land. It restarted its engine at a barely audible speed, trundling toward where Mila said the cave mouth was.

"Only sea access?" she asked Mila, who nodded. "I'm going in."

"Be careful Liri. I've had to fight my way out of every encounter with those guys."

Lirikai nodded, squeezed Mila's arm and scuttled her way down to an overhang where she stripped and let herself drop into the ocean.

The sea welcomed her as soon as she shifted into Barra'kidai, immediately darting toward the caves.

Staying well below the surface of the water, she swam along the ocean floor, guided by the changes of surf and darkness. Soon, the water level shallowed out and she drifted below the hulls of several speed boats. Shifting back into human form, she surfaced without a sound, careful to use the boats as shields between herself and where she thought the criminals would be lurking. The cave wasn't unlike the underwater cave she'd spend the last few centuries sleeping in. She listened hard, hearing some voices echo off the cave walls, but they didn't appear to be in the immediate chamber. The dim light of the setting sun allowed her just enough light to see that she was alone in the cave mouth. There were three boats tied to large rocks, but she couldn't be sure how many of the enemy would be here, or what she would find. Mila expected she would find barrels or some other kind of containers that would hold drugs or some other contraband.

Creeping up out of the water, she moved as silently on land as she did in the water following the scent of criminals. Keeping to the shadows, she edged farther, and farther still into the cave, listening to the murmur of voices as well as for any noise coming from the direction she'd emerged from. Light splashed the walls as she rounded a corner and she was careful to remain out of sight.

Edging forward, she moved around the bend of the jagged cave wall, until finally she could see something. There were some waist-high barrels made of metal, painted in muted natural colors. The scents of prey were stronger here, and she knew they were close. There were weapons propped atop some of the barrels and leaning up against the cave wall. A lot of them.

"These numbers look about right," a man's voice echoed toward her followed by the sound of fluttering papers. "We're due to move everything out tonight, so keep watch for the signals. We shouldn't have any trouble from the coast guard, they'll be occupied else-where on the coast."

The sounds of heavy steps scuffing rock and gravel drifted down the tunnel.

"What about these?" a second voice said, followed by a thud and a muffled cry.

"Don't damage them," the first voice snapped. "The buyers don't like them bruised. They like doing that themselves. Right of own-ership, or some shit like that."

"Yes sir. Are they going with the product, or a separate shipment?"

"They're going last. The drugs first."

She couldn't tell how many of them there were, but the odor drifting to her was overwhelming, more so than when she passed through the bullpen at the precinct. Too many for her to deal with alone. Barra'kidai were meant to work as a unit, not as lone soldiers. Mila had been very lucky to survive so many encounters on her own, though Lirikai knew how motivated she was to avenge her husband. Such a mission was all consuming and incredibly powerful.

There was a low sound, like what she'd heard from Carson's communication device. Another voice spoke, "Sir, they're still tracking the journalist's wife, they think they're close to trapping her this time.""Good, I don't know what the hell is going on there with that one. Is she traveling with a guard dog or something?"

"Not known."

"What is the lead?"

"She's been seen with the woman that's been working with the feds."

"Shit. I'd better get back to the precinct and find out what they know. They'll be sniffing out harder now that Keenan's been killed."

Lirikai's heart had begun to hammer in her chest at the mention of being close to trapping Mila. She had to get back and warn her.

"Call me when you've got her and get that information out of her. We need to know what she knows and if we can shut down any possibility of exposure. If she survives the interrogation, ship her out with the others. We'll get our money's worth out of her for all the time and manpower she's lost us."

His voice was rapidly becoming louder.

Lirikai padded back down the cave corridor toward the water, gasping reflexively when her barefoot landed on a sharp rock.

"What the fuck was that?" the voice boomed, feet trampling the ground behind her. "Someone's here, find them" he barked.

Lirikai held her breath, running harder for the shadows of the inlet and dove into the water, no longer holding out on stealth but speed. She shifted immediately, continuing her dive down to the ocean floor and following it as it descended farther out to the ocean. One of the boats roared to life over her head, creating turbulence in the water. She sank lower to avoid the unbearably deafening rumble. Just past the cave mouth its engine cut out, floating on the surface. They were looking for her, waiting for someone that would have to eventually surface for air. Not waiting around for them, she swam back toward the bluffs where she'd left Mila. She shifted and surfaced, then swore. How was she going to get back up? She swam farther along looking for a place to breach the cliffs. Climbing wasn't a skill she had much practice with.

The farther she swam, the harder her heart pounded. She began to pray, as she had not done in many centuries, since the Goddess had abandoned her. She prayed for a break to climb, she prayed for Mila's safety. Finally finding a break, she clumsily launched herself up the rocks, hoping her pale body wasn't noticed against the dark rocky surface. Carefully, to keep an eye on the boat that still floated near the cave mouth, she climbed as quickly as possible while keeping low to the ground. It wasn't easy, and she was leaving more skin behind on the jagged rocks than she thought possible. But her fear kept her going. With some luck, since she didn't think the Goddess was listening, she found her way back to her clothes and shoes, pulling them on over the scraps and gouges in her flesh. Manoeuvring back up the last distance to where Lirikai had left Mila, she could hear scuffling and Mila's shouts as she fought.

Lirikai clawed the rocks to climb faster, only to find Mila snarling and surrounded by armed men, one of whom held her arms tight behind her so she couldn't escape. She swore and spit at them. "If anything happens to me, John's information will go to the media." She struggled, trying to kick at another of the men dodging his way closer to secure her with ropes.

As he launched toward her, her head turned and her eyes widened at the sight of Lirikai preparing to launch herself into the fray, "No!" she yelled shaking her head. "The feds will come for-" A crack sounded as a weapon hit her and her head dropped.

"Captain thinks she has a guard dog; find it and shoot it."

One of the men broke away as the two others let her drop to the ground to bind her hands.

Lirikai remained where she was, obscured by the rocks and scrub. Everything in her screamed to fight for Mila, but her words had forced a wedge of thought to crack the instinct.

Feds—she meant Carson. Mila had referred to him and Ana as feds during their discussions.

With great effort, she controlled the urge to attack the men with weapons pointed at Mila. They pushed her into the back of one of the unremarkable cars and drove away, leaving the other.

"Where the fuck is this dog she's supposed to have?"

"How the hell should I know, quit bitching and just find the fucker so we can go."

Lirikai considered options.

The wind was still buffeting the cliff, and now and then the scent of criminal whipped past her nose, caused her mouth to water.

They were hunting a dog, and they would find her. If she tried to get back down the cliff, she risked being seen now they were no longer distracted by Mila. They were both armed.

Remaining where she was, she waited for opportunity to present itself.

Maybe, just maybe, the Goddess still watched over her priest-esses. Maybe.

Forcing herself to breathe, she waited.

Boots kicked gravel toward her.

She scrambled back down to the ledge and got comfortable.

Rocks skittered down around her. Curses were snatched away on the wind.

"Hey, who the hell are you?"

Looking over her shoulder, a man held a gun not quite aimed at her. One foot planted on a rock, the other on higher ground balancing himself.

She turned, cupping a hand around her ear, indicating she couldn't hear him. The wind blew his scent right into her face and she closed her eyes against the urges overwhelming her control.

He moved closer to her, a lone woman sitting on an ocean ledge watching the sea.

"What are you doing here?" His foot was planted on the loose rock beside her. The scent was all around her now, her teeth were descending.

Carson's voice in her mind interrupted the instinct. With a sigh, she reached up to grab the man's thigh. Startled, he looked down at her hand. He jerked when he looked into her eyes. Tightening her grip, she pulled him down in front of her while launching herself backward into the rising ground.

He flew over her head, screaming, into a heavy splash as he hit the ocean. She didn't know if he survived. She didn't care.

"Carl! Did you find that dog?"

Would it work twice? She guessed not and began to climb.

His reaction to her presence was much like the first guy's, and he smelled just as delicious. More so.

"What are you doing out here, you some kind of hooker? Where's Carl?"

She shrugged, "Nice night,"

"Where's Carl?" he repeated. He hadn't pointed the gun at her yet, but his eyes were all over her breasts.

She waved a hand in the direction she'd climbed from.

A cursory glance didn't produce Carl.

She sauntered right up to him, letting her gaze drift to the gun in his hand. A grin broke his plain face. "Gimme some head and I'll let you keep yours."

Lirikai reached out her empty hands, her fingers curling around his belt buckle, working to open it as she stepped into his space, letting her nose graze his throat, inhaling deeply. Mmm yes, this one has done many, many terrible things to those weaker than himself. He was ripe.

"Hurry up." His hand shifted to her shoulder to push her to her knees, but she was faster. Her free hand gripped the back of his neck, pulling his throat into her face and she gave into the Barra'kidai. He gurgled as she spit his adam's apple to the ground. The gun dropped as he reached for his throat, eyes wide. Stepping around him, she shoved him hard enough to send him rolling down the slope toward the cliff. She listened to the thuds and sliding rocks, waiting for the splash that came a moment later.

She smiled, licking her lips.

Just a little taste.

Her Barra'kidai purred.

Retrieving the gun, she went to Milakai's car, got in and stared at the steering wheel.

Now what?

Surely it couldn't be harder than guiding horses pulling a cart?

THIRTEEN

CARSON AND ANA SPENT hours retracing the work of local officers, conducting their own interviews with victim's families and acquaintances. It would take days to cover everyone, of course, but they'd hit up a few of the ones they thought were key to begin with.

Exhausted, he dropped his keys on the hotel room dresser, then threw his notebook on the desk and removed the brace holding his firearm. Dropping into the chair, his gaze fell to the bed. The pile of clothes left by Lirikai had been neatly folded and stacked atop the freshly made bed. He had to remember to leave housekeeping a good tip. His mind drifted back to Lirikai as his eyes remained fixed on the clothing. Lace peeked out among satin folds.

Ana had set him up; she'd read him, and probably Lirikai. But why would she bother getting involved to nudge things along? He didn't do relationships. Not anymore. Immortality had its drawbacks. He scrubbed his hands over his face, trying to clear himself of encroaching memories of the past and stop thoughts about Lirikai and the present from invading.

A click resounded from the end of the short hall and the door eased open. Lirikai's dark shape appeared. She stepped into the light, key card in one hand. Unfamiliar car keys dangled from the other. He jumped to his feet when he saw her face. Her eyes were large and silvered, blood smeared much of the lower half of her face and stained her shirt front.

Moving toward her, his hands reached for her arms, "What happened?"

"I don't ever want to drive a car again," she said.

"What? Did you have an accident?" He peered closer, looking for wounds.

"No, not really, maybe a little—there's no time for that. Mila has been taken."

"Mila? The woman you left with?"

She nodded.

"Is she Barra'kidai?"

"Yes."

"Whose blood is this?"

Lirikai's gaze dropped to her shirt front. When she looked back at his face, her expression was defiant. "A bad man's."

Carson pulled her into the bathroom and turned on the sink faucet snatching a facecloth from the rack. Soaking and soaping it up, he moved to clean Lirikai's face, she grabbed it from him, and scrubbed the cloth over her skin, then held it under the water to rinse.

"What happened?"

"They took her husband."

"Did Mila kill those people?"

Lirikai scowled at him, "She's running away from a bad bunch of people because she has information about them that her husband discovered. She was caught and now they want to get that information from her. If she doesn't die, they will sell her."

Carson straightened. "Human trafficking ring. We thought it was drugs."

"They have that too."

"Where was she taken?"

Lirikai told him about their trip out to the cliffs and her venture into the caves.

"You went in there alone?"

"We needed to see."

"And you were nearly captured too," he gestured to her shirt.

She shrugged, "I defended myself."

"What did you do with the bodies?" he prayed she didn't mutilate them, it would make things complicated to try to explain in court.

"Let them roll off the cliff. The sea claimed them."

He took the cloth from her hand, rinsed it again and wiped at a few blood smears she'd missed. "Do you know where they were taking her?""I'm not sure. But there are people in that cave, and they're being transported tonight. She might be sent with them if she survives."

"I'll call Ana and tell her to talk to the captain, she went back to the precinct."

Lirikai straightened, "one of the men in the cave said he was going back there to find out what the feds knew-that's you and Ana, yes?"

Carson nodded. Dammit. Cops were involved in this. Pulling his cell from his pocket, he called Ana. "Lirikai is back. Be careful, cops from the precinct are involved in a drug and human trafficking ring. They're running between caves and cargo ships. There's an exchange tonight."

"That would explain the gaps in the reports and shoddy inter-views, dammit. Does she know who's on the take?"

"She didn't see any faces."

"Okay," there was a long pause, "The captain just came in to the precinct, I'll go talk to him and call you back shortly."

Carson slid the phone back into his pocket.

Lirikai changed her shirt and was waiting for him. "We have to go back for Mila."

"Do you know that's where they're taking her? We have no guar-antee they'll take her there." Something shifted in Carson's mem-ory. "Who was Mila's husband?"

"She said he was a journalist. Ehm.. John Welsh."

"Shit, there's a warrant out for her. She's wanted on suspicion of his death."

"She didn't kill him."

He nodded, "They're after his information? They'll interrogate her."

"Yes, and if they don't kill her, they'll send her away with the other prisoners."

"Alright, lets head out there while Ana's talking to the captain."

Once they were outside by his jeep, Carson paused to send Ana a text to let her know where they were headed. As he glanced up, he recognized the car Lirikai had taken off in with Mila. It was in rough shape, the sides were scraped, and fenders crumpled, one mirror hung askew.

"I'm going to teach you how to drive when all this is done."

LIRI LED CARSON BACK to the bluffs where Mila was taken. He found an obscured place to leave the jeep, and she waited while he retrieved a few things from the back. From their vantage point, she could see a vast ship drifting down the coast. It was still a long way out, but she knew they wouldn't have much more time.

He appeared next to her holding a net bag with clothing inside. They climbed down to a place close to where Lirikai had gone into the water before. They stripped down, moonlight washing their skin in pale shades. Carson added their clothing to the netted bag. "You said they have weapons in the cave?"

She nodded.

"Plan is to get to their weapons. All else fails, I'll shift if I have to. You stay out of sight and free the prisoners. They are priority above all else."

"Of course."

"Try not to kill anyone."

She frowned at him.

"Self defense is allowed."

She smiled and leapt into the ocean.

An instant later he was next to her, and she swam ahead, leading him to the mouth of the cave. Looking back, he shimmered in the moonlight water, the netted bag hooked by a claw as his lithe body wove him through the ocean along behind her.

She was relieved to see the boats still as they were.

Shifting into human form, she moved to the ledge, where they pulled clothes from the bag, gave them a quick wring out, and pulled them on. Carson wedged the bag into a crevice, and they snuck along the wall. Voices drifted along the rock toward them as they crept forward.

Lirikai peered around the corner to see two armed men talking. "I'm going to the back for a round of poker while we wait," One guard said, checking his watch.

The other nodded. "Let me know if the cards are good tonight."

"They're good every night Joe, you just gotta know how to play them."

Lirikai watched him disappear toward the back of the lit cave then stepped out into Joe's line of view.

"What are you doing here?"

"My boat turned over, can you help me?"

He eyed her a moment. She stepped toward him, moving round him, drawing his focus.

"You can't be in here."

As soon as he'd turned his back enough, Carson snuck behind him and knocked him out, lowering him to the ground and taking his weapon. Farther up the path, most of the weapons Lirikai had seen earlier were still as they were. She grabbed several and ran back to drop them into the water, letting them sink under the boats. She did this several times until there were none left to be used against them in a skirmish.

Ignoring the barrels lining the path, their bare feet made no sound on the cave floor as they moved along to an opening. Peering inside, she saw about a dozen people huddled along the walls in the dim light, their hands and feet bound. There were no guards with them.

"Get them out of here," Carson whispered as continued.

Lirikai darted toward the first victim, evaluating the binds. They were all gagged and unkempt, clearly having been there for many days. Some were dressed for the beach while others looked as though they were dressed for an evening of entertainment. They must have all been taken from areas near the beach front. "We must be very quiet," she whispered, "We don't have much time to get you out of here." Moving to the first victim, she untied the gag. "Help me free the others, do you know how many guards are here?"

She shook her head, "They come and go, we never see any of them more than two at a time."

Plastic ties secured her wrists and ankles, the flesh cut and scabbed. Relieved they hadn't used chain or some other metal, she considered running back to check the unconscious guard for a knife. Instead, she bent her head low, let her Barra'kidai teeth extend enough to snip the plastic between the powerful points.

The woman gasped and jerked backward on seeing this, "Jesus!"

"Hold still." She commanded, elevating the woman's legs so that she could access her ankles. It was awkward, but the binds dropped away, and the woman scrambled away from Lirikai, eyes wide in the low light. The woman glanced toward the path to escape.

"Help me free the others," she said, her voice hard, "Or you'll wish you'd been sold tonight."

Nodding, she lurched toward a young man bound farther inside the cave, removing his gag.

"Who are you?" his voice was low, but she could hear the strain of fear.

"Help. Federal officers are on their way."

As the gags fell away, whispering began. "Stay quiet," she demanded, snipping ties with her teeth as quickly as she could. "My friend is farther inside. Don't make any noise to draw them out."

Several of the victims got to their feet, holding onto the walls for support, their limbs weak from too long without movement. Lirikai kept an eye on them as she worked. There were still a few left bound when she stood and moved toward the corridor.

"Help each other. If you don't, some of you will be caught again." She looked into their faces and knew some of them didn't care. Someone was going to make a go of it. As she moved away from the entrance to return to the remaining prisoners, she heard the quick intake of breath as one of the freed ones made her move. But Lirikai was faster. She pivoted, grabbed a handful of hair, and slammed the young woman to the floor. She landed hard, knocking air from her lungs, and she lay dazed. Lirikai put her hand around the woman's throat, "I told you to wait." She snarled, letting her teeth extend. There were several gasps and she looked up at all of them. "They intend to sell you to buyers that will do whatever they want to you. If you want to go home, help each other, or none of you will."

There were two prisoners left when shouts echoed down the corridor.

Carson.

Returning to her task, she freed the last two helping them to their feet and led them back out. Some were still strong enough to move without issue, but a few of those that had been there longer required support. Several couldn't walk without help.

Gunfire, followed by the sound of growling, and then more gunfire. She resisted the pull toward the back of the cave, trusting that Carson would be able to handle himself, as she helped the prisoners into the three boats. As soon as they were all loaded, the roar of engines filled the cave and Lirikai ran back to help Carson. Gunfire, snarling, and screams filled the cave complex. The narrow passage opened into a cave a great deal larger than the one the prisoners had been kept in. Carson filled most of it and had two gunmen trapped between himself and the rocky wall, guns pointed at him. Several bodies littered the floor. She didn't know if they were alive, and she didn't care.

There were guns pointed at Carson. They were clearly terrified, but held their ground. His scales rippled in the low light and blood streamed in several places.

"I think you've angered him."

Startled by her voice, one turned his gun in her direction, the other glanced but held his own gun on Carson.

"He might let you go if you put your weapons down."

"Fuck you!"

Carson snarled. The gun wavered.

"He just wants to know who you're working for, and I want to know where my sister is, that's all." She could smell their tightly controlled fear, mingled with the scent of their intentions. "You've lost your prisoners, business will be tricky."

"Shoot her," the one aimed at Carson said.

"What makes you think it won't attack us if we do?" she recognized him as the guard talking to other guard, Joe.

"He will."

"What the fuck is it?"

She shrugged, "You should be more concerned with what he wants. As I said," she moved farther into the space and closer to the gun, maintaining eye contact with her would-be killer. "We just want to know who you work for and where my sister is. Then you can go."

CARSON IGNORED THE POINTS of bullet penetration. Most of the spray had been deflected off his scales, but a few managed to slip between. So long as he stayed in his current form, he could hold out longer against blood loss.

Liri ran into the cave, and it was all he could do not to attack the remaining gunman pointing his weapon at her.

He couldn't believe she was actually walking toward the guy, but he held his position as she negotiated. He'd heard the boats leave the cave and was relieved the prisoners were no longer a concern. They'd likely go to the police. Whether there were dirty cops at the precinct, or not, more than a dozen victims couldn't be ignored.

"I don't know who you're talking about" the guard with his gun pointed at Lirikai said. "All the merchandise was in the front cave, go look in there." His eyes were intent on her, challenging her to turn her back on him.

"She wasn't among those escapees," she said stepping closer. "Where else would a captive be taken?"

The guard's hands tightened on his weapon, raising it a fraction so that it aligned with her head.

Carson growled, the low sound reverberating through the space confining him.

The guard jerked, his attention diverted.

Lirikai's hand shot up, slamming the muzzle away from her face. The gun fired.

Distracted, Carson slammed the man in front of him backward, cracking his head into the cave wall, and swung toward the one that shot Lirikai, snapping his jaws around him. The bad guy screamed as he bit down then released the body.

The air around him shimmered as he began to shift to human form.

"Don't change!" Lirikai shouted, "Your wounds are too severe."

He snorted his displeasure, moving his snout toward her injured shoulder. Blood streamed down her arm.

"I'll heal when I return to the sea. You will too?"

He dipped his head.

Looking for something to staunch the blood flow, she found his shredded clothing nearby and used strips of it to bind over her wound. Her skin was already turning pale. She then used the rags to wipe at some of the blood on his scales and inspect his wounds. "You have to get into the water as soon as possible."

The whine of a boat engine grew louder as it trundled into the outer cave. They could hear the voices of several men as soon as the engine cut. "Where are the fucking boats?" someone shouted. "Get the barrels loaded."

"The cave is empty, there's no one here."

"Joe's down."

"Shit."

AT THE SOUND OF booted feet running deeper into the cave, Lirikai dropped the fabric and walked out to meet them before they could see Carson in shifted form. Carson tensed, listening.

"What the hell are you doing here?" a familiar voice echoed along the corridor. "Where is Agent Carson Parenga?"

"Officers?" The reek of corruption assaulted her senses in the confined space.

Lirikai's gaze went to the two familiar faces. She'd seen them at the precinct. Ignoring them, she went farther out toward the mouth of the cave to find Mila barely able to stand, bound and bleeding, her arm in the precinct captain's grip.

Her eyes widened and she shook her head, trying to speak behind the gag in her mouth.

Rage rippled through Lirikai's body at the vision of her battered sister.

"Why is she bound?" she forced the words through clenched teeth. Each of the men were carrying pistols.

"She's responsible for all the murders. Crazy bitch has been mutilating them for some cult god or something." He shrugged, "Case solved, you feds can go home."

"Why are you here?" she asked, moving closer.

His eyes fell to the wound and blood staining her arm, "Rounding up accomplices," he said.

"All prisoners are free, accomplices taken out."

His mouth snapped shut, his jaw tight, nostrils flaring. His chest heaved as he controlled his anger.

"Boss?"

"Why don't we go back to the precinct together?" The captain said through gritted teeth. His eyes bored into her.

Mila shook her head, eyes wide.

Lirikai considered her, then looked at the weapon he carried, she turned her attention to the other two officers, also armed.

With pistols, there were too many to take on.

She stepped away from Mila, closer to the captain's opposite side.

"Don't worry, she's cuffed."

"Did you beat her?"

He smirked. "We interrogated her. She was uncooperative."

Her mouth watered as she fought the instinct to bite him.

The captain stopped smirking, stepping back when he saw her eyes.

"She is the widow of a slaughtered journalist."

"Yeah, so?"

"A journalist investigating missing people and corruption along the coast. Law enforcement profiting from smuggling." "Bullshit."

"There's evidence of your involvement."His hand swung up, pistol pointed at her head.

She sighed. Again. So predictable.

"The evidence, hand it over."

She shrugged and shook her head.

Mila tried to speak through her gag.

He tightened his grip.

"You should let her go," she said.

"Like fuck."

"Boss, she's with the feds."

"She can't tell them anything if she's dead."

"Nor can I tell you where the evidence is if I'm dead. Release her."

His eyes narrowed on her, "you want me to let her go, huh?" he turned to point the gun at Mila's head. "Funny, we couldn't get anything out of her, maybe we can make you talk instead."

Mila shook her head at Lirikai once more, then went very still and closed her eyes, straightening her spine.

"Boss, we don't have time for this shit."

The captain tossed his head, "Move the barrels."

"Drop your weapon before I destroy you." Lirikai's voice was even as she stepped toward him.

The captain laughed, shook his head, and swung the gun back in her direction.

A deep growl rumbled through the cave.

All at once, Mila's teeth erupted, slicing through her gag. She launched toward the captain, her jaws descending on his shoulder. Carson had come running into the cavern, drawing the attention of the other two cops, who scrambled for their weapons and began firing instinctively and shouting.

Knees buckling under the assault, the captain twisted and fired into Mila's abdomen a second before Lirikai launched herself at him. Mila crumpled to the cave floor as Lirikai and the captain crashed into the water. They fought as she rolled them into deeper water, under the blows of his fist as he struggled to get his hands around her throat. Slipping from his grasp, she waded farther into the water. The captain pursued.

"Captain!" one of his men screamed as Carson batted him with a massive clawed paw, sending him bouncing into the cave wall.

Seeing this, Captain Mack moved farther into the water.

Carson moved to the water's edge, taking a menacing step into the water.

The captain turned to swim for the cave mouth only to be confronted by Lirikai, who blocked his escape.

"Move or I'll feed you to it!" The captain's eyes were wild with fear.

She returned his earlier smirk. "He won't eat you, but I will." She said licking her lips.

"What the fuck?"

Her teeth erupted and, as he screamed she grabbed him, dragging him down into the ocean water, twisting deeper. She shifted, circling him as he clumsily tried to lash out at her, hindered by the resistance of the ocean. Her sleek body enabled her to slide around him with ease, biting and nipping into his flesh, dragging him farther and farther out into the ocean. When the air and resistance went out of his body, she dragged him still. She didn't stop swimming until she reached her cave where she performed the rite of the Barra'kidai. The last Barra'kidai. By the time she was done, there was only the skull of the supremely guilty, left for the Goddess of the Ocean, whether she still desired offerings or not. She wouldn't return to the surface with it to inscribe it, it would be left as it was, nameless and forgotten.

FOURTEEN

CARSON STUFFED THE LAST few file folders into the cardboard box. A quick glance around the office ensured that was everything before he slipped his hands into the handles to transfer it to Ana's office.

"Thanks Carson," she said as he dropped it on a nearby chair.

"How's the round-up coming along?"

"We're working with the Coast Guard to retrieve the barrels of contraband and investigate the trafficking ring at sea, as well as here. They obviously have internal unit issues too."

"Everyone escaped alright?"

She nodded, crossing her arms, leaning back against the wall. "Some are in the hospital for dehydration, malnutrition and battery, among other things, the others have gone home after being looked over and discharged. Lana and her crew have been visiting them for interviews."

"They're a good unit."

"Carson, how are you doing?"

He met her gaze, "I'm fine. Healing up."

She walked around her desk to close the office door.

"Are you? I saw how many slugs were dug out of you."

"Yeah thanks for calling in the GPSA medics."

She patted his arm and gave it a light squeeze.

He sighed, moving away from the contact, running his hands over his face. When he turned back to her he smiled, "I have your bag of clothes in my jeep."

She frowned, "Why don't you hang on to them for Lirikai?"

He shook his head, "I don't think she's going to come back."

"She doesn't know about her sister?"

"No."

"Oh, that's a shame. She should know. I'm sure it would make a great difference to her."

"She's been alone for so long-"

"So have you."

He snapped his mouth shut, giving her a baleful look.

"And despite what you keep saying, Carson, you're *not* an island."

"Hey, you're crushing my sense of ego here, Ortega."

Ana went quiet for a long moment. Her eyes glazed over.

"Ana?"

At the sound of her name, she turned her face to Carson, eyes clearing. She went back to open her office door, "I suggest you go out for a swim and speed up the healing process." Ana gave him a smile and a wink.

He studied her face as he approached, but could see nothing but a genuine smile as she waited for him to pass.

"The waves will be good tonight," she said as he passed through the hive of the bullpen.

CARSON REACHED TO PULL his surfboard free from the back of his jeep, catching himself as an electric twinge shot through the muscle near one of the bullet wounds. Catching his breath, he reminded himself not to move so fast, then carefully eased the board up.

He turned toward the ocean, taking a moment for the pain to pass. He watched the waves roll in, break and turn to froth. Board or free swim?

Liri drifted through his thoughts as another wave lapped up the beach sand. Moving down toward the water, he stood to watch the ocean roll for awhile, and his toes sank into the sun-warmed sand.

He had waited at the hotel. There'd been no sign of her. Carson had gone swimming in the ocean after the bullets had been removed from his body so that he could heal faster. There'd been no sign of her anywhere near the cave. He knew she had to be alright. She'd have shifted, and he'd decided not to stop a Barra'kidai doing her duty. The captain wasn't worth interfering for. Early interviews and reports were coming back indicating he'd instigated the traffic ring. He hadn't been coerced or bought. He'd created it using his status and position.

Carson knew that if he hadn't been deeply corrupt, Lirikai wouldn't have taken him. If he hadn't threatened the life of her sister and imprisoned so many people for profit. His own sense of the law didn't hold up his conscience in this case.

The captain drowned trying to escape justice, was the story relayed to the precinct.

The ocean found him and delivered its own kind of justice.

"I didn't think you'd come."

Carson whirled around.

Lirikai stood behind him, the ocean breeze blowing at her hair and dress. After a long moment, he said, "Nice dress."

She smiled crookedly, "I found it."

"Found it, huh?"

She nodded, stepping forward. He could see the uncertainty in her face. He held out a hand to her. She looked down at his proffered hand, her expression turning sad. "I couldn't leave the captain for you."

He dropped his hand, nodding, "I understand."

She studied his face as though she didn't believe him.

"After what he did to Mila-"

"She's missing you."

She jerked, startled by his words, "Missing me?" tears sprang to her eyes and she shuddered. "She's alive?"

Carson's heart broke looking at her, "Yes, Lirikai, she's alive and recovering in the hospital."

Her hand fluttered at her stomach, her whole body sagged with her relief. "Good," she sniffed back her tears, "that is very good."

He watched her transition as despair threatened to return, "Will she be imprisoned?"

"No. In light of all that has happened, the GPSA are taking her in. She's going to work with us."

A smile spread across her face and she inhaled deeply of the sea air.

Carson's heart mended a little.

"Will you?"

"Will I what?"

"Work with us."

She turned back to him, studying his face. He was sure she could read the hope in him. But she turned toward the city scape. "I don't know."

"You wouldn't be alone anymore. Mila is here, you know that now. And I'm here."

He held out his hand again.

She searched his face for a long time. "I...." She swallowed, looking away from him. "In my human life, I could not give my husband children."

He didn't lower his hand.

"I thought you should know that."

He nodded, watching her face closely. His hand didn't waver.

Her gaze rested on that outstretched hand for a long moment before she tentatively reached out. Her fingers drifted across his palm and curled to grasp him.

Looking into her eyes, he lifted their hands to brush his lips over her knuckles before he placed a kiss on the back of her hand.

She smiled at him and his heart completed the mending and swelled a little.

"First thing I'm going to do is teach you how to drive."

She scoffed, "No you're not! I'm going to teach you how to swim!"

"Oh really?" He pulled her against him and kissed her lips until she opened to him. Accepting her invitation, his tongue swept across hers and she moaned.

"Race?"

"Absolutely." He kissed the tip of her nose.

She wriggled out of his embrace and ran for the sea.

He was two steps behind, catching her dress as she pulled it over her head and released it to the wind, laughing.

Surfacing

GLOBAL PARANORMAL SECURITY AGENCY

JODI KENDRICK

SURFACING

Raya Burns gave up her peaceful, protected life with her true love in order to find her missing brother. She's spent the last decade learning just how much she's capable of and how far she's willing to go. Alone.

After a decade on his own, Ian McLachlan is more than ready to leave the peace and solitude of his lake home. His old friend, GPSA Agent Carson Perenga, has called in a favor. A prisoner connected to one of his cases has escaped and may be headed straight into Ian's territory.

When Raya and Ian's new lives come crashing back together, they have no choice but to confront the past.

If the present has them facing each other down from opposite sides of the law, what can the future possibly hold for them?

ONE

R AYA B URNS HOVERED IN the corner of the prison cell, staring at the scruffy, snoring inmate on the lower bunk.

She sighed.

It was time. It had been a long, unpleasant process, but she had a job to do.

Ignoring the second inmate, in the upper bunk, she floated closer, whispering close to his ear.

"Chuck, let's go."

Chuck flipped over, eyes wide, searching for the source of the voice in the dark. "Ashray?"

Who else would it be, after all these weeks of nocturnal visits to guide the prisoner in the process toward escape? She rolled her incorporeal eyes. "Yes, Chuck."

"We're doing this now?"

Seriously? "Yes, Chuck."

"Whoa, okay," He rubbed his eyes and scrambled out of the bunk, mindful of his neighbors hearing, and shoved his bunk mate, "Glenn."

As much as she disliked the excess baggage, it couldn't be helped. Since the cells were occupied in pairs, any activity couldn't be hidden. They'd ditch him later. For now, they had to focus on this particular step: Getting the hell out.

The second inmate grumbled, rolling over to see what Chuck wanted. There was a whispered exchange as he jumped down.

"We don't have time for this," she said to Chuck.

Glenn's eyes swept the small space as Chuck's had. She was used to this. They couldn't really see her as she was. If they bothered to focus hard enough, they might catch a wavering shape where her voice was.

"If we get caught, I'll shank you myself," Glenn snarled in Chuck's face. "Crazy fuck."

"Stay here then, just help me move the bed and I'll be on my way."

"I'm not fucking staying here to take the heat of your escape."

"Whatever man, just get moving."

Raya suppressed her impatience, ignoring Glenn's visible and offensive body ink—speaking of shanking....

The two men eased the bunk bed aside with practiced silence to expose the crude hole in the concrete.

She was grateful Chuck had been imprisoned in this old crumbling prison, and not in one of the shiny new super max facilities. It had been a challenge convincing Chuck to wait for her to guide them out, insisting she needed to get the escape route and supplies finalized. It was his problem getting Glenn to follow along.

She didn't think it was really all that hard. Despite his bravado, the loser was a coward and wouldn't have gone alone, anyway. They followed the sound of her voice as she led them along the old lead pipes and climbed the pipe braces she'd bolstered, up to the top floor. Then they moved through further breaks in the walls and along a ventilation shaft. Chuck had dropped a few pounds over the last few weeks in order to fit. She hoped Glenn's bony knees and elbows banging against the pipes and shaft walls wouldn't alert the guards.

Emerging from the ventilator shaft, they waited. Watching the guards, she instructed them on when to move and when to hold until they reached the edge of the roof top.

As they scurried across, the tower guard turned in their direction. "Get down," she commanded. Glenn dropped and Chuck stumbled toward the edge of the roof, losing his footing. She watched as he stumbled over the edge.

Oh, Christ.

Chuck's fingers clutched the ledge as Glenn stared at them from the shadows.

"If he dies, you're caught," she snapped, motivating him to help Chuck not die.

As the men struggled, with muffled grunts and scraping, she watched the guards.

They'd been heard.

One was on the radio and the two patrolling below them looked up as Chuck's feet disappeared from their line of sight.

"We don't have long." With the guards' attention turned toward the rooftop, they had to move carefully toward the smokestack at the opposite end of the building.

"Hurry."

The men moved as fast as they could without falling, scurrying down the crease between the stack and the wall. She led them along the water tower supports toward freedom, just beyond the gap she'd made in the fence surrounding the prison property.

The alarm went up as Glenn shimmied through the hole after them, crying out as he gouged knees and elbows on sharp stones in his haste.

Raya didn't stop moving, instructing Chuck as they went, scrambling toward the river.

Every bit of her stretched for it. For the safety and power of the water.

"Into the river."

They still couldn't see her clearly. As close as they were to the power of the flowing river and under the light of the moon, she knew she'd be more visible.

Glenn hesitated as he bypassed her. "What the fuck are you?"

"She's our angel of freedom," Chuck said.

There was barking in the distance as spotlights began to sweep the prison grounds.

"Get in the water."

"Fuck that, I'm going for the woods," Glenn said.

She considered letting him go as a diversion, as Chuck splashed into the water. An instant later Chuck's clothes floated, loose and shapeless. A thin translucent line whipped out of the water, striking Glenn across the exposed flesh of his throat, and disappeared again.

"What the fuck was that?" his hand reached for his throat, "Fuck, something is burning my neck, man." He glanced up, searching the bank, seeing that he was alone. "Chuck?"

"He's in the water, like you should be."

The barking grew closer.

Raya watched the wound turn red.

Glenn stumbled as he moved away from the river, tripping as he made his way toward the woods.

Glancing in Chuck's direction, she saw the inflated purple-blue bladder of a Man-O-War jellyfish floating among the prison garb.

Huh.

I guess he was tired of his cell mate.

She'd been curious to know if he was a shifter—and if so, what kind.

She had no idea how the fresh river water would affect him, and wouldn't have cared much if it weren't for the fact she had been hired to get him safely to his uncle.

She stepped into the water, unaffected by his long poisonous tentacles in her present state.

"There's a cache of civilian clothes upriver." She slid through the water. A moment later, he angled his fin and followed, leaving the prison rags as they were.

The frantic barking had reached the bank behind them.

TWO

IAN MCLACHLAN STEPPED OUT of the close walls of the elevator and drew a deep breath, adjusting his backpack on his shoulder. He searched the sign on the opposite wall, suppressing a yawn after a long night traveling; all the way from his lake home in British Columbia to New York.

It had been years since he'd stepped into the offices of the Global Paranormal Security Agency, and he hadn't expected to do so again. Ever.

But, Carson Perenga had called. And Ian owed him. It didn't matter how late—or early—it was.

A smiling assistant led him to Jack Maeda's office.

"I might be able to pull Teddy in, if you need him. Willow and Risa have gone to Antarctica with another unit, and everyone else is already out on assignment, so I want you to pull together your own team for this." Maeda was saying to Carson, frowning at his laptop screen.

"Already started," Carson said, as he glanced up at Ian's arrival and grinned.

"Good. I can't seem to find the file in the database. Ask Analiese Ortega to send it again." Finally noticing Ian's arrival, he turned his attention to him with a level gaze. "Well, look at who's risen from the depths of Loch Ness—or is it Okanagan these days? McLachlan."

"Maeda. Okanagan." He acknowledged and corrected.

The men stared at each other another moment longer.

"Well, now that we have that warm reunion out of the way, how about we get started with the meeting?" Carson said as he moved toward Ian, hand extended.

Ian took it and Carson pulled him into a bro-hug.

"Good to see you, old friend."

"It's been too long, man," Carson said with a hearty slap on the back before offering him one of the chairs facing Maeda.

Ian stood before Maeda, offering a hand across his desk.

Maeda slowly reached out and shook it.

Ian didn't miss the confusion that flashed across Maeda's face.

"You mentioned you need help with a case?" Ian said to Carson as he took the empty seat, dropping his bag next to it.

Carson nodded and leaned on the edge of Maeda's desk. "A while back, we broke a human trafficking ring on the west coast. Folks were being nabbed and moved to a ship sailing along the coast."

Ian nodded. The case had been all over the news. He glanced at Carson, if the GPSA was involved, then paranormals somehow were, too.

Carson went on. "Last night, one of the guys that worked on that ship escaped the east coast prison he'd been transferred to—some kind of agreement to be closer to family."

"He wasn't in a GPSA prison?"

"As far as we knew, everyone on that ship was human, if this guy isn't human, we're not sure what he is yet."

"So... Where do I come into this?" He checked his watch, suppressing another yawn, "at the ungodly hour of 7:30am?"

Maeda quirked a thick brow, grunting. "Carson let you sleep?" He grunted.

"GPSA was called because his escape seemed paranormal, according to the very few pieces of evidence collected. I called you in because you know the waters in that area better than anyone."

Ian nodded. He had split his time between a few different lakes in North America since he had left his ancestral home in Scotland.

"Alright, let me have a look at the particulars and I'll get started. Keep in mind, when I'm in this part of the country, I spend most of my time up at Lake Champlain, not on the coast."

Carson checked his phone, "Ana sent the files, Jack."

Maeda turned back to his computer, and a moment later the printer geared up. Carson brought the sheets back to Maeda's desk, and Ian stood to get a better look at what they were dealing with as Carson spread them across the desktop. There was a long report from Carson's human trafficking case that the prisoner was apprehended from. He'd read that later; for now, he looked at the images.

Mugs shots of two prisoners; Charles 'Chuck' Meduse and Glenn Smith, cell mates. Chuck was so unremarkable it was easy to see how he had been overlooked. The other guy was scrawny and covered in crappy tattoos, most of which were swastikas and other wannabe skinhead symbols and slogans.

Carson leaned over, pointing to him. "This one was caught in the woods in a bad state."

Ian looked up. "His cell mate tried to kill him?"

Carson shrugged. "He was found barely conscious from jellyfish stings across his throat, and muttering about ghosts."

"Jellyfish stings?"

Carson fished through the printouts still on the desk and handed one to Ian showing the reddened, whip-like marks seared into the flesh of the inmate's throat. "Looks nasty."

"The other guy hasn't been found. Just his clothes were retrieved from the river. Local forces don't know what to make of it."

"No doubt. What else do we know about the escapee?"

"Not much. Foreigner, from Canada. No priors, at least not here. Other inmates and prison guards aren't sure if he's deeply spiritual or needing medication of some kind. For months he's been witnessed talking to himself-or to someone no one else can see."

"Not his cell mate?"

Carson shook his head. "Talks more when he's alone, and usually at night."

"Psychic?"

"Maybe?" Carson checked his watch, "Ana's flight will arrive in another couple of hours."

"You're pulling her in from her post?" Maeda looked surprised.

Carson nodded. "As you said, everyone else is on assignment, and we work well together. Freddy is covering the office in her absence."

Maeda nodded.

"In the meantime, I'll catch Ian up to date on the original case over breakfast, then get packed for the drive once Lirikai brings Ana back from the airport."

"Lirikai?" Ian asked.

"Long story. Breakfast. Maeda, you coming with us? Breakfast is on you."

"Cheap old man." Maeda muttered. "Nah, I've got too much work to do. Carson, remember to grab some topographical maps and waterways charts."

Ian approached Maeda's desk and held out his hand again. "I've decided to start letting go of grudges," he said.

Maeda nodded, "Life is too long-much too long-for us to hold grudges, anyway. It's good to see you." He smiled.

"You still owe me fifty quid." Ian said, retrieving his bag.

"Jesus, Ian, that was decades ago. And didn't you just say you're letting go of grudges?"

"Grudges, not debts."

Maeda pulled his wallet from his pocket, "What's the exchange rate?"

"Interest too."

"What? It's been decades."

He tried not to laugh at the exasperation in Maeda's expression. "Aye."

He grumbled, putting his wallet away. "None of that was my fault. Not really."

"You two can catch up over breakfast." Carson insisted, waving at the stack of case file sheets.

"I've got a sudden case of indigestion." Maeda growled.

Ian snorted. "Americans."

Carson and Ian rode the elevator down to the lobby and headed for Carson's favorite local diner. That was something Ian could always count on; Carson's ability to find all the best food joints, whether they were dives or five-star galas.

THREE

RAYA STOOD ON THE western bank of the Hudson River, waiting for Chuck, who was in the bushes, changing into the clothes she had given him from her cached pack.

So far, things were going well. "Come on, they haven't found us yet, let's keep it that way."

She hoped the authorities would focus on the coast or the city. She had been hired to get Chuck to Montreal, so that's what she was going to do. The easy escape route would have been to grab a boat and go up the coast. This way was much harder. It was vital for Chuck to remain hidden, because she desperately needed this job.

They were moving on foot, heading north, with very little sleep.

Chuck adjusted the sleeves that hung beyond his fingertips. "My uncle will be in Montreal when we get there?" His features were strained.

She shrugged, "I'm supposed to get you there, I don't know who's going to meet us, yet." She considered him a moment, "Don't like that particular city?" she smirked.

"Nothing wrong with Montreal. Would have been easier going south." He glanced at her then away again.

She couldn't argue that. He wasn't alone in wishing they could take another route. She started walking, and Chuck fell in behind her.

THE DINER'S CONSTANT FLOW of customers, voices and clattering dishes had long faded to the background for the two agents.

Drinking his coffee, Ian ignored the human movement while Carson checked his phone.

"They're just leaving the airport, we can meet them at the hotel."

Ian nodded. "Good, my arse is going numb."

They'd gone over Carson's file, then he had caught Ian up on events related to the report. And on his new companion.

Ian was glad his old friend had found someone special, even if it was over a serial murder investigation. He was looking forward to meeting Lirikai. Barra'kidai were legendary even in the paranormal world. Ancient avengers created by the goddess of the oceans to detect, seek out, and destroy the filth of the world. The same goddess that had created his old friend Carson.

Carson flagged the waitress for the bill.

Ian smiled up at her as she flirted with him while Carson was distracted. She was very attractive, reminding him of another woman with smooth sun-kissed skin and thick curly black hair. A woman with a sensual smile and mischievous sparkle in her eyes. He left a generous tip on the table, grabbed his bag from the seat next to him and followed Carson.

They stepped out into the wall of noise of the awakened city. Drawing a deep breath, he fell in step with Carson.

"How long were you out at Okanagan?"

"Probably too long."

Carson nodded. "The city noise and energy are a bit of a shock to the system until it settles under your skin."

"I'm already missing the muffled world of the lake."

They wove their way along the sidewalks, crowded with all manner of people. Businessmen and women, street vendors and entertainers, hawkers and tourists. It was the same in every large city, but every city also had a distinct vibe to it.

In sharp contrast, on entering the hotel, Ian's head buzzed from the sudden lack of noise.

Carson glanced at him as they stepped into the elevator and grinned, "Lirikai doesn't like elevators either."

"Glad we have something besides you in common." His fingers gripped the strap of his backpack. The doors slid open and Ian drew in a breath. "I hate these things."

They collected Carson and Lirikai's belongings and went back down to the lobby.

Carson checked his phone, "They're just about here," he said, stepping outside as an SUV swung into the empty spot just in front of them. The trunk popped open before the vehicle finished rocking in place.

"Did you hire a stunt driver?" Ian asked, hauling the baggage into the open hatch.

Carson grinned.

A petite woman jumped out of the passenger side, her face devoid of color.

"Good to see you, Ana," Carson said, "This is Ian."

She glanced in Ian's direction, shot a hand out to shake, while her face stayed trained on Carson, voice tight. "You should have warned me that you taught Lirikai how to drive."

"She wanted to surprise you."

A nervous laugh escaped her. "Surprised!" She darted into the safety of the back seat, immediately strapping herself in.

An elegant hand patted the vacated front seat. "Carson, let's go, before lunch rush hour starts."

Ian got into the back seat next to Ana and strapped in. He looked up from the buckle to eyes trained on him from the driver seat. Lirikai was striking, and a little unnerving as the edges of her nostrils twitched. Seemingly satisfied, she reached back a hand, which he shook. Then she was all business again, chattering to Carson about the traffic.

Ana's hand reached for the handle bolted to the ceiling.

Ian's shoulder hit the door as the SUV darted into the line of traffic to a chorus of horns.

Ian glanced in Ana's direction. Her eyes were closed, lips moving. He thought he heard a whispered string of prayers coming from her lips.

By the time they reached the prison, Ian was just about ready for the safety of a lake. Any lake.

They met with the warden and reviewed the materials already in the file, along with the surveillance footage they'd retrieved in the ensuing hours. Interview transcripts were added to the file, which Ana quickly went through.

"Warden, I'd like access to the inmate's cell."

The Warden frowned, shaking his head.

To Carson she said, "I need to try to get a reading on what we're dealing with."

Carson glanced at Lirikai, his expression worried at the strain evident in her tight face and posture. They had argued back and forth at her refusal to wait in the car, but she had ended up coming in.

"Ian, will you go with Ana? It's too dangerous to even think about letting Lirikai go in there. She might lose control and we'd have a bigger mess on our hands."

"Of course."

After a few more minutes debating with the Warden, he agreed to let them in.

"Lirikai and I will be here, reviewing the security footage. Make sure Ana gets all the time she needs in that cell."

Ian nodded and followed Ana and the guard out of the office, through a series of security doors toward the main prison building.

The walls were a putrid green, while the floor tiles were so scuffed and time worn it was impossible to tell if they had ever held a pattern other than dirt skids. He focused on the doors. Thick steel doors, painted and repainted, older layers creating a topographical surface beneath the paint. They walked single file, a guard leading and a guard bringing up the rear of their little line, through the close confines of the narrow corridors until they reached the cavernous maw of the main cell block, rimmed with steel balconies and rows of barred doors holding back the inmates.

In front of him, Ana's hands curled into tight fists pressed against her thighs and her slender shoulders straightened. As soon as they stepped into view of the first cells the heckling started, mostly directed at Ana, some at the guards and some at Ian. It all went ignored. He could see the tension in his new colleague.

Up a single flight of stairs and three quarters of the way along, they stopped at a cell identical to all the others with the exception of its glaring vacancy. The guard opened it and stepped back.

Ana drew a breath and crossed the threshold, Ian a step behind.

The bunk bed was displaced from the wall, exposing the rough rectangular gap, excavated just enough to allow a man to get through. He wondered how long it had taken them to do it.

He could tell Ana was trying to focus, block out the voices and words echoing through the building toward them as her eyes slid around the sparse, yet cramped, space.

Ian stood sentinel, straight and tall, as though he could prevent the noise from reaching her.

Ana looked up at him, searched his face, her expression eased a fraction, "Please step out." When he opened his mouth to debate, she said, "I'll work faster if you do that."

Unable to argue, he stepped back out onto the grated balcony. He remained as he was, filling the space of the open door. The gathering tension eased. He centered his attention on what Ana was doing, while the guards waited to either side of the cell, curiosity evident as they cast glances in her direction.

After looking at every inch of the cell, she began to place her hand, palm down, on different surfaces. Then she picked up and cradled various mundane objects in her hands, eyes closed.

"What is she, some kind of psychic?" A guard asked, his expression dubious.

Ian shrugged, "Something like that." He really wasn't sure. Carson hadn't given him much detail about Ana.

The guard grunted and said nothing more.

She asked the guards several questions regarding the ownership of the sleeping spaces and level of disturbance of the room since their escape.

Crouching beside the lower bunk, hands out, eyes closed, she remained still for long moments. Moving to the tiny sink, her fingers drifted over other things as she looked around the space, below the bed and along the ceiling.

Ian hadn't expected her to bend down to the crude hole in the wall and slip through. He wasn't sure he could squeeze through after her.

"Ana?" He moved to step into the cell. She held up a hand, staying him.

The guards' attention was on the population behind their cell doors, protesting the unscheduled confinement during their apparent free roam time. Their frustrations were rising, the shouts more aggressive.

Ana reappeared, brushing the dust from her hands and jacket. "Let's go."

He stepped out and away, allowing her to exit. The guards wasted no time leading them back to the warden's office.

"Did you get what we need?" Carson asked Ana as soon as they returned.

She nodded.

There were more folders stacked with their original case file, and a thumb drive.

Carson spoke with the Warden a few moments, shook his hand, and the group were led back out to the public space of the building to retrieve their secured belongings.

There was a separate group of guards waiting to take them across the compound to the point of escape, explaining the suspected route.

They went through the break in the property's fence, down to the river where the inmate's clothes had been retrieved from the river, and the other escapee apprehended in the forest.

None of them spoke about the case in front of the guards, only asking questions where clarification was needed.

Once back in the quiet confines of the SUV, Lirikai started the vehicle. Ana directed her to drive north while Carson booked a motel for them.

As soon as they checked in to their adjoining rooms, Ana said, "Call Jack so I can give him my report while it's fresh. Record the call."

Carson made the call with his cell, on speaker.

She relayed in detail exactly everything Ian had watched her do in the prison cell, describing the space along with the addition of her insights into the inmates. "We're definitely dealing with paranormals. The inmate that was caught is human, the other is a shifter."

"Charles Meduse is a shifter?"

"Yes, and he's not alone. I sensed another presence in the cell and along the escape route. I couldn't see her, but she was there."

"Meduse was reported to have been talking to someone unseen. The guards thought he was developing delusions, some of the other inmates thought he was haunted." Carson said.

"She isn't a dead soul. I'm not sure what she is. I had the sense she was guiding him out. The other inmate was incidental."

"This might explain some of the images on the security footage," Carson said. "Blurred space and a faint impression of a woman's face. The warden thought it was some kind of technical distortion."

"Send it to me when you can," Jack said.

Ian reached for the file folder, leafing through the additional sheets.

Lirikai said, "There were a lot of scents to sort from along the escape path to the riverbank. The prisoners and the guards converged in the same area and sometimes it is difficult to tell them apart. The captured human is dangerous. The shifter inmate smells of greed and self-preservation. He is dangerous if he's threatened. The third presence Ana has mentioned was very hard to lock onto. Too faint."

"The third presence is driving the escape, she's the one that organized the breakout. I couldn't get a solid reading on her either. She's like a ghost, but she's living. She was focused on the river and heading north."

"The human inmate was captured in the woods, incapacitated by what seems to be a jellyfish sting. The Warden said the dogs couldn't pick up the other inmate's scent anywhere on land with the exception of the escape route from the compound." Carson told Jack.

"Ian? You know this area." Jack said.

"The waterways are interconnected here. If they're aquatic shifters, their salt water versus freshwater dependency might be a factor. The easiest, most direct, escape would be out to the ocean or anywhere along the mainland and island coasts. Otherwise, the river flows from connected lake systems north of here, leading all the way down from the St. Lawrence River, which is essentially an inland highway."

"Okay, we'll review the new material and the topography." Jack said.

Ian returned his attention to the papers as Carson spoke to Jack.

There were several stills pulled from the security cameras, which drew his attention. A narrow waver of energy caught in one shot. He'd seen something like that before.

His chest tightened.

The next still stole his breath. The subtle imprint of the female face in the distortion twisted his gut.

It couldn't be.

"Raya Burns."

FOUR

"WAIT HERE TILL I come for you." Raya leveled her stare on Chuck before heading toward the small wooden shack that was the campground office. Hitching her backpack, she cast a quick glance back to ensure he remained hidden in the bushes and prayed he didn't do anything stupid, like let anyone see his face. He'd be all over the news by now.

Awareness heightened, she opened the brittle screen door.

"Well, hello there, how may I help you?" A round faced woman greeted her, turning away from a decade-old computer screen.

"Small tent lot please. One night. Close to the river if you have it."

"Great time of year for hiking. Which way you headed?" The older woman eyed Raya's pack.

"Thinking of trying some mountain trails. Any recommendations?"

The woman nodded, accepting the cash Raya handed her for the lot rental. "Appalachian is popular. Mind, have your bear spray. Can never be too prepared, young and lovely as you are." She smiled, handing Raya her change.

"No worries, Ma'am, I'm prepared whether a predator is on four feet or two. Thank you." She accepted the receipt and campground map indicating her lot for the day.

"Ensure your campfire is out before you go. Trash goes in the bins. Enjoy your stay with us."

Raya went straight toward her camp lot. As soon as the tent was set up, she made her way around to where Chuck was hidden.

"This is tedious, we should just steal a boat."

"Which draws attention and gets us caught. You can't let anyone see you or you're going straight back to your cozy little bunk with your charming cell mate."

Chuck's lips compressed.

Thought so.

Once back at her tent, Chuck ducked inside. Raya set to making lunch like all the other campers. Pulling food from her pack, she watched families wandering among the sites, visiting summer friends and hauling water gear toward the river. She swallowed a pang of regret, quickly averting her gaze from the smallest of children.

Too late for all that now Raya. You've made your choices.

Loading up the stacked paper plates with food, she went into the tent to share it out equally. Chuck's half of the food was gone in minutes.

"Are we on our own all the way to Montreal?"

"Pretty much."

His shoulders dropped. A moment later, his eyes drifted to her barely touched food. She pushed half of it onto his plate, hoping that if he put himself into a food coma, other base needs wouldn't drift into his head.

"Much better than prison slop." He belched and sighed.

Raya stacked her plate on his and went out to drop the plates in the fire pit. As soon as she heard his snores, she went back in, nudged him to roll over and settled in the confines of the tent to sleep a few hours.

At the dinner hour, she did it all again and slept a few more hours.

As evening descended, she stayed out by the fire, banked it a full hour after dark and returned to the tent.

As soon as the shouts and squeals of families faded, they were replaced by music and raucous laughter drifting from the beach front. She pulled the tent down and stored it in the pack.

"Let's go," she said, waving him toward the woods, making their way toward the smell of a bonfire.

The air filtering through the trees grew heavy with beer and weed-laced smoke. Party goers drifted away in twos and threes or more. Seeing an opening, she grabbed Chuck's pack, and moved toward the bonfire, tossing both packs into the flames. She stood a moment, watching to ensure they caught. There was a flare as the fire engorged itself on the nylon fabric of the pack and tent.

"Hey, sweetheart, where's your people?"

Raya looked up at the sound of the slurred words. "Not far."

"Wanna party?" the young man said holding up a beer. "I bet you like to party... a hot chick like you."

"I sure do, why don't you show me where the action's happening?" He'd forget her sooner than if she'd just shut him down. Men didn't react well to rejection.

His inebriated face cracked with a smile, "Knew it!" He tottered, "This way." He swept an arm, sloshing the beer.

She followed him until they reached the edge of the light cast by the bonfire and ducked into the shadows. She had no idea how long it took him to realize she had ditched him.

She suppressed the small part of her that longed for a life of such free abandonment. Such luxuries of youth were long past. There were more important tasks to be done. Much more important.

Ensuring Chuck's safe escape wasn't one of them-it was merely a necessary step along the way.

IAN STARED AT THE still.

It couldn't be.

It couldn't be her.

It was a desperate trick of his eyes.

He *knew* the curve of that cheek, the tilt of those brows, even as obscured as the image was.

"What's the matter, man? You look like you've seen a ghost." Carson said, leaning in to see what Ian was looking at.

I have.

"Is that a face?"

"Yeah. Yeah, it is."

Ana came around to see the still. "I didn't sense the dead in that particular cell. Their energy is different from a shifter's."

Ian swallowed, glad to know she wasn't among the dead, but a ghost all the same. "Ashray. If she's who I think she is, she's an Ashray."

Carson blew out a breath. "*The* Ashray? *Your* Ashray?"

Ian's head jerked, his eyes still drinking in the obscured features.

His gut was flipping one way and rolling back the other.

That beautiful face broke his heart.

It was undeniable. He still yearned for her, given his reaction at the sight of her face. A face caught in the security footage of a prison break.

What the hell was she doing?

He tried to swallow around the sudden tightness in his throat.

Handing the papers back to Carson, he said, "I need a minute to think."

"Sure man, take your time."

Sliding the patio door open, he stepped out onto the balcony and drew in a long deep breath to get a handle on his emotions and allow space for his brain to kick in and do its thing.

Was this the path that Raya had turned onto when they were still together? When the lies and the sneaking around had begun? Part of him had thought she'd found someone else. The other part thought it was something more. No matter how he confronted her, she wouldn't talk to him. She had shut him out. He'd watched it happening and let her walk away, unwilling to follow.

Seems now he didn't have much of a choice. He'd have to follow.

Or did he? He was here as a favor to Carson, to help him capture an escaped convict. He could simply tell him key information about the rivers' and lakes' personalities and suggest places to look, then go then back to submerging his head in the bottom of another lake.

The problem was, she might be heading for *his* lake. *His* lake? Well, one of his lakes. Was it coincidence? A sick joke? Had she grown to loathe him so much, she'd go for his territory with a convicted human trafficker, knowing how he felt about human filth?

He'd never have pegged her as someone so spiteful.

But people change, as she had been changing.

Maybe this is who she is now.

Flashes of memory hammered through his head.

All their good times, sweet and fun and full of love.

With a shake of his head, the memories tilted and became more orderly images of the decline of their relationship.

Tragedy had struck, setting their relationship off-kilter. She hadn't handled the news of her brother's loss well. It changed her.

The authorities from the beach town in which he had last been known to be living had reported him missing. Given his lifestyle, they presumed overdose or suicide. Clothes and personal belongings were found piled behind a sand dune, his body swallowed by the sea. They had so many other cases to chase. Sorry for the bad news.

Raya had asked him, once, to help her find her brother. Only once. And he'd refused.

The local authorities said he'd gone into the ocean. Inebriated stupidity or willful suicide. Why else would anyone leave their clothes and valuables—wallet, jewelry—on the beach?

He was sure her manipulative mother was pushing her, as she always had, to look for him. Protect him.

Raya never asked Ian again. She turned inward, absorbed by her grief. Denial. She pushed him away. She'd be gone long periods—weeks at time—with no word on where she was going, coming back looking rough. Like she'd been out partying all night, stinking of clubs and back alleys. They began arguing. Then, she just left him. Disappeared like she never existed.

He'd spent the last few years trying to reclaim the life he'd had before their lives had collided.

Ian ran both hands through his hair, then scrubbed them over his face.

I should never have let her slip away.

He'd come to that conclusion in his reclusion.

He had returned to the world to find this, and he could have prevented it.

Despite how much half of his brain said, '*Yes, that's her! How can you not know her?*' the other half said, '*It's someone else. She would never get herself involved in something like this.*'

No, I should have been more understanding. Less selfish.

This was *his* responsibility.

The Ashray.

Maybe...Maybe he could help her now...Get her off this path she'd ended up on.

If it wasn't too late for her.

Was it?

These people she was associating with... they were exactly the kind of people he loathed. The reason for his disdain of humanity.

Did he *want* to get involved with her again?

She left him. If she still wanted him, she'd have come back.

He was here for Carson. To help his old friend do his job.

Keep it simple.

His shoulders eased.

He drew another deep, steadying breath and went back inside to the others.

Carson and Lirikai were talking quietly while Ana was on her phone. He closed the patio door behind him and waited for her to finish speaking. His mind was starting to come down from its initial overload.

Carson approached him, speaking softly so as not to disrupt Ana's conversation. "She's talking to Maeda again."

Ian nodded.

"Are you still good to work this case, or should I find someone else?" His eyes were steady on Ian's face.

"I'm doing this. I'll find her."

"You're sure it is her?"

Ian nodded.

"Okay, then what do we need to know?"

"I haven't seen her since we broke off."

"Well, she's been busy since then," Ana's voice cut in as she slipped her phone into her pocket. "Very busy," Her eyes slid to Carson. "Maeda is going to send us a file we have on her activities over the last few years. He warned us though, there isn't much information. Sorry it took so long, he had me on hold while he was conferencing with his media guy on the case. Now that we know who she is, he's going to put her photo out as a missing person."

Ian blew out a breath, gut twisting. If the GPSA has a file on her, this wasn't good. Not good at all.

"What did Maeda say about her?" Carson asked.

"Mentions. Whispers." She shrugged. "Just that her legend has been popping up here and there, linked to the underworld. Seems she's building a reputation as a mercenary."

"A mercenary?" That didn't fit with the woman he knew. "Are you sure?"

He reminded himself that they were following this individual because she'd just broken a convicted human trafficker out of prison. He scrubbed a hand over his face.

Ana nodded, "That's what Maeda said. We'll know a little more when he sends us the file that we have on her."

Maybe he was wrong after all. Maybe he'd just wanted to see her face in that still-frame distortion. He picked it up from the table. It wasn't like she was the only Ashray on the planet, as rare as they were. Or possibly, this was some other type of shifter....

While the shot was obscure, to his eyes, it was definitely her face.

"Maybe I'm wrong," he muttered.

"I hope so, too," Carson said. "What of her family? Are they Ashrays too?"

Ian shook his head. "Her father died in an accident when she was young. Her mother and brother are human, as far as I know." He went silent a long, long moment. Their humanity had been a point of contention between her and her mother. A bitter one. The gift had skipped a generation.

"You're not sure?" he pressed.

"Her brother went missing while we were still together." He didn't mention that it was part of the death of their relationship. "Her mother blamed her for it. Somehow, she always expected her to use her abilities to protect him. And failing that, to find him. She wasn't able to."

"That's a harsh situation," Lirikai said, her voice soft.

"Harsh woman; bitter and resentful."

Ana's phone buzzed. She checked the message then brought her laptop over to the table and sat down. A moment later, they were crowded around the small screen reviewing the file Maeda had sent. There were a few obscure photos similar to the screen capture they had, but nothing definitive. There were similarities in the images.

She was a water spirit. An Ashray. A ghost.

"Unless we catch her in her solid form, we can't get a solid ID. All we have are a list of mentions and speculations in this file. Impressive rumours about her abilities, though." Ana said.

Ian stood back. "She's hard to track. As an Ashray, she doesn't leave behind a scent, like other shifters."

Ana nodded, "Her energy signature is distinct."

"Her scent is detectable while in human form during the day. That's when she's vulnerable. She can only shift at night."

"Okay, let's review all the files again and figure out the best approach."

Ian nodded, "At this point, I think the inmate's scent might be easier to track if he is, in fact, a shifter as well."

"Which I can do without much problem." Lirikai said.

Ian glanced up at her.

"It is what I do. I track criminals by the scent of their...intentions. In the old days, we would track such individuals and deliver the goddess's justice at the bottom of the sea. Protect the innocent from the wicked."

"Now we have legal systems for that." Carson said to his lover, with a quirk of his lips. He turned his attention back to Ian. "We just need to know what we're up against. I'll get the maps so we can study our options."

Ana nodded "I'll print this new file too. If we can follow the timeline of where she's been seen, maybe we can figure out where she's heading now. I'd still keep our attention focused north. That's the impression I picked up at the prison."

Ian really didn't think he was wrong. While part of him desperately prayed he was, the other part of him hoped he wasn't.

The part of him that longed to see her again.

FIVE

"We should have stopped hours ago."

Chuck's voice hit Raya's last nerve, right in the back of her skull.

"Enough." She rounded on him with enough vehemence to force him back several steps. All night she'd had to remind herself why she was in the middle of the wilderness with this asshole, deflecting questions, complaints, and persistent propositions. She shuddered. Never in a million.

In the last hour, the harder they pressed on, the more aggressive he became.

He grabbed her wrist. "You're going to make me? What? As far as I can tell, you're here to guide me to my uncle." The more miles they had between the prison guards and themselves, the bolder he became.

"I already told you not to touch me. Release my arm."

His fingers bit deeper into the skin, pressing the bones. "What are you going to do, turn into a puddle? Yeah, it's morning, I know you can't shift," he sneered, pulling her closer.

"Yes, the deal is to deliver you to your uncle," she said through clenched teeth.

He grinned, "He must be paying you very well, to go through all this. I can take what I want and dump you here and get back on my own."

"Maybe," she said, jerking her wrist to dislodge his grip. He held fast. "He also wants something you have. Without it, he said, you shouldn't show your face."

Chuck blanched, then swallowed. "So?" he said, his voice losing some of its bravado.

"So, sounds to me like you're not exactly in his good graces, are you now?"

"You still haven't told me why I need you."

She shrugged, waving a hand toward the tree lined river. "Before I began your instructions on how to break you out of your prison, I listened. I listened in very carefully. You talk too much, you know."

"What do you mean?"

"You don't know when to keep your mouth shut. Bragging to your cellmate, the other inmates about who you were, how important you are, who your uncle is. The properties, the cars and boats. Not all at once, of course. In your everyday blathering, it was easy to learn an awful lot about you."

He glanced down as she pressed the blade tip of a large hunting knife he hadn't seen before to the soft flesh next to his Adams' apple. His fingers released her wrist, stepping back, the razor edge left a tiny incision. His hand went his throat, coming away with fresh blood smeared across his fingertips. "You B-"

"Ah-ah," the point immediately rose to his eye level. "Don't finish that thought." She stepped forward. "It wouldn't take me long to find out what you have, that he wants. It's what I do. You, however, don't know the location of where we're supposed to meet."

"You said we were meeting him in Montreal."

"Did I?"

He frowned.

She could see the doubt in his face.

"No one would know to link me to you. You need to stay hidden, as I said many times. I can simply walk away; you're welcome to fend for yourself."

The desire to ditch her was evident on his tired face. She was just as tired as he was. Both at their limit. She'd pushed on longer than usual the night before, in order to put as much distance as possible between the prison and themselves. Humans wouldn't be expected to have come as far.

The whine of a motor in the distance broke the face-off, forcing both of them to step into the cover of the bushes and trees.

While Chuck was watching the boat pass, she slipped away in the dense brush and made her way to her cache site. After several moments, she heard his raised voice call for her, followed by a string of curses.

Ignoring it, she stuck to her plan and made her way to the target campground. She'd let him stew for a little while before collecting him.

Prick.

She could do with five minutes of peace anyway.

This campground office was much like the last one, with the exception of a small television mounted on the wall rolling the local news. The old man behind the counter aimed his remote at the screen, silencing the audio as he shuffled in her direction with a friendly greeting.

Her interaction with him was much the same as with the woman at the last campground, with the exception of the hair rising on the back of her neck. He studied her face with far too keen an eye.

"Just one tent?"

"Yes, sir."

"Where you headed?"

"Appalachian trails."

"Quite a distance from here."

"So I hear," she said, "Any advice?"

He squinted, and after a moment he shrugged, "Just be mindful of predators and hunters, never know when one will pop up."

She nodded and thanked him, then headed for her lot to set up their camp.

When she went back for Chuck, she found only his pile of clothing in the shade of an outcropping of rock and pine trees.

"Shit."

Had he gone, or was he just cooling off from the intense summer heat?

She waited, scanning the constant flow of the Hudson for the purple-blue iridescent bubble of air that supported him in the water. It was difficult to see under the sun's glare. She thought she spotted him floating among the rocks. "Chuck, let's go," she shouted, and turned to step back into the woods.

A sharp sting struck her cheek followed by flare of pain. "Mother fucker!" she spun back toward the river, pulling her knife.

A clear, thin cord shot toward her from the water, wrapping around her wrist. She grunted from the pain of the poison burning the sensitive skin, "Come out, you son of a bitch!" she snarled as her blade slashed at the cord, releasing her arm, and she backed further away from the river. Another tentacle shot toward her, falling short, and retracted back into the water. She sheathed the knife.

"Fuck. Fuck!" Her fingers wiped the blood dribbling along her cheekbone, the fire of his poison mingling with it, seeping into her blood stream faster than the wound on her wrist. She sheathed her knife, stumbling back through the woods, running for the campground. The last image she saw was the enormous smudge of a bright yellow and pink inflatable ducky before she fell to the dirt path, unconscious.

IAN AND THE TEAM made their way to a small community hospital not far from their motel.

The call had come in not an hour past that someone matching Raya's description had been seen and taken by ambulance from a campground further up the Hudson than they'd expected.

Releasing her photograph to the local networks as a missing person had worked, and they'd received calls from the campgrounds she'd been to, as well as some campers that had seen her. However, they hadn't anticipated a trip to the hospital. A family had called the ambulance when she collapsed on the path in front of them, on their way to the campground beach.

Ian told administration he was her partner-the one looking for her. The story they concocted was that she suffered from depression, stopped her meds and took off. He told them how relieved he was to have found her again, safe.

The hospital staff weren't sure what was wrong with her. They surmised it may be a severe allergic reaction to some kind of poison parsnip or oak or ivy, maybe. They were keeping her stable and comfortable.

The team hung back in the hospital corridor while Ian stood in the open doorway staring at the bed, heart hammering.

"Do you want us to stay here?"

"No. I'd like a few moments."

"We'll look for the cafeteria, then come back in a bit."

Carson's hand squeezed Ian's shoulder before he took Lirikai's hand and followed Ana down the hall.

Ian's feet were rooted.

For the first time in his life, he was frozen in place while his insides churned.

She'd left him, after weeks of relationship disintegration. Half-truths and lies, avoidance and periodic disappearances.

He'd confronted her, and she'd dissolved what they were in that very moment.

When she walked out, she left him in a state of confusion, distrust, shock, and heartbreak.

All of that warred within him now. Surging. Renewed. Fresh.

He still loved her.

She was his heart.

He'd known it when they'd met all those years ago.

He just thought she knew it too.

It seemed she had, at least for a while.

He drew a deep breath, swallowed down the renewed hurt, resentment and confusion and stepped toward the bed.

She lay so still.

Pale.

Her face was relaxed in induced sleep. A bandage taped to her cheekbone was a stark white slash against the rich sunlit bronze of her skin. He reached for her hand, staring at the bandages encircling her delicate wrist.

"Ray." His whisper was loud in the silence of the room as he brought her fingers to his lips.

Sedated as she was, he didn't expect a response.

Her hair was a thick cloud of dark curls around her head, her lashes were silky fans, her brows delicate jet arches. His gaze dropped to her wide, full mouth, wanting to see her brilliant smile again.

His right hand held hers, thumb stroking her fingers while his other scrubbed over his face with a deep sigh.

This was so fucked up.

She was here, in this bed, because she'd broken an inmate out of prison and gone on the run.

Why?

Not to mention the GPSA file hinting at her exploits over the last years-the years since she'd walked out on him.

His jaw clenched as he stared at the beautiful face he loved, trying to reconcile the two realities of who he knew her to be with what she had become.

He wasn't sure he could.

His fingers brushed the tape holding the bandage on her wrist. Carefully, he eased back the edges hoping to not find what he suspected was there.

It was. Several rows of whip-like purple welts burned into the flesh identical to those found on the second escapee encircled her wrist.

"Bollocks." There was no denying her connection to the same inmate.

So what happened? Whatever it was, he was going to find out what was going on.

He'd come onto the case as a favor to Carson. A consultant. Now, he was going to see this through to wherever it took them.

Gently placing her hand back on the blanket next to her, his fingers lingered over hers for another moment before he left to search for Carson. It would be a little while longer before the sedation lifted.

SIX

THE DISTINCT SCENT OF hospital disinfectant crowded Raya's senses first. Then the sounds of voices and the sense of movement in the distance.

Raya's eyes fluttered open, and squeezed shut against the glare of sunlight piercing her eyes. Her head throbbed, her face and wrist ached.

She clenched her fists against the heart pounding need to leave the building.

This wasn't good. She hated hospitals. Really hated them.

And she was hallucinating.

Amid the sun glare was a hazy image of what she could have sworn was Ian.

Tongue plastered to the inside of her mouth, she tilted her head away from the window. Several figures were in various states of lounging, between her bed and the door.

She blinked, trying to focus on the unfamiliar faces. "Who are you?" she croaked.

A tall, dark-haired man stepped toward, while one of the women with him discretely closed the door. "Carson Perenga. GPSA."

"Shit," she groaned. Not just a hospital. Busted by law enforcement. She'd failed. And failed bad.

"Ray." The deep, distinct voice drew her attention back toward the widow. Her breath lodged in her chest.

"Am I doped up, or is that you, Ian?"

"It's me."

So bad.

Turning her face away from both men, she instead stared at the ceiling, hoping to find sense in the tiny holes of the tiles. Surely, she was locked in a nightmare.

Her nails bit into her palms as her fists clenched tighter.

"Why the hell are you here?" Her voice was hoarse, harsh, even. She squeezed her eyes shut to stop the sudden surge of tears from escaping as her heart flipped and rent. After years of suppressing her emotions and maintaining a controlled state, those two words had just ripped open all the pain and memories she'd shut away—locked away for good, she had thought.

She'd never expected to hear that voice again. Should never have hoped for it.

Especially in these circumstances. Her heart ached and she swallowed hard. She couldn't look at him. She couldn't face the judgment in his eyes. She didn't want to relive the pain of the circumstances around their breakup.

Because she couldn't tell him the truth. He wouldn't understand.

She considered her options.

She was caught. These were feds.

Would they arrest her?

Or help her?

Why the hell was Ian here?

The lake. Of course. She had considered the possibility he might be there before she initiated the project. Her last report had him in the west at Okanagan. She'd just hoped he would stay far away.

She needed to get out of here. She had a job to finish. There was too much at stake and this was no time for wallowing in the heartache of betrayal.

She reeled it all back into the safety of her anger.

"Why are you here?" she said again, through clenched teeth. Her head still throbbed; her body ached.

He stood and approached her bed.

She turned her head and leveled her stare on his face, coming into focus. Her brain promptly went to war with her heart and her hormones.

She'd nearly forgotten how handsome he was. That was a lie—she'd tried to forget. And she couldn't ignore the fact that despite the circumstances, every part of her reacted to him like the gravity between the moon and the tide. Her fingers twitched toward him. She flexed her fingers out in an effort to dispel the stiffness, but they just resumed their curled state as she waited for him to speak.

His broad shoulders shielded her from the sun and it took a moment for her eyes to focus on his face in shadow as he moved in and out of the light.

Still strong and serious. His brows were drawn down, and his eyes held a deep weariness as he regarded her. His normally full mouth was tight. She realized she wanted to ease the lines and see him smile again, just for a moment or two. With a blink, she discarded that thought.

"I'm here for you." He said.

Her heart foolishly jumped.

No, he was here with the GPSA.

"Well, here I am."

"Where is Charles Meduse?" Agent Perenga asked, breaking the spell that was threatening to draw her too far into the current of Ian's aura.

"Who?"

Ian picked up her wrist. "Your inmate lover."

She tried to snatch it away, but he held fast as she choked on the word. "Lover?"

He didn't really believe that. Did he? She looked into his eyes. No. He was pushing.

She pushed back. "I have many lovers, can you be more specific?"

His frown deepened and his lips thinned even more.

Good.

One of the women stepped forward. To Agent Perenga she said, "This is a waste of time, I can track him."

Perenga seemed to consider this as he turned back to Raya. "Who is Meduse meeting? Who hired you to break him out?"

Chuck was just a lead.

Looks like they're after the same thing I am.

Maybe.

"Again. Who?"

The other woman remained by the wall. "She isn't going to talk. There's too much at stake."

"If she won't cooperate, we'll have to arrest and detain her."

"On what charge? Camping?"

"On suspicion of aiding and abetting a fugitive felon from a prison."

"There is no proof of such a ridiculous claim."

"Isn't there?" Perenga said, voice even.

Raya let her silence speak for her.

"You'll have to move her during the day and hold her in a place with no flowing water source. No pipes or underground streams." Ian said.

Her face whipped his direction.

Traitor.

Perenga nodded. He turned to the woman next to him. "Lirikai, track him, but don't engage. I want to see who he meets with. That's more important right now. We can retrieve him later."

She nodded, brushed a delicate hand down his arm and went out of the room.

"Ortega, stay here with Ian. Get what you can."

"She's hard to read." Ortega said, voice so low Raya almost missed it. "The emotional confusion is blocking everything else out right now."

Perenga nodded. "Keep trying." To Ian he said, "I'm going to secure a holding facility."

As soon as he left, Raya studied the small woman left behind. "What are you, a fortune teller?" She taunted with a smirk.

Agent Ortega straightened her slight shoulders, not rising to the bait.

"How long have you been a mercenary?" Ian's voice stung her.

Her heart flipped. Raya clamped her emotions in place with a steel trap and remained silent.

"Working for money. I thought you were a peace-loving naturalist. Money had little value. At least, that's how I remember you, until just before the end."

"Do you remember? Truly?" She shot back. "Do you remember how you betrayed me?"

"Betrayed you?" Ian's voice rose. "You spent weeks lying and deceiving me before you left me."

"I left you because you betrayed me. The lies were necessary."

"Like fuck." He leaned toward her. "Since when is it necessary to lie to someone you're supposed to love?"

"When he refused to support you."

Ian stepped back. "When didn't I support you?" His voice softened, floating over her, confusion evident on his face.

"The only time in all the years we spent together that I asked you to help me. The only time. If you couldn't do that one thing, then we couldn't *be*."

The color drained from his face.

She swallowed the heartache lodged in her throat.

"Why didn't you help me, Ian?" Her words steamrolled toward him. "Couldn't be bothered to leave your precious lake and go out into the wider world? Too much trouble to disrupt your peaceful existence to look for Dominique?" She could see the truth of her words strike him.

"They said he was dead."

"*Probably* dead."

"Your mother had no right to drop responsibility for his life on your shoulders."

"It was *my* choice."

"There was evidence, Raya. His clothes, identification, his ring-"

"There was no body."

"The sea took him, Raya."

"That's what they told us. I've learned, that's what they tell everyone."

He straightened his shoulders, as he did when he was uncomfortable.

"Raya, I..." He blew out a breath, turning to the window.

She ignored the slip of emotion in his voice, the flash of conflicting pride and...regret?

"I thought you loved me enough to help me with this one thing I needed help with. *He* had nothing to do with what happened to your family all those years ago. I mistakenly believed *I* might have been more important than your grudges and prejudices. I was wrong."

The silence was a barrier that widened with every passing second.

"You are." He turned back from the window, expression set.

Anger surged through her. "Clearly I'm wrong, you don't need to-"

"You are more important." His words froze the breath in her chest.

Her heart expanded and retracted as she studied him. The regret was raw.

"It's too late."

SEVEN

Ian replayed the memory of her expression when he told her she was more important.

The words were out of his mouth before the thoughts had entered his head. It was like some other part of him had overridden his battered pride and deeply buried shame.

A fissure of shocked disbelief cracked the anger etched into Raya's lovely face. She slammed it closed. Those words meant something to her.

She refused to say anything more after that.

The hospital discharged her to his care and they were on route to the interim holding facility. Ian had recalled that a mutual friend of his and Carson's had a cabin up in the mountains, suggesting it as a possible option. He hadn't been there since before their friend had built on the land, so had no idea what the place was like.

Carson called Odson, and they were in luck. The cabin was available and lacked running water. There was a rainwater holding tank, otherwise they would need supplies.

Carson drove while Ana used her phone to find a nearby village where they could get supplies.

Ian's gaze was pulled back to Raya's profile.

She hadn't spoken to him again. Her attention was fixed on the rolling landscape outside her window, or straight ahead through the windshield.

"There's a small convenience store in the next town. If you turn off this main road, we should find a grocery store." Ana said to Carson.

As the car slowed to make the turn at the intersection, Raya's door snapped open at the same time she released her seatbelt and jumped out.

"Raya!" Ian yelled as he struggled to release his own seatbelt. "Stop, Carson."

Getting out of the SUV he took off after her across the road, nearly getting himself hit by oncoming traffic.

She disappeared into the dense brush lining the road and he barreled in after her. He had the advantage of long legs to keep up to her gazelle-like pace as she nimbly dodged overhanging branches and ground debris.

"Raya, stop!"

She didn't.

He was nearly upon her, despite the extra effort his larger body exerted to avoid the same obstacles she had.

"Don't make things harder for yourself. Give it up."

His hand stretched for the back of her shirt.

She spurred forward. His fingers closed on air.

Raya dodged around a cluster of trees and changed direction, putting extra distance between them, running along a rock ledge.

Goddess, she was fast.

He remembered the days spent hiking and running together. This was different. It was like she trained for this kind of scenario.

It was daylight, so he knew she couldn't shift. She was likely trying to lose him in the forest until she could find a place to hide from him and the agents.

His legs pumped hard and he leapt, reaching.

Making contact, they rolled hard over the uneven forest floor, grunting as hard branches and rocks hit limbs and ribs.

They came to a stop with him atop her. She fought as he struggled to grab her wrists to pin her to the ground.

"Give up," he growled as his beast-self rose to the surface after the chase and capture.

"I'll never give up." She snarled back.

She somehow managed to fold herself so that her knees and feet came up between them, and sent him flying away from her. She instantly scrambled to her feet, hands clenched into fists.

"Don't be so stubborn." He said, gasping for breath after having the force of her feet lodged in his gut.

"*I'm* stubborn? Look who's talking, you goddamned hypocrite. You're the one that is stubbornly holding on to centuries' old grudges and outdated ways of thinking."

"That has nothing to do with what's happening right now. You can't expect to not face the consequences of breaking a human trafficker out of prison, Raya. When did you lose your mind?"

Her eyes narrowed on him. The rosy hue of her cheeks darkened several shades more before she came at him.

She was a churning whirlpool of fists and feet, striking him like dead wood in a frothing river rapids.

He hadn't expected her to attack him. He'd been as naive as a careless young lad entering his first battle, guard down. He deserved it when her shoe flashed before his eyes, causing the world to go black.

STUBBORN? GIVE UP?

Not. Fucking. Likely.

The suppressed rage of a lifetime of being dictated to rose up in the form of her fists.

The loss of her father at a young age. The manipulation and resentment of her mother ever since. The self-harm and loss of her only brother.

Ian's failure to support her when she needed him most. She hadn't realized how deep and raw the erosion of those last years were until faced with the reality of his proximity now.

He still expected her to walk away—because he wanted her to.

This was more important than his precious pride, or her wounded heart.

This was her brother's life.

This was the lives of many others besides.

She had to get Chuck to Montreal so she could fulfill the next part of what she'd set out to do so many years before. And she couldn't do that from a GPSA prison.

This was the first time in years that she found herself hesitating to act.

They were giving her no choice.

He was giving her no choice.

He was another obstacle to overcome.

She let her rage power the strikes of her fists and feet to drown out the knowledge that she was striking Ian.

Ian.

The fissure in the dam had crumbled the barrier and the torrent was wild. She used the emotional super charge to find her equilibrium again.

She was too close to let them stop her now. She couldn't fail.

She sprang forward, taking advantage of his shock.

Every impact struck her heart, below the rage. The shock on his face seared her soul. She already regretted it, but couldn't let it hinder the need to escape. She had to try.

She'd learned how to drop a man much bigger than herself since the last time she'd seen Ian.

And she did.

A fraction of a second later, she drew a weary breath and turned to run, only to be met with the furious face of Agent Ortega, arm extended in her direction with a device in her hand, her chest heaving from the pursuit.

Raya's eyes swept the device. It was a Taser. Agent Perenga crashed through the woods toward them, still at a distance.

She raised her fists. "You'll go down faster than he did. Just let me go."

"No." Ortega's eyes were locked on Raya. "You owe me a new pair of shoes, Burns."

"Maybe if I can finish this job, I'll be able to afford it. Last time. Walk away."

Ortega adjusted her aim.

Raya hoped Ortega was more desk than field agent, and a poor shot, as she gauged the distance.

Was she faster than Ortega's trigger finger?

She had to try.

Raya turned in an attempt to outrun the reach of the Taser probes.

Ortega didn't have a slow trigger finger, nor was she a poor shot, Raya conceded as the probes struck her back, causing her to crumple to the ground not far from Ian's inert body.

She was so fucked.

EIGHT

IAN RODE IN THE backseat next to Raya, her wrist cuffed to his to prevent her from running again. Ana rode up front with Carson, and Lirikai hadn't checked in yet.

Ian's face and abdomen ached; his pride was shredded.

Raya maintained her silence during the long drive north and up into the mountains. The landscape here was veined with rivers and creeks feeding into the Hudson. They stopped only once for supplies. They had to get to wherever they were going before dark.

Ian couldn't stop himself from glancing in Raya's direction. With her attention trained on the passing landscape, it was easier for him to drink in what he could see of her face. No matter that she looked the same, she felt different to him. She even smelled a little different. The sweet innocence of her scent was altered.

Proved when her fist had connected with his face.

He should be furious that she'd struck him. He was still in disbelief.

She definitely was not the sweet Raya Burns he'd known. *That* woman would never commit violence on another individual.

This was *his* fault.

He swallowed his guilt.

He should have helped her look for her brother. Instead, Ian just accepted that he'd died of a drug overdose or committed suicide while vacationing on the coast. That's what the local police told them when they handed her Dominique's belongings, that's what Ian went with.

Not Raya.

She wanted more proof. They both knew the hunger of the sea and how unlikely the probability that she would give up a body.

Raya's mother expected the impossible of her.

"How is your mother?"

She started at the sound of his voice. "Dead."

"I'm sorry." Despite being human, she was still Raya's mother, and a compatriot.

Raya sighed, and nodded at his acknowledgment. "I know you didn't care for her. Her liver finally gave out." After another long moment, she added, "I brought her remains home to Aberdeen and buried my father's ashes with her. Resting together where they started, back in Scotland. Before life turned to shit for them." She sighed. "Now it's just me."

Alone.

Instinct prompted Ian to slip his fingers around hers on the seat between them.

She looked down at their hands. A break in the trees allowed the sun to catch on the cuffs linking their wrists. Her hand slid out from under his, fingers curling against her thigh.

The loss of her touch was razor-sharp.

Carson turned the car onto a dirt road—if you could call it that. It reminded Ian more of the old narrow tracks criss-crossing the countryside before automobiles were a thought. He appreciated the modern suspension as they bounced along under the thick canopy of trees for an eternity before coming to a stop in front of a shack.

"Lovely," Raya muttered.

Ana's sigh echoed the sentiment.

"Just like the old days, eh, Ian?" Carson quipped.

Stacked log walls sagged over a stone foundation, topped with a crumbling, lichen-covered roof. "Looks like Odson built this place himself." Ian eyed the place.

Carson shrugged. "You seen him lately?" He asked as he parked the car and popped the trunk.

"It's been a couple of decades, but aye." He grabbed two of the large water jugs from next to Raya's backpack in the trunk. With Raya in tow, still attached by the cuffs, Ian headed toward the cabin.

Inside the cabin it was easier to see its fortress-like qualities. The interior structure was bolstered. Every corner was precise and immaculate. The support columns were intricately carved in the old style with mythical beasts and flora. Drawn to them, he stared a long time.

"Ian?" Ana's voice broke the reverie that was blocking out the present.

"Yeah?" He smiled, shoving the sudden nostalgia down where it belonged. Buried.

Ana handed him more supplies and turned back to the car.

"Are you going to uncuff me at some point? Being tugged back and forth is getting tedious." Raya said.

"Are you going to start talking about Charles Meduse and your camping trip?" Ian asked.

"May as well get comfortable. Until we can figure out which GPSA facility can house you best, you're stuck here with them." Carson nodded toward Ana and Ian as he went back outside.

"Wait, what? Why do I have to stay here? There's no working toilet, Carson." Ana's voice drifted off as she followed him.

Ian gave Carson a full description of the topography of the lake region and the waters' personalities to relay to Lirikai. He told Carson he should be doing the scouting, since that's what he had called him in to do. Carson insisted it was more important he stay with Analiese and Raya.

"Maybe you can find the right words to get her to work with us." He finally said.

By the time Carson abandoned them to the quiet of the mountain forest, they had enough supplies to last quite a few days.

Ana paced back and forth outside, hand extended to the heavens, trying to catch a signal on her cell. She didn't believe him when he told her there likely weren't any cell towers out here yet—if there ever would be.

She went back inside a quarter hour later, cursing and muttering under her breath.

"Come on, we may as well make dinner," he suggested, looking through the cupboards at the dishes. "Raya, do you remember how to make scones?"

They found the cabin to be powered by a solar powered generator. Cords of wood were piled around back for the wood stove, in the event the generator failed and they needed to cook.

She gave him a level look and rolled her eyes. Ignoring it, he grinned. "Ana, Ray and I will teach you how to make the best scones on the planet."

"I don't think you should let her near the cutlery. I've read her files."

"Really, now?" He turned toward Raya with a raised brow. "Well. This ought to be interesting; may as well regale us with these mercenary tales. Good with fists, feet *and* weapons?"

She had been desperate to escape earlier that day. How far would she go to gain that freedom?

Raya turned her impassive face toward Ana. "Knives or spatulas," She shrugged. "I can make either equally effective."

Ian shoved a plastic bowl in Raya's hands followed by a whisk. "Come on now, Ray, don't try to frighten the lass." He intentionally thickened his burr, drawing her attention, and smiled. Since she'd grown up in eastern North America, she'd always said how much she liked the sound of his accent when he wasn't masking it.

Her frown dropped back into place.

It was worth a try.

Carson preferred her cooperation to incarceration. Ian agreed.

At one time, he would have said he knew Raya better than anyone. Did he still? Even though she'd changed so much?

He slid measured ingredients across the counter and, having nothing else to do, she began mixing while Ian chatted with Ana.

Raya remained silent beside him. She was slowly losing the brittle tension that stiffened her body.

He didn't know if he could get her to tell them what they needed to know. Given the reputation she seemed to have earned, he'd have to give her a damned good reason to say anything. A damned good reason.

Aside from keeping her confined, that's what they were here to do.

NINE

RAYA'S EYES WERE GLUED to Ian's regrettably bruised face as they sat at the tiny table eating the scones and drinking tea in near silence.

The sudden roll of Ian's brogue earlier had jolted her back a decade. He knew that the wicked combination of that brogue and his boyish smile used to drop her panties faster than anything else in the world. And the scones.

He was working her.

She couldn't let him see it wasn't taking much effort to have an impact on her.

No matter how this was bringing back memories; memories of him making her scones for breakfast in nothing but an apron. The view from behind was a wonderful distraction while she waited.

She blinked away the traitorous memory as the buttery food slid over her tongue.

She was so focused on Ian, she was nearly startled to recall Ortega was there watching her, small and timid looking. Raya clearly saw Ortega's catlike patience as she surveyed her.

Raya had had plenty of opportunity to build her poker-face over the years.

But this, with Ian, had never been a factor.

She was going to have to make some decisions.

Her job was to get Chuck safely to his Uncle via Montreal, with a slight detour to retrieve something he valued. Raya suspected the item was the real goal in all this and the nephew was actually just a bonus of sorts.

Why wasn't her employer telling her what it was? A flare for the dramatic? Was it so she wouldn't have time to over think and change course if it was something of monetary value? Clearly, he didn't yet trust her enough. A test of some sort, no doubt.

Either way, she needed to complete the job. She needed to get close to this man. He was the key.

Her eyes slid to Ian again. Why was he here? What did he have to gain from this? He never mentioned working for the Global Paranormal Security Agency before. He was a recluse. Part of GPSA's job was to protect humans from rogue paranormals, which was entirely out of his character.

She recalled the banter between him and Carson. A favor for a long-time friend, no doubt.

He couldn't do her a 'favor' to help her find her brother.

The scone turned gritty in her mouth and she placed the remainder back on her plate. Their cuffed hands rested side by side on the scarred wooden tabletop.

They were going to send her to a GPSA prison. Her throat was too tight to swallow. If she went to prison now, she'd never be able to find Dominique. She had to find out if he was still alive or truly dead.

She looked up to see agent Ortega assessing her.

"What do you want from me?" she asked, even though she already knew.

"We want to know who Chuck Meduse is going to meet. When and where."

"What do you plan to do with me?"

Ortega sighed, considering her. "Depends."

Raya raised a brow, waiting for her to elaborate.

Ortega thought a long moment before answering. "Obviously, breaking an inmate out of jail is illegal. However, you know we couldn't prosecute you through the human judicial system, you'd have to go through GPSA's system. As Charles Meduse *should* have done." She leaned back, re-crossing her legs on the chair and shrugged. "Reduced time. Depends how good your intel is."

Reduced time.

That wasn't enough. Raya seriously considered her options. "Has my detention been made public?"

"Not yet. The only reports were those of an unknown female taken from a camping ground to hospital to be treated for exhaustion and dehydration."

"Who in your department knows I've been caught?"

"Our team and director."

"Keep it that way, and I'll help you retrieve Chuck, for full immunity."

Ortega's eyes narrowed. "Full immunity. That's a big ask. We'd need more—a lot more. Besides, how could we be assured you can be trusted?"

Raya turned her attention to Ian, who was observing in silence, his keen eyes on her face. She looked at the cuffs for a long moment before she turned her focus back to Ortega. "We're after the same thing. You want Chuck's boss, right? Chuck's Boss is his uncle. Maybe you know that already. What you may not know is that he wants Chuck to retrieve something of value before going to meet him. Which I was supposed to ensure that he did. That's what he's paying me to do."

She looked at Ian. "I'll let you have him after I get what I need from him. I need information about the trafficking network."

Ian blinked, lips compressing.

"That's what we're after." Ortega said.

"I need the intelligence for the organization I'm *actually* working for. An organization that exists solely to infiltrate and break this network."

"Why not just work with GPSA? I highly doubt they aren't aware of this organization you mentioned?"

"This is bigger than your serve and protect organization."

"So, you're working as a mercenary to infiltrate this crime organization." Ian said, his disbelief weighing his voice. "Is this for real?"

She nodded.

"You really have changed."

"You haven't."

He jerked from the sting of her words.

"I'll need to report to Agent Perenga and our director." Ortega said.

"If you wait too long, it'll be too late."

"We have no choice until he comes back."

HOW HAD SHE GONE from wanting to find her brother to this?

Ian's stomach rolled and tightened.

If the two weren't connected, how had she landed on this incredulous path? As a mercenary. Working for some shadow organization.

All this time?

He scrubbed a hand over his face trying to process what she'd said as he looked at her, trying to find the truth in her words, in their current situation.

It seemed everything had changed between them in a snap of her fingers. So many times, he'd thought of the night she asked for his help.

He regretted the devastation on her face when she'd asked him to help find her brother and he shut her down.

That should never have happened.

He'd been a stubborn, selfish, arsehole.

It shouldn't have mattered that he believed her damned mother guilt-twisted her into going, just as with everything else she wanted Raya to do.

Raya and her brother spent their lives firmly under their mother's thumb, to the point where he had fallen into addiction, no matter how much Ray had tried to help him.

To Ian, it hadn't been a surprise when they were told he was missing and presumed to have committed suicide or overdosed at the beach where he was living.

Her mother had instilled this impossible sense of responsibility for the kid, no matter that he was a full-grown man that had maintained a youthful appearance, with red hair and freckles that stood out on pale skin, like their mother's. Ray favored her father's rich brown skin and thick curly hair—he'd often caught her staring at the one family photo she had.

Ian really believed the kid was lost and he'd just wanted Raya to have some peace. Devoid of her mother's demands and the responsibility of looking out for her kid brother all the time. And selfishly, he'd wanted her to live in peace with him, away from the chaotic world of humans.

He never dreamed she would go down this path.

She was an Ashray, with an inherent need to seek sanctuary and live in places of beauty.

Yet here she was, living the life of an undercover mercenary, hip deep in the lowest of human filth.

No. This wasn't the human underbelly. This prisoner was a paranormal working within the network. How many others were there? He'd come to think of humans as primitive little savages after they destroyed the relationship of peaceful co-existence between themselves and his family. But paranormals using their strengths to enslave the weak wasn't acceptable either.

He looked up into Raya's defiant face, staring him down.

She'd become someone else.

Her accusation that he hadn't changed stung.

Why? Why would he be stung by that? He'd been around for centuries, what did it matter if he changed or not?

Somehow the fact that she believed he hadn't, mattered to him.

He wasn't sure he liked how much she had changed.

Had she changed so much in the ways that truly mattered?

This wasn't about chasing a life of darkness for gain. It was about finding information for a covert organization to combat global human trafficking.

What the hell?

What if that was just a lie? A lie to convince them to let her go on her merry way?

He'd believed her lies before. Lies to hide her activities because she knew he'd try to stop her from looking for her brother.

He should have helped her find closure. Her mother's involvement shouldn't have mattered. Ian should have just supported Raya. Helped her. Maybe none of this would have happened. She wouldn't be facing time in a GPSA prison—if she was lying.

They'd still be together. Not in this ridiculous situation.

She broke an inmate out of a prison. He had to admit, that was a fucking ballsy thing to do.

He'd spent far too much time moping in his lakes.

Ian couldn't be sure one way or the other of the truth. He glanced at Ortega. If this was all a lie, Raya was facing serious prison time. Could he live with himself knowing she was shut away in a cell?

If she was telling the truth, then she was working in a fucking dangerous climate, and only looking to sink deeper.

Where would it end? Would she drown, and her bones be swallowed by the ocean, too? Or could she surface triumphant and be free, once and for all?

He held Raya's gaze. "Maybe it's serendipitous that Carson called me, and that I actually agreed to help him. Or maybe I just got tired of the boredom of being alone with my own thoughts." He drew a deep breath and blew it out. "Either way, I'm here to help." He slipped his hand around Raya's slender fingers, brushing his thumb over her soft skin. "It's late in the game, I know." He stopped to draw another deep breath. "I'm going to help you, Ray, as I should have done years ago. I failed you."

His heart cracked at the sudden gathering of tears in her eyes. A fissure of deep regret shot through that crack when she blinked them away, straightened her spine and gave him a sharp nod, mask snapped back in place.

TEN

IT'S LATE IN THE game, I know. ... I'm going to help you, Ray, as I should have done years ago. I failed you.

Those words rolled through Raya's mind over and over.

I failed you.

She'd never known Ian to apologize to anyone in the years they were together.

No one had ever apologized to her. Ever, in her life.

Ian, in his way, had.

Yes, it was late coming.

She couldn't deny how hard those words hit her. Like a throat punch.

She sighed, staring at the far wall of the dark room, laying on her side, the heat from Ian's body radiating against her back.

Still cuffed together, until agent Perenga returned with the keys, they lay in the cabin's one bedroom, while agent Ortega curled up on the couch, the door open between them.

Ignoring the awkward angle of her arm with her right hand resting on the bed behind her, next to Ian's, Raya tried to process the turmoil of her thoughts and emotions. This job was not going the way she'd planned. She and Chuck should have been reaching their final camp soon, then retrieving his uncle's precious object before going on to the yet to be determined meeting point.

What the hell was she going to do now?

Would the other agents catch Chuck?

From all the hours spying on Chuck before engaging him and instigating the breakout, she'd listened. He talked up the condo he had in Montreal. Where he stored his sports cars and kept expensive art. Where he partied with beautiful women who threw themselves at him. Gag.

What a yammerhead. She was pretty sure the only reason Chuck worked for the Quebec City crime boss Jean-Guy LeVoleur was because he was his sister's son. Otherwise, she had no doubt he'd be cemented under a sidewalk somewhere, because the guy never shut his yap. A *secret* condo that he kept to himself, that he didn't think his uncle knew about.

Well he knew of its existence, just not its precise location. That was part of Raya's job. If she couldn't get Chuck to the condo to get the thing, then it was up to her to retrieve it herself.

Either way, she preferred to deliver Chuck at the meeting. She had a reputation to maintain in order to navigate the underworld. An unavoidable necessity.

She hadn't lost control of a job so badly since the early days when she fumbled her way along. In this line of work, she'd had to learn fast.

Lost in her thoughts, she didn't notice the change in Ian's breathing and was startled when he rolled onto his side. His heavy arm arched over and around her, with her back suddenly pressed against his chest, her backside to his groin. With her right hand wedged in the small of her back, the rim of Ian's navel was distinct against her curled fingers.

Surprised, she remained still, Chuck gone from her head to be filled by the sensation of Ian's body against hers.

He grew hard against her.

She should ease away from him.

The familiar, old desire to rub her ass against him was overwhelming. The invitation for him to slip into her. The memory of how he used to fill her slammed her body, and sent a coil of heat shooting down her belly to pool in her panties. The lightning reaction of her body to his took her breath away.

She ached for him.

His scent enveloped her. She closed her eyes, resisting the urge to breathe deeply of him. His big hand curled next to her chest, just under her chin. Part of her wished it would slip over her breast. Her nipples hardened. It was so difficult not to move her hips against him.

So familiar. His body was like home.

She should move away, regardless of probably waking him.

She didn't.

Instead, she closed her eyes and slowly—very slowly—relaxed her body. The heat of his body seeped into the muscles of her rigid back. The more she allowed herself to ease into him, the tighter his arm pulled her to the comforting realm of his chest.

Her throat tightened.

She had no idea how much she missed this—how much she missed him—until this very moment. The fingers of her free hand curled over his and pressed it to her beating heart. Like it had just suddenly kick-started again after years of being dormant.

It hurt.

She didn't stop the tears when they came this time, allowing the edge of her pillow to absorb them as she finally fell asleep.

"IAN."

His eyes snapped open at the whisper of his name.

Ana stood by the open door of the bedroom. "It's morning."

He nodded and she disappeared.

He took stock of his situation.

Curled into his chest like she was meant to be there, Raya's breathing was steady in sleep. His hand was entwined with hers, pressed to her chest. Her bottom rested against his groin and thighs and all he could smell was her hair and the natural scent of her skin. Fresh like a natural spring after a long winter. He studied the fine hairs curled at her nape, resisting the urge to graze his lips over the soft skin. Her breasts were soft against his forearm and her firm arse brought back a rush of memory that had him hard without another thought.

Sensing his arousal, she leaned back into him and he swallowed a groan, staying as still as possible, for as long as possible. It was delicious torture. He remained as he was. His greedy mind was lost in a feast of delectable flesh amid soft moans of delight, his memories of their passion vivid in the dull morning light. He knew this body so well. He knew what made her breath catch and what made her moan, and especially what made her scream.

He grew harder. Bad idea. He strained against his jeans' zipper, having slept as they were, fully clothed. His body craved hers in a way he hadn't acknowledged before now. There'd been no thought, no interest to find someone else when she left him. Now, with her lithe body pressed to his as she was, there was no doubt in the hunger that was surfacing.

Ana wandered past the open door, folding the blanket she'd used and straightening the pillows on the couch.

He had to focus on that.

No matter how much he craved slipping into Ray, watching the passion in her expression and the little sounds he knew she would make as he loved her—it wasn't going to happen. No matter how much he ached. The need was a vice around his chest.

Her breathing lightened and he knew she was awake. After an eternal moment she leaned away. The cool morning air rushed to fill the new space between them. Sitting up on the edge of the bed, she looked down at him. Her expression not as hard as it was the day before, as she studied him.

"Good morning." He said, voice husky, brogue thick.

She smiled, and he could feel the sun rise in his chest.

ELEVEN

RAYA SERIOUSLY CONSIDERED HER options as she looked around at the cabin in the early morning light.

She was still cuffed to Ian. The key was miles and miles away, secured in agent Perenga's pocket.

She'd never had the opportunity to master handcuff lockpicking, so that was out. As was severing Ian's hand from his wrist. She was dedicated to her job, but maiming him wasn't an option. She wasn't so ruthless that she'd take such drastic measures to free herself from Ian. Were it Chuck, she'd think about it. The other douche-bag, Glenn, she wouldn't think twice.

All this time, she'd been watching and listening to Ian and the GPSA agents—and to her gut—trying to find a bead of light in the shadows of her situation. If she was honest with herself, which she usually was, that bead of light was Ian, of all things and people. She was beginning to believe maybe she could work with these agents.

Maybe.

The cabin's three occupants tried to find things to fill their time throughout the long day.

Ian was becoming twitchy from the confinement. He was setting her on edge. He never could stay inside for long.

"You up for a little walk? Stretch our legs for a bit?" He asked Raya.

"Is that wise?" Ortega asked, looking up from her laptop.

He held up their linked wrists, giving the cuffs a jiggle.

"Ian." She said removing her glasses, face intent. "If Ms. Burns wishes to rid herself of you in that dense forest. She could do it. We both read her file. And while I would go after you and haul her ass back here. I don't want to have to go out into those blackfly infested woods."

Raya couldn't stop the laugh that escaped her. Despite herself, she was beginning to like agent Ortega. "She's right." She said to Ian, turning her attention to his face. She was nearly taken aback by the intensity of his gaze.

"Would you?"

"Depends." She couldn't seem to help the breathless reaction either. She realized she actually didn't want to rid herself of Ian. Even though she had work to do, every particle of her wanted Ian to be part of it. It was like the heart ache and anger of the betrayal between them was beginning to dissipate.

"On?"

On? Oh right.

"If you promise to make more scones." She said the first thing that came to mind to set him at ease.

He lifted a brow. "Clothed or not?"

Ian. Naked. She swallowed.

"Okay, I don't need to hear this." Ortega said. "Just don't make me come looking for you."

Ortega was armed and kept her distance from Raya in case she forced her to use her weapon.

Raya had already decided to bide her time. At least until they got down off the mountain and she could get out of the cuffs without maiming anyone.

She knew that was why they cuffed her to Ian in the first place. She might think twice about hurting him, whereas severing anyone else's limb for freedom might be a price she'd quickly pay.

"Not." She challenged, sweeping him with her eyes.

If she was going to escape, she may as well make it easier.

She was rewarded with his slow grin.

"Ian." Ortega said. "Be careful."

Ian nodded to her as he stood.

The woods surrounding the cabin had a magical, primitive qual-ity to them. Alive in a way that was wholly distinct from the wilder-ness around the lake, where people dwelled all the time.

They walked a little distance through trees, following a narrow trail. Trees were marked at regular intervals, unlike the forest the previous day, where she'd struck Ian in an attempt to escape. Despite all her skills, escaping hand cuffs wasn't one of them. A problem to be dealt with during her next bout of leisure time.

Breathing deeply, she eased her guard. Then she reached out with her magic, seeking a water source.

"There's nothing up here." Ian said.

"A girl has to try."

He snorted.

"I forgot you could sense my magic."

"So did I." He glanced at her.

The trail curled around the rocky surface as it gently descend-ed. The birdsong was deafening as the sun rose higher, peeking through the tree tops above them. The terrain began to fall away on one side.

They rounded another boulder and the trail opened to a cliff top view.

Raya gasped.

They overlooked a vast valley; a rolling carpet of trees.

It reminded her of the old days, together. When they spent days hiking through the woods around one of Ian's lakes. Including this one.

She looked down at their cuffed wrists, side by side. She brushed the back of her hand against his. She felt his attention on her as she looked up into his face. This was the first time they'd been alone in nearly a decade. Stubble shaded his cheeks and jaw, somehow making his lips look softer.

She licked hers, desperately wanting to taste him.

Drawn to her mouth, his gaze caressed her.

She slid her fingers along his palm, inviting his grasp.

Fingers linked, palm to palm, she stepped toward him.

He watched her face as she moved closer.

The air fizzled between them, sending tingles across the flesh of her chest and belly.

She pushed through it until she stood, her breasts a breath from his chest.

So close.

She thought of the previous night. Sleeping with her back to his front. Delicious fantasies of his body moving against hers pebbled her nipples and dampened her panties.

She recalled how well he knew her body, and she knew his.

Glancing down the thin space between them, she lifted her hand to his chest. It was still a solid wall of warm muscle as it rose and fell with each breath beneath her palm. His free hand curled over hers, covering his heart. He leaned over her, lips close to her ear.

"It's still yours."

His whispered brogue ripped through her, slamming her throat, her heart and her core.

The tip of his nose ghosted along the shell of her ear down to the soft, vulnerable flesh below it.

Oh. Oh, he was *so* working her.

And she relished it.

She tilted her head, offering her throat to him as she stepped into his space, pressing her body to his, completing the connection.

An instant later, she found herself pinned with her back to a massive tree, their cuffed hands pressed to the bark over her head.

Ian's free hand gripped her thigh, pulling it up over his hip. She could feel his desire pressed to her hot center.

Dear Goddess, she wanted him to fill her. Wanted him to remind what it was to feel whole again. To feel like a woman full of desire.

She remembered what she was like, before she'd shut herself down.

Her insides throbbed as she wantonly lifted her hips, wrapping her leg around him and drawing him closer still.

Ian could never be close enough.

She slid her free hand along his back, slipped into his jeans, and gripped his ass.

"Ray." He warned, face close to hers. Nose tip to tip. They inhaled each other's breaths.

"It's been so long," she whispered, brushing her lips across his. Her tongue darted out, tasting him. Her hand slid from his ass to grip his hard cock. "Much, much, too long."

His chest rumbled with a deep growl, his body rigid as he struggled for self-control.

She was so ready for him.

Her hand slid up and down his length.

Taunting. Daring. Encouraging.

His body jerked against her.

He forced his eyes open, looking into hers. The sun made them glow like highly polished mahogany.

"Here? Now?"

She nodded. "Yes, now, Ian. Right now."

She craved the security of his body, the connection with him. To not be so alone. Just for a little while.

They helped free each other of their pants in seconds. Then she was guiding his tip to her hot wet core.

She drew a breath of anticipation.

He remained a moment longer nestled between her moist folds.

She tilted her hips so that his crown was at her entrance.

He thrust home.

She cried out.

Home.

They stood as they were. Her back against the trunk of the ancient tree, his face buried in the crook of her neck. Chest to chest in this wild place on a mountain top. The drop to a rolling valley just feet away from where they stood.

Glancing up into the lattice of tree branches, tears filled her vision.

It's still yours

Regardless, she wouldn't ask Ian to be hers again, though she never stopped loving him. Even through her sense of betrayal and anger. She never stopped.

"Fuck me, Ian." Her voice was soft in her demand.

He lifted his head, looking straight into her eyes.

"Hard."

He claimed her mouth and as his tongue swiped hers, he thrust hard, as she'd asked him to.

Her legs wrapped over his hips, the tree bark bit into her back through her shirt.

She relished it as he pumped into her over and over. Relentless.

Raya held on tighter and tighter, desperate for the closeness of his body, his essence.

She'd missed him so damned much.

She crested.

As deep as he was within her, it wasn't enough.

He kept going until she crested again. He followed her into the abyss.

TWELVE

JEAN-GUY LEVOLEUR WALKED THE length of his hotel suite, hands clasped behind his back. The television on the wall was set to the local news. He'd made the three-hour drive from Quebec City to Montreal in anticipation of the meeting with the Ashray and his nephew Charles.

He glanced at the time in the corner of the newscast then to his silent phone on the hotel room desk.

She should have checked in by now.

Something was wrong. He could feel it in his gut. She had a reputation of flawless job executions.

No doubt Charles fucked things up. He snorted and turned back to the large windows overlooking the old quarter near the waterfront. It wasn't as beautiful as his city. It lacked...elegance.

The sooner he could go back the better, though he knew he needed to be here himself to complete the job he'd hired her to do.

It was too important. There was too much on the line.

The door swung open to admit his personal assistant.

"What is it, Marie-Ange?"

"No reports yet, just messages from your contacts. They're expecting the next shipment from your sector in a few days."

He nodded. He'd already delayed things by a week. He couldn't hold off for much longer.

He needed to secure the operation before taking the next usual steps.

And that all depended on Charles.

Jean-Guy needed access to his apartment before he moved ahead. He had to handle this discretely or his whole sector of the ring could fall because of his nephew's sentimental stupidity. What could he do? Charles was his sister's kid.

If he were anyone else...

Anyone else wouldn't be a problem; he'd just deal with them. Simple.

Charles complicated things for him. Immeasurably.

Dealing with Charles required incredible patience, if he was to be entrusted with his entire legacy. With no children of his own, Jean-Guy needed to ensure the survival of the business in the family. Charles was the only choice. He just needed a little more time to mature. More time to understand the way of things.

He sighed and paced the length of the windows, staring out at the gray buildings, gray sky, and gray river front.

He was so close.

"*Merde.*" Jean-Guy swore, glancing at his watch again.

Charles.

Where the hell was the Ashray now? Where was Charles?

Jean-Guy's heart pounded in his chest and his skin flushed. He drew a deep breath.

Calm.

IAN'S GAZE RETURNED TO Raya across the table.

They faced each other over a Scrabble board they'd found tucked away in a cupboard. She was seventeen points ahead in their third game.

In the forest, spent, they'd righted each other's clothing with still more lingering touches before returning to the monotony of the cabin.

He couldn't get enough of her.

They had so much history and yet, there was so much heartache between them, too.

Could she let it go? Could he?

He'd already decided he no longer wanted to hold onto the past. This, with Raya, was different.

They'd hurt each other deeply. Equally.

When he was truthful with himself, he'd never let her go. He'd meant it when he said his heart was still hers.

She'd invited him into her sweet body again. What of her own heart?

Ian wanted all of her.

Words filled the board while the air was silent.

Ana was curled up with a book from the small collection stored with the board games and cards.

Ian never would have figured Odson to be the board games and books type. He supposed everyone got bored in isolation.

He didn't mind it—not when Raya shared it.

It was temporary, he knew. And that was fine with him.

He was thankful she hadn't taken advantage of his vulnerability in the forest to escape. Especially considering how messy the cuffs would have made it.

He glanced up at her again.

Would she try again, as soon as they were free of each other?

No doubt.

Their fucking hadn't changed the fact that she was on a mission.

He straightened and drew a breath, considering the letter tiles in front of him, as he considered his choices for the future.

He'd promised to help her discover the fate of her brother.

He'd admitted his heart was still hers.

Raya had accepted neither his help nor his heart.

He cleared his throat and chose his last few playable tiles and slid them into the spaces between words Raya had placed, launching him several points ahead of her.

It didn't matter.

She was too important to him to withdraw his support and love from her now. He realized that in the last few years. He wasn't going to fuck up another opportunity. Whether she realized it or not, when they worked together, they were both the richer for it. He knew that now.

She placed her last tile, finishing the game and tying the score.

The rest of the afternoon and evening passed in a cloud of quiet riffs of conversation, tea, and little things to fill the time until the hour grew late again.

"I'll wash up the dishes." Ana said with a yawn.

"Why don't you bed down; we can do it." Raya said.

Ana's perfect brows rose as she looked from Raya to Ian, who nodded and stood to collect the abandoned cups and plates from the table.

"Go on, then," he said, reaching for the still warm kettle to use for the washing up. Without running water, they'd had to get creative, like in the old days before indoor plumbing.

"Alright. I won't be far if you need anything." She said, heading for the couch.

Dishes washed and set aside, Raya followed Ian out of the screen door to dump the water from the bowl they'd used.

"It's perfect up here." Raya said, face upturned toward the stars and wisps of space dust visible between the overhead crowns of oak and maple.

Ian set the bowl aside and joined her in a few moments of stargazing.

"I've often thought about the many nights we spent together, just like this." Her chest rose and fell. "Those were good days."

"They were."

She turned toward him. "I can't go back, Ian."

"I know."

"I wish things were different but-"

"I understand."

The rest of her words died on her tongue as she looked into his face, seeing that he truly did. Her free hand rose up, her fingertips gently traced the bruises she made. "I'm sorry."

"Nothing to apologize for." He kissed her palm. The memory of her flying fists and feet still stung, more his pride than anything else.

There'd no doubt been a flowing water source in the valley. She could have fought, again, for her freedom, despite the cuffs. She hadn't. Instead, she'd invited him into her.

"You've certainly learned how to protect yourself."

Her laugh was short. "You have no idea."

His eyes narrowed on her, his gut rolling over. He could imagine. He recalled what people were like. And diving into the underworld as she'd done...

Dropping his gaze to their cuffed hands, he slid his fingers between hers, which in turn tightened on his. "We should get some sleep too."

They didn't know what would come the following day.

He nodded and retrieved the bowl on their way back inside.

Ana was curled into a ball, wedged in the corner of the couch. Ian paused to adjust the throw that had slipped from her shoulder before going into the bedroom with Raya.

Raya closed the door and slipped the lock.

Ian's gaze snapped to her face.

Her eyes were trained on his, in the darkness of the room.

She reached for the hem of her shirt and pulled it up over her head, letting it drop to the chain of the cuffs tethering them. Then she reached for his before unbuttoning her pants and letting them drop to the floor. His joined hers as his gaze swept her perfect body. Full breasts and hips, muscled thighs and strong toned arms were testament to the hard hours of physical training she must have endured over the years. Her fingers slid with gentle familiarity over his taut abdomen, making his dick jerk with need.

She licked her lips, stepping closer. He grew harder.

She was so fucking beautiful. He wanted nothing more than to slide into her hot wet channel.

First, he needed to worship her.

This could very well be the last time she welcomed his touch.

Dipping his head, his lips brushed the tops of her breasts. Her head fell back with a sigh. With his free hand, his fingers ghosted her spine till he found the clasp of her bra.

He was rewarded with a groan as his mouth closed over first one peaked nipple, then the other.

His arm slid around her hips as he turned their bodies so that he could back her toward the bed. He followed her as she eased back onto the mattress. Staring down into her face, her gray eyes were luminous in the moonlight streaming in through the window.

So beautiful.

He kissed her with all the gentleness in his soul until she parted her lips and invited him in.

His tongue swept hers.

She groaned, her free hand clasping his back, nails gliding along his skin. With each plunge of his tongue, his cock throbbed with need.

He wasn't going to just fuck her this time.

He had years to make up for.

Neither of them knew what the dawn would bring.

With reluctance he relinquished her mouth and made his way down her body.

Throat, collarbone, breasts. The curve of her belly button, hip, and inner thigh.

Hooking his fingers under edge of her panties, he slid them down her legs so that she was fully exposed to his gaze.

Beautiful.

He sought to devour more of her.

He licked and nibbled.

She gasped and sighed.

Her fingers slid along his jaw. "Hold me."

He kissed her wrist, then her soft skin just above her core, working his way back up to her mouth, turning her so that she was cradled in his arms. With her smooth back pressed to his chest, his cock rested along the cleft of her lovely bottom.

He kissed her nape, teeth grazing the sensitive flesh below the delicate shell of her ear. Their fingers were intertwined as his hand moved over her breasts.

Her gasps made him pulse.

Hands still linked, and ignoring the fabric draped from their wrists, she guided his hand down to the apex of her thighs, sliding each of their middle fingers into her hot channel.

She was ready. So fucking ready for him.

Tilting her hips, her arse rubbed against his cock, making it buck.

As she hooked her ankle over his calf, he aligned himself, their fingers moving away to make room for him.

He slid into her.

This time he gave her an inch with each slow flick of his fingertip on her nub until he was fully buried within her.

She turned her head so that she looked at him over the curve of her shoulder, lids heavy with need. "Ian." She said, her fingers gripping his harder.

He took his time, no matter how much his body craved a quick release. It screamed at him to pump and slam.

He resisted.

Savor.

His mouth claimed hers again.

With each slow swipe of his tongue against hers, he slid out to the tip and in to the hilt.

Her soft gasps and moans became sharper, breathier, until he knew she was almost there.

One last thrust of his tongue and his cock and she was coming so hard, her grip on him was a painful bittersweet haze, forcing him to surge even deeper into her, their palms cradling their joined sexes, holding on to the moment.

When thought returned, he lifted his forehead from her shoulder and looked at her. Her face was turned to his, her eyes large and luminous in the moonlight.

He could see the unshed tears. The words remained unspoken between them.

But he knew.

He knew she still loved him.

THIRTEEN

Raya was lost in her thoughts, staring in the general direction of the brunch dishes on the table. Across from Ian again; she was almost growing used to the cuffs that still linked their wrists.

The familiarity was lulling.

Her body had responded to that familiarity, pulling her heart along with it. Her brain had to get things in order. Regardless of the fact that Ian was right here with her and he'd apologized for the past, she still had work to do.

She had to find out what happened to Dominique. That's what *all* of this was about.

And she was finally on the cusp.

Get to Jean-Guy LeVoleur via Chuck. LeVoleur was the head of one of the transportation sectors. If she could get close to him, get his trust, she could gain access to his business information. That's what the *Organization* needed. She also needed to find clues that would lead her to her brother. She just *knew* it was all connected. Every step taken to find him had led her in this direction.

Her heart twisted. She should never have left him alone. He was far too gentle.

She grimaced. There was a time she'd been gentle too. Soft. Impressionable. She glanced at Ian. He stared at her with that unique intensity that touched her heart and made her belly flutter.

The distinct sound of an engine pulled everyone's attention from brunch and from each other.

Ana downed the last of her coffee and went out to meet Agent Perenga.

Raya looked across the table at Ian. He was still studying her closely.

"Agent Carson Perenga." She said.

Ian's brow rose.

"He's a good friend?"

"We go back many years."

"Long before you and I met? I've never heard you mention him before."

Ian shrugged and pushed his empty dish aside. "He's been busy working for the Global Paranormal Security Agency, saving paranormals from other paranormals. And humans from paranormals."

"Not your thing."

He shook his head.

"Until now."

He sipped his coffee. His eyes lingered on her face before he spoke. "I believed in fate, back in the days when we were happy, you and I. Then I lost that belief when we fell apart. Lately, the quiet life hasn't been enough. Not for a long time."

His words made her heart drop. She turned her mug between her palms. Sunlight streaming in from the kitchen window glinted off the cuffs that still linked their wrists.

Agent Perenga still had the key.

When he unlocked them, would she still slip away? Her eyes slid from the cuffs to Ian's face. His remained on her face, his expression guarded.

"And now?"

"Fate? I dinnae know." He cleared his throat.

Raya's heart skipped a beat at the slip of his natural brogue. For a moment, as she stared at him, the emotion in his eyes was raw. He blinked, then sipped his coffee like they were discussing travel plans.

She couldn't explain it either.

It was uncanny, that the one time he stepped outside his usual anti-people attitude to help his friend, they were sent crashing into one another again after all these years. What did it mean—if anything?

"He's trustworthy?"

"Carson? Yeah. All about doing what's right."

"What about his superiors?"

"Jack Maeda is good folk. I've known him a long time too. And he reports to Joey Kane."

"I've heard of her." She nodded. "And who does she report to?"

Ian shrugged. "How should I know? What does it matter?"

"Exactly. You don't know. And it does matter. A lot."

"They're all working toward protecting everyone. Humans as well as paranormals."

"And somewhere in that chain, someone may be exploiting the system."

"You think the GPSA is compromised?"

"I didn't say that...but I don't know for sure. Could be somewhere above GPSA's umbrella."

She twisted her mug between her palms again, tracing the rim with her thumb.

Options. Risks.

She glanced back up at Ian's handsome face.

Complications.

Several days of stubble coated his jaw and cheeks. The deep-seated memory of the sensation of that stubble grazing over her body, so many years ago...and along her throat just a few hours ago, sprang to the forefront of her thoughts, sending a shiver rippling through her.

She huffed and shoved it away.

Distractions.

She had to focus on her job. On finding Dominique.

FINALLY.

She was getting somewhere. The Ashray's defenses were finally lowered long enough that Analiese could get a reading on her.

She'd made it pretty frikking hard. She was so damned guarded.

Now, Ana could at least pick through the images and impressions enough to create a very rough picture from the fractured pieces.

The second Ian and the Ashray had walked through the cabin door the day before, she could feel the sexual energy fill the small space. Sensual satisfaction. It rolled over and through her like a tidal wave, triggering her own desires, best quickly locked away again.

Focus.

This job was important to Raya Burns because she believed it was somehow connected to something else...her brother's disappearance? She couldn't detect any other underlying motive.

It was the clearest and strongest impression she'd been able to pick up since she'd started trying to read the woman. Ana was exhausted from trying to be 'on' all this time to glean the slightest subconscious information.

There was also not a whiff of a doubt that the woman still had very deep-rooted feelings for Ian and she was incredibly conflicted by this. It was also clear that the longer she was with him, the weaker her guard became.

Until Carson drove up.

The sound of his closing car door had been a trigger switch and the Ashray's walls slammed back in place.

Ana went to meet Carson outside.

She doesn't trust us.

Well, we'll just have to find a way to get her to.

Carson closed the last few steps. "Good morning."

Ana nodded. "Coffee? We still have some in the pot."

"Any luck with our new friend?"

"Some." She relayed the little she'd been able to glean from Raya.

Carson nodded, thoughtful. "I've been talking to Maeda and Kane."

"This is serious."

"Yes. It's big."

Ana raised a brow. "The feeling I'm getting from you is disturbing."

"Don't do that. And yes, it is disturbing." He blew out a breath. She could see he was as tired as the rest of them were.

"Sorry. I've been *on* for so long now, I'm picking up everything. Has Lirikai reported in?"

He nodded. "She's good."

"That's a relief."

"We need to get her to work with us." He said with a nod toward the cabin.

A grunt escaped Ana. "We're going to have to find a damned good angle. But I think we may be able to. I'm getting a clearer picture of what's under all that steeliness." Ana sighed, turning to regard the saggy cabin. They both stared at the hovel-like dwelling. No one would ever guess just how deceiving the outside was compared to what lay within. Once you get past that outer layer, there was so much going on inside.

Ana's ability sort of worked that way. She had to see past the exterior and get a sense of what was really inside for the true story. What and how things were compartmentalized, how strong those divisions were, how deep the foundations went.

"Come and grab what's left of the coffee and Ian's scones." Ana said, heading back toward the door.

Carson nodded and followed her. "I'm always up for one of Ian's scones."

As she held the door for him to enter, she had the sense that he was holding back something. Something important. Her gut tightened, hoping that whatever it was, it wasn't going to throw their progress sideways.

"Time to take you back down the mountain." Carson said to Raya.

Analiese noted that the stiffness of her posture and mask-like expression returned.

One step forward, two steps back. Ana swallowed a sigh and poured the last of the coffee into a mug for Carson, then went to get her small bag. They left the remainder of the supplies they'd brought up to the cabin.

Downing the coffee, Carson locked up the cabin and everyone filed into the car. No one really said much. Ana sat up front with Carson, still trying to glean energy from Raya and sometimes from Ian.

She could feel their emotions. She could sense their desire for each other, which was almost overwhelming. And the deep, deep longing.

It was so strong. And yet, to look at them, they were a pair of strangers occupying the back seat of the car.

She continued to concentrate on their emotions as Carson drove.

IAN SLID HIS FINGERS alongside Raya's on the seat between them. The tip of her little finger stroked his, then went still. She didn't pull away.

As soon as their car reached the main road, Ana called Lirikai for directions to where they would meet.

Once at the meet point, Carson pinned a wary eye on Raya as he unlocked the cuffs binding her to Ian. "Ian, I want you to go talk to Lirikai. Raya will stay with us.

Ana moved into their line of view with a hand on her taser, her eyes glued to Raya's face.

Ian nodded and headed for Lirikai's car with a glance in Raya's direction. She wasn't looking at him. She'd kept her gaze averted from him since Carson arrived to collect them from the cabin.

"Meduse is still somewhere in this lake." Lirikai said to Ian as he got into the car. "I followed his scent along the banks for a long time before he started crossing back and forth."

"Was he looking for something?" Carson asked.

She shrugged. "Maybe food or clothes? His scent is heavy with desperation."

"There are campsites everywhere on both sides of the lake, he should have been able to steal something by now."

"He probably has, to have gotten this far." She turned in her seat to look at Ian full on. "I don't like this guy. He hasn't hurt anyone yet, but when people get desperate, they give up or get violent."

Ian nodded. "The sooner we catch him the better, obviously."

"Yes. We need him to get to his boss. As your Ashray is doing. This man is the small jellyfish." Her lips quirked. "We want the bigger jellyfish."

"You want me to help Raya get to him?"

"It's risky. We could just follow them. Carson prefers to have her cooperation."

He nodded. "Well, you're going to have to find something she really wants. She wants to know what happened to her brother. Can you get that?"

"We're working on it, but it isn't easy. Disappearance cases are hard to solve for a reason. We want you to find out everything you can from her."

"Right."

When he signed up for the job, he was helping Carson find a runaway prisoner, not interacting with the lost love of his life, who'd completely changed from the woman he'd known, only to dive headlong into a crime syndicate case.

I don't know her anymore. He had to keep reminding himself.

Did he ever?

He thought he did at one time. He was clearly wrong.

He'd had an idea of who she was—a soft, delicate, beautiful woman that had been treated very badly. A woman that just wanted to live life in peace. Like him. And he'd thought he'd be the man to shelter and protect her from the world, in the sanctuary of his lakes, far, far from the insanity of humanity.

He hadn't taken it seriously when she'd said she wanted to know what happened when her brother disappeared. He really hadn't. He'd thought her mother was pushing on her to use her ability to find out, and she was doing it out of a sense of family loyalty and guilt.

Maybe she was. Ian didn't know. Whatever it was, it was enough to drive her in a direction he certainly never would have thought she, of all people, would go.

A mercenary working in the underworld.

It was an incredible leap.

She clearly was not the woman he'd thought she was.

And yet the familiarity of their bond tugged at him. It pulled at his flesh. It triggered memories of their time together. Another lifetime together. Another world, one he had believed long dead.

Their bodies certainly still responded to one another. Thought and emotion were far more complicated than the simplicity of a familiar touch.

Could there be a new world? A new lifetime for them with new memories to be made? He thought of the previous night. Their bodies knew each other, as did their magic.

Did he still want her? Physically, yes—always.

He said he'd help her find her brother. And he would do what he could, but that was different from trying to breathe life into something that she wasn't interested in rekindling.

FOURTEEN

"WE WANT YOU TO work with us."

Raya stared at Agent Perenga's face. "Of course you do."

His lips compressed.

They were standing outside the car. She could have made a run for it, might even have made it. Move in, take down Ortega before she could draw her Taser, and then round on Perenga.

She'd have to be damned fast. She held back.

She wanted to know where this was going before she did.

The Agent had clearly wanted her cooperation from the time they'd found her at the hospital until now.

That old glimmer of hope for help. The one she'd given up on after law enforcement had repeatedly turned her away during her search for Dominique.

"What are you offering?"

"I told you, we want the same thing you do."

She shrugged. "What are you offering?" she repeated, crossing her arms.

"Support."

She quirked a brow.

Her attention was drawn to the other car that Lirikai and Ian were emerging from.

"And my *record*?"

He drew in a deep breath. "My bosses have agreed to ignore it, *if* you work for us."

"I told you, I'm already working for-"

"Yes, I know, a hidden group. Deeper than the GPSA. I've been caught up. And my superiors are reaching out to them to confirm your claims. Until then..." He shrugged.

Raya felt the color drain from her face. If they knew she'd been caught by GPSA and there was a leak somewhere, this could affect everything she had worked for. She needed to be seen as capable and unbending.

"If anyone finds out I've been caught, the whole operation will be compromised."

"No one will. Maeda and Kane are discrete."

She needed an impeccable image to continue to move along the underground channels that she'd spent years gaining access to.

The heat from Ian's body rolled toward her as he stepped into the space beside her

"Once you find Chuck and help him get this valuable thing his boss wants, you're going to be delivering it?"

She nodded.

"We want to bring him in."

"I need him." She snapped.

"To get information about what happened to your brother." Carson acknowledged.

She glared at him, then nodded.

"We'll provide support when you go in to complete the job."

"Raid his place."

"We can find it if you help us tap and track." Ortega said.

"What makes you think this would work?"

"You have a reputation of impeccable success. He knows you deliver. That's why he hired you. There's no reason to suspect you wouldn't."

"As long as he doesn't know I've lost Chuck. He is the key." Her teeth ground together at the thought of her failure.

"Well, lucky for you, Lirikai has been tracking him all this time. Ian knows the lake better than anyone, so he'll get you to Chuck. We'll all be keeping an eye on you."

Raya wasn't expecting the sense of relief that overwhelmed her. Tears stung her eyes. She turned her face away from the others. Looking at the visible expanse of Lake Champlain, she blinked and ham-fisted her emotions into a state of control.

She took a deep breath. The lake was beautiful. Ian's lake. She didn't want to think about the time they'd spent here together, which didn't seem like long enough—even then. He had a cabin of his own nestled on a rise overlooking an inlet near the deepest part of the lake. It couldn't be far from here.

Could she trust them?

Her brain screamed to ditch them as soon as possible, get the job done, get the information needed from the mob boss and get the hell out and on her way.

Could she get the information? She had planned for much more time spent working for the man, gaining access to his compound, infiltrating his systems. More spying and sneaking. For how long?

If—*if*—GPSA were really going to help, it could be an easy way out. A quicker way to get to the information she craved most. The fate of her brother. To know if he was alive or dead. If he was alive, then she had to find him. If he was dead, then she needed to find a way to bring closure and peace to her soul after accepting her failure. Her failure to protect him.

She glanced at the agents, all staring at her. Waiting. Then she looked at Ian. She couldn't read his expression. There was tension in his full lips. She recognized the signs of his inner conflict.

He said he'd help her find her brother.

It was a long shot.

Turning her attention back to Agent Perenga, she drew a breath. "Anything you find in that compound, I want access to it. Even if I do find information about my brother, my work doesn't end there. I'm committed to doing what I can to break this trafficking ring. They've taken so many people, and have no intention of stopping any time soon. I know too much to walk away. Seen too much."

Ian frowned.

Perenga reached out a hand. "Deal. Welcome to the GPSA."

She shook his hand, then Lirikai's. Ortega's gaze slid from her to Ian then back again. She too, extended her hand.

Raya hesitated before taking it.

Fortune teller.

At this point, she no longer had anything left to hide. She shook Ortega's delicate hand.

At the contact, Ortega's hand clenched on hers, then her eyes rolled back in her head and she tipped backwards.

Perenga caught her. "Analiese?" His voice was harsh with concern.

"Put her in the car." Lirikai said, opening the door.

Perenga slid Ortega's slight frame onto the leather seat, easing her head against the headrest. "She'll be alright. It's happened before. We just have to wait for her to come around." He said, straightening. "You two better get going. Lirikai will catch you up."

CHUCK MEDUSE WAS SERIOUSLY rethinking his brilliant plan to sting and ditch the Ashray bitch.

He hated being told what to do—by anyone.

He'd had to do something.

She was taking him to his uncle, after retrieving something from his place.

She didn't know what he had to retrieve. That was good.

That also meant that he needed to get there as soon as possible.

Uncle Jean-Guy knew.

Fear gripped his gut. Chuck was his nephew. He didn't believe *he* was in any danger. If he were anyone else, there'd be a puddle of piss soaking his feet, but he was family.

What the Ashray didn't know, was that the 'something' was actually a 'someone.'

Someone Chuck was desperate to protect from his uncle.

Maybe he'd been too hasty in ditching the Ashray. Maybe he should have followed her plan, used her resources to get back.

An outdoorsy guy, Chuck was not.

And just maybe, he might have been able to talk her into helping him instead of doing the job his uncle had hired her for.

He scratched that thought. She had a reputation of getting the job done. His uncle wouldn't have hired her otherwise.

Fuck. He stared at the shoreline, watching vacationers enjoy the water.

He needed to get out of the water. The fresh river water was wrong for his shifted self. He needed salt water to survive long periods off land.

He had no clothes or other supplies. He'd slept naked in some bushes shivering all damned night, with no one around from whom he could easily steal what he needed.

The Ashray had made it exceedingly clear just how much he needed to keep his face hidden. Even out here, people had access to the news and could recognize the escaped convict.

He moved on, heading north through the water.

Why this way? Why didn't his uncle just leave a boat for them somewhere or send a driver for them? He could have had men pick them up anywhere outside the prison.

What was the deal?

Something was going on with him.

Was he trying to break him down? Make him desperate? It was fucking working.

He obviously had a strong enough reason to go through the effort of hiring the Ashray to break him out of prison.

At first, Chuck had thought it was because he was family. Maybe his uncle had a soft spot for him. More likely a favor to his mother. Then the Ashray had mentioned his secret place in Montreal and picking something up from there.

No. It was self-preservation. Uncle Jean-Guy wanted to ensure his position was safe. And the person Chuck had hidden at his place was a threat.

Chuck's heart hammered in his chest. He could take some comfort in knowing that his uncle obviously had not yet found what he was looking for. Chuck had to get back as soon as possible, and find another safe place to stay. The question was, why now? After all these years, why now? How did he find out Chuck had deceived him?

He had to think. And that was hard to do when you were exhausted, cold and hungry.

He eyed the boats docked nearby.

It would be easy to steal one.

It was also the fastest way to give away his position if he were seen, too—as the Ashray had also mentioned.

Steal a boat and get there faster. Steal a boat and get caught.

He continued upstream. He would decide when it was dark. Hopefully, he'd be able to come across some supplies. He was getting so damned hungry it was hard to think straight.

FIFTEEN

RAYA STARED, UNSEEING, AT the passing landscape.

Ian directed Lirikai as she drove to a local marina and they secured a boat rental. She told them where she'd last seen Chuck's floating iridescent bladder. It was early enough in the day that lake traffic was minimal.

Lirikai handed Raya's backpack and knife to Ian.

"Ana will be okay?" Ian asked her.

She shrugged. "Carson said she would. I haven't seen her pass out like that before, but I don't know her as well as he does." She dropped the rental key into his palm. "Good luck," she said to him, then turned to Raya. Lirikai handed her a small device which she recognized as a tracker. "If you fuck us over, I'll come for you myself."

Raya bristled at the threat. "You really think you-"

"Come on, we're wasting time." Ian pulled her arm toward the docks.

"I don't take threats lightly, Ian."

"Barra'kidai don't threaten, they promise."

"I don't give a shit what she is."

"Get in the boat."

She cast a baleful look in Lirikai's direction. She stood watching them from beside the car.

"I don't like her."

"You don't have to. Let's go. You drive, and as soon as we get far enough out, I'll go in and start searching for him. If he follows the currents, he could be among the islands." He dropped Raya's belongings into the boat.

Raya started the engine and they were soon headed for the center of the lake. They passed several fishermen and an anchored sailboat.

She cut the engine. Ian immediately began stripping down.

She couldn't help herself.

As his shirt came up over his head, exposing his well-defined abs, her mouth watered. Her tongue had explored every one of those ridges and valleys. His jeans sagged on his hips, the belt slung far below his bellybutton. Her fingers itched to slip into the loose gap.

"Ray?" His low voice snapped her back. "You okay?"

She blinked and huffed. "Yeah, fine. Thinking."

Focus, Raya. We have work to do.

"I have a cache of supplies stashed toward the end of the lake. Chuck's going to need something to wear once we find him."

He assessed her as he slipped his shoes and socks off. "Okay, meet me back around here."

She should look away. Watch for boaters or folks along the banks. Her eyes slid back to Ian.

Focus.

She licked her lips. Her fingers twitched, drawn to his warm flesh again.

When they'd been together, neither could go long without touching the other.

His jeans hit the bottom of the boat and her panties were suddenly damp.

Raya groaned, low in her throat.

She'd buried the memories of how beautiful his body was. Tall, muscled, with graceful proportions. His tanned skin was coated with a light dusting of fine hair that caught the sunlight.

She turned away from him, gripping the steering wheel of the boat to stop herself from reaching for him.

The boat rocked gently, followed by a light splash.

She drew a deep breath, knowing he was in the water.

Releasing the steering wheel, she moved to the edge of the boat. He glanced up at her before letting himself sink below the surface of the water. She watched his pale, wavering form sink into the darkness of the lake.

At the same time the water rippled unnaturally, her flesh tingled.

He was shifting below the surface.

She'd forgotten that her magic recognized his too. A funny little thing. When they were close to one another and one shifted the other could feel it.

She felt as though she'd been punched in the heart.

She'd never felt that connected to anyone else. Her connection with her brother was different. So much...thinner.

A form, lighter in color compared to the lakebed, rose up under the boat. She recognized Ian's head and long neck gliding under the boat. Soon the mass of his powerful body slid past as well and narrowed again to the pointed tip of his tail.

She cranked the starter of the boat and gunned the engine, avoiding the area above where she could make out his shape, and headed for the cache.

He'd be scenting the water, given how small and hard to see Chuck was. He'd be next to impossible to find and she wasn't sure if Ian's sonar hearing could pick up a delicate mass like Chuck's jellyfish form.

The pack was exactly where she'd left it, hidden among thick brush not far from the mouth of the Richelieu River. It didn't appear as though it had been disturbed since she'd placed it there weeks ago.

This job had been so long in the planning. It was nearly done.

Drawing a deep breath, she retrieved the bag and got back into the boat, tossing it next to the one she already had.

Could she trust that the GPSA agents would come through and back her up?

They wanted the same thing she did.

Would they arrest her when the time came? Round her up with the others? If that happened, would the *Organization* bail her out, or cut their ties to maintain their anonymity?

At this point she wasn't sure she cared so long as she got the information she needed about her brother.

She was tired, trying to keep from drowning in the murk of the world she'd submerged herself into.

As driven as she was to complete this mission she'd tasked herself with, she longed for the simple life she'd shared with Ian. Maybe, when she had her answers....

Raya was getting closer. So close. She could feel it.

The wind scrubbed her face and whipped through her hair as she sped the boat back to where she'd left Ian.

From the moment they'd been given the news of Dominique's likely death by ocean suicide, there'd been an underlying current of heaviness in her gut. She hadn't been surprised that he'd been reported missing. He'd disappeared from the face of the earth. Swallowed by the sea, they'd told her. In her heart, she hadn't believed it. The vibrating tension of an invisible cord that bound her to her little brother remained. It was like a precise, maintained music note that hadn't cut or faded completely. She was going to find out the truth, one way or another.

As she looked out over the expanse of the lake visible to her, she considered what Ian had said to her all those years ago.

Denial.

He'd said that she was holding onto childhood memories of someone who was no longer the child she knew. Maybe, but neither was she the child she once was. At her core—and his too—there was still that part of both of them that was. It didn't matter that it was buried deep below the layers of life experiences.

This is what her gut was telling her, or perhaps her wishful thinking.

Maybe she was in denial. This wasn't the first time she'd questioned herself on the matter. And it likely wouldn't be the last.

Her instinct told her to keep searching. So, she did.

She blinked away the sudden onslaught of tears and breathed deeply of the silky air flowing over the lake's surface.

Seeing Ian again—being close to him after all this time—had set her off balance.

She needed to get a grip.

Acknowledge the truth to herself.

She still felt something for him.

She still wanted him.

They were both changed.

Raya huffed. He truly had changed. Something she never thought would happen. He'd been so set in his ways.

His promise of help was like an outstretched hand drawing her up from the depths that she'd sunk to, inviting her to the surface of the living world again.

She still had a job to do, and it was still more important than anything else. That had not changed.

In the boat, she waited, letting the peace of the lake and its surrounding mountains ease her heart.

This was one of Ian's homes.

She'd always understood why he loved it so much. It was another world, and it was so very easy to be lost in it without time.

When her brother had gone missing, she could no longer afford the luxury of existing in the fog of a time and place set apart from the rest of the world.

She was sorry that Ian hadn't been able to understand that.

She straightened, peering over the edge of the boat. His form became visible as he approached. Energy rippled over her as he shifted into his human form. She turned away as he climbed in. Once his jeans were back on, he directed her to where he'd found Chuck.

"Among a cluster of large rocks on the east bank."

She nodded and started the engine for the last time.

"I'M NOT LETTING YOU go alone, Ray," Ian said again.

They'd guided the boat into a small tree-lined inlet and cut the engine, letting it drift closer to the gentle sandy rise.

"You don't have a choice."

Ian stepped closer to her, forcing her to look up into his face.

Ignoring her scowl, he leaned closer, allowing the subtleties of her scent to infuse him.

She wasn't cowed by his looming presence. Instead, she locked her eyes on his.

His mouth quirked at the defiant glint in her beautiful eyes.

"This is how it works, Ian. I do the job. Alone. I'm expected to deliver. Alone. Therefore, I will complete my job as expected. Alone. You tagging along like a little bodyguard would fuck everything up. So stand down." Her voice hardened on the last word.

He blinked. Another reminder of how much she'd changed.

Pride flared in his chest. He'd always known she was strong.

She wasn't hiding it anymore.

His gaze swept her determined face.

"You are so goddamned beautiful." His voice was husky and thick.

Her eyes widened, clearly not expecting those particular words. Then they narrowed again. "I go alone, Ian."

She didn't move when his right hand reached for her. She didn't stop his fingers from sliding up the side of her throat to her jaw or step away when he moved closer still.

He didn't miss the subtle shiver his touch incited.

"I have missed you, these years past." He whispered from his heart.

He eased closer, drawing out the descent of his mouth toward hers, giving her the chance to pull away at any point.

There was a soft fizzle as his lips made contact with hers.

By the next breath, she was pressed to him, her arms around his torso. Her mouth devoured his. She opened to his tongue, welcoming. The familiarity of her sweet taste overwhelmed him. He'd already gone hard at the first touch of her lips, now he swelled painfully for her.

His head reeled with memories of their past lovemaking and the desire to bury himself in her warm body again and again was overwhelming.

He never could get enough of her. Never.

They were supposed to be resuming a chase.

But she was asking him to let her go.

He wanted to remind her of what they'd once had; something beautiful, pure and primal.

He wanted to entice her back to him.

Ian gripped Raya's arse, rocking her hips against his, leaving no doubts about how much he wanted her.

She was just as hot for him. He could feel it through the layers of their jeans.

Her mouth wasn't enough. He wanted to taste more of her sweetness.

His fingers twisted the button of her jeans and eased the zipper down, granting him access to the lace of her panties. A second later, his fingers slid into her core.

Goddess, so was so hot and wet.

She groaned into his mouth.

His fingers slid in and out of her tight channel, his thumb grazing her nub.

"Ian I-" Her breath hitched and she came, gripping and flooding his fingers with her warm honey. Her hands gripped the muscles of his back.

He was so engorged it was painful, but he'd made her come. Fast and hard. Again.

Bittersweet.

He licked her juices from his fingertips.

Her face turned rosy, and he chuckled.

She panted, staring up into his face. The mask was gone and he could read every nuance.

There she was. The Ray he knew, her face alight like the sunshine that warmed them both.

He kissed her. Deep and heartfelt, sinking everything he was into that kiss. He pulled away as slowly as he'd approached her.

He pulled the zipper of her jeans back up and fastened the button. "We're not finished yet." He whispered.

The sound of another boat engine in the distance brought them back to the here and now.

"I'll see you in Montreal." He promised.

With a lingering glance, she got out of the boat, taking her knife and both backpacks, and was soon swallowed by the trees encroaching on the shore of the lake.

SIXTEEN

RAYA STARED AT CHUCK'S tired face.

She focused on that as her body still hummed from Ian's attentions. The moment had been so damned impulsive. She couldn't help letting him touch her. She'd craved it.

On the open lake, everything between them had flooded back; the ease of who they were, together.

It was dangerous accepting him. She'd thought her heart was cold after so many years. It was just dormant, waiting.

She hadn't expected to crest so damned fast; it was embarrassing. It was just another reminder of how much she missed him in her life, and deeply desired him.

And he'd promised more.

She understood what that meant and she couldn't afford to let it distract her from what she needed to do now.

Chuck was fully dressed and they were five minutes into what he thought were negotiations after he'd inhaled a protein bar from the cache pack.

She let him talk.

They really needed to get moving, but this could be fruitful.

As he talked and talked, she schooled her features and posture while her excitement soared.

He was going to make this easy. About fucking time.

Chuck was wrapping up.

Love of his life. Protect them from his uncle.

"Why?"

He shuffled, looking down at his feet.

"If you want me to consider throwing a job, you have to give me the reason—and a substantial amount of money. No bullshit."

He looked up at her with a spark of hope.

In all the time she'd eavesdropped on him in jail, not once had he mentioned someone important to him in that apartment. He had bragged it was his little love nest. The place where the parties happened.

She assumed he'd been bullshitting his prison peers. Was he bullshitting her now?

When she agreed to break him out of prison, she'd assumed LeVoleur wanted her to retrieve an object—money, art, jewels, or even information. A person was much more complicated and expensive. She ground her teeth.

Chuck was exhausted and desperate. He would tell her anything he might think she would bend to.

He drew in a deep breath, eyes trained on her face.

"He was one of the intended merchandises. I pulled him off the ship."

She was not expecting that. He? Now all the prison bullshit about the women and the parties made sense.

"Nicki can place my uncle on that ship. Name some of the other victims, identify his men and some investors. I have absolutely nothing else my uncle could possibly want."

"And this victim is your lover now?" She couldn't hide the incredulous tone from her voice.

He straightened. "We connected."

She swallowed the words on the tip of her tongue, took a breath and counted.

Her mind reeled. This person could be the key she needed to find her brother. Was there a chance he was abducted from the same beach her brother had disappeared from, if the trafficking ring worked the same locations down the coast?

It was a thin chance. Very thin.

"Start walking. Tell me more about this lover of yours and the night you met—where and when, and I'll think about it."

Relief flooded his expression. She didn't miss the tears that sprang to his eyes before he dropped them. "We met at the beach..."

Don't go soft, Raya.

She guided him north.

He kept talking.

He'd been talking all throughout the first leg of their journey, before he'd stung her, but the chatter had been so very different.

A couple of days alone and vulnerable in the wilderness seemed to have done what a couple of months in a state penitentiary hadn't.

She had to think this through.

The mob boss had sent her to break his nephew out of prison, trek him up to Montreal to retrieve something of value from his secret apartment and take both to him at a meeting place to be determined later.

What was she missing?

Why hadn't she been told that this thing of value was a person? Did he know? Was it a guess?

Why hadn't he, as Chuck had whined, provided transportation? She'd assumed it was in order to maintain as low a profile as possible, so that Chuck wouldn't be tracked to the border and to Montreal. Less chance of being seen. Was it punishment for Chuck's betrayal?

She had to focus on her job. Make him disappear from the prison like a ghost. Get Chuck to the meeting place unseen.

She'd deal with LeVoleur's attempt to swindle her later.

She glanced back at Chuck. If he wasn't bullshitting her about this secret rescued lover, which she was deeply skeptical of, maybe—just maybe—Chuck was more of a key to her problems than she had initially realized.

It was going to be damned hard trying to view him from a different perspective.

Or maybe none of his confessions made any difference at all.

ANALIESE CRACKED HER EYES open to the two looming faces of Carson and Lirikai.

Her instincts jerked her body back into the leather of the seat. No matter that she knew them both, having two powerful beasts that close to her was unnerving. Even if they wore human faces, her 'fight-flight-freeze' instinct knew better.

"You gave me a fright, Ana." Carson said, his expression full of concern.

"So did you." She mumbled.

He frowned and eased away from her, giving her space. "I don't like when you do that."

"Pass out? Me either. It's not like I do it on purpose."

He reached for a water bottle that was in the central drink holder and passed it to Ana.

"What happened to you?" Lirikai asked, clearly impatient to get to the point.

"Vision?" Carson asked.

Analiese nodded as she uncapped the bottle and sipped. "Powerful."

"And?" Lirikai prompted.

Ana looked down at the bottle in her hands as she sifted through the images and overwhelming emotions that had crashed over her when she'd touched Raya Burns' hand.

She recalled the clear look of defiance on Burns' face right before blackness had dropped Ana like a stone.

Burns knew what Ana was about to do and she hadn't backed away from it.

She'd opened the gate and given her full access.

Why?

A cry for help? A way of conveying information without breaking her code?

"Well?" Lirikai said.

"I need time to process."

"Talk it out." Carson reached into his pocket to extract his phone and opened the recorder app.

Talk it out, like she did with Maeda. She'd only started talking out the process with Maeda in the last few months, as he helped her strengthen and hone her ability. She wanted to be more useful than just a desk agent coordinating the west coast office. When Carson had called her for this case, she'd jumped at the chance. And so far, all her hard work with Maeda was paying off.

She closed her eyes and started talking, letting Raya's images flow off her tongue.

They were jumbled. Memories, emotions, dreams.

"This job is important to her. Personally and professionally."

Images of Ian overwhelmed everything. It was confusing. Anger. Hurt. Love, such a deep love, it took Ana's breath away for a moment.

"We were right to keep Ian close to her."

Ana gasped. "She's been aboard some of those ships, Carson." She drew in a shaky breath. "We were lucky to get to those survivors before they got to the ship," she said, referring to the case they had worked which had led them to investigating Chuck's prison break.

"What are they being taken for?"

Ana shook her head. "I don't know. She doesn't know, either. They're not well cared for, at least not on board the ships, they aren't."

A young man's face loomed in her mind, pushing her heart up into her throat.

Raya's driving force. Whatever she was doing, this was driving her.

Her brother? Shocking red hair with freckles, and gray eyes the same as Raya's.

The image wavered between the young healthy memory to a later, older one; gaunt, pale, and so very unwell.

Ana pushed those memories aside and tried to find something related to the mob boss they were preparing to target.

Raya's feelings about the man were crystal clear. She abhorred him. She maintained the same controlled barrier in his presence as she'd tried to maintain when she'd been trapped with Ana and Ian in the cabin.

Ian had been a fissure in that wall. A fissure that had expanded enough to allow Ana access to glimpses of Raya's inner world.

And the true sense of desperation that was driving her to complete this job he'd hired her to do flawlessly.

She needed to get close to him.

She needed information from him.

She really is working for a higher purpose. Ashray the Mercenary was just a legend.

Raya was in for the long haul, going deeper into the underworld. The crime boss was a step to yet another knot in the network.

"Carson, I don't know if we can raid the compound. She's supposed to be going in long term."

"I know."

There was a hitch in Carson's voice that Ana almost missed. Her gaze shot to his face.

A maw opened in Ana's gut. She drew a deep breath, trying to separate Raya's memories and emotions from her own.

Whatever they did, it would affect Raya's ability to infiltrate the mob boss' network. Raya was working her way deeper and deeper for crucial intelligence. It was incredibly dangerous.

It really wasn't only about her personal quest to find her brother. She was fully committed to do what she had to.

"She could flip on us."

"I know that too. We're aware she'll do what she needs to do."

"Ian isn't going to like this."

"No. No, he won't," Carson said, suddenly looking very tired.

"Having them together gave me a chance to get in. This could lead to further complications later on."

"I'll deal with Ian when I have to."

"This mission, it's big, isn't it?" Lirikai asked, her voice solemn. "We will support her?"

"We just have to wait and see what happens. Be prepared for anything. I'm going to call Maeda to see if he can reach out to Teddy. We may need some help on this." Carson said, then grinned at Analiese. "Missing your cushy office?"

She smiled back, "I'm sure Freddy is keeping things warm for my return."

"Poor kid."

SEVENTEEN

"CARSON, I STILL DON'T like this," Ian said as he stepped up onto the dock, where he met with his old friend and his new colleagues.

"She has the tracker?"

Ian nodded. "Lirikai gave it to her. I have a feeling she isn't going to make this easy."

"They never do." Carson muttered. "It doesn't matter. We know she's going to Montreal to meet with Chuck's boss, so we'll be ready."

"It's still difficult to wrap my mind around how much she's changed."

"Everyone changes. That's life. Sometimes, to the outside world it's a sudden turnabout when the reality is that it was really a slow burn change. Looks to me like you're the slow burn type."

"Me?"

"Yeah. You've changed. Microscopically, I'll admit, but there are still changes."

Ian snorted.

"Well, you're here, aren't you? I figured it was an incredible shot in the dark that you'd haul your ass out of your lake to come and help us investigate this case. And look at you! You're practically a GPSA agent. *And* I didn't miss the fact you're letting go of your grudge against Maeda. You're almost a whole new man!"

"This guy thinks he's funny. And you've gotta put up with him every day?" Ian asked Analiese as he slid into the backseat next to her.

She was already belted in, hand gripping the support handle above the window. "You get used to it." She winked. She quickly adjusted her grip as Lirikai started the car. "I don't mind doing some of the driving, Lirikai. You must be tired." She prompted, hopeful.

"Don't you worry Ana, I'm just fine. I actually really enjoy driving."

"Damn." Ana muttered, sliding lower in her seat, then changed her mind, and sat upright again with a sigh.

The car swerved from its stopped position and they were on the highway in seconds, headed north.

Ian could hear Ana's teeth grinding.

"Keep an eye out for State patrol." Lirikai said to Carson.

"I am, don't worry there. Your speeding tickets are going to put us in the poor house, honey."

"What's a poor house?"

"Never mind."

Ian's mind drifted as they began chatting softly between themselves about Odson and something that was happening with a tribe of dragons off the east coast near Bermuda.

Glancing toward the window, he unhooked his hand from his own support bar, not having realized he'd reached for it.

He tried to relax and let his thoughts return to Raya.

The instant he'd touched her, it was like no time had passed between them.

What now?

They couldn't go back to the way things were before. He didn't know if there could even be a 'they' at all. Was it an option? Did he want it to be? Would she?

Raya had changed too much, but maybe not in the ways that really mattered.

He always knew she was strong. She had to be. That was never in question.

Now that he realized how selfish he'd been, he had a lot of work to do to make it up to her.

He sighed. The landscape whipped past.

The car's speed eased as they passed a parked state trooper. As soon as they crested a hill, Lirikai increased the speed again.

As much as he was wary of Lirikai's driving, he was fully aware that were he the one driving, he'd probably be flooring it all the way to Montreal.

Raya's new life—and Carson's job as a GPSA agent—was at an intersection that had Ian right in the middle. The reality of the situation was seeping into his bones, making them itch.

Ian had walked away from the human world so very long ago, when they'd run his family out of their territory with violence.

His family had maintained a long-standing friendship with the local Pictish tribe. His tattoos were a reminder of that alliance. Some visiting missionary had come along and labeled Ian's family 'Evil Monsters', causing the tribe to turn on them.

They'd left their lake, no longer wanted by their neighbors, and had elected not to slaughter the ignorant fools. Instead, they'd found other lakes to inhabit and learned to stay hidden. His mother had taken it hard. She'd loved her little humans.

Homesick, he had gone back from time to time, once the memory of his family had faded and locals no longer feared the monsters in the loch. Now, they capitalized on them.

For centuries, Ian held on to that experience from his youth. Right up until it affected his relationship with Raya. He'd been blind to the tension it caused in her. No that wasn't right. He wasn't blind. He'd willfully ignored it. Added to it.

And here she was. On her own, deep in the underbelly of not just the filthy human underworld, but that of the paranormal underworld too, it seemed.

Exploiters will exploit the vulnerable.

He glanced up at Carson and Lirikai, their voices a constant murmur of conversation.

Carson was created to protect the humans. Lirikai, as a Bar-ra'kidai, sought vengeance on the exploitive. And Ana?

For them, it didn't seem to be an Us versus Them. Paranormal versus human.

Ian had to shed his old way of thinking. He hadn't even noticed when it stopped serving him.

In the past, he'd wanted Raya to live a sheltered life with him. Away from the pressures of her human mother's influence and the outside world.

He still wanted to protect her; he was driven to. He loved her too much to just step back and let her walk away again. Alone.

If she was going to walk in through the maw of the underground, he'd be there to split that gullet open if she needed an out.

They were going into a place where he might not be able to shift, to battle with his teeth and powerful size.

The last time he'd battled in his human form it was all swords and shields and fists and feet. And sometimes foreheads. That was fifteen centuries ago. He doubted Carson had a sword or a solid mace in his trunk.

He blew out a breath, catching sight of the disappearing mountain range out of the opposite window and noticed Ana's gaze locked on his face.

"What?"

"As GPSA agents, we carry guns when we need to." She smiled. "Your emotions are flooding the car."

"Think Carson will have a spare?"

"I do. I can share, if you know how to shoot?"

He chuckled. "Point the open end at the target and squeeze?"

"Carson, we should find a place to teach Ian how to shoot."

"Oooh, target practice!" Lirikai said, glancing at Ian in the rearview mirror.

"He isn't licensed."

"I won't tell if you won't." Ana said.

Carson turned and looked at Ana. "Seriously? Did *you* just say that?"

"Total self-preservation. I don't want to get shot in the ass if he happens to steal one from somewhere."

"Thanks for the vote of confidence, guys."

RAYA STOOD ON THE road between two tiny parked sedans, staring at the front of the townhouses, with a plastic bag from a near-by *Depanneur* clutched in her hands. The city was all shades of dawn-gray.

This was not the posh condo Chuck had talked up to his prison mates for the last few months. No wonder they hadn't figured out where he lived. It was low key and in the heart of the city.

This was an historic two-story building that she wished she had the keys to. Reaching into the bag, she withdrew the other half of the chocolate bar and stuffed it in her mouth as Chuck poked around the flowerpots. She'd reluctantly gone into the corner store after his fifth request for a jug of chocolate milk for his love. A little thing he always did for him when he came home.

"Whatever, just stay out of sight. And if you try to run, I will find you. You know this." She grumbled, then realized she was ravenous and bought an armload of junk food which she reluctantly shared with Chuck on the last block and half to his place. She'd kept her eye on him through the window while she was in the shop, in case he decided to make a run for it; she would have.

Chuck hadn't. Maybe his desperation had him gambling all-in on her soft heart or mercenary greed.

"Ha!"

A moment later, he stepped off the matchbook sized front garden with a key held aloft like a prize. Quickly scraping the mud from his shoes on the side of a neighboring stone wall, he bounced up the short flight of stairs.

The cross into Canada had been slow. She'd managed to guide Chuck safely along, much like she had during the prison break. She called LeVoleur when they reached tiny village of Carignan, Quebec, before abandoning the Richelieu River to go overland toward the St. Lawrence River.

Although LeVoleur was delighted they were both still alive, he reproached her tardiness in contacting him with her report.

He confirmed that he wanted her to retrieve an individual, vital to the health of his business. Now that she'd proved herself capable this far, they would discuss the retrieval fees on her arrival.

Fucker.

Raya swallowed the chocolate, casting a quick glance up and down the dimly lit street, and followed Chuck past the beautifully carved front door.

Chuck closed the door with a soft click as Raya squeezed into the narrow foyer alongside him. Even in the near-lightless space, she could see the glimmer in his eyes as he held his finger up to his lips and slipped out of his shoes. She did likewise and followed him toward the back of the house to the kitchen.

This really was not what she was expecting.

After weeks and weeks of planning, spying, waiting and walking—so much walking—this moment felt surreal. The misleadingly shabby cabin in the mountains had been weird. Standing in the homey kitchen of the man she broke out of prison for working with his crime boss uncle, running a human trafficking ring, felt more so.

She stared at the faded sticky notes on the fridge. They were all love notes, written in two distinct styles. She decided the cramped, messy notes were Chuck's. The elegant script of the other reminded her of the notes Dom used to leave in her room when he needed to her to swap out the laundry, or do some other favor for him.

She swallowed hard and drew a breath. Goddess, she missed him.

This was not the Chuck she'd shadowed in the prison or secretly observed at meetings with LeVoleur before making contact. This was someone else, living a completely different life.

Was she in the right place, or was he trying to screw her over too?

She stood in the middle of the kitchen, staring.

He opened the fridge, shoved the chocolate milk onto the top shelf, and grunted. "We're out of bread. Do you want anything?"

She blinked.

Who was this man?

"Washroom?"

He pointed his thumb to a door off the end of the kitchen.

She walked into the tiny powder room that held a cloud of apple cinnamon infused air.

Sitting on a toilet after several days of using bushes felt like a luxury, no matter how tiny the powder room was. As she washed her hands, she glanced around for the source of the fragrance and found a small plug-in. The scent reminded her of her childhood. Her father would often bake apple pie, heavy on the cinnamon. She inhaled the spicy sweet air, letting the tremor of longing ripple through her.

Raya stared at her reflection in the small ornate mirror above the sink. There were dark smudges under her eyes, and her shoulders drooped. This job had taken unexpected turns at every possible junction. The constant need to pivot was incredibly draining and she was still processing it all, mindful that the exhaustion could affect her judgement.

She dried her hands, then stepped back out into the kitchen.

"Chuck?" A man's uncertain voice pulled their attention.

Raya's gaze shot to the darkened entry. The dull morning light teasing the patio doors barely illuminated the figure standing in the doorway, clutching a hockey stick and staring at Chuck by the open fridge door.

Her heart stopped. "Dom?"

His head whipped in her direction and the stick clattered to the floor. "Oh my god, Ray? What the hell are you doing here? Either of you?" A second later the fridge door slammed shut and Chuck had his arms wrapped around Dominique.

She watched her brother kiss Chuck with intense longing and urgency.

She swallowed hard and turned her gaze to the view out on the back garden.

Her heart had finally kick-started again.

What. The. Fuck.

Chuck's lover was her brother.

Dom *is* alive.

Is this really happening? Or is this some kind of weird dream?

Maybe she was actually still in the forest, wandering in a haze of hallucinations.

Wave after wave of emotion threatened to bring her to her knees. Closing her eyes to stop the tears, she pressed a palm to the door frame as her world tilted. She sucked in a deep breath, feeding oxygen to her brain to process what was happening. She needed to get control over her shock. First Ian, now Dom.

She'd finally found him. Alive. And in those fleeting seconds, she could clearly see he was healthy. Everything she'd done since he'd gone missing was for this moment. To see his face for herself.

Everything had become so convoluted.

Think.

She was supposed to deliver Chuck's lover to the head of a powerful crime ring.

It was too much. And she didn't have time to break. Not now.

"Ray?" Dom's voice was soft at her side. Uncertain. Like when they were small and he stood in the door to her bedroom clutching a stuffed animal in the wee hours of the night after a bad dream. "I don't know why you're here, but I'm glad to see you. It's been a long time."

She turned to look up at her little brother. Relief warred with anger. "It has."

The uncertainty in his expression twisted her heart. The second her arms lifted a fraction, his were wrapped around her waist, his face buried in her shoulder. "I've missed you, Ray."

Her arms held his shoulders in a death grip, she was sure they'd both be bruised, they held each other so hard.

"So, this is weird." Chuck's voice snapped the tenor of the moment.

Raya opened her eyes, blinking away the tears. Beyond the glass of the patio door, the sun was finally cresting. A blazing ball of orange, suspended between the jagged horizon of the city-scape and the thick gray clouds blanketing the sky.

She stayed in the moment a little longer, allowing the sun to fill her vision and her heart, to welcome her brother's embrace.

He finally pulled away. The light of the rising sun illuminated his shock of copper hair and eyes, turning them from gray to smoky quartz. Like her own. Like their father's.

"We have a lot to talk about." She said.

"No shit." Chuck said. "Tea?"

Seriously. Who the fuck *was* this guy? "Yes, thanks."

EIGHTEEN

S<small>TANDING AROUND THE ISLAND</small> counter with steam rising from teacups, Raya stared at her brother. The sun made its way above the layer of cloud. In the dull light from outside, she stared at her brother, really looking at him now.

There was no doubt he was healthy.

The last time she'd seen him—months before he disappeared—he'd been gaunt from addiction. He no longer looked skeletal, or had the deep bruising under his eyes. His skin was smooth and his hair had lost that stringy droop. It stood out in thick red waves.

"I see the resemblance, now that the two of you are side by side, but I'd have never guessed otherwise," Chuck said, looking from one to the other.

Dominique turned to Raya. "Okay, I saw on the news that Chuck had escaped prison-"

"So you're fully aware he's a convict?" Raya cut in.

"-but how do *you* figure into this? And yes." He said, chin rising a notch. "I am."

"You know what he's been convicted of?"

He nodded. "He doesn't do that anymore."

She stared in disbelief, eyes darting between the two. Chuck glared at her, mouth compressed.

This was wrecked.

She rolled her shoulders, took a generous swallow of tea, which scalded her tongue and throat, and decided to go right at it. She cleared her throat. "I'm here to collect and deliver you to Chuck's uncle. A crime boss. You know that too, right?"

Dom blanched. "I see." His gaze slid to Chuck.

"Nicki, she broke me out of prison to do this job. She's not going to finish it. Are you?" he challenged her. "You're going to take the money I offered and walk away."

"I'm so confused. Raya doesn't break anyone out of prison or have dealings with crime lords. And she never, ever does things for money. She's a peaceful, gentle soul."

Chuck erupted. His laughter bounced off the countertop and kitchen cupboards. "Gentle. That's funny, Nicki. How come you never told me you had a sister? Or even better, a sister that is a shifter? Or that she's *the* fucking Ashray? That might have been helpful information, love."

"It never came up. How do you know about shifters? And what do you mean 'the' Ashray"

"Are you aware Chuck is a shifter too?"

Dom turned big eyes on Chuck "What? No. What are you?"

"He's a jellyfish." Raya couldn't suppress the smirk.

Chuck puffed up. "I'm a Man-O-War jellyfish."

"He's actually kind of pretty." She sipped her tea, glancing at her brother's open-mouthed expression.

"I don't know either of you," Dom said, staring from one to the other.

"Likewise," Raya said putting her cup down.

"What's that supposed to mean? I'm not the one with a title beginning with 'The', breaking people out of prison. Or revealing that I'm a shifter." This last accusation landed on Chuck.

"You-" Raya stopped at the elevated sharpness of her own voice, took a breath and resumed at a controlled volume. "The last time I saw you, Dominique, you were doped out and on the verge of death. Do you remember that? Do you remember the argument we had when I tried to help you? I bet you don't." She couldn't hold the raw emotion back any longer. "You went missing. They told us you were dead. Mom blamed me. She guilted me into finding you because I failed to protect you in the first place. Just like she blamed me for everything since Dad died."

"I-" Dominique's voice broke.

"No, Dom. You dropped off the face of the earth, you don't get to be righteous. I have spent all this time—*all* this time—doing everything I had to, in order to find you. Alive or dead."

"And now you're going to hand him over to my uncle." Chuck cut in.

"Right now, I'm fucking tempted, Chuck."

"So you're not?"

"I didn't say that."

Dominique and Chuck went so still her own breathing sounded like a roaring furnace in her ears. She took a controlled sip of her tea and placed it very deliberately back on the marble countertop.

IAN SLID HIS FOOT forward as far as he could under the car's dashboard. They had been parked along the narrow street for a while, now. "How long are we going to sit here?" he asked Carson, as a black car with tinted windows rolled past theirs.. They'd changed seating positions, with Carson behind the wheel and Ian upfront. Lirikai and Ana were curled up against their respective windows.

He yawned and reached for his third cup of coffee.

They'd spent the dark hours monitoring the waterways bordering the southern half of Montreal, looking for Raya and Chuck. Even though Carson had given her a tracker, he didn't trust she'd use it, and he wanted to know where she was.

She still hadn't activated it.

Just before dawn, they were spotted crossing the river to the island city, going straight inland to a quiet little street lined with century-old townhouses. He glanced at the ornate door she'd gone into for the hundredth time.

The black car slid past them again and pulled into the line of parked cars at the far end of the block. "Company?"

"Looks like." Carson grunted into his paper coffee cup. "This may get interesting."

"She can't shift after sunrise."

"I've seen her file. She'll be fine."

Ian had also experienced Raya's capabilities. The instinct to protect his mate lunged to the surface. The hand resting on his thigh began to tap.

"Patience."

The doors of the new car swung open and four figures rose up from it in the dim morning light.

His beast growled.

His hand hovered over his thigh as his breath lodged in his throat. "They shouldn't have been able to fit in that little car."

"It's Montreal, everyone drives small cars. They're used to it." Carson nodded to the cars parked in front of them.

Ian's right hand drifted toward the handle of his door.

"We don't want to complicate things."

"*We* don't?" He eyed the four large complications headed straight for the door Raya had disappeared through.

"Watch and wait."

"Dog's bollocks."

"Yup, this sucks." Carson took another sip.

NINETEEN

RAYA JUST NEEDED THIRTY seconds to think things through.

LeVoleur was expecting her to deliver Chuck and his lover. Obviously, something to do with witnessing operations. What else could it be? Why now, after all these years?

She'd let Chuck believe he could buy her off in order to get his cooperation. He didn't know the real reason behind the work she was doing. All of it was to find her brother Dominique.

Correction. It *had* been all about finding Dominique. It had become much more complicated since she'd been enlisted by the *Organization* to help break the ring. There were still so many others out there being sold into human trafficking. That hadn't stopped—and wouldn't.

She couldn't walk away now, as tempting as it was.

Ian's image rolled through her brain so hard it brought with it the memory of his scent and touch. She sucked in a breath.

We're not finished yet.

Could she walk away from Chuck and Dom? Let them live in peace while she found another way to do the job she'd taken on?

Chuck was a convicted human trafficker—and Dominique knew about it!

She groaned.

So fucked up.

Her gaze lingered on her brother's face, drinking in the sight of him. For so very long she'd waited for this moment.

"How did the two of you meet?" she asked him.

"I told you. Nicki and I met at the beach." Chuck said.

"So you did." She turned to her brother. "I want to know how you ended up with a guy that deals in human merchandise, Dom."

Color flooded Dom's face. "I uhm...I was living with some friends in the party district, close to the beach where the tourists kept things lively. Every week there were new faces to hang out and have a good time with." His eyes dropped to his hands.

Her gut tightened and her heart twisted. She knew what that meant. She reached out and slid her hand over his.

"This particular week, Chuck walked into the club with a bunch of guys. I approached him. And we just..." He shrugged. "We just hit it off. We met up each night. He was different from the other guys I'd met."

She thought of Ian. She'd never met anyone else like him. They just clicked when they met. Still did.

This was different. Ian didn't work for a crime boss stealing people from vacation havens. Chuck was nothing like Ian.

Dominique drank some of his tea. "His buddies insisted on having a big end of vacation bash one Saturday night before going back to wherever they were from. The partying was more intense than the previous nights, of course."

"Of course," she said, voice flat.

"I went into the bathroom to take another hit from the stash one of the guys had. Then I went looking for Chuck. I ran into his buddies instead. I'm not sure what happened. It was a bad hit. I woke up in a cold, dark room in nothing but my underwear. I wasn't alone; there were others. We were in a steel box."

Raya knew exactly what he was talking about. She'd been on two ships with humans imprisoned in steel cargo containers. She squeezed his hand. "How did you get out?"

Dominique lifted his gaze to his lover. "Chuck. He got me out the night the boat was supposed to leave. I've never been so scared in my life."

"I couldn't just leave him there." Chuck said, his voice catching in his throat.

"What about all the others?"

He looked away, toward the back garden and shrugged. When he turned back to her, he wore a deep scowl. "It's not like I ever wanted to be part of that. When you work for my uncle, you do what you're told."

"You could have worked for someone else? You know, got a real job." She snapped.

"It was quick and easy money to begin with. Little things here and there. The more respect you earn, the more important the job. The more he trusts you. And that trust is powerful. And before you know it, you're doing all kinds of stuff you never would have imagined."

"So, you worked for your uncle stealing people for profit, so you could feel good about pleasing him."

"He did. That all stopped after we got together."

"Did it? Then how was Chuck caught on a ship full of kidnap victims on the west coast, which landed him in prison, Dom?"

"He didn't have a choice. He pushed for Chuck to do the job, even after he told him he wasn't doing it anymore."

"Right. Nothing to do with money, maybe? This is a nice place."

"Who the fuck are you to judge me? You're a fucking mercenary, for Christ's sake. You get paid to hunt people down." He turned to Dominique. "I offered to pay her off."

Dom snatched his hand away from Raya's.

She straightened. "It isn't nearly what your uncle is paying me."

Chuck's mouth dropped open, his eyes sliding to Dom. "You wouldn't. You wouldn't turn him over. Not now."

"What did you call me, Chuck? *The* Ashray? I'm a mercenary with a reputation that your uncle paid for. A reputation of getting things done. I'm hired for a job. I do it. Simple. I've come a long, long way from the person you used to know, little brother."

Should she tell them that she wasn't really a mercenary? That it was all a front to find him? To get the information she needed to break the network? Could she find another way to get that information, without handing him over to the crime lord?

She doubted LeVoleur would let her anywhere near him if she failed this job. Infiltration would be so much easier. Easier access to his inner circle, gleaning bits of information that might not be kept on a computer, phone or some other physical database. Some things just weren't committed to paper or digital files.

So far, all of her jobs were confined to the crime world. Criminal on criminal work. This was the first time she was having to deal with an innocent.

She studied Dominique's face then let her gaze slide to Chuck.

Could Chuck have that information? Being so close to the boss, he must know things and people. She'd spied him at the few key meetings she'd been able to infiltrate. Did LeVoleur trust Chuck to keep his mouth shut? Were she a crime boss, she wouldn't trust Chuck. Or was he as much at risk as Dom was, now that LeVoleur knew Chuck had stolen his merchandise from him and set up house?

Ray didn't trust him.

"Chuck, why does your uncle want Dom? And why now?"

"He was on the ship, he saw faces."

"Who did you see, Dom?"

"I don't know who they were. While we were being held, a large group of businessmen came in. It looked like some sort of tour. They all had different accents and some spoke in other languages."

"They must have been very important, Chuck. Who were they?" she said turning her full attention back to him.

"Why?" His eyes had turned assessing. He was trying to guess the motive behind her line of questioning.

The identity of those men might be the key to breaking the network. The crime boss wanted Dom because he was the one victim that had escaped, *and* had seen the faces of important men. Those men likely needed to keep their identities safe from public knowledge of their clandestine activities.

She looked from Chuck to Dom. They were on borrowed time.

Raya had to somehow get Dom to the GPSA, then to her contacts with the *Organization.*

"Your uncle is expecting my call."

Chuck glared at her with murder in his eyes from across the countertop.

He slid sideways around the counter and lunged at her.

Raya sidestepped, locked her hand on his throat and used his unbalanced momentum to pin him to the tiled floor.

He groaned from the impact.

"Second strike, Chuck. Third, and you're out. Understand?"

She glanced up at her wide-eyed brother, then let go of Chuck's throat.

Chuck gasped for air and scrambled to his feet.

"Do you understand?"

He nodded, backing toward Dominique.

She reached into her pocket for the burner phone from the last backpack she'd planted. Her fingers grazed the tracker Lirikai had given her from Carson.

"I'm going to step out into the back garden to think."

The tension in Chuck's expression eased. Hope.

She went to the front door to retrieve her discarded boots. On her way back, she brushed her hand along her brother's shoulders which made him start. "I just need a few minutes. Don't get any more brilliant ideas, Chuck." She slipped into her boots and slid the patio door open. She stepped out, inhaling the fresh air.

With a final glance at her brother through the open door, she strode across the small deck and down to the flagstones, hands in her pockets.

What the fuck do I do?

She couldn't deliver Dominique to the crime lord. He'd kill him.

She needed to get him to a safe place. He'd been safe here for a long time. Could she just leave him here while she made other arrangements?

How long could she hold off on calling LeVoleur before he became suspicious? She'd contacted him at the last cache point, so he was expecting to hear from her by midday. The flowers lining the path pulled her attention.

She crouched down to look at the beautiful healthy petals while she laced her boots. Fragile. Vibrant. Healthy. Like her brother finally was.

She inhaled deeply of the fragrance that infused the early morning air.

Priceless.

She smiled as a bee landed on lily and got to work. The work this little guy did would ripple out, helping other plants to thrive.

She stood and turned to head back inside. She could hear Chuck and Dom's low voices cut by the ringing of the doorbell.

"Are you expecting company?" she asked Dominique.

"No. No one ever comes here, especially at this hour, and it's Sunday, so no deliveries, either." They both looked alarmed.

"Get your shoes." She said.

"Good idea," a voice said as a figure moved to block the open patio door. "Nice place, Chuck."

"Fuck." Chuck gasped.

"Francois," Raya said, recognizing the man as one of LeVoleur's enforcers. "Boss is impatient, is he?" How the hell had she not heard him come over the fence?

Francois shrugged. "He wanted us to make sure you had a ride. Thought you could use it after all that walking, or swimming, or whatever it is that you did."

"Thoughtful," Raya said, as she considered options. His bulk filled the doorway. She could take him down. Beyond him a second figure lingered in the back yard.

"He is, isn't he?" Francois grinned. "Chuck, be polite and open your front door for our friends."

Chuck, she knew, was exhausted after their long journey from the prison. How far could they run, if they needed, once she took down the two guys in the back yard? How long before the goons at the front door either forced it open or came around the back as well?

These guys wouldn't kill Chuck or Dominique. The boss wanted to see them first. She still had time to figure something out. She reached into her pocket as she reached for the last of her tea.

"Don't want be wasteful." She said as she slipped the tracker into the pocket of her brother's lounge pants while he stared at the neckless man in his kitchen. "Get your shoes; time to go," she said, as though rounding up a couple of wayward children.

"Chuck?" Dom's voice was strained.

"You're a heartless bitch." Chuck growled at Raya. "You're condemning your own brother."

"Brother, huh?" Francois smirked as he loomed next to Chuck, eying Raya and Dominique with curiosity.

Raya looked at her brother. Her heart twisted as her mask fell back into place. "The brother I knew died years ago," she said, loud enough for Francois to hear.

Dominique jerked as though she'd backhanded him, but he didn't say a word.

She resisted the urge to say anything more. To ease the sting of her words.

She couldn't risk it.

If—*if*—she could get him out of this alive, he would understand.

For now, she had to buy enough time to figure out just how to do that.

TWENTY

IAN'S BODY WAS STRUNG. He couldn't relax with those guys lurking on the front step to the house Raya was trapped in. The other two guys had disappeared up the street, most likely looking for a way around the back of the solid row of townhouses.

Minutes later the front door opened, and the two thugs stepped aside to make room for Raya to emerge from between them.

"Here we go," Carson muttered, as the sound of another vehicle approaching pulled Ian's focus from Raya.

A black SUV pulled alongside their car and rolled to a stop across from the open townhouse door.

Raya descended the stairs and two more figures emerged from the house. He recognized the first one as being the inmate from the prison. Then the second one came into view, followed by the two guys that had gone around the block.

"Holy fuck." Ian said, hand reaching for the door handle again as his gaze whipped back to Raya. "That's Ray's brother."

"Don't." Carson's voice stopped him. "Ana-"

"Yes, she turned the tracker on. It's active."

"This should be fun." Lirikai said, the glee evident in her voice.

"There are probably two more guys in that SUV." Carson murmured. "Ana-"

"Yes, Carson, I'm already texting Jack."

Ian turned to look at Analiese as she bent over her phone, her thumbs flying. She glanced up at him with a grin. "Long work relationship."

"I should be driving." Lirikai said, her hand on Carson's shoulder.

"No time for that," Ana said, before Carson could answer her.

As soon as everyone was piled into the two black vehicles, Carson started the car. He waited for them to turn the corner, then pulled away from the curb in pursuit.

"AH, THERE YOU ARE!" Jean-Guy LeVoleur beamed as Raya stepped off the elevator. "I knew I made a good decision when I hired you. Phenomenal."

She tipped her head forward, "Mr. LeVoleur."

He guided them toward the penthouse suite with an adjoining boardroom. "I much prefer my home and offices in Quebec City, but this is serviceable. Would you like to sit?" he swept a hand toward a nearby leather couch.

"Thank you." She said, settling herself into a laid-back posture, creating the illusion of complete ease. Internally, there was a boulder settling in her chest. "It was very considerate of you to have the cars sent for us."

LeVoleur nodded, pleased by her acknowledgment. "After your last message, I had men watching for your approach. I thought you might be tired after your journey, and I was eager to be reunited with my wayward nephew, Charles," he said, finally turning to look at Chuck.

"Uncle." His voice was tight, his body rigid. Dominique stood next to him.

LeVoleur moved to stand before Dom. He studied him for a long moment, then turned away with a grunt and went back to Chuck. "You've put me in a difficult position, Charles. A dangerous position on one hand, and an exceedingly uncomfortable position on the other. I hate being at odds with your mother; she knows how to make my life miserable."

"What will you do with him?" Chuck asked, his attention glued to his uncle's face.

LeVoleur's thick brows rose. "You care for him that much, do you?"

"I do."

The boulder in Raya's chest grew a little bigger as she looked from Chuck to her brother, side by side, straight and tall, heads up and eyes forward.

He, too, had grown stronger in the last years. He'd always been physically strong, until the addiction took over. That was clearly in his distant past.

If he was afraid, he didn't show it.

She was proud of him in that moment.

As much as she really disliked Chuck, she grudgingly admitted to herself that, despite everything else, he'd been good for Dominique. They'd made a life together. A home. Until Chuck had gotten himself caught and incarcerated. Dom had stayed and waited for him.

She thought of Ian.

Would they have had such a life, had things been different?

They had for a time.

Until this man's operations upended her world. Not just hers. Many, many others, too.

Her meeting with LeVoleur would end shortly, and she would be expected to depart, now that her job had been completed.

What would become of Chuck and Dom, if she walked away now? He'd made his decisions with eyes wide open.

Her mother's voice slid up the back of her spine.

Protect your little brother. He's your responsibility. He's just a helpless human.

Ian's face loomed in her mind. He didn't have room in his life for humans. And he hated the unbearable sense of responsibility her mother had dumped on her shoulders all her life. It was the main reason he'd been unable to get along with her.

She hoped the tracker she placed in Dom's pocket was functional, and Ian's GPSA friends were on their game.

LeVoleur paced the room. Everyone else stood waiting, silent. Two guards stood by the main door, another two lingered by the edges of the room. To stop their escape? Or something more?

"You betrayed my trust, Charles," LeVoleur finally said. "You know how I feel about trust. It's very important to me. You also know what happens to those that betray me."

Chuck nodded. His Adam's apple worked up and down his throat several times.

"I'll deal with that situation later. Right now, I want to discuss business," he said, dismissing Chuck as he turned toward Raya.

She stood and followed him into the board room. Two of his guards slipped through the door and closed it behind them before taking up posts at either side of the room.

"Marie-Ange, call the others. Confirm the meeting time." LeVoleur spoke to a woman who'd been in the board room. At his command, she nodded and left the room.

Moving further into the room, Raya went to the window with a magnificent view of the city. The river was a glimmering ribbon behind the skyscrapers and heritage buildings.

She waited for LeVoleur to join her before she spoke softly so that his men would not hear. "Human retrieval fees are much higher than object retrieval."

"I'm aware."

She turned to look at him.

"You needn't scowl at me, Mademoiselle. I have no intention of fleecing you. I merely wanted to see how you handled the situation."

The entire break out and trek through the mountains had been a test.

"To what end?" she demanded.

"To ensure you lived up to the whispers. You are quite capable." He nodded.

"I know I am." She held his gaze, unflinching, waiting for him to elaborate.

"I'm proposing another job."

"You haven't paid me for the first one yet."

The money he owed her was substantial. She could use it to help Dominique find a new life.

He smiled. "That will be taken care of within the hour. I have something very specific I want you to do. Something *only* you can do. A special job. I want you to see the site."

She was aware of the door opening and the gentle clink of glasses that drew her attention to the back of the room. She jerked her head back to the view out the window.

Her heart stopped and the blood coursing through her body flooded her veins. She missed part of what LeVoleur had said.

TWENTY-ONE

WITH A FINAL RUNDOWN on the plan, the group split up and entered the towering hotel through different entrances.

Ian followed Ana to the elevators while Carson moved toward the long line at the check in counter. Lirikai disappeared down another hall entirely.

"From the tracker, I can't tell exactly what floor she's on, just the general area of the building. I'd bet my grandmother's poker luck they'll be on the top floor; mob bosses tend to enjoy luxury. The hotel schematics map out the penthouse suites." She punched the button for the fourteenth floor. "Quick stop to the housekeeping supply closet first."

Ian ignored the distinct feeling of the walls closing in during the trip up and focused on controlling his breathing.

As they stepped off the elevator, Ana fired off a text on her phone. "Lirikai is on her way."

She found a spare custodian jacket and housekeeping smock. With a quick glance down the hall, she wheeled the cart out of the closet and headed for the elevator. The doors opened and Lirikai handed them both gold key cards. The doors closed and Ana pushed the button for the second elevator car to take them up.

"I hope there isn't already a chambermaid working on their floor." The doors opened and Ana swiped her card, then jabbed the button for the penthouse.

Ana grabbed an ice bucket from her cart and shoved it into Ian's hands then pushed the linen trolley to the left and knocked on the first door. "Housekeeping."

Ian went right. Two of the guards that escorted Raya out of the townhouse that morning stood at the end of the hall just outside the double doors. He made a quick turn down the short vending and ice machine hall. There was another door marked employees. Using the card Lirikai had given him, he peeked inside and found another cart with glasses and water pitchers. There was a laminated map of the floor taped to the wall which told him exactly what each room was. He quickly filled the bucket and pitchers with ice and water and backed out of the tiny room.

The guards moved to block his progress as he reached the double doors.

"Refreshments for the board room, sirs."

"Don't disturb them." He opened the door to allow him through.

Ian nodded as he silently pushed the cart into the room and moved toward the corner where he set down the clean glasses and sweating pitcher. As he gathered the used glasses to the lower shelf of the cart, he glanced around.

His heart jumped when his eyes met Raya's. They widened in surprise before she dropped her gaze and turned away.

She was listening to a stout man in a tailored suit talk, as he faced the panorama of the city outside the window. Ian guessed that was LeVoleur. Two more guards stood to either side of the room. One stared ahead, the other monitored Ian's movements.

Ian nodded respectfully to the guard, then proceeded to poor fresh glasses of ice water to be placed on the sideboard.

"I would be very interested in a tour of the site before I decide to accept the contract." Raya said to the man. "I'll let you know in a couple of days after I've had a chance to rest and consider."

"I'm afraid a couple of days from now would be too late. I have arranged a room for you just down the hall. Go and rest and refresh yourself. I'll take you for that tour later this evening," he said, turning away from the window to face Raya.

She appeared to consider this for a moment, then nodded. "I wouldn't want to impede your schedule. Tonight is acceptable."

He nodded. "Francois will walk you out."

Ian was about to push the cart through the open door after Raya and Francois when the mob boss' voice stopped him. "You."

He froze midway through the door. Had he given himself away?

He turned to see the man with an arm raised and finger extended toward him. "Water."

Ian rested the open door against the cart so he could walk over to the sideboard to retrieve a fresh glass of ice water. Approaching the mob boss he held it out to him.

The man stared hard at him.

Dread settled in his gut. Had he blown it already? Had he put Raya at risk? He couldn't be sure.

His heart pounded, more thoughts racing through his head as the man stared at him another moment before reaching for the glass.

"You move very quietly for such a large man. You do your job well." His eyes swept the neat rows of glasses at the back of the room. "I'm always looking for men like you to join my team. Little jobs. Easy jobs. Someone who takes pride in his job." He pulled a business card from a pocket inside his jacket and held it out for Ian. "If you'd like a job that pays more call that number."

"Thank you, sir."

Ian took the card and made his exit. By the time he reached the hall, Raya and Francois were nowhere in sight. Ana's cart was parked at the far end of the hall. He acknowledged the two guards who still stood outside the board room doors, and continued pushing the cart back to the short hall where the employee room was, and left it as he found it. Glancing around at some of the open boxes of supplies, he grabbed an arm load of linens and toiletries and headed toward the parked supply cart, fully aware of the guards' attention on his movements.

As he was placing the supplies on the cart, Ana emerged from a room. Seeing what he was doing she smiled and said in a voice that carried "Awe, you are so kind to do that for me."

"Anything for a pretty lady such as yourself." He said, hand to heart. "Will you join me at break time?"

She glanced at her watch, "I'm nearly finished. Would you mind taking these to that room right there?" She asked, grabbing some of the soaps and towels. "And I'll join you shortly?"

"Of course."

With the supplies in hand he gave the door a light rap. When it opened, Raya stood in the doorway. "I'll just put these in place for you."

She stepped aside for him to enter then let the door close.

"I'm alone."

He shoved the towels and bottles on the bathroom counter just inside the door then pulled her into his arms and held tight.

She stood rigid at first then relaxed after a moment.

"Ian," her voice was soft. "Dominique. Dominique was in that house, he's what I was meant to retrieve for LeVoleur."

"I saw him."

Her mask slipped so that her lovely face was a mixture of heart-felt relief and terror. "Goddess, I can't believe I found him, here of all places! With Chuck, of all people! He's in trouble, real trouble."

"We have to get you out of here."

"I'll be fine. I know what I'm doing. The tracker is in Dom's pock-et. I don't think he noticed I slipped it in. I need you to promise me you'll protect him. No matter what."

"If things do go sideways and it comes down to you or him, you know I'll always protect-"

"Him, Ian. I need you to protect *him*."

He was about to shake his head.

"Promise me. I can't lose him again. Promise me."

It was the last thing he wanted to do. The look in her eye and the strength of her resolve twisted his heart. "I'll do what I can."

She searched his face, wanting something more. She finally nodded.

His thumb traced the edge of her plump lower lip. "I still..."

She bounced up onto the tip of her toes and locked her lips to his. His arms instantly enveloped her, crushing her to him. The taste of her sweet mouth reminded him how much he loved her. How much he wanted her to be in his arms for the rest of their lives.

She had an important job to do, and he was going to do everything he could to ensure she succeeded.

She suckled his lip, then released it with a sigh and pressed her forehead to his jaw.

He could feel the words between them, though she maintained her silence.

"I have to go."

She nodded and stepped back.

It took everything he had in him not to pull her back to him again.

His eyes held hers a moment longer before he turned away and joined Ana in the hall by the elevator.

"All set?" she asked, voice light and bright as she pushed her cart toward the opening doors of the elevator.

"All set." He smiled.

RAYA CLOSED HER EYES when the door clicked shut after Ian.

She had a job to do.

As much as she appeared confident on the outside, her stomach was a knot of worry.

Another job offer.

It was what she wanted. To get closer. Go deeper. Get to the heart of the network.

Yet Dom's life was on the line.

If he were anyone else, how would she approach the situation?

She didn't like collateral damage. Still, she needed that distance. And she wasn't sure how she could achieve that.

She walked to the window that looked out over the city of Montreal. The reality of Dom's presence in this situation had started to settle into her while they were still at his house. Now that she stood here alone, it overwhelmed her in waves.

Ian was here. Another potential point of danger. During their time together, the years had been peaceful and quiet. He'd told her tales of battles in the old days. She knew he could fight if needed, though in a world of semi-automatic guns? She wasn't so sure.

Turning away from the window, she lay down on the bed and closed her eyes. She had to wait for nightfall.

The tears came.

She'd done it. She'd found Dominique and he was alive.

For now. Her mother's voice rose up from the back of her mind.

But alive. She insisted.

She gave into the blackness of exhaustion.

Her eyes popped open. The room was illuminated by the city lights, the sky differing shades of charcoal and indigo.

Dominique.

Reaching for the pull of the water she could sense running through the pipes and underground streams, far below her, deep under the surface of the city streets.

It fueled her essence.

The scent of living water filled her nose as she inhaled deeply and let her particles disperse, becoming part of the moisture in the air, and began to drift. Finding what crevices she could, she moved throughout the hotel floor. Through vents, around electrical outlets, out and in through open windows and doors, by-passing LeVoleur's men, Chuck, and Jean-Guy himself enjoying the company of some women in a scene she'd later need to scrub from her brain, until she found her brother in a room identical to the one she'd just left.

He was alone.

She materialized beside him by the window.

He jumped.

"You know it's always freaked me out when you did that. I never know where you're coming from." He turned toward her. "Did you see Chuck?"

She nodded. "He's fine. Pacing."

"Worried." He sighed, shoulders dropping. "He's been worried about this since he helped me escape."

She watched him. Gauging. Trying to come to a decision. Up until now, it seemed as though every other decision had been clear. Do or don't.

"Dom, what did you expect your future would be like, living with someone like him?"

"We were trying to bide our time until we could find a quiet way out."

"I don't know if that's possible. The work he's involved in-"

"Was. Was involved in. He was caught on the west coast because he had no choice in the matter. He never wanted to do the work."

"There is always a choice."

He straightened, staring down into her face.

He couldn't argue that. "People change."

"They do. What about the destruction left behind in their wake until they reach that lofty realization?"

"Who-the-fuck-are *you* to say that to *me*? You're a fucking mercenary. No better than *any* of them. At least Chuck was trying to get out. You're sinking your teeth as deep as you can."

She wanted to tell him.

If she did, how badly could it go if he told Chuck and Chuck tried to use it to get out of what he had coming?

"He could make amends."

Dom stared at her.

"He could work with the authorities to stop more people, like you, from being abducted and sold. To track and find the ones that have been trapped for years."

"Chuck? You want Chuck to make amends. What about you, you fucking hypocrite?" His voice was venomous.

She didn't flinch.

"Mom made it my life's responsibility to protect you, Dominique. Because I had the ability to do things you couldn't. From the time she realized you were human, she *made* me your guardian. She couldn't bear the thought of losing you after dad died."

"Dad's death wasn't your fault."

"I was there, Dom. When the accident happened; I couldn't help him."

"You were young. It wasn't your fault. I know what mom is like."

"Was."

He froze for a solid minute. "She's dead."

Raya nodded.

He let out a shuddery breath, rubbing a hand over his face.

"She gave in to her oblivion."

His eyes filled with tears.

She squared her shoulders. "Dom, they told us you drowned at that beach. By accident or suicide. They expected you were probably dead, with nothing further to be done. She demanded I search for you, but I had to know, too. I couldn't spend the rest of my life not knowing, Dom."

He looked up at her.

"That's all I've been trying to do since that day. Find you. Dead or alive. Just find you. And I have."

"Ray, I'm not your responsibility. Never was. That's why I left. I had to get away from this...drama between you and mom." The tears spilled down his cheeks.

"You *know* me, Dominique."

He faced her. Studying her now, after so long apart, his eyes searched hers.

She watched as he began to make the connections, his expression changing from anger to wonder. He blew out a breath.

He opened his mouth. Then closed it to try again. "You've always looked out for me. It's really not about the money."

She shook her head. She finally let her hand reach for him. "It never was."

He understood.

"What do I do?" he asked her.

"Trust me."

He nodded, sniffling.

"You can't tell Chuck. Not yet." She said quickly when he raised his head to look at her again. "Not *yet*."

She reached for his hand, squeezing it, then looked out the window.

"Please." Her voice pleaded with him. "I wasn't expecting to find you like this. I have to find a way to get you back into a safe place and finish the other things I have to do."

He turned to the window and pointed to a street to their right. "That's my house. I've been happy there."

"If I hadn't found you, someone else would have. LeVoleur would have made sure of it. You have to realize that that sanctuary was always temporary. Help me find you a permanent one."

He straightened his shoulders, eyes clearing. Drawing in a breath he asked, "What do I do?"

"I just need you to trust me, no matter what happens. Stay close to Chuck if you can. I can see how much he loves you and will do what he has to, to keep you safe. And do not let on that anything has changed. I was never here."

He nodded. "Ray, I'll do whatever is needed to protect him, too."

"I will get you out. But I need to go in deeper."

Something flickered in his eyes. She thought it might be pride. She couldn't be sure.

"The Ashray, huh?" he grinned.

"I had to woman-up and get shit done."

He chuckled and pulled her into his arms. "I love you, Ray. I've missed you."

"I've missed you, too." She couldn't hide the emotion in her voice as she wrapped her arms around her little brother's waist. "I have to get back to my room."

She hesitated. "Nicki, huh?"

He grinned. "That's what Chuck likes to call me and I needed a new name anyway. You can still call me Dom."

"You're sure?"

He nodded and kissed her forehead. "Be safe."

"You, too."

His eyes followed her as she dissipated and drifted away.

Rematerializing in the room assigned to her, she went into the bathroom to wash her face and collect her thoughts and emotions.

Staring at her reflection in the mirror, she reviewed the sequence of events, trying to find the underlying pattern.

Was she in over her head?

She was so close to the next step down into the network.

Another league below the surface.

LeVoleur wasn't the heart of the network, but he was close to it.

How do I get Dom to safety without blowing my cover?

Ian was here. The GPSA agents probably were too.

She wasn't alone.

Her eyes closed and she swallowed hard.

I'm not alone.

I'm not alone.

I'm. Not. Alone.

She drew in a shaky breath.

There was a knock on her door.

Time to go.

TWENTY-TWO

THEIR SUV ROLLED UP to the security gate at the Port of Montreal, where the driver showed the guard some sort of paperwork. Night was fully settled and Raya could feel the pull of the river. It whispered to her magic, full of life and power.

The water always called to her at night. Like most nights lately, she had work to do, so she ignored it.

LeVoleur had offered her a new job. This was her chance to get the information she needed, and hopefully save her brother while doing it.

She'd taken a big risk—an incredibly big risk—trusting Dom. She hadn't trusted anyone in years. And she was hinging it all on her gut trust in Ian, that he'd pull through with agent Perenga and provide help if she needed it, or stay out of her way.

Above all, she needed two things. Her brother alive and free, and key information about the network.

She didn't know what the job was that LeVoleur wanted her to do. It seemed that her apparently ruthless loyalty to her personal mercenary code made him believe he could trust her to get things done.

She'd worked so hard to build that legend and now it was paying off.

She may have destroyed parts of her soul in the process, but she made her peace with her creator on a nightly basis. If there was an afterlife, she truly didn't know what lay in store for her. So long as she was able to save her brother and do her true work, she was okay with whatever she had to face.

The driver continued on, steering them past port workers, along rows of stacked shipping containers in faded dirty colors of rust, dust-bowl gold, and silt-smudged blue. Above them, the lights of a bulk carrier lit the port, bow pointed east toward the Atlantic Ocean.

She'd wondered.

All previous known trails were coastal, remaining far outside the interior and in the safety of open international waters.

If this was what she thought it was...this was bold.

"I'm expanding my business ventures." LeVoleur leaned toward her with a grin.

Were the men Dominique had seen on that other ship, all those years ago, investors?

"What does this have to do with the job you're proposing? I'm not a sailor."

"You, my dear, are a ghost. I need a ghost to ensure the quality of my employees."

She raised a brow as she looked at him.

"You have proven your reputation. You keep your contracts no matter what. My nephew made my operations look weakened. I don't know if there are others that might feel they can do as they wish with my merchandise as well. I suppose you can say I'm feeling a little vulnerable. And with Charles being my sister's son, I'm reluctant to make a true example of him. You see the difficulty he's put me in?"

"Hmm, I do." She paused as though considering. "However, I tend not to limit myself to one long term employer. You want to hire me, full time, to spy on your employees? I'm expensive."

"Free agent. I know. I'm sure we can agree on terms favorable to both of us."

"I will have to give this offer some deep consideration. I've always enjoyed my choice of jobs. I've never come under any one employer's payroll. I don't like being tied down."

The car passed a crane and rolled to a stop not far from an access bridge to the ship.

"Shall we go for a tour?"

IAN WATCHED OUT THE windshield as Lirikai guided the rental along Notre Dame Street at a safe distance behind the mob boss' SUVs.

Analiese was monitoring the tracker and watching the map on her phone. "We're coming up to the Port of Montreal."

Lirikai pulled the car over when the SUVs turned onto a service road toward the river. They could see the fencing and security gates from their stopped position.

"There's a public park just beyond here." Analiese said, moving the map across her screen.

"Good. We can park and approach from that side. They're probably headed for that ship." Carson said. "Avoid security cameras where possible. It's easier to manage post-op clean up if we don't have to confiscate footage, especially if anyone shifts. Once that stuff gets out, it's hard to get it back under wraps."

Ian nodded. "I've spent most of my life staying hidden from humans."

Carson snorted, "You're spotted all the time."

"Only when I get bored and want to mess with the tourists. Freaks them out, and it's amusing to see them scramble."

"Lirikai, slow down and take the next right." Analiese said. "Keep right. According to the satellite view, there's a park storage lot butted up against the port property."

"With those flood lights everywhere, it's going to be hard to get around unseen. If we can't find a way through or around the fence, go along the river." Carson said.

"I'll get the waterproof bags from the trunk." Analiese said, getting out of the car once it was stopped. She handed one to each of them as they approached the back of the car to grab any other gear they may need. She reached into her duffle bag and withdrew a holstered gun, checked it over, then handed it to Ian. "Remember-"

"Aye, I know. Safety off, point at the bad guy."

Ana handed them each an earpiece.

"Spread out, stay out of sight, avoid cameras. And keep an eye out for crew on that ship. We don't know if they're armed and looking for trouble. We have to assume there may be shifters among them," Carson ordered.

"I scented shifters at the hotel property. There may be some here," Lirikai said.

"You good, old friend?" Carson cast a look of concern toward Ian.

"It's been a long time since I've gone into battle. I'm not sure about this thing." He held up the holstered gun.

Carson shrugged and inserted the earpiece Ana had given him, nodding toward Ian to do the same. "They can be a useful deterrent."

"I also miss the old days of swords and sharp teeth," Lirikai said with a grin, and darted off into the shadows.

Ian followed Carson along the fence toward the river. "Ana, do you copy?"

"Copy."

"If you can't find a way through the fence, stay with the car in case we need a quick and direct escape."

"Copy that."

They crouched in the shadow of some bushes close to the river's edge. Carson's eyes were trained on the illuminated ship. It was the only one currently docked at the port. Through the foliage, they could see the two SUVs. Raya looked small surrounded by the mob members.

The instinct to protect her rose up hard in him.

"Stop snarling." Carson snapped.

"I'm going down to the river."

"Don't engage, she needs time to do her job."

"If she's in trouble-"

"Then we all have her back, Ian."
He nodded and made his way toward the water.

TWENTY-THREE

LeVoleur led Raya up the short ramp to the ship's deck. Workmen were busy checking over their stations, with random thugs occupying spaces nearby, watching her and their boss.

They went up to the brightly lit bridge, where the pilots navigated the ship across oceans and lakes and along treacherous river routes like the St. Lawrence.

On seeing their approach, the ship's pilots backed away from the table where they were in deep discussion, and turned weary faces to LeVoleur and his guest. More thugs occupied the far corner of the space.

"Gentlemen, this is a new employee of mine, we're just giving her a tour of the place before she joins you as the new head of security."

The Captain's brows went up, looking from Raya to LeVoleur to the man standing guard in the corner.

Raya smiled at LeVoleur. "I haven't yet accepted your offer." She said, walking toward the large windows overlooking the ship's deck. From this height, she could see the guards posted across the deck and on the ground around the port surrounding any access to the ship. The bow was pointed toward the Atlantic and floodlights glittered off the water's black surface. Beyond the port was a green space, where she could see movement in the dim evening light. Squinting, she could make out two shadowed forms moving toward the riverbank.

"You will. Everyone finds it hard to refuse my offers. Isn't that right, Louis?" He laughed and patted the ship's captain on the shoulder. LeVoleur's voice drew her attention back to the conversation and to the Captain.

His lips compressed as he gave the mob boss a short nod.

"So long as we can all work harmoniously together, we can make a great profit together."

The corners of Captain Louis' mouth drew down further.

"It's not very...homey on board, is it? I tend to like my creature comforts."

"Ah, this way toward the personal quarters. I did my research before acquiring this vessel. I wanted to be sure it was suitable to our needs." He held a hand out, directing her toward the door out of the navigation room. As soon as he turned toward the door, Raya saw the captain and the pilot sag a little.

She could see why LeVoleur was eager to have her come and spy aboard the ship. At least some of the crew didn't appear to be committed.

The private quarters were as basic as she'd expected, fancied up with some expensive towels and bed linens. Her finger traced a hotel logo embroidered into the edge of the pillow case.

"Charming little space."

"Ah, see, Francois, I knew the towels would do the trick."

He pointed out key rooms and their functions as they worked their way back down to the deck level, then he led her down even further into the cavernous cargo holds. Most were filled with raw materials from the Great Lakes. There were a few containers here and there tucked away at the back, set apart from everything else.

This ship was set up much like the others she'd infiltrated. Human cargo would be in those containers.

"Tell me, what is it you think I can do here? You clearly have plenty of security."

"A man can never be too careful. Consider your role as security for my security. A fail safe." He smiled.

"I'm not interested just now. I have several jobs lined up already."

LeVoleur's smile faltered. "You're turning down my offer?"

"As I said, I have other work I'm committed to. Other contracts that deserve my attention, as much as yours did."

"You know, I was surprised to find out that my little problem turned out to be a relative of yours. I really was not expecting that." He held up a finger, shaking it. "And I bet you weren't either," he said, turning toward her.

She froze, waiting for his next words. How did he know? Had Chuck told him to save himself?

He went on. "I was surprised that you would just hand him over to me like that. Very surprised. And incredibly impressed."

Icy tension pierced the muscles of her shoulders.

"So committed. Dedicated to your reputation. Flawless. Cold." He moved closer. "Ruthless." His voice rasped and his eyes flashed as he approached her.

She said nothing, waiting.

"Still. I imagine it couldn't have been easy. Not knowing what my intentions were for your brother. So fascinating to learn this. Fascinating. I still find it hard to believe."

Her chin notched upward.

"Made it easier to find out more about *you* though. Broke through that thick veneer of mystery. Less a ghost and more a—p*erson*. The last living member of your family. The information almost humanized you. But, you're not human. Are you?"

She held his gaze when he looked at her.

"*We* are more than them." His fingertips drifted up her arm, his pupils dilating.

She suppressed the overwhelming shudder that threatened to wrack her body.

Disappointment pulled at his features at her lack of response. His hand dropped. "Would you like him back, as part of our contract? After I've questioned him, of course. I have to know what he knows. And backtrack where he's been and who he might have talked to, etcetera."

He was testing her. She had to tread carefully. If she showed interest in Dominique's safety, he would question her motivation. If she was completely disinterested, he might kill him as she expected he would anyway.

"What would I do with him? Especially if you insist on having me work here."

"He could keep you company." He shrugged. "A familiar face among strangers. Until you get to know me better. I'd certainly like to get to know you much, much better." His lascivious eyes swept her.

She was used to it. It was expected. She still didn't fucking like it when a man looked at her like she was something to satisfy his whim.

No matter that her reputation was of a hardened mercenary, it always came to this.

In the end, after a little time together, it came down to the fact that she was little more than a piece of ass. Another conquest to be added to the trophy wall, like a hillbilly lording over his man-cave shed.

The look she gave him dared him to touch her again. LeVoleur read her expression and stepped back a pace, turning away from her.

"And what would this *company* cost me, from the price you have yet to offer, so I can decide if any of it is worth my time? Working aboard the confines of a ship is of little interest to me."

"Hmmm, hard bargain. I like it. Shall we go up?" He waved his hand to ascend back up to deck level where she could see Dominique and Chuck were being held amid several armed mob thugs.

Her heart hammered in her chest. She turned to LeVoleur, frowning. "You spent an awful lot of money to hire me for the enormous effort to break your nephew out of prison and retrieve his lover for you."

"Yes."

"And, just like that, you're going to offer him to me for company aboard your ship."

"Yes."

"What would you have done with him, had he not been a relation of mine?"

"As I said. I needed to know what he knows. What he has seen. Then put him right back where he belongs. I was expected to deliver a certain amount of goods. Well, I'm sure you know how it is when you're hired to do something and come up short." His smile didn't meet his eyes.

He's going to sell him. Pick up like the last decade hadn't happened.

"Can't say that I do."

His smile faltered.

"I am curious though, why such the effort now? I mean, Dominique went missing years ago. Seems rather...late."

"Hmm, yes." LeVoleur walked up to Chuck and studied his defiant face. "Francois saw you with your lover, here." He sniffed as his gaze slid to Dominique. "A face like that, all those freckles and red hair, is very memorable. I sent you to the west coast job to get you away long enough for us to find him ourselves. My men came up empty. Then you got yourself arrested." He sighed. "At least you didn't land in a GPSA prison. Now that would have been challenging."

Impossible, more like.

"Anyway, my investors heard of your imprisonment, and knowing what you do about the business, they were concerned. So, I thought it best to round everyone up and deal with your mess, Charles."

"He doesn't know anything. He never did." Chuck said.

"Hmm. I'm disappointed you think me so naive to believe that. No, I'm sure he knows probably as much as you do."

Chuck opened his mouth to speak.

"Don't," LeVoleur snapped, "Don't you dare stoop to begging," he said, switching to French, "My family—my blood—never begs."

Another vehicle arrived, rolling to a stop beside the other SUVs by the access bridge.

LeVoleur turned to Raya. "If you don't want him as part of your contract, he will be put back into circulation. I mean to recover my money, one way or another," he said the last to Chuck, whose face reddened.

Dominique blanched.

Before Raya could answer, he went to meet the new arrivals. No one on the deck of the ship moved.

All of LeVoleur's men were armed. Some could be shifters, but she didn't know how many, or which ones.

"Welcome, welcome!" LeVoleur's superfluous greeting was a sign that he was becoming agitated.

This was important to him.

She turned her attention to the new arrivals approaching. All white-haired older men with impeccable appearances and a haughty tilt of their noses. She recognized two. Her mind worked to recall where she'd seen them before.

"Thank you for coming all this way. I do hope you've enjoyed touring the region before our meeting."

"Yes, Jean-Guy, very quaint. Good to see you again," one said; an older man with deep scowl lines, drooping jowls, and an east coast accent.

Investors?

As she struggled to place the other faces, Raya's body tingled. The undeniable sensation of Ian's magic rippling against her essence pulled her attention toward the river.

She moved toward the starboard side of the ship. Everyone's attention was on LeVoleur as he escorted his visitors to tour the ship as he'd done with her.

Seemingly forgotten, she inched her way into the shadows. When Dom turned to look for her, she held up a finger and dispersed.

TWENTY-FOUR

IAN STRIPPED, STUFFED HIS clothes into the waterproof bag Ana had given him, and slipped into the inky water. As soon as he was out far enough, he swam close to the ship, keeping to the shadows.

Carson followed, running along the bank, close to the under-brush to stay out of sight of the floodlights with mounted cameras. He was a better shot with a gun, so Ian decided to go beast for now. If he could get close enough, he might be able to hear what was going on. Keeping to the shadows, he glanced around the river to ensure there weren't any observers before sinking below the surface to shift.

The water rippled around him as his body stretched; muscle, bone and sinew morphed. The river water displaced, making room for his mass as he grew, next to the ship.

Waiting for his sensitive hearing to adjust to the ambient sounds, Ian listened next to the hull of the ship. Crew called to one anoth-er as they worked. Cargo was being moved from one section to another. And the low murmur of other voices. Many voices, weak and full of despair. Off at the far end of the ship, he could hear someone crying.

Dear Goddess.

Yet another bolt of the reality of Raya's life over these last several years slid home.

He lifted his head, mindful to keep it below the line of the deck.

Then he felt Raya's magic.

"What the hell are you doing here in your beast, Ian? You can be seen by anyone." Her voice scathed him.

He didn't bother turning, knowing he wouldn't be able to see, nor answer her, in his present form.

She huffed. "There are visitors here. They look like investors. LeVoleur wants me to play babysitter aboard this ship while it's on route to pass off the human cargo. The ship is leaving tonight."

A low growl rumbled through his chest.

"I'm not going if I can help it." She said. "Stay out of sight, I'm going to see what else I can find out."

Her presence floated away like a fading melody.

Ian sank to his human state as he returned to Carson. Putting Ana's earpiece back on, he relayed what Raya told him to Carson's team.

Carson nodded. "Ana, call Jack, he'll need to reach out to his contacts with local law enforcement."

Ana's voice sounded in his ear. "Already done. His GPSA agent embedded with them is standing by with the Coast Guard. And Teddy's on his way."

"Teddy! Good, catch them up."

"Copy."

"We're going to see if we can get on that boat," Carson said to Ian.

"I'm positioned close to the vehicles," Lirikai said through the earpiece.

"Hold."

"Copy."

"Want a ride?" Ian said to Carson.

Carson grinned as Ian handed him his bag of clothes. Shifting back into his beast, he stretched his tail out so Carson could run up the length of his spine.

Sliding through the water back toward the ship, Ian eased alongside it then positioned himself so that, after a quick glance for guards, Carson could climb over the rail of the deck. He quickly found a lifesaver hanging nearby and tossed it over. Ian again reclaimed his human form and scrambled up the rope.

Taking the bag of clothes from Carson, he dressed before sneaking around the back, trying to get the holster Ana had given him in place.

RAYA LEFT IAN'S SIDE, and floated her way into the ship, looking for LeVoleur and his business partners.

The ship was leaving tonight, he'd said back at the hotel. She had to do this now, before it started navigating the treacherous waters of the river toward the gulf.

She found the investors in the cargo hold, grouped around an open container with an armed guard. LeVoleur was off to the side, talking to Francois.

She hadn't been wrong.

There were several dozen people in the one container, as she'd expected. Judging by the stink of the steel box, they'd been in there awhile already.

She floated closer to LeVoleur.

"Thanks to your loyalty, I've got Charles back where I can keep an eye on him. Stupid that he thought he could get away with deceiving me like that. Disappointing. I was preparing him to take my place. No matter. I will deal with him, and in the meantime, you will continue to work in his position until he can see reason."

"Yes, sir." Francois grinned, looking pleased with himself. "And the other one?"

"If the Ashray doesn't want him as part of her contract, throw him in with the others. If she does, she can have him until the ship makes contact at sea. *Then* he can go with the others." He sneered. "I don't want him back in this hemisphere again."

"If she objects?"

LeVoleur swept Francois with his gaze and grinned. "You can have her."

Francois frowned. "Yes, sir." He swallowed hard but nodded.

Good. He's afraid of me.

Raya moved back out toward the deck, floating toward Chuck and Dom.

"Be ready for anything." She whispered, making them both jump.

Sliding into the shadows, she rematerialized, strolling with her hands clasped behind her back as though she'd been touring the deck all this time.

Moments later, LeVoleur reappeared with his visitors, pulling her attention to their faces again. Where had she seen those two before?

The first clicked. She'd seen the more austere of the two at one of LeVoleur's meetings she'd spied on years ago, before she'd made contact with the underworld. The other...

The group were almost to the bridge to disembark from the ship. They stopped to wait their turn and the last in the line, the one that Raya couldn't figure out where she'd seen him before turned, noticing her looking at him.

Being the only female on board, she stood out.

His attention honed in on her, eyes widening as he recognized her at the same time she recalled how she knew him too.

Jones.

One of the liaisons between the Federal government and the *Organization*. They'd crossed paths, once, when she had been summoned for a debriefing after a successful mission.

Mother. Fucker.

TWENTY-FIVE

RAISED VOICES DREW IAN'S attention toward the open deck. Inching forward from his position at the stern of the ship, the lit deck eased into view.

Raya stood alone in the middle, guards spread out around her. LeVoleur strode toward Chuck Meduse and Raya's brother, Dominique. Several older men in suits were in the process of descending to the pier. The last of the line was turned, pointing at Raya.

His indignant shouts carried across the deck of the ship. "This project is compromised. That woman is an international agent, LeVoleur, and I suggest you get rid of her."

LeVoleur spun, wide-eyed, in Raya's direction.

Fuck. This wasn't good.

He recalled her concerns at the cabin on the matter of a corrupt link somewhere between GPSA and her Organization.

"Shit." Carson's voice sounded in the earpiece. "Shit."

"What is it?" Ana said.

"Deputy Director Jones, in the chain of command. Well above my pay grade. Somewhere above Kane. This isn't good."

"Oh, this isn't good at all." Ana's voice was quiet.

"I'll take care of him." Lirikai said.

"Don't let those men leave the port, Lirikai. And don't eat them either. We need them."

"You know the scent of all this corruption is making me salivate."

"Copy?"

"Copy," she answered, with a heavy sigh.

LeVoleur was talking, voice too low to hear. He now stood in front of Raya, talking down at her, clearly enraged.

She shook her head.

LeVoleur spun back toward the older man.

"I'll goddamned well do it myself." The old man shouted, as he pulled a gun from inside his blazer and leveled it at Raya. She dematerialized as a shot resounded. The bullet disappeared into the darkness over the water.

She rematerialized with her forearm across his throat, the point of her knife pricking the sagging flesh below his ear.

"That...was rude," she said as he struggled to free himself from her grip.

"Release him," LeVoleur commanded.

"He shot at me," Raya said.

"I don't care, I told you to release him."

Raya didn't move.

In light of her defiance, LeVoleur drew a gun of his own and aimed it at Dominique.

"That man is an integral part of my operations. Let him go."

After a moment, he cocked the gun.

"If you fire that gun, I will slit your throat, LeVoleur."

His eyes widened, then he grinned. "Not so removed from your little brother after all, are you?" Despite his bravado, his aim faltered.

He'd just threatened the Ashray. And she was having none of it.

Pride swelled Ian's heart.

The old man grunted as blood trickled below the tip of Raya's blade toward his crisp collar.

"Hold." Carson's voice was soft through the earpiece.

"If that kid dies..." Ian ground out through his teeth.

"LeVoleur doesn't have any reason to kill him. He can't sell a dead man."

Ian was skeptical.

Movement pulled Ian's attention to a large figure moving in from the side. It was one of the neck-less goons from that morning and he was drawing a gun.

"Dom!" Raya yelled, having seen him at the same time Ian had.

The large man cocked the gun and fired in the same moment Chuck Meduse slid in front of Dominique, hand outstretched. A long clear cord whipped out of what should have been Meduse's hand, wrapping around the man's throat with a snap as his own body jerked back into Dominique with a grunt.

"Chuck!" Dominique yelled.

They both dropped to the deck, and chaos erupted.

The shooter also dropped to the ground, desperately clutching at the translucent cord wrapped around his throat, his face turning first red, then purple. The cord released him, retracting back into Chuck's limb. His face was pale as blood oozed from his chest.

More thugs moved toward Chuck and Dom. Raya's elbow came down on the old man's head, knocking him unconscious.

LeVoleur was bellowing.

Raya ran toward Dom, telling him to run. Seeing the turn of Raya's priorities, LeVoleur aimed his gun and fired at her. She dissipated and rematerialized next to a couple of guards, taking them down seconds before LeVoleur's bullets passed through the vacated space, some hitting his own men.

Several of the guards shifted.

The old men that were still conscious ran for their guarded vehicles, where Lirikai met them with horrific extended teeth. Ana aimed a Taser and her gun at them.

Raya was occupied evading guards. Carson had moved in and was fighting hand to hand with another.

Someone ran toward Ian with a long steel rod. He engaged the goon, while still trying to keep an eye on Dominique. He'd promised to keep him safe.

LeVoleur turned, wild-eyed, on Dominique, who still cradled Chuck as he bled.

"You! All this for you, you little piece of shit!" He advanced, gun drawn. "Charles, you stupid fuck. You ruined my legacy, the one you were meant to take over. For what?"

"I didn't want it, uncle," Chuck said, chest heaving with pain.

Raya cried out as she took a hit, her attention on her brother as LeVoleur advanced.

Ian sent the guy he'd been fighting sailing over the edge of the ship with a heavy splash, then ran toward Dominique and LeVoleur, trying to pull Ana's gun from its holster as he moved his body into the space between them. He aimed the gun at LeVoleur.

"I need him alive!" Raya shouted as she brought down a tiger shifter, then turned as another one of LeVoleur's men ran toward her.

A muscular figure with shoulder length blond hair jumped into the fray, shifting into a badger, attacking the man before he reached Raya. A panther followed close behind, launching for the neck of another one of the mob goons.

As LeVoleur swung his gun toward Ian, Raya moved in, her arms around LeVoleur as she'd done with the old man, knife at his throat.

LeVoleur fired his gun.

Pain exploded in Ian's chest as he knocked the gun loose, sending it clattering across the deck.

"Ian!" Raya screamed, wide eyes on the blood blooming on his chest. Fury transformed her features into a menacing mask.

Sirens wailed in the distance, echoing off the city buildings.

Ian managed to remain standing; the gun he pointed at LeVoleur wavered.

LeVoleur laughed at him, despite Raya's knife pinned to his throat.

"You're not going to kill me." They were standing close to the edge of the ship.

His eyes darted toward the edge a second before he threw his head back into Raya's nose.

She held fast, knife digging deeper. Her hand shook as her eyes flicked back to Ian's wound.

"You're not worth the effort to keep you alive." She growled.

LeVoleur grimaced in pain.

"You destroy people's lives."

Blood began to trickle faster from LeVoleur's throat as Raya's knife sliced deeper.

"Raya, you said you needed him alive," Ian prompted, panting.

"I changed my mind. We have all the evidence we need on this ship, plus the investors, and Chuck."

"Charles is my nephew. He won't tell you anything."

"Are you sure about that?"

LeVoleur's eyes slid to Chuck. The first of the emergency responders had arrived and were surrounding the port. Dominique was supporting Chuck as they carefully made their way off the ship.

The pain in Ian's chest grew. He needed to shift to dislodge the bullet if it was still in his flesh.

Carson finished handcuffing the last of the criminals he'd brought down and had just turned his attention to LeVoleur. "You're done. Let's go."

The sound of electricity crackled in the space in front of Ian. Raya screamed as the air around LeVoleur turned white-blue with ozone. Raya held tight, arms locked around LeVoleur.

The electricity was coming from LeVoleur and growing brighter.

Water and electricity didn't mix, and Raya was a creature made of water.

"Raya!" Ian bellowed, surging forward. It was too late.

LeVoleur forced Raya off balance, sending them both over the edge of the ship into the river.

Ian went in after them.

The water was alive, shocking him as soon as he touched it. The pain was worse than the bullet wound.

Raya.

Ian shifted.

He'd never experienced anything so excruciating as he did in those seconds between man and beast.

Once his beast was solidified, his thick hide dampened the effects of the electricity.

Raya hadn't let go. She was fading as she held onto the biggest electric eel Ian had ever seen. And it was still sending out waves of electricity in an effort to dislodge her grip.

With a final surge of a blue-white filament, Raya let go, her knife sinking to the bottom of the river as she floated free of LeVoleur.

Ian's brain fogged with panic at seeing her limp form.

He couldn't lose her now. He also couldn't let her efforts be for nothing.

Reason wriggled into his brain. Her magic wouldn't let her drown.

LeVoleur writhed through the water away from Ian and Raya.

With a growl, Ian's jaws snapped. Then again as he stretched his long neck forward, his teeth sinking into the eel, trapping it. Raising his head out of the water, he sent it flying up onto the deck of the ship before plunging back below the surface.

He aligned himself so that his neck slipped under Raya's inert form. As soon as he was sure her body was balanced, he carefully lifted her out of the water, where Carson was close by to help pull her onto the deck.

He dropped back into the river one last time to retrieve his clothes and shoes that had drifted loose during his shift and slipped them back on. He swam to the flotation device Carson had used to help him up onto the deck before and moments later he was at Raya's side. She was still unconscious. Dropping to his knees, he pressed his ear to her chest.

"She started breathing as soon as you got her out of the water," Carson told him.

He was sure she wouldn't have drowned in the water. There was no telling what that kind of electric charge would do to her, though, and he hadn't wanted to risk leaving her there any longer than necessary.

He listened carefully. Her heartbeat was faint and irregular, but it was still beating.

LeVoleur lay naked and bleeding from the wounds Ian had inflicted with his teeth. Lirikai loomed over him.

"He's not going anywhere." Carson said. "Are you okay, Ian?"

"Yes, shifting released the bullet and triggered the healing process."

Carson nodded. "Good, I'd hoped so. Getting shot sucks."

"Especially in the ass," Ana said, striding toward them. "Teddy's here."

Carson nodded. "I saw him. Never been so happy to see a badger in my life."

Ian peered into Raya's pale face, whispering her name.

Her eyes fluttered open and Ian's heart cracked with relief.

Her hand wavered toward him, landing on his cheek. "Have I ever told you how much I love your accent?"

"Not in a long, long while." He answered, laying it on thick.

She smiled.

Carson clapped him on the shoulder and moved back to where LeVoleur was. Ana went with him.

"Dominique?"

"He's okay."

Her eyes closed. When she re-opened them, they were full of tears. "I found him, Ian."

"Aye, you did, love."

She quickly blinked away the tears. "I feel like shit."

"Can you stand?"

She nodded. He helped her up and supported her for a few moments as she got her balance. "I'll be okay. I want to see him."

He smiled at her and kissed her forehead.

TWENTY-SIX

RAYA LOOKED UP FROM where she was seated next to Dominique, who held Chuck's hand as he lay on a gurney just outside of an ambulance.

Ian appeared before her.

The port was crowded with emergency vehicles, jammed into the spaces between shipping containers. Firetrucks, police cruisers and ambulances were barriers to enclose the scene. Coast Guard boats bobbed around the ship, so escapees could be retrieved from the water. Port employees, ship workers and criminals were being assessed and shuffled off for further processing.

"Carson is going to take Chuck and Dominique into GPSA's direct custody. Maeda and Kane are going to take over from here. You're expected to meet with them, too."

"Where is LeVoleur?" Raya asked, glancing around the red and blue lit chaos.

"Secured in an ambulance. Still breathing."

"So am I, thanks to you," Dominique said, reaching over to him, hand outstretched. "Thanks."

Ian shook it. "It's good to see you again."

Dominique nodded. "Good to be seen." He glanced at Raya with an awkward smile. "We have a lot of catching up to do."

"Aye, we do," Ian said, turning his gaze to Raya.

She looked from one to the other and laughed, shaking her head. "And we will." She reached out and squeezed Dom's hand.

"Time to go," Agent Perenga said from behind Raya. She turned to see him looking from Dom to Chuck. "We have a very long night ahead of us." He watched as Chuck's gurney was loaded into the ambulance.

Dominique tugged on Raya's hand, pulling her into a hug. "I'm okay, Raya. I'll be fine."

She hugged him so hard he wheezed, but he didn't complain. He returned the strength of it equally, his cheek resting on her head.

"I love you, little brother."

"I know you do, and I love you, too." He released her, glancing from Ian to Raya. "You really need to live for yourself. No matter what happens after tonight. I will be okay." He kissed her forehead and turned to take his place at Chuck's side in the ambulance.

Agent Perenga spoke briefly to the EMS driver then returned to Raya and Ian.

"What will happen to them?"

He shrugged. "The board of inquiry will assess them, see how cooperative they are, or aren't, and go from there."

Raya nodded, accepting this.

"This case just gets deeper and wider," he said to Ian.

"You have no idea," Raya said.

"I may, a little. Analiese told me about what she saw when she touched your hand. Sounds to me like we have an awful lot of work to do."

"Yes, we do." She looked up to Ian, seeing him study her face. "I'm not done yet." She said.

Ian slipped his fingers between hers, pulling her hand to his lips. "*We*...are not done yet."

She smiled as her heart fluttered at the look in his eyes.

"Teddy and the local GPSA agent, Pia Jensen, are waiting to talk to me. I'll see you both later," Agent Perenga said, giving Ian's shoulder a hearty clap.

RAYA OPENED HER EYES to see the early morning sunlight bathing Ian's sleeping face.

Her heart swelled as she stared at the illuminated angle of his jaw as the light caught on the new stubble, then at his lips, relaxed in sleep. She traced the tip of her thumb over a thick brow.

A moment later, she rolled away and rose from the bed, reaching for her discarded silk nightgown and wrap. Tying the belt, she stepped out onto the open terrace and drank in the sight of the loch below the cottage.

Ian's birthplace.

A fine morning mist lingered over the loch, which stretched out of sight in either direction. Wandering out further, her hands clasped the iron rail as the sun burned off last of the fog and made the water glitter like crystal shards.

She drew a deep breath, savoring it.

Home.

Ian had gone with her to pay her respects at her parents' grave site in Aberdeen before they drove to Inverness, where they were to spend the next couple of weeks.

The *Organization* had been satisfied with their procurement of LeVoleur and the shipload of victims. The investor that had tried to shoot her had also been taken into custody. The *Organization*, the government and GPSA were launching a deep investigation into his activities and connections.

While LeVoleur maintained his silence, Chuck gave the GPSA and the *Organization* everything they needed.

It appeared he did indeed want a life free of his uncle's criminal world. He and Dominique wouldn't be able to go back to Montreal. They'd have to make a new life elsewhere. And all the money she'd made as The Ashray was going to help them do just that-after she replaced agent Ortega's shoes.

Raya felt the warmth of Ian's body before his hands slid around her. She shivered, knowing she'd never get too used to the sensation of his touch.

"Want to go for a swim later?" His brogue was thick next to her ear. Her nipples pebbled.

"Maybe." A smile played at her lips. "Think any tourists will be around?"

"We can look for them."

She giggled.

She felt his chest rise against her back as he drew a deep breath. "Good to be home?"

"Aye. I shouldn't have stayed away so damned long. I was foolish." He turned her to face him. "Foolish about so many things."

Her fingers drifted over his cheek and jaw. He kissed her fingertips.

"I've caused us to lose so much time."

She shrugged. "We can look at it that way, I suppose. Maybe we needed it, Ian. Maybe we both needed that time to step up to the next level of who we are. Besides, the reunion has been incredible." She grinned, rubbing her body against his.

He hardened against her belly. "If we keep this up, I willnae be able to walk."

"We aren't going anywhere for a while." She whispered.

Ian's eyes were locked on her face.

She shivered at the intensity of his gaze.

"I love you so much, Raya. I nearly died when I thought I'd lost you again."

"Ian." Her voice was so very soft. "It will happen one day. Hopefully a very long time from now, but it will. And with the work I do..."

"I'll be there with you, Raya."

"To protect me. As much as you can."

"Will you let me?"

"Sometimes. Will you let me protect you, too?"

He smiled. "Sometimes."

"Then we have an agreement."

He nodded.

She slid her hand into the front of his lounge pants, wrapping her fingers around him.

Ian's hands pushed her gown up, then lifted her so that her bottom rested on the railing.

"Now," Her voice dropped, turning husky. "Talk to me in that dirty brogue of yours, and I'll think about letting you in."

He lowered his mouth next to her ear, where his lips grazed the shell. "I'm going to make you scones for breakfast, love." He bit her earlobe. "With fresh butter."

Raya wrapped her legs around his hips and guided him to her entrance. She moaned as he slid home.

This was turning out to be a wonderful lakeside vacation indeed, and beautiful start to a second chance with the love of her life.

POLESTAR

GLOBAL PARANORMAL SECURITY AGENCY

JODI KENDRICK

POLESTAR

The guiding light of the north unites two fragile hearts on the verge of shattering.

A call in the middle of the night summoned GPSA Agent Analiese Ortega to the field of an ongoing case. After a recent devastating loss and deeply burrowed self-doubt about her abilities, Ana insists she isn't ready to return to work.

With lives at stake, what choice does she have?

Agent Magnus Bjornson has seen it all, been jaded by most of it and amused by little else the world has to offer. Something about his new colleague thaws his iceberg heart despite the ongoing injustices they continue to face with this case.

Together, they strive to end it all.

ONE

ANALIESE ORTEGA'S EYES SNAPPED open, heart still racing from her nightmare. She blinked, scanning the dark room for what had startled her awake.

Bzht. Bzht. Bzht.

She blew out her breath and reached for her phone as reality replaced the nightmare.

"Carson," she mumbled, rolling onto her back, rubbing her face with her free hand. She didn't bother asking if he knew what time it was, because he wouldn't be calling at a ridiculous hour if it weren't necessary.

"There's a chartered plane waiting for you at Santa Ana airport."

"I hate that airport."

"It's close."

"I'm not ready."

There was a long silence before Carson answered. "I know. I'm sorry about Antony, but we need you, Ana."

"Farida can do it."

"On assignment in New Zealand."

She struggled to think of another agent from the Global Paranormal Security Agency that could take her place.

Some other objections.

Set by her bedside, her gaze found the only photo of Antony she couldn't let go of.

Pain twisted her heart.

My fault.

She shoved the sensation away, locking down her emotions.

Carson continued. "The data from our informant is paying off, Ana. We have a lead." He paused. "You've been there from the start. I know you want to see this case through."

Dammit. I do.

Ana threw off her duvet. Her feet hit the cool floor and propelled her toward the patio doors of her bedroom, overlooking the beach.

The surf rushed in and rolled out. Once more.

"I need to shower and pack."

"The pilot will wait, but don't keep him waiting too long. He gets grumpy."

"Noted."

"Pack warm."

"Why? Where am I going?" She spun around, eyes finding her closet door.

"Iceland."

"Iceland! Carson, you know I hate cold places."

"Don't we all." He sighed.

"Just don't have Lirikai pick me up when I arrive. My nerves can't handle her driving."

Carson chuckled, "She misses you."

"Carson, please."

"Don't worry, your ride is already taken care of. Besides, Lirikai is working elsewhere at the moment."

Oh, thank God.

"You know I like her—I really do."

"I know."

She could hear the mirth in his voice.

"She's just..."

"Intense."

"Yes. Intense."

"Her driving is improving."

Ana grunted. Carson laughed.

She hung up the phone, then tossed it onto the foot of her bed as she straightened the duvet and fluffed the pillows. Opening the sliding glass door, she stepped onto her balcony, breathing deeply of the sea air, giving herself a few moments to fully awaken.

And absorb the warm California air.

She'd be going to the boardroom for a briefing first, so office wear.

North.

She'd have to dig deep into her closet.

Do I even own cold weather clothes?

Her shoulders drooped. She'd have to layer. A lot.

I hate the cold.

I'm not ready for this.

Ana allowed herself a few more moments to reconcile. Carson needed her.

Ready or not, people's lives are at stake.

"Right then, no time to waste."

MAGNUS BJORNSON YAWNED, PACING the tarmac outside of his chartered plane.

He glanced at his watch again.

"An hour late," he growled.

Refueled, the plane waited. He'd already been through all the checks. Twice. He didn't mind long hours in the cockpit, but disliked unnecessary added time. Especially when a storm was expected between himself and the landing site. This extra wait time could cost them more than just an hour at the other end of the journey.

He sighed and went into the hangar office to make coffee.

About to take his first sip of the hot brew, rapid footsteps amid the sound of rolling wheels drew his attention to a tiny brunette dressed for a boardroom, hauling two suitcases. She could have fit into either of them with space to spare.

The coffee was too hot, but he drank some anyway as he observed the hangar official with his passenger.

It was going to be a long flight.

He considered the rest of the brew, gulped it down, and tossed the paper cup in the trash bin.

"I'm already late. Please tell the pilot I'm here and we can take off right away—unless someone else is traveling with me? Is anyone else expected?"

"No ma'am. Just you."

Her narrow shoulders lowered a fraction. "Okay, just watch that one doesn't roll away while I bring this one up." She motioned toward the bright teal case as she tightened her grip on the lime green one.

"But madam, I can take those for you. Just leave it here."

"No, it's okay, I've got it," she insisted, dragging it up the first step as though she were a champion weightlifter pulling a maxed bar.

Magnus smirked.

He patted the official's shoulder as he moved toward the steps locked below the opening and grabbed the case with one hand, then mounted and grabbed the second case with the other.

"No, it's okay, really, I—Oh." She said, when she turned to stare into Magnus' face, who still stood taller than her despite being lower on the steps. Her gaze shot down to his easy grasp of her oversized luggage.

"You should go in," he suggested.

"I really could take one."

"I insist. We're already late."

"Right. Okay." She nodded and scurried up the steps and into the charter.

Magnus sighed as he followed.

I bet everything she owns is in these two cases.

She reappeared in the door, preparing to descend again.

"Agent Ortega?"

"I forgot my laptop bag by the front door."

Thankfully, the official had noted the oversight and was already trotting back with the bag.

"Thank you so much." She smiled and disappeared inside.

Deciding to ignore the dimples her cheeks made when she smiled, Magnus secured the cases in the back, then did final checks as he moved toward the cockpit.

"Is the pilot ready?" Agent Ortega asked, fastening her seatbelt.

"He is," Magnus said, closing and securing the door. He nodded to the official below.

"But I didn't see him up front." She glanced toward the back of the plane.

"I'm the pilot," Magnus said, stepping into the cockpit. "Anything else I can do for you before we get on our way?"

She blinked.

"Uhm. No. Thank you," she said. "Sorry about all the luggage. Perenga said 'pack warm' and I panicked a bit. I don't like the cold."

Magnus grunted. "You get used to it. Wheels up in ten. Stow your bag." He nodded to the laptop bag on the seat beside her.

"Of course."

Magnus wasn't fazed. He was familiar with the expression of disbelief due to his appearance.

Six foot five, impeccably kept long hair and beard, Nirvana t-shirt and jeans. No, he didn't dress like a pilot. Nor did he think he had to in order to do his job properly.

Although, the agency often tried to convince him otherwise.

Agent Ortega clearly adhered to the agency's dress protocol in her crisp office skirt-suit, white button-up and heels.

No wonder she's so uptight. No room to breathe.

As he cast her one last glance, he noticed she had retrieved an eye mask from her laptop satchel before tucking the bag beneath her seat.

He closed the door and got to work.

TWO

ANALIESE LURCHED AT THE sensation of falling in darkness, then skipping over a series of speed bumps at racetrack speed.

Her heart hammered wildly, and her limbs flailed, slamming against too-close objects.

Chest heaving, her hands clutched the arms of her chair as soon as she found them, then she reached up and ripped the mask off her eyes to dispel the nightmare.

Plane. Charter. Giant pilot. Going to Iceland.

Had she slept the entire flight? She glanced at her watch, then pushed the window shade up.

Chaos filled the small window.

Rain poured down the glass. The plane swayed. The steel-tinted sky lit with a flash, followed by a deafening crash.

Ana slammed the window screen shut, then threw herself back against her seat, eyes closed as she prayed. Her fingers gripped the seat handles, feet securely against the plane floor.

Her gaze darted to the small door, blocking her view to the pilot. This particular plane had a thin wall dividing the cockpit from the rest of the cabin. Probably to stop passengers, like herself, from screaming at the pilot in terror.

A dull 'pong' drew her attention to the ceiling.

The pilot had illuminated the seatbelt sign.

No shit.

The plane lurched and continued to descend.

Breath stuttered through her chest. One of her nails cracked as her grip tightened on the seat.

She hated flying almost as much as she hated the cold.

"If I die… in a plane crash… in the North Atlantic… I'm going to friggin' haunt you, Carson Perenga," she spat through her clenched teeth.

She was almost sorry for all the complaining she'd done while at the mercy of Lirikai's driving. Almost.

At least, in that case, she was already on the ground.

She waited for the 'brace for impact' message to come over the com. Instead, the plane leveled out and eased downward. She held her breath till the wheels touched the ground and they rolled to a stop. The seatbelt sign went dark, then the engine went silent.

Ana disengaged her nails from her seat and unbuckled her belt, still cursing Carson's name.

The scowling giant pilot squeezed through the cockpit door. "Slight delay in plans. We'll stop here to ride out the storm."

"We're not at our destination? Where are we?" Ana shoved the window blind back up again, now that it was safe to look outside. There was nothing but rain-lashed barren rockscape pockmarked with small bodies of water between a few stubborn trees.

We're nowhere.

"Fogo Island." His expression remained unchanged.

She wracked her geographical memory, trying to recall where Fogo was as she stared at the pilot.

"Newfoundland," he provided, then turned toward the exterior door to release the steps. "We departed a little bit late, and the storm arrived a little bit early, so here we are."

Ana recalled Carson's warning on the phone *'The pilot will wait, but don't keep him waiting too long. He gets grumpy.'*

She'd only been an hour late. It had taken her that long to find all her 'winter' gear and choose the right shoes for the office. Carson had neglected to tell her if she needed field or boardroom wear for the duration of the case. She had to be ready for anything. And she was currently dressed for the office. Not a frigid rainstorm off the coast of apocalypse-scape.

"Where are we going?" She pulled the edges of her thin jacket close as a gust of wind wound through the cabin once the door was open.

"Out." He descended the steps.

Ana found a large hand extended through the open door to help her down the steps.

The pilot's bear-like grasp was warm as it engulfed her hand. She gasped. Her fingers felt as though she'd inserted them into a warm energy current. Images flashed through her mind's eye, too rapid to grasp before she could throw her barriers up to block the transfer of energetic information.

She descended quickly, sliding past his trim torso to the tarmac, trying to shake the sudden onslaught of images and sensations.

Ana grit her teeth trying to control the influx of information.

I'm never going to get used to that.

He gestured toward a squat building, indicating she should enter. Trotting forward, she glanced back to see that he was securing the plane, impervious to the rain soaking his clothes.

The door was locked, so she waited under the narrow overhang, holding her jacket closed, shivering as rainwater dribbled down her bare legs to pool in the toes of her office pumps.

She'd expected to be chauffeured to an office like Maeda's—or her own, for that matter.

Ah. Field work.

She sighed. She would soon find out if this was worse than Odson Blackridge's mountain cabin. She prayed that this facility at least had running water and an indoor toilet. Cell service would be nice.

Though, as she peered through the driving rain and saw absolutely nothing, she had her doubts.

Finally, the pilot strode in her direction, unhurried by the downpour. She blinked at the alluring vision of the tall man, t-shirt plastered to a mountain range of muscle and valley. Withdrawing a key ring from his jeans pocket, he unlocked the door and gestured for her to precede him.

Shivering, she darted inside the black interior.

A few seconds later, lights flickered on. "No customs agent on duty?" she asked through chattering teeth.

"Private runway. They know our tags and leave us alone." He strode across the open space of the small hangar toward an office door set in the wall between a work bench and a large tool chest. "I'll radio in to let them know we're grounded for the time being."

Radio.

No cell service.

Damn.

Ana followed him through the door.

"Oh, thank God!" she blurted on seeing a bathroom door, and rushed toward it. After the stress of that unexpected landing and the icy rain, Ana had a sudden emergency of her own.

MAGNUS' GAZE TRAILED THE pint-sized agent as she bee-lined for the lavatory and slammed the door shut.

He sighed and made his way toward the kitchenette to fill and set the kettle to boil before powering on the radio.

He contacted Joey Kane, his superior, confirming his position and status. They'd continue on as soon as the storm let up—with a change of destination.

Negotiations weren't going as smoothly as Kane had hoped.

"Sorry to do this, Magnus. We need Agent Ortega's skills on this, but until we resolve this disagreement, we need to delay revealing too much to our *partners.*"

"Understood. An extended journey it is, then."

He switched off the radio and returned to the kitchen to pull mugs from the cupboard.

The agent approached, rubbing her hands together, shivering in her damp jacket.

Magnus poured water over the tea, handed her a mug, then went to fetch a space heater from the utility closet. "Sit over there." He set the heater on the floor next to the chair and plugged it in.

She followed his instruction, grasping the mug with both hands. "How much further to Iceland from here?"

"We're not going to Iceland. Ireland."

"No, I'm pretty sure we're going to Iceland. I wouldn't confuse 'pack warm' for frigid Iceland with Ireland. Ever."

"Plan's changed."

"Since when? Why?" Agent Ortega jumped to her feet, still clutching her mug.

"Since the order came when I radioed in."

"What's going on?"

Magnus shrugged.

Agent Ortega scowled at him. "Listen, Mister—what's your name?"

"Bjornson. Magnus Bjornson."

"Of course it is. Look at you," she muttered. "Mr. Bjornson. *My* orders were to meet my team in Iceland. I packed for Iceland. Two very large suitcases. For Iceland. Until I can confirm that *my* orders have changed. You will fly me to Iceland."

He lifted a brow, looking down at the bossy woman shivering in front of him with a pink nose. "Agent Bjornson," he corrected, leaning over her. "Your orders depend on mine. And I have just been told to fly you to Ireland. So unless you want to walk around this little island in the driving rain to find your own ride, you will accompany me to Ireland."

She sniffed, bright spots appearing on her tanned cheeks. "And how much longer do I have to *fly* with you? If that's what you call flying? What was *that,* anyway? I think I lost ten years of my life in that landing."

Magnus stiffened. "That maneuvering saved your life. Had you arrived *as expected*, we'd have missed that storm and be nearly to

Iceland by now. Then someone *else* could have flown you on to Ireland now that the plan has changed."

When she opened her mouth to speak, she swayed on her feet. Magnus grasped her wrist to steady her.

She gasped and dropped her mug as her eyes rolled back.

The mug hit the concrete floor with a crash as Magnus jerked her forward toward himself to stop her from falling backward. "Agent Ortega?"

He caught her as she slumped against him. Her head lolled; eyes closed. While supporting her, he checked her vitals and eased her into the chair.

What's wrong with her?

"Agent Ortega?" he said again, easing her back into the chair. "Ortega?" His hands swept her forehead and cheeks. Her skin was pale despite her pink tipped nose and rosy cheeks.

Magnus swept her slight form into his arms and carried her into the small bunk room, tucked away beyond the kitchenette. Gently laying Agent Ortega on the cot, he pulled off her shoes. Her bare feet and calves were wet and cold. He eased her upright so he could remove the soaked jacket. The thin silk blouse beneath clung to her damp skin, outlining the contours of her lacy bra.

"Shit."

Easing her head back onto the small pillow, he went to fetch the space heater, to plug it in next to the cot. He cranked the knob, so that the filaments ticked as they grew to bright hot orange. It wasn't heating the room fast enough.

"It's not even winter. How can anyone catch a chill so damned fast?" he grumbled, rubbing her arms and legs to warm them up while the heater worked to bring the room temperature up.

The sensation of her silky skin beneath his palms didn't go unnoticed, just ignored.

Trembles wracked her body.

Quickly, Magnus unbuttoned her blouse, peeling it from her skin to drape it over a couple of hooks screwed to the wall next to the door. Then he pulled his own t-shirt up over his head.

Dragging a chair from the office, he sat, then carefully pulled Ortega onto his lap. He wrapped his arms around her lean form, ensuring her back was pressed to his chest. After a few moments, the trembling eased.

"Antony." She sighed, easing her head back onto his shoulder.

As soon as he was sure the agent could maintain body heat on her own, Magnus slid her back onto the cot, pulling the blanket around her shoulders and torso, then moved to rub the warmth into her feet and ankles.

The electric heater continued to tick furiously, working hard to warm the concrete and steel room.

After about ten minutes, Magnus went back to the plane, bare chested, to fetch one of the agent's suitcases. When he returned to the hangar, he left Ortega's suitcase at the foot of the cot, grabbed his wet shirt, and draped it over the back of the chair, pulling it back into the office.

Retrieving his own mug of tea, he sat down, impervious to the cool air. As a polar bear shifter, the cold didn't bother him.

He positioned his chair so that he could see Agent Ortega through the open door. She was a burrito on the thin cot. Her dark hair framed her small, round face, making her look younger than she probably was. And vulnerable, which she probably wasn't.

The only sounds were the steady ticking of the heater over the howling wind driving the rain against the steel roof of the airstrip hangar.

In the morning, he'd refuel the plane and get his new colleague to Ireland.

It would have been easier putting her on a commercial flight, but Kane had insisted that Ortega arrive as soon as possible, hence the private charter.

Magnus rubbed a hand over his face. Whatever they needed her for, it was important. Given their verbal exchange before she passed out, the sooner he delivered her, the better for both of them.

He didn't appreciate anyone slamming his flying skills, not even a feisty little agent from the Global Paranormal Security Agency.

THREE

ANA WATCHED THE LANDSCAPE through the same small window of her plane seat.

The Irish coast was beautiful. And green.

Not the north, as she'd worked herself up for.

She stifled a yawn and glanced toward the closed cockpit door concealing her giant pilot.

Ana's thoughts returned to the moment she'd awakened to discover that she was half naked and burrowed into an uncomfortable cot next to a blazing space heater. Then, unexpectedly, had taken in a full view of her pilot dozing bare-chested on an office chair in the next room. His long, long, jean-clad legs braced the chair against the wall behind him where his head rested. His large hands lay clasped over his belt buckle.

Her eyes trailed over the tattoos adorning the muscle. On the small table next to him were the remnants of the mug he'd given her the night before. She frowned, unable to recall anything after... what? What had happened?

God, she couldn't remember anything beyond feeling so damned cold.

And here she sat, flying to Ireland.

Bjornson, he'd said his name was. Agent? Yes, Agent Magnus Bjornson.

Tall, blond, and silent. He was a shifter of some kind. She'd gleaned that much from the unintentional contact.

He'd barely said anything to her since he caught her staring at him from her little bundle on the cot where she'd slept. As he seemed to have slept all night on an office chair.

She sighed.

What stupid shit did I say last night?

All she could piece together was the recollection of feeling... but it was gone again before she could grasp it.

Her heightened anxiety made chaos of her emotional barrier. The self-control that her boss, Jack Maeda, had been working to help her hone was rice paper thin. And with all the rain and the wind, being called to duty, and the storm forcing the plane down, it had all just torn through.

She glanced at the door again. Had Agent Bjornson touched her? If he had, she didn't recall it, and normally she did.

Sometimes, when all her barriers became depleted, the slightest touch could bring her to her knees with information overload. But it would stay with her, like an echo chamber, until she could snatch every piece and categorize it.

This was different.

Her vision had gone blinding white. Then she fell into darkness.

Emotions, thoughts, impressions. None were tangible. Not enough. Too much.

Either way, she decided that until she had better control over her channeling, she wouldn't touch him again.

Not that she *should* touch him again, because she *shouldn't*.

Although, part of her secretly wished she could remember if he had touched her at all.

Ana's cheeks burned as images of all those tattooed muscles rolled through her brain, where the psychic impressions wouldn't.

She cleared her suddenly dry throat.

For the best.

I prefer clean-cut men; she reminded herself. *Like Antony...* her heart crumbled at the reminder.

Antony's smiling face rose in her mind's eye, blotting out everything else, followed by his other expressions. Confusion over her explanations of her work. Resolve when he'd ended their long-term relationship. Fear over her insistent warnings that something was wrong. Pity when he left on his voyage out to sea. Routine training exercise.

The end of her world loomed with his disappearance.

She shut down the rest with a deep, deep breath and turned her focus back to the window.

This was her life now.

She'd always been devoted to her work at the GPSA. And after so many recent heartbreaking experiences, it was her life's work now.

No time for distractions, like attractive Viking-ish pilots, or dead relationships.

Her grandmother had warned her.

Ana hadn't listened.

She was listening now.

The plane descended the last few hundred feet. She barely felt the wheels graze the tarmac as they coasted to a smooth stop.

Much better than last night's landing.

Agent Bjornson emerged from the small cockpit door once he parked the plane and turned the engines off.

With her laptop bag slung over her back, Ana was already trying to free her suitcases from the aft baggage compartment. She glanced back as he opened the door hatch and lowered the steps.

A moment later, his large hand hovered over hers, straining on the suitcase handle. "Go."

"But I can get this one—."

He grunted, and she moved aside, surprised by his gruff non-verbal order.

She huffed, slid past him, and exited the plane.

They were on another private landing strip with an accompanying office and hangar.

Fine. If Agent Bjornson wanted to be her baggage handler, so be it.

Her conscience pinged her.

What was wrong with her?

He'd helped her last night. Maybe she had awakened shirtless, but she'd also been bundled onto a cot with a blasting space heater while the man had slept on a frikking office chair in a cold room.

Don't be an asshole, Ana. Get your shit together and mind your manners.

"Thank you," she said as he approached, exposed biceps flexed, carrying her cases like two shopping bags.

His second grunt sounded something like *'welcome'*, but she couldn't be sure. He didn't head toward the office door as expected, but veered toward the side of the small building and a parked car.

At the car, he stopped, reached into his pocket, and pressed a button on a universal key fob. Releasing the trunk hatch, he tossed the cases into it and closed it.

Agent Bjornson opened the front door on the left of the vehicle, rounded the car, and got in on the right.

She sighed. He was her chauffeur, too.

Settled in next to him and belted, she leaned toward the door to create more space between them.

She didn't want any more accidental readings. She couldn't manage it while she wasn't in full control of her abilities. "Where are we going?"

"Kane Estate."

Ana sucked in a breath.

GPSA Headquarters.

This was more important than she thought.

MAGNUS GLANCED AT HIS passenger while navigating the car up the long drive toward the manor house. He ignored the circular path, steering the car around the back toward the carriage house's converted garage. Pressing a button to open the door, he parked the car, retrieved Agent Ortega's baggage, and led the way through the back halls of the house.

Ortega's heels clicked a staccato behind him as she kept pace with his long strides.

Mentally, he grumbled over her sharp accusations about the integrity of his flight skills.

He quashed the temptation to lengthen his strides and increase his pace.

Thankfully, she maintained her silence.

"Magnus! Give the girl a break!" Agent Raya Burns' voice echoed up the hall. "You're making her run a marathon in heels with the pace you're setting, man."

Magnus halted, swinging around, narrowly missing Ortega with the life-size suitcases, to see Burns' head poking out of a side room they'd just passed.

"No worries... Burns... I can keep up. Good to see you again, by the way... And thanks for the replacement shoes," Ortega said between gasps.

Magnus rolled his eyes, set the luggage down, and backtracked to speak to Burns. "Maeda?"

"Kane's office," Burns said to Magnus. Her gaze swung back to Ortega. "They fit?"

Ortega gave Burns a thumbs up as she rubbed a stitch in her side.

Magnus sighed. "How long have they been there?"

"Couple hours. Ortega's room is in the east wing across from mine."

A couple of hours? Not good. Not surprising, but not good.

He grunted, retrieved the bags, and resumed his quest to deposit Ortega in her room and get on with the investigation they'd gathered for.

"I can do that," Ortega called after him. "I told him I can carry my own luggage." He heard her say to Burns.

Burns snorted. "There's no elevator in this place. Hey Magnus, she has a sweet face but don't let her touch you with her woo-woo hands or she'll steal all your secrets."

"My woo-woo—" Ortega huffed. "Funny."

The clicking heels also resumed behind Magnus, catching up to him shortly after rounding the corner and thankfully turned to dull, rapid thuds when he cut through the study for the service stairs.

Finally, he deposited her bags outside the room Burns had mentioned.

"This place is incredible," Ortega said, stopping next to her bags.

He gestured toward her door.

"Thank you," she said, looking up at him. "Really. For getting me here and hauling my bags." She stuck her hand out in front of his midsection.

The corner of his mouth twitched at the professional gesture after their last *interesting* twenty-four hours together.

Burns' words about woo-woo hands echoed back to him. Whatever that meant. Besides, the only secrets he had that she could steal from him were about his work, and she was already here for that.

Accepting the handshake, the firm effort she put into it surprised him.

"There is a house manager if you need anything. There are phones in the rooms, like in hotels. Since Kane and Maeda are still in a meeting, I'm sure you'll have a bit of time before they send someone for you."

She nodded, not making any effort to go into her room.

"Anything else?"

She bit her lip. "Just an apology." She blew out her breath. "For being so rude last night—"

He lifted a hand to stop her words. "Forgotten. See you around."

He spun away as she drew breath to say something else, and walked away before she could. At the end of the corridor, he opened the door to his own room. Glancing back, he noted Ortega was struggling with the second of her two suitcases.

And Perenga wanted to send this woman to Iceland? The man was losing his faculties after gods only knew how many centuries he'd spent in this planet's oceans. If Ortega could be afflicted with hypothermia from a rainstorm, she'd never survive actual cold weather.

Or maybe they'd redirected the plane here because Perenga realized how much of a mistake sending that woman into the frigid landscape would be.

He shrugged, pulled his shirt off, balled it up and threw it into a hamper as he strode toward his shower.

Not my problem.

I did my job. Now she's Perenga and Burns' problem.

As he stepped under the steaming water, he couldn't help but recall the sensation of her vulnerable body balled up on his lap, shivering in his arms. Her silky-smooth skin smelled of California sunshine, vanilla coconut, and a scent that was uniquely hers.

He blinked away that wreck of a thought-train, snatched the soap from the shelf and began lathering.

She's not my type, anyway.

Magnus was used to women who had a powerful presence, could hold their own on a physical level, and wouldn't fly away with a sneeze.

But, if he was honest with himself, as he usually was, he grudgingly admired her stubborn determination to handle those ridiculous suitcases herself.

Adorable.

And those dimples... when she actually smiled.

Magnus snorted and turned his back to the water stream.

Despite her tantrum, she'd never acted as though anyone ought to serve her. Quite the opposite. He attributed the poor behavior to fear and fever right before she passed out.

He frowned, recalling Burns' words again.

What the hell does that even mean?

He shook away the thought after trying to reconcile the weird statement with the pretty round face, pert little nose over full, pillowy lips.

Soft.

He was sure of it.

He grunted away the thought, glanced down and sighed, noting the erection that told him just how soft he thought Ortega's lips were.

That wouldn't do.

He faced the hot stream again and cranked the faucet, blasting himself with frigid water.

No. That wouldn't do at all.

FOUR

ANA PERCHED ON THE edge of an elegant, silk-embroidered chair stuffed with horsehair, in the most luxurious eighteenth-century library she'd ever been in.

Barely aware she was present, Jolena Kane and Jack Maeda still argued by the floor-to-ceiling French doors overlooking a rolling green that ended some distance away at a dark band of woods. Their coffees, in hand, were also forgotten except to use as emphasis on certain points.

Ana sighed and sipped her own drink. By now, they were on their third iteration of the same debate. Apparently, they'd forgotten her, too, despite her being summoned almost as soon as she'd closed the door to her room after hauling her suitcases in.

Two full-sized suitcases. What was she thinking?

I panicked.

With nothing else to do, she carried on in the theme of the moment and ignited an internal argument with herself over every moment since Carson Perenga's call woke her with the word 'Iceland'.

She shivered and sipped more of her hot coffee.

To a lifelong California girl, images of Iceland evoked frigid, barren landscapes of rock, snow, and ice. Sure, the northern lights would be pretty, but the light show wasn't worth the risk of frostbite.

So, she'd packed almost everything she had in her closet that could be considered colder weather wear. That done, she reminded herself that the routine was to be summoned to your superior's office for a briefing, settled into a hotel to review the file and freshen up before getting to work the following morning.

Pretty much like what was happening now. Here, in Ireland. Not Iceland.

Not for her, just yet, anyhow.

"Look, we were barely able to squeak that ship out of territorial waters before their coast guard arrived," Kane said to Maeda.

"Perenga and McLachlan know what they're doing. They can handle themselves in the deep-sea sectors. It's Ortega I'm worried about."

Ana's gaze snapped to the director. He scowled at Kane, his superior.

"Noted. That's why she's here, instead." Kane's attention flicked to Ana. She turned, finally drank from her cup, and set the vessel on a nearby gilt end table before moving toward her.

Ana set her own cup aside, careful not to rattle the porcelain, and stood to face Kane at eye level. Well, almost at eye level, the other woman stood several inches taller than she did.

"It's good to see you again, Agent," Kane said, extending her hand.

Ana shook it. "Thank you, Madam Kane."

"Feel free to call me Joey, here at the estate. Jack's been keeping me apprised of your progress on this case."

Ana nodded. "I've been working with the rescued survivors and Raya Burns during debriefings when she returns from the field."

"But you've been on leave for the last month."

Ana swallowed. Nodded. "Yes."

Kane's expression softened a fraction. "I was sorry to hear about Private Antony Ruiz. Please accept my condolences and those of the other members of the Organization."

"Thank you, ma'am. We had already separated before... before our team cracked the Montreal trafficking sector. But still on friendly terms until... well, until a few days leading up to the accident."

Kane nodded. "It's hard losing someone you love. And it hasn't been long." She glanced at Maeda. "Your director insists you need more time, Ortega. I ordered Perenga to call you in, despite Maeda's protests."

Ana looked at Maeda's grim expression. He wasn't a soft man. Professional and demanding, often setting Ana through grueling exercises to hone her ability so she could be a stronger tool for the GPSA. People's lives depended on all their abilities to go above and beyond what even the most skilled human agents could do.

Maeda knew what Ana's capabilities were. She respected him to no end.

He was also the only person who knew what had happened, and how deep Antony's loss went.

Ana straightened her spine and shoulders. She'd told Perenga she wasn't ready.

"People's lives are at stake," she finally said.

It wasn't really a choice. She had to set her personal grief and guilt aside.

She went on, "You mentioned a ship, so there are more survivors. When do I talk to them?"

"I had Magnus bring you here instead of Iceland because we've run into jurisdictional resistance, so we have other agents working on that. The ship is being escorted to the north coast where the survivors will disembark. We're working with Garda and the Irish Coast Guard. They know we're a branch of Interpol, but nothing more. They'll care for the survivors and provide us with access to interview them."

"Can I get aboard the ship?"

"I'll make it happen," Kane said, "Maeda is going to consolidate the data and draw up a new plan of action. We're getting close, and any of these survivors could hold the key to where that trafficking hub is located."

"I know. I'll do everything I can." She glanced at Maeda, whose expression hadn't changed as he watched her.

She swallowed. She didn't need to be psychic to sense his disapproval.

"You'll go first thing in the morning. I'd prefer to be there when they disembark, but Garda will want to have their medical needs attended to before we can have them. Magnus Bjornson, Raya Burns and Aaron Connor are your primary team on this." Kane studied Ana's face for a long moment. "I know you're the right person for this case, Ana. That's my superpower." Kane's lips quirked.

Ana's shoulders eased a fraction. "Yes, ma'am."

"Get some rest. There won't be much time for it in the coming days."

"I'll walk you back to your room," Maeda said, striding toward the mahogany paneled door to open it for her. He led her along a different path from what she'd seen before, and she wondered if she'd have the time to get to know the estate's secrets before she went home.

If I go home.

She sucked in a breath at the unexpected thought, but it was true. As a field agent, there was always the danger that one of the team wouldn't make it home.

"Kane's right," she said to Maeda's back as she followed him.

He glanced back over his shoulder. "I don't know that she's right, but she's not wrong."

Ana snorted. "Cryptic as ever."

He slowed his brisk pace. "You know what I mean."

"I know, but we don't have a choice."

He stopped walking. She stopped to face him.

"If your emotions block your ability—."

"I know. And I told Carson I wasn't ready. How can I be?" her voice cracked, "My ability was useless to save Antony and his crew, Jack. I tried to warn him, and it made no difference. He died. They all died anyway. How can I trust that? I thought he could save them if he just knew—." She swallowed down anymore words.

Jack nodded. He understood. He always did.

She'd been having nightmares since the accident. A routine naval exercise gone wrong. Antony and his crew were never recovered from the ocean.

Controlling her grief, she straightened. "But I have to at least try. Any information I can glean is better than no information. You said so when you started training me."

"As long as you can allow enough information in to interpret it correctly and not let your personal emotions taint it."

He resumed walking. Ana followed until they arrived back at her door again.

"Go through the practices tonight. Rest and find your balance."

"Thanks, Jack. For everything."

"You're a good agent, Ana. I know you need more time. Anyone would after a loss like that. But, yes, time is essential, and we need you." He rubbed a hand over his cleanly shaved scalp. "I'll see you in the morning before you leave," he said, and departed back the way they'd come.

She watched him till he rounded the corner and turned back to her door. Hand on the knob, she glanced to the other end of the hall, where she'd seen Magnus go earlier.

Is that his room?

Memories of Magnus Bjornson over the last twenty-four hours flickered through her mind. She was going to be working directly with him.

She twisted the doorknob and entered her room.

Shower first, then practice.

I have no time to waste on thoughts of bearish pilots that smell nice. *Really* nice.

AT THE SOUND OF hurried footsteps, Magnus glanced up from pouring his coffee into a travel mug.

Agent *Ortega, no doubt.*

Seconds later, the woman in question entered through the open door of the breakfast room.

Today she wore a pantsuit and more reasonable shoes.

Her dark hair tumbled down so that it framed her face, making her dark eyes look larger in her small face.

She straightened her shoulders and breezed toward the spread of croissants, scones, muffins, and pastries he had no names for.

The scent that was uniquely hers, mingled with coconut and vanilla, drifted past his nose.

"Good morning," she mumbled, reaching for the raspberry jam and a scone. "Not hungry?"

"Nope." Magnus had eaten a full breakfast between his six a.m. run around the estate grounds, first in his human form, then in his animal form, and a morning shower. His coffee in hand was, in fact, his third of the day—so far.

Studying her down-turned face, he noted the concealer powdered across the delicate skin below her eyes as she stifled a yawn.

Raya Burns' laughter echoed in the corridor before she appeared in the door, followed by another familiar face.

Magnus smiled at his teammates. "Nice to see you up before noon, Connor."

"That's *Agent* Connor to you, Bjornson. And you should try it, you know. You could use the extra hours' beauty rest."

Magnus snorted.

Connor turned to Agent Ortega, proffering a hand. "Aaron Connor."

"Analiese Ortega. Stationed on the West Coast—California," she added as she accepted Connor's hand with a wide smile.

Magnus sipped his coffee as he observed her friendly interaction with Connor.

She hadn't smiled at *him* like that, although she *had* offered her hand as a professional courtesy.

The fine bones of her slim fingers had all but disappeared in his grasp.

Unbidden, he recalled the sensation of her smooth skin under his palm as he tended her unconscious form at the hangar. He cleared his throat, shoving the image of his vulnerable colleague from his mind, and sipped more coffee.

"I see you brought the boots I sent you," Burns said to Ortega.

"You sent Ortega boots? You've never sent me boots, and we've been working together for years," Connor complained.

Mischief glinted in Ortega's eye as the corner of her mouth quirked. "Well, the incident involved a mountain forest run and a taser." She shrugged her narrow shoulders. "Burns owed me."

"Come on, Ortega. What happens on the mountain, stays on the mountain," Burns growled.

Magnus chuckled, recalling Burns' report of events that led Ortega and Perenga to working with their team. "I'm impressed. No one has ever tased Burns before."

"Shit, you must be fast with that thing," Connor said, looking from Ortega to Burns.

"Fast and fierce when it comes to my favorite boots," Ortega said, biting into her scone.

Burns grabbed a couple of pieces of fruit. "I heard Lirikai owes you a new skirt."

"She does. Where is she, anyway?"

"We sent her to Iceland in your stead. Not happy about it, either," Connor said, as he grabbed his own breakfast, and followed the small group over to a table.

"Would anyone be? Better her than me, though." Ortega shuddered. "I hate the cold."

"Bjornson would be. He's the only nutter around here that loves it. Colder the better," Connor said, pulling a chair out for Ortega before she could put her breakfast on the table to do it herself.

Magnus grunted as she smiled at Connor again.

Ortega sat. Her gaze flicked up and down Magnus. "All that Viking blood, I bet."

Connor snorted. "You'd think. Bear blood. Polar Bear."

Ortega's dark brows arched, her expression changing to one of interest. "I've never met a polar bear shifter before."

Magnus' cheeks warmed. He couldn't say why.

"We all know you're a mind reader, and you know Raya is some kind of water spirit." Connor went on. "And I'm a white tiger. Now we all know everyone's secrets."

"Why, agent Ortega, I do believe you've made our Magnus blush." Burns' smooth voice turned mirthful.

"Too damned hot in here," Magnus grunted.

"Yeah, cuz it's not minus sixty-two in Ireland," Connor said. "But I believe you're right, Ms. Burns."

"Leaving in ten minutes," Magnus said, rising from the chair he'd barely occupied. "Don't be late."

"Fastest way to get on his bad side," Connor said to Ortega. "Stickler for punctuality.

"Oh, I know that already. I, uhm...was an hour late getting to the plane to come here."

"Huh, and you're here all in one piece. No chew marks or limbs missing." Connor's gaze flicked between Magnus and Ortega. "Ah, but then, you're cute."

Magnus stalked toward the door, growling, "Don't be late."

Burns' laughter followed him out.

FIVE

THEY RODE TO THE port in the same car she'd arrived in the day before.

Ana sat in the backseat with Raya. From her vantage point, she studied Bjornson's profile.

Pilot. Driver. Polar bear shifter.

Magnus had tied his long blond hair back in a French braid, exposing tattoos adorning the side of his neck below his hairline and behind his bearded jaw, disappearing below the collar of his leather jacket.

She couldn't see which vintage grunge band was on his t-shirt today.

What is that cologne he uses?

She blinked, turning her face away from her temporary teammate, toward the passenger window.

Focus, Ana. It doesn't matter what he smells like. He's your colleague and you have work to do. Do your job, crush the trafficking ring, and go back to your desk in California.

Her gaze drifted back. She couldn't recall the images that had flashed through her mind when they'd touched, when she'd been too distracted to close herself up.

Just the vision of whiteness before she'd passed out.

Her cheeks flamed.

I can't believe I passed out like that. Or the stupid things I said right before.

Awkward start. It was the fever.

She nodded to herself.

Yes, just an awkward start. Set it aside and don't be weird about it.

Resuming her gaze out the window, the port came into view.

Stacked containers hid the body of the ship, but the tower was unmistakable.

At one time, she'd been fascinated with ships of all kinds, because Antony had been a sailor and loved all things water-going.

Not anymore.

I hate this.

Her fingers flexed over her thighs as she rubbed her palms along the fabric of her pants.

Memories crashed through her.

Not mine.

Shared memories she gleaned from survivors and crew alike.

Prophetic images that warned her of Antony's accident.

Not the same.

She had to separate the situations from each other. One was work. The other was personal.

She squeezed her eyes shut. Drew a deep breath through her nose and eased it out between her lips.

Pressure on her forearm drew her attention.

Raya Burns' hand rested on Ana's sleeve, her expression one of compassion. She didn't say anything.

Raya knew.

She knew because she'd seen it, too.

Ana had seen it *all* first through Raya's memories.

Survivors trapped in shipping containers on the freighters. Barely fed or hydrated, dirty and cold, some sick. All headed for a life of enslavement to the highest bidders. Bidders that comprised human and paranormal buyers alike.

Anytime paranormals were involved, the GPSA was called in. And this team had been tracking this specific ring for some time before Ana had called Carson Perenga in to investigate a murder case that led them all together. Here.

She never could have imagined that the mutilated bodies that had turned up in her community on the west coast of California would bring them to this.

An international human trafficking ring, facilitated and organized by paranormals, which had led them to Raya Burns and her team.

The things she had seen in Raya's memories bit deep into Ana and still hadn't let go.

It changed her. Resolved her will to do all she could to help stop it.

Until Antony.

She'd changed, and she'd lost everything.

Ana forced a wan smile for Raya and whispered, "I'm good."

The look Raya gave her said *'bullshit'* but she maintained her silence and released Ana's arm.

Bjornson stopped the car outside the port office. The official on duty came out to meet them.

"Show time," Connor said, before stepping out of the car, Ana right behind him.

"Magnus, stay with Ana, no matter what. I'm going to look around while Connor entertains the officials," Burns said to Bjornson.

Even if Burns couldn't shift during the day, she still knew how to get around unseen. She knew how to be the ghost she became after nightfall.

A moment later, Ana sensed Bjornson at her back.

Used to working alone and taking care of herself, it surprised her that she found comfort in his presence as she turned her gaze toward the freighter looming above the port.

Sure, she'd worked with Carson, Lirikai, Raya, and Ian McLachlan on the last leg of the case, but that was different. Carson was like a big brother to her. Everyone else... sort of grew on her.

But this felt different.

The scent of Magnus' cologne mingled with the sea breeze encircling her.

Not now, Ana.

Focus.

She frowned at how easily she was becoming distracted by this man.

Not even Antony had distracted her in this way. At least, not until his death.

A surge of guilt warred with the sense of relief at realizing something other than the accident occupied her mind.

Neither were appropriate, at this time.

There was work to do.

Balance. Focus. Work.

The port official led them to another building on site, further away from the ship.

Ana eased the tension in her shoulders.

She'd board the ship later. People first.

As she trailed Connor and the official, she extracted her grandmother's crucifix and rosary from her jacket pocket. Looping the rosary around her wrist, she gripped the crucifix and beads in her palm, then checked her other pocket to ensure her phone hadn't slipped out.

Her thumb worried the smooth garnet beads as she sought balance, whispering her mantra with each breath.

Balance. Focus. Feel.

Her senses expanded around her, testing.

The general bustle of the place. The crisscross of natural and human energy.

The official's sadness. Connor's determination. Bjornson's concern.

She sucked in a breath as they stepped into the building.

She'd been expecting it, but it still took her breath away. Every time.

Inside, emotional energy corralled and turned over on itself. A heavy cloud.

It'll be worse on the ship.

They walked through an industrially decorated lobby, along a short corridor and through a double set of doors. Cots and chairs lined the large room where dozens of people slept, sat, or conversed. Medical personnel and local law enforcement were busy doing their jobs.

"They arrived in the wee hours. Near starved and filthy. Some are still getting cleaned up or having their first proper meal in weeks," the port official said.

Ana breathed through the suffocating storm cloud of collective heightened emotion. Her attention turned to a young woman curled up on a cot, staring at the empty one next to her.

Despair oozed from her.

Fear rippled toward Ana from a young man seated on the floor with his back pressed to the wall.

Anger rolled around the room as someone else raged at a police officer who was trying to take a statement.

Ana remembered to breathe. The ridges of the crucifix bit into the pad of her thumb.

Connor and the official were a dim memory as she moved around the room.

Bjornson, silent, moved two paces behind her.

Another young woman stood, leaning against the far wall, facing the room.

Numb.

Different.

She focused on this one.

Ana moved toward a table with a water carafe to fill a glass, then approached the young woman. Once she was in front of her, she realized the woman was much younger than she'd initially thought—a teen? Seventeen? Younger?

"Thirsty?" Ana held out the glass.

The girl turned her haunted gaze to Ana, lifted to Bjornson, then back to Ana and the glass. She shook her head.

Encouraged that the girl understood English, she pressed on.

"Can we talk?"

The girl shrugged.

"There's an empty office we can use," Bjornson murmured next to Ana's ear.

She turned to see the open door he indicated.

"There, okay?" Ana asked the girl.

Her gaze flicked toward the vacant room before she pushed away from the wall and preceded Ana toward it.

Still holding the glass of water, Ana straightened her shoulders and drew several steadying breaths as they followed.

You can do this, Ortega.

Set up for conducting business or interviews, the small room held a chair on one side and two on the opposite.

The girl dropped onto one of the two plastic chairs.

Ana set the glass on the table before her, then settled on the chair beside the girl, facing her.

Bjornson moved toward the back of the room, where he stood vigil.

"Do you mind if I record our chat? I'm an investigator."

Another shrug.

Ana extracted her phone from her pocket, found the voice app, turned it on, and set the device on the table. "I'm Analiese Ortega. What is your name?"

"Sascha," she mumbled, accent thick.

"Where are you from?"

"Varandey."

Ana repeated the answers for clarification on the recorder. "Have the authorities contacted your family yet?"

"No. I have none."

Ana studied Sascha's face. It was gaunt with a lack of basic needs. Her face and hands bore bruises, cuts, and scrapes. Ana suspected there'd be more under her clothes.

"You fought."

Sascha nodded. "I didn't want to get on another ship."

"Another ship," Ana repeated, thoughtful. "May I hold your hands?"

Sascha's gaze flicked to Ana's face, to her upturned palms with the crucifix and rosary and back to her face again. "I don't pray."

"No praying. Just talking."

"You are... a seer?"

"Something like that."

After another moment's hesitation, Sascha placed her frigid fingers over Ana's. Ana slid her hands forward, palms up under Sascha's. She drew another deep breath to allow the remnants of her mental barrier to fall away. She held Sascha's gaze as their energies fizzed.

Ana's hands felt as though they were frosting over, and she fought against a wave of fatigue.

Sascha's numbness was her own mental barrier, protecting her.

The emotion behind that barrier pressed upon them both, waiting for a fissure that Sascha wasn't ready to crack.

Yet.

Ana held firm, seeking.

Finally, after long moments, images flickered through.

But she wasn't seeing survivors like Sascha.

It was the familiar nightmare of Antony's naval vessel.

Ana released Sascha's hands, flexing her fingers.

Focus Ana. Focus!

She tried again.

This time, gaunt faces appeared as she searched Sascha's emotional memories of the last few weeks.

Despair. Fear. Rage.

Ana pressed deeper, seeking the faces of the perpetrators. Whispers of locations. Anything that could send them in the right direction.

Nothing.

Suddenly, the visions changed. Ana no longer guided the flow of memory and emotion. Sascha's numbness dissipated and everything else surged forward, stealing Ana's breath away.

She went rigid under the onslaught as Sascha's memory jerked back to the last beating at the hands of the guards. The last beating because a small group of men stopped it, fought back, protected her and the others in the dank room.

Their faces were familiar to Ana.

"Save them!" A disembodied voice shouted at her.

She flinched away from Sascha again, severing the energetic connection.

Balling her fists on her lap, she drew several deep breaths.

"Who were the men that protected you?"

"I don't know," Sascha said, trembling.

"The room wasn't on a ship."

"No. It was some kind of transfer place."

"Can you tell me more?"

Sascha shook her head as her body trembled.

Ana didn't want to push her too hard, but she wanted to know more about this transfer place.

"Can't you hear him?" Sascha said, eyes fixed behind Ana's left shoulder.

Ana glanced over her shoulder. She saw no one else.

"No. Who is there?"

"I don't know who he is. He just keeps screaming at you," she sobbed.

Save them.

Ana straightened. She'd heard it just once. She was so focused on Sascha, she didn't sense anyone else.

Still couldn't.

"Can you describe him?"

Sascha shook her head, squeezing her eyes shut. "No, I don't want to... dark hair... uniform of some kind. Same as the guys that protected me. Please, I don't want to talk anymore."

The numbness dissipated and emotion surged forward, overwhelming the space surrounding them.

Ana gasped as Sascha sobbed.

"Okay, Sascha, thank you. Thank you for talking to me," Ana said, voice soft as she struggled to reconcile the girl's emotions washing over her.

She closed her eyes, drew a deep, steadying breath, and when she opened them again, the chair across from her was empty.

As it had always been.

Elbows braced on her knees, she leaned forward until her forehead rested on her trembling hands.

"Are you all right?" Magnus' deep voice was quiet in the small room.

"Yes." She glanced at her phone on the table next to the untouched glass of water. She picked up the phone to speak into it. "Interview with bi-located victim in shock before she returned to her body." Ana's hands continued to tremble as she described the interviewee and what they said, since she couldn't be sure how much the recording would pick up of the conversation.

The phone slipped from her fingers, bouncing on the carpet.

Magnus scooped it up, sat across from Ana, and held it for her to finish her report.

When she finished, she turned the recorder off.

"Is it always like that?"

She shook her head. "You're pretty calm for someone that just watched me talk to an empty chair."

"It was a first." His lips quirked. "Who was the other person?"

"I-uhm... don't know." She swallowed.

Antony.

No, it couldn't be Antony. Wouldn't be Antony.

I can't sense anyone else.

"Probably another victim that didn't make it. But she mentioned a group of men trying to protect them in there. Uniforms. She mentioned *'some kind of uniforms'.*"

Magnus nodded. "If you're good to continue, I'll contact Kane and find out if there are reports of missing servicemen, which doesn't fit the usual abductee profile."

"No, it doesn't. But yes, I'll move on to the other survivors. We have a long day ahead of us." She rubbed her palms down her thighs and gripped her knees.

Magnus placed a hand over one of hers. "Let me know how I can help."

Her gaze flicked up to his.

You can't.

"Thank you," she said, standing. "If I think of something, I will." She slipped her phone into her pocket and moved toward the door.

Drawing a breath, she straightened her shoulders and stepped back into the room of survivors to interview.

SIX

MAGNUS NEVER LEFT ANA'S side during the hours of interviews. He didn't think he could, even if he'd been ordered to.

No matter how pale she became or how much her hands trembled, she repeated the process again and again, recording each conversation.

There were no other eerie one-sided interviews like the first.

He'd been present when the tribal shamans conversed with the spirits.

This was different in as much that it lacked the ornate ceremony which normally accompanied the practice.

And yet, in her way, there had been similar points of respect. Permission, an offering, and an expression of gratitude.

Still, Magnus would admit to himself, if never anyone else, the experience had unsettled him. He preferred physical communication. Tangible. Anchored in *this* reality.

As he observed Agent Ortega throughout the day, the care and consideration which she approached every individual she spoke to never wavered.

In between sessions, she uploaded every recording to the cloud where any of the team members could access them. He knew Kane and Maeda would have them transcribed and reviewed within a few days. Neither cared to waste time or effort.

It wasn't until late evening, when the team packed up for the day, that a young woman approached agent Ortega.

"Sascha," Agent Ortega said.

The young woman nodded, hands wringing, gaze on the industrial carpet beneath their feet.

"How are you feeling?" Ortega asked, her voice soft.

"I—we... We spoke earlier?" Sascha asked, lifting her tear-swollen eyes to Ortega.

"We did."

This was the young woman Magnus couldn't see. What was it Ortega had said... bi-located? Not dead. Just... separated somehow. His heart twisted a little as he continued his role as observer.

"I don't understand. I thought it was a dream, but then, I've watched you talk to the others all day. And I don't think it was?"

"No, not a dream, but similar," Ana said, not elaborating.

Sascha seemed to accept this with a slight nod. "I've been thinking. Remembering. I don't want to, but I can't help it."

"It will take time, but you're safe now, Sascha."

Sascha blew out a breath, looking around the large room, and finally nodded.

"I know it here," she pointed to her head. "But here," she laid her hand over her sternum, "not so much."

Ortega gave her time to form what she wanted to say next. Magnus knew there was more. He could feel it himself, and he wasn't a psychic.

"Your recorder. Turn it on."

Ortega extracted it from her pocket and did as instructed.

"The man shouting at you, that you couldn't hear... had dark hair, as I said before, and a uniform of sorts—like the other men in the transfer station but blackened with dirt or smoke. He had a name tag that caught the light."

Magnus moved closer on hearing this.

Ortega didn't move, waiting.

"Ruiz. I think it read."

Ortega's whole body jerked, then went so still, Magnus doubted she drew a breath.

"Are you sure?" she finally asked, voice almost inaudible.

"Yes," Sascha nodded. "This I'm sure about."

"What else do you remember?"

"Just that he kept screaming *'save them, Ana, save them'*. It was very frightening."

Ortega remained quiet for a long moment.

"The men in the transfer station... did they have tags too?"

Sascha shook her head, swallowed hard, and dropped her gaze. "I'm sorry. I can't do this anymore. I had a friend... they took us at the same time. I don't know what happened to her." She lifted her gaze to Ana. Her eyes brimmed with tears.

"Of course, Sascha. When we find her, we will do what we can to reunite you. Thank you for talking to me. Earlier and now. And in the coming days, if you wish."

Sascha reached out to touch Ana's hand, as though testing her solidity. Ana squeezed her hand in return. "Eat some food and get rest. You did wonderfully today."

Sascha sniffled as Ortega released her hand, then threw her arms around Ana as she sobbed.

Ortega embraced the young woman and let her cry as long as she needed. Magnus stood at Ortega's back, observing it all, chest tight.

Everything they heard, every piece of data they collected today, would be added to all the rest of the data they'd collected over the years since they started investigating these traffickers.

We're so close. So, damned, close.

Gods, I want to shut these fuckers down and make them pay for what they've done to so many innocent people.

So many victims stolen. Families fractured, communities mourning.

And for what?

So someone can make money.

He swallowed his revulsion and calmed the rush of emotion before approaching Ortega and the survivor, Sascha.

Sascha let go of Ortega and moved away without another word.

He glanced up at movement across the room. Connor and Burns waited by the door.

"Time to go," he whispered by Ortega's shoulder.

She turned to look up at him, eyes haunted, as she acknowledged his words with a nod.

In that instance, he wanted nothing more than to pull her into his arms and give her the comfort she'd given so many others this day.

Instead, he followed her out of the room to join the others who'd moved out into the hall. They both studied Ortega with grim expressions. Burns rubbed Ortega's shoulder, but said nothing.

They walked back to the car and Magnus drove them back to Kane's estate.

Each team member was silent as they reflected on their day's work, mentally preparing for the next.

"YOU'RE TELLING ME WE lost another fucking ship?" Adolf Wulker's heart pounded as he stared at his subordinate.

"Yes, sir, but we used our connections to put up some jurisdictional roadblocks. They shouldn't be able to trace the ship's point of origin."

"But another ship, with all of its cargo, is lost. That shipment had a very particular order for a very important client." Wulker's fist slammed the top of his solid oak desk, making loose objects jump and rattle.

"How did we lose it in the first place?" He held up a hand, stopping the other man from speaking. "No. Never mind, I don't care. This careless loss of merchandise is going to stop. Now. See to it."

The assistant dry-swallowed and croaked. "Yes, sir."

Wulker waved him away.

"An unfortunate by-product of any trade business. A reasonable insurance write-off." The forgotten blonde woman in the corner of the room said, as she rose to her feet.

Recalling her presence, Wulker scowled at her. "This one was lost in *your* territory."

She breezed toward him. "My brother was aboard that ship, but I trust he'll have evacuated with the crew, yes?"

He couldn't help himself. Despite his annoyance, desire surged through him as his gaze swept her pouty lips, full breasts, narrow waist, and generous hips.

Adolf nodded.

"I'll talk to my people," she murmured, pressing her soft breasts to his chest.

Unable to resist, his hand drifted down her waist to her ass and groped as she leaned in to kiss him. As his arousal grew, his hand shifted, splitting into two distinct tentacles extending from his cuff, drifting lower down her hip. One encircled her thigh, the other drifted up under the hem of her short skirt, teasing.

She moaned.

He grinned, enjoying the power he had over her.

He stepped back, releasing her. His limbs merged, returning to human form. "Set up a meeting. We need to discuss a change in procedure."

She frowned at the extra space he put between them. "Of course."

"Impress the importance that this meeting be face to face."

"My former father-in-law won't be eager for that, no matter that we've... persuaded him otherwise."

"I'm well aware of how difficult he is to control, despite the formidable power of my venom's persuasion. I'm also aware he doesn't welcome outsiders to clan territory, nor does he like to leave his people for any length of time. As you've reminded me. But if he wishes to continue to provide them with security and prosperity, then he will meet with me."

"Where and when shall I propose this meeting take place?"

"I'll keep it simple. The stronghold. As soon as possible."

She arched her brow, nodded, and left the room.

"An unfortunate by-product indeed," he murmured as he approached the vast window of his office overlooking the skyline of Barentia across the narrow channel.

Maybe once the meeting details were set, he would accept her less-than-subtle offer of intimate play time.

For now, there was work to do.

Work first, play later.

However, Adolf did allow himself to indulge in just a few moments of fantasizing about their future bedroom escapades. He did prefer to plan *everything*, after all.

SEVEN

ANA'S BREATH SHUDDERED AS she popped her earpiece in place before embarking on the freighter.

She moved aboard the ship, both hands grasping her phone, carefully positioned close to her midsection so she wouldn't accidentally touch anything.

That would come later.

Magnus, her ever-present shadow, moved silently several paces behind.

She still found it difficult to grasp just how such a large man could move with such stealth.

Equally, while she couldn't comprehend her instinctual acceptance of his nearness consciously, she willfully accepted it.

Regardless of her comfort level, her fingers still drifted over the reassuring presence of her taser tucked safely away should she need it. The ship had been checked, but it was always a possibility that someone could hide if they knew the nooks and crannies well enough.

She glanced over her shoulder.

Magnus' gaze swept the deck of the ship, assessing. Fierce, determined concentration.

Anyone looking to tangle with that man was on a mission of serious self-harm, or had lost their reason.

Forcing her attention back to the task at hand, she switched on her recorder and began her own method of investigation.

Balance. Focus. Feel.

Speaking in a voice low enough for the earpiece to pick up her voice, yet quiet enough that most humans couldn't pick out the words, she made her way across and through the ship, documenting everything she observed.

Physically and psychically.

She welcomed the familiar haze.

Aware of her surroundings yet lost in the mental images and sensations bombarding her, she struggled at first to just let them flow around and through her.

Her breath came fast under the onslaught. Every muscle in her body fought against it, tense and rigid. Until she repeatedly reminded herself to surrender.

At the top of the metal stairs leading down into the hold, she hesitated.

Revulsion rippled through her.

That self-preservative part of her was screaming not to descend.

That way led to too much pain.

What sane person would willfully inflict the torrential pain of others on themselves?

Her breath hitched.

But isn't that why Antony left you in the first place?

Because you no longer operated like a sane person?

He died believing that.

"Agent Ortega? Are you alright?" Magnus' voice was muffled in her current state.

Magnus.

"Ana?" His voice broke the spell.

She blinked. "Yes, I'm fine."

She descended the stairs. It was several degrees colder below deck and growing colder the deeper she went.

The temperature change was both natural and supernatural.

"A few of the victims died down here," she murmured, moving ever closer to the holding crate.

The GPSA team hadn't found any digital trackers, documents, or maps left behind. The crew must have disposed of them into the ocean or taken them with them when they escaped.

Otherwise abandoned, the ship had drifted with its cargo.

It was that information that they needed.

The departure point and destination point.

Balance. Focus. Feel.

First, she had to document what she could register below decks.

She drew another deep breath and allowed her instinct to guide her. Moving along one corridor, she followed it until it opened up to the main hold and kept going until she stood before the steel containers.

In her mind's eye, she could see all of them, victims and crewmen alike, in various states, dependent on what their strongest emotions were at the time they were in this place.

A suffocating jumble. Still, she opened herself up as wide as possible, flowing through it all until *something* tugged at her.

The energetic signature of shifters, not the signatures of the human cargo.

Focusing on those, she moved toward another area where rusty splotches stained the floor.

Pain.

She tensed as her protective barrier slammed into place, blocking everything out.

"Dammit!"

I need better control.

She drew a breath. Held it and tried again.

But all she could sense now, was the distinct polar bear shifter signature that she identified with Magnus now that she knew what he was.

"I need more space. Wait here," she said, and moved away from him, crossing the stained floor to the other wall.

But it didn't make any sense. The signature was stronger here, where it should have been weaker when she moved away from Magnus.

Save them.

Antony.

Ana froze, swallowing a sob of frustration.

How can I do my job if my guilt over Antony's accident keeps interfering?

She straightened her shoulders, determined to ignore the echo of Antony's voice from her nightmares.

Moving further away from Magnus, she tried to grasp the faint tethers of energy that had drawn her here to begin with.

Still rife with polar bear shifter energy, she followed it anyway. Maybe it wasn't Magnus she was picking up on after all, since it led away from him.

Curious, she followed the energy trail. Which led her to another section of the ship.

A vast room containing the ship's engine, with pipes and machinery jutting out of it in what seemed like controlled chaos to Ana.

The signature that guided her here lost its direction and seemed to surround her now. Unable to pinpoint where to go next, she resigned herself to placing a hand on the steel railing between herself and the engine.

But not just yet.

Realizing she'd forgotten to talk through her path, she quickly recapped where she was.

"Energy signature similar to Agent Bjornson's led me to the engine room from the cargo hold. I'm going to make first physical contact here." She finally placed her hand on the rail and continued to move forward as she searched through the images of crewmen that had been here until she found the person associated with the signature.

The vision of a young man, similar in build to Bjornson, crouched along this rail, injured.

She followed it to the end, where a bank of steel paneled controls faced her.

Save them.

An overpowering sense of urgency surged through her. She dropped her phone into her pocket and placed both hands on the massive control box. Moving around the side of the control panels, she saw a gap between it and the wall, close to floor level.

The urgency increased, and she found a section with a missing panel.

"Here," she shouted to Bjornson as she got down on her hands and knees. "There's something here."

Unable to see into the darkness of the cramped space, she reached out a hand, seeking whatever hid in the box.

She hadn't expected her hand to land on what felt like a foot. A cold human foot.

Startled, she cried out and fell back.

Bjornson appeared beside her. "Are you alright?"

"There's someone in there. I don't know if they're alive or not."

He left her to peer into the space, pulling out his phone to aim its light into the darkness.

"Shit. We've got a body hidden inside the engine room's control panels," he spoke into his earpiece. "Vital status undetermined."

As soon as the shock of finding a human body rather than an object passed, Ana approached and replaced her hand on the foot, trying to sense their spirit. "I think they're still alive. Yes! He's alive, but barely."

Within minutes, an emergency response team arrived and got to work extracting the survivor.

Now they just had to determine who this man—polar bear shifter—was, and why he was there.

MAGNUS ANXIOUSLY STOOD ASIDE while the medical team worked to free the man hidden inside the engine room's control panel.

"Magnus, he's a shifter." Ana's voice was quiet.

He looked down into her upturned face, tight with concern. "A polar bear shifter, like you."

The blood drained from his face. If that were the case, why hadn't he recognized the scent right away? And what the hell was one of his kind doing aboard this ship? Who was he?

Magnus crouched next to the opening again while the crew worked to remove the steel framing of the box surrounding the pipes and wires to determine how to extract the man safely.

He inhaled, scenting.

Yes, now he could pick out the distinct, faint scent familiar to him, but it wasn't right. Familiar yet distorted. It was... other. Someone he knew. Polar bear, yes, but tainted.

Finally, after cutting through the steel paneling, the team lifted it off, allowing the light to wash over the hidden man.

The side panel came away, and the man rolled free, unconscious.

"Fuck." Magnus barked, chest tight, as he shoved team members aside to get a closer look at the man's face. "Aksel Matochkin."

As gently as he could, he lifted him off the floor and carried him to the awaiting gurney so the medics could work on him right away.

He backed off to give them space, listening as they assessed.

"We need to get him to GPSA Medics," he said to Ana.

She nodded and pulled her phone from her pocket to make the call.

By the time the medical team could safely bring their patient out of the ship and transferred to the docks, the GPSA medical staff were already landing via a nearby helipad to take him into custody.

Magnus helped load Aksel into the helicopter, identifying him as one of his clansmen.

His instinct was to accompany him to see to his care and find out how the hell he was on this ship.

But that would have to wait. Answers would have to wait. For now, Magnus had to trust the GPSA medical team to do their jobs while he did his.

He and Ana still had work to do aboard the ship.

EIGHT

ANA RUBBED HER FINGERS across the back of her neck, kneading the muscles as she listened to the rest of her teammates give their reports to Kane, now that they were all back at the estate.

After the extraction of Magnus' clansman, Ana had continued her investigation with little success. The only directional intention she could glean was 'north', which was pretty darned useless as far as she was concerned.

She looked up as Magnus crossed the back of the room again.

He was with them in body, but his mind was visibly with his clansman.

"Bjornson, will you sit? Your pacing is making me twitchy," Aaron Connor snapped, cutting into what Raya was saying.

Magnus scowled at Aaron, but dropped into the leather chair next to Ana.

Raya resumed.

Ana tuned out Raya's words as Magnus' energy swarmed her, stealing her breath away.

"I'm sure he'll be alright. Our medics are the best." She reached out, hesitated for only a second to ensure her psychic barrier was in place, then laid her hand over his on the arm of the chair.

Magnus blew out his breath, looking down at her hand on his. "I know. He flipped his hand over, so they were palm to palm, giving her fingers a slight squeeze.

Shivers rippled through her at the intimate contact. She struggled against the urge to slide her fingers between his, anchoring them together.

She looked up into his face, his eyes locked on hers, thoughtful. "He would have died in there if you hadn't found him."

"Maybe, maybe not," she said, trying to make light of her role.

Magnus snorted. "He's a polar bear. If he's unconscious, he's in a bad way." He glanced at the door.

"Magnus, what else can you tell us about our patient?" Director Kane asked, drawing the focus of the meeting back to Bjornson.

Palm still tingling, Ana withdrew her hand from Magnus' light grasp.

"There really isn't anything more I can add to the report I filled out earlier."

Kane picked up the sheaf of paper. "Aksel Matochkin, twenty-two years old, kinsman by marriage via your former wife, Ulla Matochkin."

Magnus nodded.

Former wife?

Magnus was—had been married? Ana wasn't sure why it surprised her, given that she knew nothing about the man next to her. It had only been a few days since she boarded his charter.

"When's the last time you saw Aksel?"

Magnus drew a deep breath and blew it out on a heavy exhale, staring at the floor. "The day they banished me."

Banished?

Ana's gaze shot to Magnus' solemn face, then to Kane and the others.

They all know.

Despite not being a shifter, even Ana knew that banishment from a clan was bad.

Very bad.

And he worked for Kane and the GPSA? How the heck did that make sense? What could he possibly have done that was so bad, that the only answer was banishment? Or death.

She glanced at him again and decided she was glad it was the former.

But if he worked for Kane, it couldn't be *so* bad, could it?

She'd never got that kind of vibe from him, not even when she'd accidentally read him on that first night. Which knocked her out. Along with the fever. She still blamed *that* mostly on the fever.

Or… had it been something more?

She searched his profile, tempted to lower her barrier and prod. But that would be an invasion of his privacy.

Not something she would deliberately do to her teammates unless directly ordered to do.

Deliberate reading or not, she couldn't ignore the waves of guilt and regret that emanated from him. And something more. Deeper. Heartache.

The urge to take his hand and offer him comfort again was overwhelming.

Heartache for his former wife?

She clasped her hands on her lap, fingers locked together as she passingly acknowledged her own fleeting feelings of disappointment and jealousy.

Jealousy?

You've barely known the man a few days, she reminded herself. *What's wrong with you?*

She entertained the notion for a few seconds. Only a few. That was all she needed.

Tall, amazing hair, muscle-y in that bear-like way and smells really, really great.

Then she promptly shut that line of thought down.

Colleague. Grumpy—in a cute way. Colleague. Professional. Gentleman. Colleague.

She recalled waking in her burrito-blanket-roll, eyes opening to the image of his bare-chested form sleeping upright on an office chair.

Who does that?

That doesn't sound much like the type of guy that gets himself banished from his clan, does it?

Ana!

She squeezed her eyes shut to control her wayward thoughts.

She was so busy self-analyzing that she missed when the topic changed.

"... when he wakes up. Otherwise, you'll have to investigate this further," Kane said.

"You mean go home and talk to my father?" Magnus spat the words. "You know, I might not make it that far if they have orders to kill me as soon as I cross the territorial boundary."

"They won't, and you know it."

"No, they'd want to know why I was there first, then kill me."

"So, you give them a reason that would get you in to see him."

"Death or marriage."

Kane raised a brow. "Explain."

"Normally when someone is banished, that's it. They're dead to the clan. However, as the king's heir and son, proof of death would be necessary, therefore my body would need to be returned."

"And marriage?"

"Along the same lines as death. The registrar needs to record vital information in the clan histories. They must keep the information tracking the lineages. If I were to marry, this would logically lead to an heir that could return and challenge for leadership at some point, despite *my* position of banishment."

King's heir and son? Magnus was a polar bear prince?

Ana was dying to know why they banished Magnus from his clan.

"Okay, that's perfect. If we can't rouse your brother-in-law to consciousness in the next day or two, you're going to your father to report your marriage."

"What?" Magnus shot to his feet.

"Well, you can't go and report your death now, can you? Marriage it is."

He snorted, throwing his hands up. "And who am I supposed to present to him as my wife?"

Kane seemed thoughtful as she regarded him. "Not Burns. They'd smell her and know instantly she isn't human, which would raise suspicions. That leaves Ortega."

"What—what?" Ana popped to her feet next to Magnus. "I can't marry Bjornson!"

"Hey, no one said anything about actually getting married," Magnus growled. "Besides, Ortega's too frail to even survive the trip there."

"I'm not frail!" she objected, fists landing on her hips.

"Sweetheart, anyone who gets hypothermia from a rainstorm is frail," Magnus rounded on her, brows furrowed.

"Well... I..." She crossed her arms. "Whatever, I don't want to go anyway, so it's a moot point."

"Want to or not. Your orders are to go to Barentia and pretend to be Magnus' bride-to-be if his kinsman doesn't wake up to explain what the hell he was doing on that ship."

"BRIDE-TO-BE..." MAGNUS GRUMBLED AS he sat next to Aksel's hospital bed, which had been set up in a room at Kane's estate. GPSA medics that knew how to handle shifter physiology closely monitored him.

Despite the ridiculous proposal, the underlying seriousness of Aksel's state was undeniable. He was alive—barely, but he wasn't healing either.

Magnus studied the younger man's bruised face. He'd been carefully cleaned up, his broken leg encased in a cast. The grime had obscured many cuts and bruises, testament to the fact he'd been beaten—severely. Many times.

Magnus swallowed hard. Aksel was still a kid the last time they'd seen each other, and it hadn't been a happy parting.

Obviously. There was nothing happy about a banishment where everyone was expected to treat the banished like a pariah as they cast him out, hurling objects and bitter words.

Before that day, Aksel had been like Magnus' own little brother. He'd certainly loved him like he was his blood.

Blood didn't matter anymore. Nor did kinship. None of those things existed in Magnus' world since he'd been cast out.

I can't go back.

His father had ensured that.

He rubbed a hand over his face and beard, scrubbing the memories away as he moved to sit in the chair at the foot of Aksel's bed.

Why the fuck was Aksel on that ship? He wasn't human—he was a powerful member of Barentia's polar bear shifter clan. So how is it possible for him to even be in this state? Prone, vulnerable and near death, unable to heal, let alone awaken and tell Magnus what happened to him.

Even when Magnus had experienced the worst of the worst in clan life by being banished, no matter what they'd thrown at him, or insults they'd hurled, he'd still had his physical strength to keep him alive, alone in the frozen northern wastelands.

When he'd almost died of starvation, or drowning from swimming for days, exhausted, he'd still healed.

Aksel wasn't healing.

Why?

Magnus' gaze swept over Aksel's prone form. The blanket covered most of his body, leaving his clan markings visible above it. A mixture of his Matochkin home clan and Barentian adoptive clan.

Magnus swallowed down the long-buried homesickness that threatened to rise. He hadn't seen such familiar body art, other than his own, in a decade.

As he looked at the young man's exposed tattoos, Magnus noticed one that stood out, stark and fresh on the base of his throat, but partially obscured by his thick beard.

Magnus rose from his chair and approached the bed, bending to inspect Aksel's throat.

His stomach dropped, his heart stopped, and he closed his eyes. *Fuck.*

Leaning on the rail at the foot of the bed, he forced himself upright.

He gave himself a moment to collect his despair and his rage before reaching for his phone to call Kane.

"We've got a problem. A big one."

NINE

ANA GLANCED AT THE text that flashed across her phone, which lay on her bed while she dried her hair and sighed.

'Meet in my office asap.'

She'd only had enough time to shower after the long, long day and what seemed to be an even longer meeting.

I can't believe Kane even suggested I pretend to be engaged to Magnus. What a ridiculous ruse.

And yet, nothing about Kane's demeanor hinted at any type of humor.

She glanced at the phone again.

Kane wouldn't call them back to her office if it weren't important.

Ana scrubbed her hair as quickly as she could with the towel that encircled her head, then threw on her silk nightgown and reached for her robe. Shoving her bare feet into her fuzzy slippers, she belted her robe and left her room as Raya was leaving hers, still fully dressed, her brows deeply furrowed with concern.

She gave Ana a cursory once over and smirked. "Cute slippers."

"Any idea what this is about?"

Raya shrugged. Her concerned expression returned, "Nope, but we should hurry."

At that, they jogged the rest of the way.

They arrived at Kane's open office door, where she was still at her desk. Connor sat in the leather chair that Ana had occupied earlier in the evening while Magnus stood by Kane's desk with a haunted expression.

Ana's stomach churned.

What could have happened in the last twenty minutes that was so urgent?

Aksel Matochkin was stable and in the care of GPSA medics. Had he taken a turn?

Kane gestured for them to sit.

"What's happened?" Raya said as she took the other chair.

Ana perched on the same antique chair from the first day, arms crossed.

"Aksel is marked."

"Shit," Connor spat.

"Oh no," Raya whispered, turning wide eyes on Magnus. "Oh no."

"Marked? What do you mean?" Ana demanded after seeing their reactions.

"Magnus, would you show Ana the picture?" Kane said.

Magnus withdrew his phone and swiped his screen, producing an image.

Ana rose from her seat and approached to see a human throat with a black ink sigil at its base.

"A tattoo? On his throat?" She looked up at Magnus, who nodded. "What does it mean?"

"It seems to be some kind of hex," Raya said, her voice full of disgust.

"Magic?" Ana said, incredulous. "But... why?"

"It's most likely the reason he isn't healing. It's keeping him weak."

"And unconscious?"

"Not by design. He's unconscious because he was beaten so badly and cannot heal naturally because of the sigil. Medical science is doing its best to support his body where his shifter ability can't."

"But I still don't know what this sigil means. Why would he have it? Is it something to do with the trafficking ring?"

"Yes," Kane said. "It's the mark of one of the sector heads that we're tracking. We've only seen it a few times, and it's never resulted in anything good."

"What do you mean?" Ana's hand shot to her chest, fingers tugging on the edges of her robe as her anxiety spiked.

Dark magic is way out of my league.

"It means that unless we can find a way—which we haven't yet—to break this hex, the only way we can communicate with Aksel is through you."

All the blood drained from Ana's face and a chill swept through her like a north front.

"I—I see." She drew a breath. "And what if I can't?"

"Then we're going into clan territory completely blind," Magnus said.

"LIKE HELL I'M GOING into polar bear clan territory!" Ana squeaked at Kane, eyes wide, still gripping the front of her thin robe across her throat. She freed a hand to swipe the air in front of her. "N—No. I agreed to Iceland, for Carson—who's not even frigging here, by the way! But the Barents Sea? No. No way." She turned toward Magnus, jabbing the air in his direction with a pointed finger. "No."

Then she spun around in her fuzzy slippers and stomped out of the Director's office, the bottom edges of her robe billowing out behind her.

Burns stared after Ana, mouth gaping. "I've never seen her lose her shit like that before. She's always so damned calm, like an unruffled cat."

"Seems that cat just got her tail stomped on. Good job, Magnus. Great way to break the new recruit in."

"Shut up, Connor," Magnus growled as he followed Ana out—and not sure why he did.

Just to calm her down and make her see reason, he told himself, since Kane had insisted that she was the only agent that could do this mission.

Which he seriously, seriously doubted.

There has to be someone else that can do it. Someone that won't shrivel at the sight of snow.

Still, Magnus didn't like to see her so rattled. Especially not after how she'd handled herself for the last couple of days. She'd been so empathetically solid for all of those survivors they'd interviewed. So calm and collected as she led their team through the ship to find his near-dead clansman.

And she hadn't even been working on these cases nearly as long as he and the others had.

Just before he caught up to her billowing robes, halfway down the hall to their rooms, he admitted to himself he respected her.

Her professionalism and compassion in the face of such hardship.

"Ana."

"No." Her index finger jabbed the air as she swung her arm out behind her, but she didn't slow her pace.

Two more strides and Magnus reached for her arm, trying to slow her without hurting her. "Listen."

"I. Am not—." She heaved a deep breath. "Going. To The *North*. I'm not." She shook her head, eyes wild as she looked at him, then up and down the hall in case anyone else was coming to force her into the barren frozen wilderness. "Not happening."

"If you would just listen—."

"Nope. Nuh-uh. As I said, I was willing to go to Iceland for Carson because he's like a brother and he's always had my back. Thank *God*, I ended up here instead. And now, what? You're going to try to make me go into hostile territory? I'm not trained for that. It's so much worse than Iceland." She sobbed on the last few words.

"You're exhausted."

"You're demented," she snapped.

"And you're being rude again." Noting the red splotches of color appearing on her cheeks. Just like it did before she passed out in the hangar. He tried to take a softer approach. "Ana, you've pushed yourself really hard these last few days. Get some rest and we can talk about this tomorrow."

She'd handled herself impeccably, and now, at the mention of going to his homeland, she was losing her shit? It was the Iceland incident all over again.

"Magnus, I can't."

Something about those three words and the haunted look in her eyes cracked his heart. Her lower lip trembled.

"I told Carson I wasn't ready. Maeda knows it. This is way over my head."

Magnus reached for Ana, wrapping his arms around her trembling body, trying to comfort her.

She sagged against him. "If I couldn't save Antony, how can I save anyone else? And now there's black magic involved?"

Magnus didn't answer. He didn't have one to give, so he just held her. After a moment, her hands slid around his waist, and she held him back.

Closing his eyes, he rested his cheek on the top of her damp hair, inhaling the fragrance of her.

Coconut and vanilla and Ana.

The way she fit in his arms...the way hers felt around him...felt... *Right*.

He smiled against the top of her head when he felt her thumb stroking his spine.

Ana turned her face, resting her forehead against his chest, and drew a deep breath.

"You always smell so good," she murmured.

"So do you." He lifted his head from hers, inhaling her scent again.

Memorizing it, as though he hadn't already.

She leaned back just enough to look up into his face. Her eyes shimmered in the low light of the hallway they still stood in.

He wished they were in his room, or hers.

She searched his face.

What is she looking for?

His gaze dropped to her plump lips, waiting for her to say what she was thinking, or ask a question.

He hadn't expected her little pink tongue to dart out, to moisten her lips.

That tiny movement undid Magnus. A growl rumbled through his chest.

Her fingers clutched at his back now as her face tilted up to his descending lips.

Her mouth was ripe and lush, warm and inviting as the entire length of her body pressed to his.

He was suddenly hyper-aware that the only barrier between them was her thin nightgown and robe.

Dear gods, he wanted to take her to bed.

He hardened against the warmth of her belly, and she pressed into him even more.

Her tongue swept his lower lip, drawing him in.

He growled a second time, forcing her back a step to pin her body between his and the ornate wallpaper.

She gasped against his lips as his thigh moved between hers, pressing into her heat, eliciting a moan.

"Magnus," she gasped.

His name, like that, from her... too much.

His hands moved up to her shoulders, caressing their way up her collar bones to her delicate throat to cradle her face as he kissed her.

His voice was low, almost a whisper of restraint as he spoke, a breath away from her soft lips.

"Ana, sweetheart, if you don't want to finish this," he paused, drawing a breath, "then we should part ways here."

Her sweet breath shuddered against his, her body pliant, her lips parted.

All he had to do was lift the hem of her gown and she'd be his. It was all he had in him to resist the temptation to slide his palm along her thigh, to draw it up around his hip and settle into her heat.

She didn't move as she considered his words.

His heart pounded in time with his throbbing cock.

He drew a deep breath to clear the lightheadedness, but all it did was embed the scent of the woman locked in indecision before him.

Slowly, she dropped her forehead to his chest as she slid her palms around from his back to his abdomen before she leaned back against the wall.

Releasing her face, Magnus' hands retraced their path back down to her shoulders. He slid them along the length of her arms till he found her hands.

Taking them in his, giving them a little squeeze before releasing her, he backed a step, pulling her with him as they continued down the hall, the fingers of his right hand still entwined with those of her left until they found her room.

At her door, he lifted her fingertips and brushed his lips across her knuckles before letting go of that last little bit of contact and regaining full control over his body.

She reached for the doorknob, then turned to look at him, about to say something.

His heartbeat quickened.

She settled on, "Good night, Magnus."

He nodded, "Good night, Ana." He turned, striding toward his room. He heard her door click shut just before he reached his.

TEN

ANA DRAGGED HERSELF OUT of bed, stumbled toward the shower, and forced her chaotic, exhausted emotions into a semblance of order.

After a kiss like that, how could anyone sleep?

Every inch of her body was hypersensitive and wound to the point of snapping.

All she could think about was the taste, smell, and feel of Magnus.

Magnus! How the heck had that happened?

She turned on the shower faucet with a snap.

It had all seemed to happen so quickly and without warning.

A moment of comfort quickly turned into something more.

When had she decided she wanted him before her brain knew it?

A small inner voice told her. She knew exactly when.

She tested the water before disrobing and stepped under the stream of warm water.

That first night on the tarmac when he'd taken her hand and helped her board the plane after lifting her suitcases like paper bags.

She soaped her loofah.

The sensation of being enveloped in his arms... heaven. She'd never, ever, felt so secure as she had in that moment. Like the world outside of their little impulsive sphere didn't matter.

God, that kiss—had almost made her feral.

The memory of his growl, low and deep, reverberating through her, igniting every erogenous zone in her body.

She slid her soapy hands over her skin, reveling in the cascade of warm water, imagining Magnus' lips following the trail of water over her taut nipples.

This wasn't helping to calm her nerves.

Her fingers found her core, gasping as they brushed over her sensitive, throbbing nub.

She needed the release that hadn't found its natural end last night. It had only grown. Her fingers worked to find it.

Magnus.

The gentle rasp of his silky beard against her skin, his soft lips and the sweep of his tongue on hers.

She gasped and moaned, pulsing around her fingers, body finally sagging under the cleansing water.

She drew a deep, shuddering breath, opened her eyes and stared at the tiles until they focused again and finished her shower.

There was work to do, and she couldn't afford to be distracted.

MAGNUS STOOD NEXT TO Aksel's inert body. The medical equipment monitoring his vitals assured him he was still alive.

Kane stood by the window, glaring at her phone, furiously tending to emails while they waited.

Magnus glanced at his watch and, like magic, Ana appeared in the open doorway.

She paused, gave him a curt nod, and glanced in Kane's direction, who waved in acknowledgment, then approached the bed.

With Aksel's bed between them, Magnus assessed Ana's expression.

She focused on Aksel, her demeanor serious and professional.

As though last night had never happened.

Neither said anything until Kane approached, dropping her phone into her jacket pocket. "Are you ready?" she asked Ana.

"There's never any guarantee with this," she warned.

"I know. I'm also aware that you've already given a lot over the last few days. But we need this."

Ana's gaze swept Magnus' face before turning back to Aksel.

"Okay." She pulled her phone from her pocket, set it to record, and drew a deep breath. "What do you want me to focus on?"

"The sigil," Kane said.

"How he ended up on that ship." Magnus answered at the same time without looking at Kane.

"They're probably connected, right?" she murmured as she turned her focus away from the other occupants of the room and trained her energy on Aksel, then opened her senses.

For a long time, she stood beside the man, seeking to connect with his energy.

"His signature is still weak. All I can detect from him is that he vibrates on the same level as Magnus. That's how I knew he was a shifter, and what kind." She frowned. "He didn't draw me to him. It must have been something else that led me to find him. He's not reaching out—like he's locked inside."

"The sigil," Kane repeated.

Ana set the phone on a level spot on the mattress and extracted her Gran's garnet rosary from her pocket. She wrapped the beads around her left wrist and gripped the crucifix between her thumb and forefinger.

Ana held her right hand over Aksel's bare forearm and planted her feet.

Balance. Focus. Feel.

Her fingers hovered over the fine red hairs of his freckled arm a moment before descending the last few inches to rest on his cool flesh.

A wave of frigid water washed over her, stealing her breath away, followed by flashes of a white barren landscape, the face of a beautiful blond woman, and then the sensation of fists connecting with flesh and bone before the pain of impact on her face, and gut.

It all hit her in a matter of seconds, leaving her gasping and doubled over.

"Ana!" Magnus' voice pulled her from the haze of pain and suffocation.

Her hand snapped open, releasing Aksel's arm.

She dragged a hard, gasping breath into her lungs. "I'm okay," she croaked, struggling for more air before describing what she saw.

Her gaze flicked over Aksel's still inert form, curling her right hand into a tight fist. "It doesn't mean anything. You can guess all of that just by looking at him."

"Try again."

"Kane, just give her a minute. She's already exhausted from the last few days," Magnus growled.

Kane turned to him, brow raised. "I am well aware, Agent Bjornson." To Ana, she said, "Agent Ortega, when you're ready to resume your work, place your palm over the sigil."

Ana warily looked from Magnus to Kane to Aksel's pale, bruised face.

Maeda had warned her against direct contact with such things during their training sessions.

After that first reading, she wasn't sure she was ready to touch the sigil. It could do anything to her.

Lifting her left hand, she pressed her lips to Gran's silver crucifix, whispering a prayer as she repositioned her stance next to the bed.

She ignored Magnus and Kane, focusing all her attention on Aksel's face.

This was about *him*. A victim, like all the others, she hoped to God would be a survivor, unlike so many of those they couldn't reach.

Flexing the fingers of her right hand, she pressed her palm to the black ink sigil at the base of Aksel's throat and closed her fingers in a firm grasp.

This time, it was a wave of suffocating black ink that washed over her, rather than frigid water, forcing her to her knees.

Still, she didn't let go.

Her grip on Aksel was her lifeline to reality.
She couldn't let go.

ELEVEN

MAGNUS LUNGED FORWARD, DESPERATE to separate Ana from his kins-man.

"No!" Kane slipped between Ana and him and shoved him back with such unexpected force that his back hit the wall several feet behind him. "Let her do her job."

Magnus was startled by a glow in Kane's eyes he'd never seen before as her voice pinned him in place.

Then he realized she hadn't physically touched him.

What the fuck?

He snarled at her. "Release me."

"Not until you understand you cannot interfere."

He struggled against the invisible bond.

"I know this is harming her and what the risks are, Magnus. We have no choice. She is meant to do this, as are you."

"What the fuck does that mean?" He couldn't unpin his spine from the wall or force his arms forward more than an inch or two.

"It doesn't matter. We need all the information she can get about this sigil, Magnus."

The raw emotion in her voice took some of the fight out of him.

"Burns and Connor left this morning to meet with Lirikai, Perenga and McLachlan in Iceland. They're getting closer to the location of the hub. But this sigil changes everything. We have to know more before we move in."

His gaze fixed on Ana's kneeling, trembling form. He stopped struggling against Kane.

She released him without another word or movement.

He scrubbed a hand over his face and back through his hair. "We've seen it a few times before. Why the concern now?"

"As agents, you're not kept up to date on all the survivors' post-rescue. You go on to the next job, and the next." She turned her gaze to Aksel. "Every one of them is still in a disconnected state. That sigil is the only difference between those victims and the ones that we've recovered that have healed and are trying to move on with their lives."

"So, Aksel might remain like this?"

"Yes. Maybe? We—I don't know."

"And how will this affect Ana?" He swallowed the lump rising in his throat.

"I don't know that either," Kane said, voice raw.

When she returned his direct gaze, her expression was full of concern, regret and resolve.

There was nothing he or she could do.

It was up to Ana.

ANA AWAKENED IN A black filmy undertow.

Pulled and pushed in all directions, unable to draw breath.

Trapped. Weak. Disconnected.

Prey to the whispers.

Something tapped against her palm. Her hand closed around the object, grasping at anything she could use as she struggled against the crushing blackness.

It was Gran's crucifix.

Focus. Feel.

Balance soon followed.

She stopped fighting against the need for air and control, allowing her body to drift with the current.

She surfaced, gasping for air, and opened her eyes to a looming iceberg.

Only the polestar kept it company above the empty sea.

The iceberg's tip was blinding white and pristine, while the lower section at the water level had veins of black streaking upward, seeking to devour it.

On its face, there must have been a ledge as she focused on the form of a bear, clinging and exhausted.

Ana swam toward it, as much as she could, through the thickening black mire, sucking at her legs to drag her back under.

She trembled against the cold as her body threatened to seize. *Not now! Not now.*

"Aksel!" she screamed without stopping.

The bear turned its weary head in her direction but didn't move.

The downward drag on her body nearly had her below the surface again. Panic flared through her, but the crucifix in her palm reminded her to focus.

Shivering, she focused on relaxing her body, feeling the direction of the water—the actual water not the inky oil slick that tainted it and surrounded the iceberg.

Water was Ana's natural element. It was her emotional conduit. She sought it now to enable her to reach Aksel.

She opened her eyes when her shoulder bumped into something smooth and solid.

Aksel peered down at her from his ledge.

Her hand slipped off the icy surface as the current threatened to sweep her right past him.

His paw slapped the side of the iceberg, claws anchored in the ice so Ana could pull herself out of the water.

After several minutes of struggling, she climbed his furry arm and collapsed next to him, chest heaving.

"Thanks."

He huffed.

"I'm with Magnus," she finally said.

He didn't move or make any effort to shift in order to communicate with her.

"Are you in bear form to stay warm, or are you stuck like that?"

This time, his huff contained a despondent growl.

His morose state rippled over her.

Pushing herself into a seated position, she placed a hand on his damp, dirty fur. "We're going to try to help you. But we need you to help us figure out how."

The next huff *felt* like a sardonic laugh.

"Where are we?"

He turned his head, leveling his gaze on her, one polar bear brow raised.

"Yeah, fucked if I know too," she said, uncharacteristically using the *'F'* word as she surveyed the empty ocean. "Okay, listen Aksel. We found you aboard a cargo ship, hidden in the engine room, badly beaten and unconscious. That's all we know. That and that you have a sigil tattoo at the base of your throat. We need to know what happened to you and anything you can tell us about the mark. So, if you could take your human form and explain it all, that'd be totally awesome."

The bear stared at her, and she had the distinct feeling he wanted to chomp her head.

"Fair enough, but if you eat me, I can't help you."

The next impression was something like, *'how the hell can you help me?'*

Going with the hunch, she said, "I'm guessing you'd like to know how I'm going to help you. Well, whether you're aware or not, we are not physically on this iceberg in the middle of the ocean. We're somewhere in your psyche. Your body is in a comfy hospital bed with IV's hooked up to you. Magnus is standing by and worried about you."

There was no response as she stared the polar bear in the face.

His nose twitched, scenting.

Then he shoved her shoulder with his snout.

Who the hell are *you?*

How much should she tell him? Could this sigil link somehow convey information back to its originator?

Maybe she'd already said too much.

"My name is Ana. I'm able to reach you through my psychic ability."

Shaman.

"Sort of, but not really. I don't have the skills and experience your shaman would."

She considered what she knew of shamanic wisdom, which wasn't much, and realized that maybe that's what he needed—his clan shaman.

"Is that what you want? Do you want us to take you to your shaman?"

He growled.

"Oh, oh dear, okay, that was a clear 'no'. But why not?"

Why wouldn't Aksel want to go to the shaman?

She sat next to him, arse frozen to the iceberg as she tried to work through the problems and frustrated that he couldn't just communicate with her in plain English. Then she realized she didn't even know if Aksel spoke English, anyway.

But he understood her.

Because they were in his psyche.

And yet, even here, he was trapped in his bear, while his physical body remained trapped in his human.

She dropped her face into her hands. This was way beyond her pay grade. None of this was anything Maeda had ever worked on with her. They'd never gotten this far.

Because usually, she grew tired and lost her connection.

How long had she been here already? Was she trapped here, too?

Oh, dear God, that would be so bad.

Tell me about it.

She popped her head up and looked at Aksel. "You can hear my thoughts?"

He dipped his head with a little tilt.

Her body shuddered against the cold, her hand gripping Gran's crucifix.

No, she wouldn't be trapped. But that didn't mean she should stay here any longer than she needed to.

She had an idea.

From this ledge, they could only see in one direction. Maybe, just maybe, the open ocean wasn't all Aksel had access to here.

She stood, stretching out her stiffening joints, and flexed her hands against the cold.

Ana tried to find a place to climb. There weren't many footholds on the face of the ice. Most of it was too slick for her to grip.

"Aksel. Can you help me get to the top of your iceberg?"

He turned his head, looking up to its snowy peak beyond the black veins creeping up from the ocean. Now that she watched them for a few moments, she noticed they continued to creep upward—consuming.

A wave of sudden dizziness overwhelmed her, causing her to stumble as she tried to step onto a more solid spot.

The black, oozing water pooled around her feet, impeding her ability to ascend.

Aksel's fur was covered in the stuff. Did it weigh him down too?

"We have to try, Aksel. I need you to help me *see* more."

If there is anything more to see.

They both thought it.

But he looked down at his paws. The water encroached on him too. He stood and staggered forward.

The water seemed to reach for him, to drag him back.

He looked down at it, then seemed to notice how it coated his fur. He engaged in a full body shake to dislodge the blackened water from his body.

It flew off in a cloudy spray, splattering the iceberg and open water beyond.

Some of it gathered itself, pooling and oozing back toward Aksel's paws.

He climbed.

Ana struggled to climb alongside him but couldn't get a grip.

On.

"Climb *you?*"

He huffed and repositioned his rear leg and dug the claws into the ice so that she could use it.

"Okay, if you insist," she said with a last glance at the black puddles that seemed to try to find them through the dips and valleys in the ice.

Once she was on, she gripped his fur in her fists and tried not to put her knees and feet in awkward places to impede his ability to reach the summit.

The higher they went, the heavier the pressure on her mind.

Aksel felt it too.

She felt it in the way he struggled to move ever upward, his sides laboring with the effort.

But finally, finally, they crested the iced peak and Aksel dug his claws in so as not to slide back down to where he'd worked so hard to climb from.

"Oh, my god." Ana breathed.

Beyond them, the sea was filled with dozens, if not hundreds, of other icebergs of all shapes and sizes and in various states of being consumed by the black water, turning the ice and snow to varying shades of white, gray and black.

There were a few more polar bears occupying other icebergs. There were also humans—many of them. A few other creatures occupied the floating surfaces.

They floated between two visible coast lines, small ports on either side.

The inky water stretched between the two land masses; the land as streaked with black as the ink burrowed like seeking vines.

Then she understood.

They *were* all connected.

They were all connected by the black, inky magic of this sigil.

"We have to somehow break the sigil."

But how?

TWELVE

ANA GROANED AND MAGNUS instantly lunged forward to scoop her up from the floor.

She was small and limp in his arms as he strode out of Aksel's room, seeking any other room where he could lay her on a comfortable surface.

"This way." Kane led him to a nearby sitting room with plump couches.

He gently laid Ana on one, placing her shoulders on the padded arm, and reached for a cushion to prop behind her.

Her eyes fluttered open, searching the room around her as her body trembled.

"I'm... it's so... cold." Her teeth chattered.

"I'll get some hot tea—get her warmed up," Kane said, leaving the room.

Magnus pulled Ana forward and slid behind her so that her back was to his chest and wrapped his arms around her, much like he'd done that first night in the hangar.

"Aksel... so many..." she struggled to get the words out. "Connected. Consuming..."

"Just rest right now," he murmured against the top of her head, relieved to have her back. He bundled her closer, reaching across the back of the couch for a wool throw to tuck around her.

By the time Kane returned bearing a tray with a teapot and mugs, Ana's trembling had settled into random little shivers.

Kane selected a steaming mug and crouched next to the couch. "Ana." Her voice was soft, encouraging Ana to look at her.

After a moment, Ana's head, resting on Magnus' chest, tilted so she could look at Kane.

"I brought your phone."

"Turn the recorder on," Ana murmured as she reached for the hot tea. "Thank you."

She recited everything she saw and felt in Aksel's mind.

Kane and Magnus listened, steaming mugs in hand.

Magnus' heart dropped at her descriptions of Aksel's isolation and the view she described of all the other icebergs, both with more of his kinsmen and other victims.

She said they were all connected.

Where are they all?

"What does it all mean?" he asked when she finished.

"I'm really not sure, Magnus. But, he emphatically didn't want me to go to the clan shaman for help." She sighed. "I'm sorry. I didn't get anything useful out of all that."

"What can you tell us about the shaman, Magnus?" Kane asked, refilling his mug.

He shrugged. "The shaman that I knew growing up was my father's closest friend and advisor. His duty was to oversee all royal rituals and activities, but above all, to protect the king from non-physical threats. He had a Guardian Chief for the physical ones. I haven't seen him or anyone else from Barentia since they banished me. I haven't been back, and I haven't had any contact with anyone—not even my son."

Ana jerked in his arms, sitting up and moving away so she could turn to look at him, her expression incredulous. "You have a son? You have a son you haven't seen in a decade?"

"Yes," he said, his body tensing.

She frowned as she considered this, but said nothing more about it. Instead, she turned to Kane. "Why do you want us to go into his clan's territory?"

Kane looked at Magnus.

"Joey, she should know," Magnus said to Kane, using her given name, which he rarely did.

"Know what?" Ana demanded.

Wearily, Joey held Magnus' gaze before turning her attention to Ana. "It's my fault Magnus was banished."

"I wouldn't say it was *your* fault," Magnus objected.

"It was. Is. If I hadn't pushed your father so hard, he probably wouldn't have turned against you when you tried to help make him see reason about the prophecies."

Magnus snorted. "Maybe. But there were also an awful lot of underlying clan politics that pushed him toward his decision."

"Prophecies?"

A pang struck Magnus when Ana moved away from him, renewing the distance between them as she slid to the opposite end of the couch. She huddled in the wool throw he'd wrapped around her.

He turned so that both his feet were firmly on the floor, elbows on his knees, as they continued their discussion.

"Look, Joey, you've always known something was going to happen there. That was the whole deal in the first place. Something is happening and we need to find out how it relates." He rubbed his hands over his beard and through his hair. "How else would Aksel end up on a human trafficking ship with a hex tattooed into his throat like this?"

Magnus had never seen Joey with any kind of expression that resembled uncertainty before.

"Why are you back-peddling now? Why *now*, when you were just pushing us to move forward on this yesterday?" he demanded. "We're so close, Joey. *So* close."

"Is it because of the shaman? And what's this about prophecies?" Ana asked again, setting her mug on the floor next to the couch.

"Yes. The way forward isn't as clear to me now. I need to think this through. We'll discuss the prophecies later, but it's all part of the reason Magnus needs to go to Barentia."

Ana cut in. "If we can somehow break the sigil, wouldn't that free Aksel? Then he could wake up and just tell us what we need to know? That black inky stuff seemed to consume the icebergs and I don't know what that means for him—or the others."

"It's not so simple as that." Joey's voice was gentle as she reached a hand to Ana's knee. "Even if there was some way to remove the tattoo, it magically embedded the ink in his skin and bloodstream."

"Magic like that has very few counteragents."

"Death is usually the main one," Magnus said, "Of the creator, or the recipient."

"Are there any other tattooed victims nearby that I could interview? I might get more information from someone that is trapped in human form," Ana asked.

Joey shook her head. "They're all being cared for at facilities close to their homes, although GPSA is monitoring them and keeping us informed."

Ana threw off the blanket as she stood, then began pacing. "Okay, I really don't think I can do anything useful with my gifts. But at the very least, I *can* pose as Magnus' fiancée if that gets him through the door, and close to whomever he needs to talk to. Since I can't actually help save anyone, this is the very least I can do." She paused mid stride and shrugged. "If it's a dead end, then we move on. Who knows, maybe this will give Magnus a chance to see his son."

Magnus blinked. He cleared the sudden lump in his throat. "That would be irrelevant to the mission."

"Like hell it is," Ana exploded, color blooming in her cheeks. "Sons need their fathers. Fathers need their children. You—." She closed her eyes, straightened her spine and drew a breath. "Everyone has the right to see their family."

A smile tugged at Magnus' lips. "That's not exactly how my society works, but I appreciate the sentiment, Ana."

"I can feel it, Magnus," she said, impassioned, her fist over her heart.

Magnus' gaze darted to Joey, who studied Ana closely.

His heart thudded in his chest, his emotions and thoughts tumbling between Ana and his clan—his family.

My god, she is beautiful when she is unrestrained.

The idea that he might see his son... after all this time.

Fear iced his spine.

He'd avoided thoughts along that path over the years. It did no good to entertain them.

Banished meant erased, in most cases.

The only reason he'd possibly be allowed back at all was only because he was the king's son, and his bloodline needed to be tracked. Hence the recording of unions and offspring.

A decade had passed since he'd last set eyes on his tiny boy. He'd be approaching manhood now. Still a boy, but not for much longer.

As quickly as the thoughts appeared, he brushed them away again.

That way was dangerous. To his heart, and his soul.

There was no room in Magnus' life for family. Not anymore.

I won't go through that again.

No, best to focus on the mission. Always the mission.

The bigger picture.

He would go, just as he'd been prepared to when Kane had first ordered it.

And he would banish thoughts of seeing his son from his mind.

If he didn't, he might not leave again.

He would fail the mission, because he'd take his son with him this time, which would incite a war that would ruin everything.

ANA DUG THROUGH HER two open suitcases, seeking the warmest of her warm clothing.

Seated on the floor between them, damp hair piled on top of her head, thin robe loosely belted around her freshly showered body, she groaned.

Right back where she started. Stressing and panicked over what to wear.

But this was different.

So different.

Iceland wasn't like Barentia.

Iceland was cold, yes, but it also had people. People that she might turn to for help, should something go wrong.

Ana laughed.

She was fucked.

So. Fucked.

She'd panicked over Iceland, was relieved to land in Ireland... and now?

Iceland was a cakewalk compared to Barentia.

Barentia would eat her alive.

Literally.

An ancient civilization of Northmen and women, never tamed like the rest of the world. Insular and strong in their brutal ways.

No, that was unfair.

She thought of Magnus.

He wasn't brutal at all. As far as she'd experienced so far, he was more... gentle teddy bear than fierce wild northern polar bear.

Even when she'd ranted at him like an idiot.

God, what an idiot.

She sighed, throwing her cotton underwear back onto a pile she'd already moved several times.

She eyed the segregated pile of lace and satin thongs and bras she normally wore.

Definitely not practical.

But her favorites.

She sighed, picking up the small pile, trying to decide what to do with them when there was a knock on her door.

"Come in." She got to her feet, expecting a member of the household staff come to deliver a message from Kane.

Magnus stepped inside, closing the door behind him, quickly surveyed the disaster, eyes landing on the cluster of thongs dangling from her fingers.

Ana couldn't whip her hand behind her back fast enough.

She blushed when a thick blond brow rose over his twinkling blue-grey eyes.

She cleared her throat. "How can I help you?"

The corner of his mouth quirked as his expression turned mischievous. "Pack light—but maybe not too light, you'll want to be warm. Wheels up at six."

"Six!" Ana spun around, assessing her mess. "Just how cold will it be?"

When Magnus stepped close enough to peer over the mess, she had to resist the urge to lean back into his warm, wonderful smelling personal space, but it was hard.

He always smelled so good, and it seemed the more often she caught a whiff of whatever scent he wore, the more she wanted to sniff him.

And with it, came the recollection of how wonderful it felt to have his arms around her.

She tilted her head, turning enough to look up into his bearded face as he considered her piles of clothes.

Long, thick blond hair loosely braided back from his face. Deep-set eyes, and a straight nose over full lips, framed by his impressive beard. His grooming was impeccable, he smelled amazing and he just... enveloped her in a cocoon of security when he was so close.

She wanted more of that. More of him.

Her gaze swept his wide shoulders and thick biceps.

Her palms itched to explore his muscled arms, the ridges and valleys of his torso... and more.

Her eyes sought his lips, remembered that kiss in the hallway the previous night, and how it had left her wanting so much more.

She bit her lip. Did he want more of her, too?

That kiss... left her with the impression that he might.

"I don't see much that's appropriate for Barentia temperatures. We'll just have to make sure you stay close so I can keep you safe and warm."

"Safe and warm?" she repeated as his words made their way through the haze of distracted visual exploration she'd been engaged in. She blinked, turning toward him.

Ana looked up at Magnus, his eyes locked on her lips.

Her breath hitched as her face tilted up toward his.

"I'm partial to blue," his low voice rippled through her.

"Blue?" She licked her lips, inching toward him, mesmerized.

A light tug drew her attention to the hand that still clutched her forgotten underwear. A sapphire blue satin thong dangled from Magnus' forefinger.

Ana's cheeks flamed. Desire swept down her body, pooling at her core. Her nipples peaked as she stepped closer still.

Chest tight against the overwhelming desire, she sucked in a breath, dragging his delicious scents into her.

She'd never been sensitive to scents before, but it seemed she was becoming intoxicated by him. She couldn't get enough.

Magnus' warm hand slid behind the edge of her silk robe, pulling her to him.

She gasped as their chests collided.

He took advantage of her open mouth, slipping his tongue across the tip of hers between her parted lips, inciting sparks of erotic sensations all over her body.

She crackled.

Her fingers shook as raw desire raged through her, surprising the logical part of her brain, which seemed so very far away now.

What was it about Magnus that made her feel so primal?

She wasn't a shifter. She didn't have those instincts.

Do I?

His lips left hers as he nibbled his way along her jaw to her throat.

She bared it to him. Her fingers clasped his arms for support as she pressed her body into his.

The sensation of his beard along her sensitive flesh made her shudder and groan as he inhaled her scent.

His large hand slid down her back to grip her bottom as he pulled her against his steely erection behind the barrier of his jeans.

Desire slammed through her, stealing her breath away.

What's happening?

One moment she was sorting clothes, the next she was throwing herself at a man she'd only known for a few days.

A colleague, her small, logical brain, reminded her.

This isn't me.

Is it?

Her robe fell from her shoulders, leaving only the thin night dress which barely covered the tops of her thighs.

Nothing else.

Magnus leaned back, one hand still on her rear, locking her in place so that she could feel his hard length and he could feel her moist heat.

The other hand cradled her cheek and jaw. "You're so beautiful." He murmured, gaze fluttering over her features.

Her hands dropped to his waist, tugging at his shirt, desperate to press her palms to his hot flesh.

"Kiss me, Magnus." It was more a breath than a whisper.

Her brain screamed *'make love to me'*.

She had wanted it since she saw him that first night and buried it; like everything else she wanted.

He growled as his lips descended to hers.

Like the night before, the rumble of his growl shot straight to her core.

Her hands slid down. She unbuckled his belt before attacking his jeans, to free him in seconds as her hand slid behind the waistband of his boxers to grip his rigid length.

His growl deepened and the erotic need surged through her, gripping him hard and stroking.

He pulled his shirt up over his head, tossing it to the floor among her clothes.

Her hands shoved at his jeans. The boxers fell with them.

She stared at the sight of him, tongue darting over her lips as he pulsed with need.

Her gaze rose to meet the hunger in his eyes.

Would he devour her?

THIRTEEN

MAGNUS STARED INTO ANA'S dark eyes, liquid with desire. Her scent enticed his animal brain, so that there was only her.

She was killing him every time her gaze explored his body, tongue peeking out between her plump lips. He wanted nothing more than to feel the flutter of that little pink tongue and soft lips all over his body.

Soon enough, but not yet.

He dragged a breath into his lungs. The scent of her arousal enveloped both of them, and he'd barely touched her.

Mine.

Ana is mine.

Mate.

His mate. The fact had locked in place when their lips met the previous night.

There was no longer any doubt in his mind. She was *his*.

Magnus wasn't sure she'd reached that conclusion—yet.

But, he also had to ensure that she knew he was hers too.

He grinned down at her barely controlled restraint.

Her self-control only seemed to slip when she was around him. Magnus wanted Ana to lose all of it.

By the time they left for Barentia in the morning, they would be covered in each other's scents.

There would be no more doubt for either of them, and certainly none for anyone else that might challenge their claims to each other's bodies—or their hearts.

She didn't know she already held his in her small hands.

Ana was the psychic one, but Magnus knew things too.

He knew, like nothing he'd ever known in his life, that she would cherish it like the fragile ice sculpture that it had become after Ulla had forced him out of his home.

Magnus also understood that as big as her heart was, so full of compassion and kindness, it was just as fragile as his own. And she wouldn't easily give it over. She trusted him, but not enough.

"What are you grinning at?" she demanded, brow furrowed.

"You. You're a wild hell cat and you don't even know it."

Ana snorted, stepping back, indignant. "I am not."

He shrugged, his grin widening. "If you say so."

She eyed him suspiciously as he leaned in to claim her lips again.

His tongue swiped her lip, eliciting a low moan. She leaned into his chest, forcing him back against the wall as though the mere mention of the word 'wild' had unlocked something in her.

Her roaming hands found his chest and abdomen, sliding ever lower.

He caught her hands before they gripped him again. Linking his fingers through hers, he spun them around, pressed her back to the wall, and pinned her hands against its surface above her head.

The motion pushed her breasts up. Her hips fell forward, pressing against his, rubbing his hard cock between their bodies.

He stilled against the sudden near-loss of his own control.

Little minx.

Magnus deepened their kiss. She grew supple against him before he moved downward, grazing his lips over her silk-covered skin, earning little gasps as he went. He nuzzled and nibbled each breast, then the valley between, dragging his nose along the flat expanse of her belly, downward still.

His hands gripped her hips as he crouched before her. Her fingers clutched his shoulders as she stared down into his face, her breath in little puffs between her parted lips.

The grin returned to Magnus' mouth as he dragged the silk up from her thighs.

Palms on his shoulders, lifting herself away from his seeking mouth, she twisted in his grasp. She squeaked, "Magnus, I—."

But he hushed her with a breath against the sensitive, exposed flesh below her belly button and above her mound, where he placed a kiss before looking up into her wide eyes, staring down at him.

Through his mounting desire, he registered her panicked expression at her naked vulnerability.

She's never been properly worshiped.

With all the gentleness in his being, Magnus slid his tongue and lips over little spots on her thigh, working his way back up to her hip and across her belly.

When he glanced up again, her head had fallen back against the wall, although the pressure on his shoulders hadn't eased.

She was afraid.

Not of him.

She read others. He read *her*.

Lips pressed to her lower belly, he murmured, ever so softly, ever so low. "Open for me, sweetheart." Then his tongue circled her belly button before placing another kiss.

She moaned.

Her arms trembled as she struggled against herself, her fingers gripping his shoulders.

He looked up into her flushed face, holding her gaze. Her lower lip caught between her teeth.

His cock jerked. He ignored it.

She must have seen it because just then, the corner of her mouth curled.

Dear gods, she was sexy as all hell, and Magnus wanted nothing more than to bury himself deep inside her.

Emboldened by her effect on him, she turned so that he had full access to what he wanted.

Magnus loved how her breath still came in little pants of anticipation.

He inhaled, drawing her scent deeper still, before he placed the tenderest of kisses to her hot, moist center.

She shuddered at the contact, breath hissing through her teeth.

His tongue flicked over her, causing her arms to buckle.

Ana caught herself against the wall, palms flat.

Magnus slid a hand up her ankle, along her calf, lifting her knee over his shoulder.

Looking up into her face, he held her gaze as he lowered his mouth and set to devour her properly.

Ana hissed. Her nails scratched at the wall. She growled and spat. And she screamed as she came.

He lapped it all up.

Her body trembled around him.

Easing her foot back to the floor, he swept her limp form into his arms and finally carried her to the bed, where he continued to lick and kiss every inch of her.

He couldn't get enough of her. The more he tasted, the more he wanted.

By the time he slid into her, he'd ensured that she understood they belonged to one another.

As he moved inside of her, she rose to meet him, pulling him in deeper and deeper.

Claiming him.

Magnus' eyes locked on Ana's as she crested again. He gave her everything that he was, as they toppled over the edge in each other's arms.

She claimed his mouth one last time and released him with a grin.

"You wanted a hellcat. You got one."

He chuckled against her mouth before he rolled them to the side, wrapped his arms around her, and watched her beautiful face until she fell asleep.

BEFORE DAWN, MAGNUS ROUSED Ana from her languid slumber.

She groaned, rolling out of the bed, her feet slapping the floor on her way to the shower.

Ten minutes later, Magnus was nowhere to be seen. She found a backpack containing her clothes and anything else she would need for the trip. The rest of her belongings were neatly replaced in her suitcases and pushed aside.

She quickly dressed in the clothes set beside the pack, dried her hair and tied it back.

A knock at her door drew her attention. She opened it to find one of the household staff delivering a pair of insulated boots and a much better jacket than the one she had.

"From Mistress Kane. There is food for you and Mr. Bjornson in the breakfast room."

She glanced at her watch before accepting the boots and coat. "Thank you," she said, closing the door.

Ana quickly slipped the boots on and laced them up. One last glance around the room, noting the wild state of the bed sheets and blanket, she tugged them back into place and plumped the pillows.

Grabbing the coat and pack, she left for the breakfast room, trying not to think about all the things they'd done in that bed just hours before.

All of *that* would have to wait.

There was work to do.

FOURTEEN

MAGNUS GLANCED AT THE dials and adjusted a few settings on the cockpit panel.

Next to him, Ana occupied the co-pilot's chair, tense but quiet. At least she didn't have a mask over her lovely eyes this time.

She tentatively glanced out of the window again, each time for a little longer.

And when the sun crested the horizon, her gasp of awe sent a thrum through his heart.

The view from well above bird's eye was incredible. One reason he loved flying.

The other, the speed and danger-control factor, was also the reason he enjoyed driving fast cars and motorcycles.

Something Ana would learn about in time.

He cast her another glance, wondering what he would learn about her?

Soon, she relaxed and spent most of her time peering down from her side window.

"That's Norway below us?"

"Yes, we'll be landing on the easterly tip then going the rest of the way by amphibious plane. Barentia doesn't have a landing strip."

She nodded.

"What do I need to know about Barentia?"

"Stay close. There won't be a warm welcome. I'll find an excuse to stay at least a day or two. You're not a polar bear, or even a shifter, so expect some intimidation."

She nodded.

"Don't be afraid to make your taser visible. Keep your handgun well hidden."

Her fingers drummed her knee as she looked down at the ocean and mountains.

"What are these prophecies that Kane mentioned?"

Magnus sighed. He was the one that had said Ana had a right to know. But Kane hadn't offered any more on the subject. "It's best if she explains it all."

"Cliffs' notes?"

"Kane's been around a long time. *Long* time. And she's been collecting information about ancient prophecies. That's why she came to Barentia in the first place. She believed there was a link between my homeland and the information she was studying."

"Which is?"

Magnus shrugged. "She and my father and the old shaman had long, long discussions on the matter. Something to do with a gateway of sorts."

"What does this have to do with the trafficking ring we're investigating?"

"Nothing. Everything." He rubbed a hand over his face. "She asked for two things. Help with the prophecies and help fighting against the growing practice of shifters exploiting humans. My father sent her away and told me never to deal with her when he was gone—when I became king of the clan. Barentians never get involved with human affairs. When I pushed him on it, he said that we would do as we'd always done; keep to our own and shut the world out. That I wasn't ready yet. The shaman said little on the matter, beyond how vital it was that we protect our territory, to keep the darkness away."

"Sounds very cryptic."

"Yeah, well, my father was incensed that I went to talk to Kane myself and find out what she had to say on the matter. Her view was that whatever was coming, every civilization had a responsibility to fight against those that would use this darkness which the shaman had mentioned. Made sense to me."

"Your father disagreed."

Magnus nodded. "We continued to argue in the following weeks and months. Kane tried again. He demanded she never return. I, being young and impatient, challenged him. Turns out Ulla also disagreed with my viewpoint, and had been putting words in my father's ear. There was another heir—my son. The clan didn't need me."

Magnus gave his attention to the flight gauges for a few moments, to shake the lingering emotions for his ex-wife.

Ana maintained her silence.

"Uphold our insular traditions, or go. The Clan or Kane. My heart said to stay and shut the fuck up. My gut told me I had to go."

It was far, far more complicated than that.

"You trust her? More than your father?"

Magnus shrugged. "Instinct."

She didn't ask why he didn't just wait out his father's rule, or why he chose a stranger over his family—his son.

He'd had a decade to study his choices. Swallow his regrets.

To work with Kane, even though his absence from Barentia meant she didn't have the ally she'd sought *in* that territory.

Some days, it felt like it was all for nothing.

Considering the struggle to protect humans from exploitive paranormals, Magnus had done a lot, but it wasn't enough.

"So, you're not welcome. Humans aren't welcome. They know we're agents."

"They know *I* work for the GPSA. They may assume the same of you, or not. But as a human, they can't automatically assume you're a threat of any kind. Anyone else would put them on their guard."

Magnus flicked several switches and began their descent toward land.

"Ready?"

"As I'll ever be."

FEAR POUNDED THROUGH ANA'S chest as they left the seaplane tied to a simple dock and began the trek up the snow-covered path toward the fishing village.

Somewhere on the eastern tip of Norway, they'd landed and switched to the smaller amphibious aircraft for the rest of the journey.

She struggled to control her heart rate.

Pulling her phone from her pocket, she checked for cell service, holding it up in various directions, trying to catch *something*.

They would smell her fear, making her an easy target.

She laughed at herself, tucking her phone away.

She was already an easy target. A human on an island full of powerful shifters, but she also wasn't helpless. Her fingers ghosted over her weapons before she drew a breath. On its release, she opened her senses.

Time to get to work.

Barentia, like everywhere else in this part of the globe, was comprised of mountainous islands rising out of the steely waters of the north. The world was all shades of gray and blue, white and black, with little variety in between. Even the coniferous trees appeared more black than green.

Without looking at her, Magnus reached out to squeeze her glove-covered hand as several villagers came out to see who'd interrupted their daily routine of coastal life.

Magnus' name drifted between individuals until a stoic older woman emerged from the gathering crowd of astonished faces.

Surprise, disdain, and hostility rippled through the air.

Magnus' appearance pleased some villagers, but you wouldn't know it to look at their craggy, sea-worn faces.

She felt it.

They looked from Magnus to Ana, and moved aside.

The old woman stood at the top of the path. She looked like any of the other villagers. Magnus stopped before her, head bowed.

Ana didn't understand Barentian, but through observing their facial expressions, body language and psychic energy, she got the gist of what was going on.

Magnus and the older woman exchanged a few words before she turned her back on them. Magnus followed her. Ana followed him.

The elder woman led them to an ornately carved wooden structure where a boy awaited her. With a few sharp words from the woman, the boy's gaze darted between her, Magnus and Ana, then he set off like an Olympic sprinter along another path that led away from the ocean.

Magnus whispered to Ana as he held the door opened for her to precede him inside the building. "The boy will send a message to alert my father that we have arrived."

Moving into the space felt like stepping into an energy cloud. The hairs on her arms rose.

Magnus whispered close to her ear. "As a banished one, I'm not welcome in resident's homes, but the temple is a place open to all."

With Ana's senses open, and the high energy of the place, Magnus' proximity made her skin tingle even through the layers of clothing until he stepped away again.

She nodded, gaze sweeping the beautifully crafted interior lit by braziers. At the far end of the open space, an altar filled the far wall.

The village temple. The woman was no doubt its priestess.

Ana approached the altar. Touching nothing, she inspected the symbols and offerings.

None looked anything like the sigil imprinted on Aksel's throat.

The elder appeared next to her.

Ana turned toward her, met and held her gaze before offering her hand. "I'm Analiese Ortega."

"Beyla Jorgansdotter." The woman shook her hand with a firm grip. The corner of her thin lips tilted upward as she assessed Ana.

With a short laugh, she turned toward a table with a pitcher and glasses, speaking to Magnus over her shoulder as she poured.

"She says I've brought you here to clean up my mess," Magnus said.

"What is she talking about?"

Magnus relayed the question and translated the elder's answer.

"She says things haven't been the same since I left the clan. My father is different. More conflict among Barentians than is usual. And in recent years, a gang seems to have formed."

"A gang?"

"Young Barentians rove from village to village, recruiting the strongest among them to join their gang, and off they go." He paused, listening as the elder continued to talk. "At first, they thought the king was forming an additional guard to protect the territory from what the priests and priestesses knew was the coming darkness, but it seems not to be the case."

"What *are* they doing?"

She shrugged. "No good," she said in English, her accent thick as she handed them each a glass.

Ana sniffed at the liquid.

"Barentian ale," Magnus said with a smile. He drank the entire glass. "Ah, I've missed this stuff."

"What did she mean, your father is different?" Ana took a tentative sip.

"I assume it means he's accepting outsiders to the island now, since we weren't met at spear point when we arrived at the dock."

"Except that's what you argued about and were banished for?"

Magnus nodded.

"That doesn't make sense."

"No, it doesn't."

Heavy footsteps sounded outside the door before it opened. The young boy appeared, chest heaving, speaking between breaths.

"He notified the relay. We can go," Magnus said.

Ana turned to offer her thanks to the woman for her hospitality.

The elder went to the altar, glanced along its surface and re-trieved an artifact, cradling it on her palm as she returned to Magnus and Ana.

The elder reached for Ana's hand, surprising her.

Magnus translated her words. "Don't let the darkness touch your heart when it comes; but even the light can be a barrier. And when it's imperative to open your heart, the bear will be your polestar."

Ana looked at the talisman in her hand. A polar bear carved in polished ivory. Flipping it over, she studied the etched symbol on its back. The top of the talisman had a drilled hole with a metal link so it could be worn on a necklace or bracelet.

"Thank you," she said, pulling Gran's rosary and crucifix from her pocket while the woman continued to speak to Magnus direct-ly. Ana attached the bear talisman next to the crucifix, considering it. She was about to tuck it all back into her pocket when, instead, she looped it around her wrist and tucked it under her shirt cuff.

Maybe it's just the weird warning about light and dark.

Or how the village elder reminded her of her grandmother.

Or something else entirely that Ana couldn't define.

Priestess Beyla Jorgansdotter led Magnus and Ana back out of the temple so that they might continue their journey.

The villagers had remained outside all that time, and observed their departure inland. Their somber faces, hopeful auras, and the elder's strange warnings coiled through Ana, twisting up her insides, adding to her deep unease about this mission.

Despite the mention of outsiders no longer denied access to Barentian territory, she doubted an extraction team could rescue them, should things go wrong—as her gut told her they inevitably would.

FIFTEEN

DURING THE LONG WALK, Magnus ruminated over what the village elder had told him.

Everything about Barentia *looked* the same.

Everything about Barentia *felt* different.

Subtle differences that would be a trickle-down effect from their leader.

Why would his father change his stance on outsiders, especially after he'd done the extreme act of banishing his only son and direct heir?

"They don't look it, Magnus, but I could feel that many of them are pleased to see you." Ana had said to him as they left the village boundary behind them.

Her words should have made him feel better.

They didn't.

He noted how quiet the road was between the coastal village and his father's stronghold.

A stronghold that didn't seem necessary to a culture of polar bear shifters that had rejected most outsiders for the last few centuries.

Mostly human outsiders, of course. And most other paranormals that weren't polar bear shifters like themselves, which were usually vetted before setting foot in the territory.

Like his former wife, Ulla, and her younger brother, Aksel; children of the ruler of the Novaya Zemlya clan that occupied the Matochkin strait, whom it was named for.

A political alliance.

Although they deterred most outsiders, there were still rival clans that would seek to conquer and control Barentia for their own gain.

Hence, the massive stone stronghold that housed Magnus' forebears.

Other clans had tried and failed to take it over. Barentia had always been too strong.

They'd been strong because they'd kept their borders tight. Easier to do when you occupied a frozen archipelago in a northern ocean.

Unease slithered at Magnus' nape.

The elder had said Bjorn Thornsson was different. He didn't look out for his people as he once had. They hadn't seen him in a long time because there hadn't been a gathering or festival in years.

Magnus had been gone for a decade.

Barentia, like a glacier, was slow to change. Annual gatherings and festivals were a vital activity in their way of life.

What other changes would he see when they reached his former home?

He glanced at Ana, walking alongside him, bundled in borrowed cold-weather gear. With her face framed in a faux-fur trim, the tip of her nose was pink, and her cheeks bloomed under the pale blue sky.

Magnus wore his usual clothes, with the addition of an extra layer under his leather jacket.

They both bore backpacks with more clothing and supplies.

He frowned, recalling the elder's cryptic words to Ana. She clearly sensed there was more to her.

But then, she'd been cryptic about everything she'd said.

At first, Magnus attributed it to the fact that he was a returned banished, and he should have been shunned by all he met.

It was the way.

He had expected resistance at their arrival, and had been surprised they'd allowed him off the dock, let alone parted for him to enter the village and their most sacred space.

They had all remained silent.

The elder had chosen her words carefully.

Like someone could be listening.

IT WAS LONG DARK by the time they reached the foot of the fortress built into the base of the island's weathered mountain.

They had exchanged few words, preferring to focus energy on the journey.

"Cozy," Ana muttered, "Don't suppose it has indoor plumbing and a reliable heating system?"

"If they don't send us away immediately, they'll probably relegate us to a hut outside the town's boundary. *If* we're lucky. More likely, we'll be sleeping in the tent that I have bundled in my pack."

Ana groaned, her expression pleading that it wasn't the case.

"Don't worry, I know many ways to keep you warm." He winked and saw that she couldn't help but smile.

"Shall we get this over with?"

Magnus nodded. The smile dropped from his face as he stepped forward.

Toward his past.

Toward the father that banished him from his world.

The ex-wife that had undermined him.

The son that no longer knew him.

The rest of his friends and family that had all turned their backs on him.

None had protested the banishment. None had come forward for him. He'd been alone. Until he joined Kane's Organization. What else was there for him?

He'd questioned everything in those days; Kane, her motives, her sanity. Others that worked for her. In time, he'd learned to trust her, as his instinct had urged him to do, but he still questioned her regularly. As he'd done with his father. It was in his nature.

Unlike his father, Joey Kane respected him for it.

When did it all go wrong?

He sighed, staring up at the familiar stone walls built into the mountainside.

As far as he could recall, everything changed after the birth of his son, Elias.

It should have been a happy time, full of wonder and rightness—and it was, for a little while. His world revolved around his brand-new little cub. He'd never experienced pride and love like that before. Magnus held those memories deeply buried under the permafrost, protecting his heart.

Everyone changed.

While at the time it was difficult to discern what was happening and who was instigating the direction of things, time and distance had since made it easier to see what was happening.

Ulla.

Still, Magnus was cautious where to lay the blame, despite how contentious their separation had been.

Family break-ups were messy, and everyone had some responsibility to claim.

A decade was a long time.

AS ANA PASSED THROUGH the smaller door set into the massive iron-banded wooden gates, she remembered to keep her mouth closed as she took in her surroundings—she was so in awe of the place.

She breathed a sigh of relief as the high walls blocked the arctic wind from freezing her through to her bones. She didn't care that Magnus insisted it wasn't winter. She'd already decided she'd never, ever, be in the arctic during that particular season. The current climate was bad enough.

They stood between two stone walls, lined with snow and ice in every crevice and cranny. The ground, clear of either, was surfaced with a stone road and a cobbled foot path.

She gave a little laugh. "This place is incredible. It reminds me of a dwarven mountain castle from the movies."

"That's because we worked together to build the place."

Ana stumbled on the cobbles. "Wait-what? Dwarves are *real?* You're joking, right? This place has to have been built centuries ago. Where are they now?"

"Yes. No. It was. No idea."

"Huh." She considered this as they moved toward the next reinforced door. "Where is everyone?"

"Ordered to remain out of sight. Banished are to be considered among the dead and treated thus. The land of the dead is a barren landscape, devoid of the living. The two worlds never cross. Mine is an exceptional circumstance."

"I'd argue against the 'never cross' part," Ana murmured. "But, yeah, I think I get it. So, the villagers we met before..."

"Caught off-guard, I suppose. If they knew it was me coming to their dock, they likely would have disappeared, too. Except for the temple priestess."

"The convener for the two worlds."

Magnus smiled as he turned to look at her before passing through the next reinforced door. "Were you Barentian, you'd have been given to the temple because of your ability."

"Lucky for both of us, I'm not."

Ana's heart panged when Magnus' smile left.

"I suppose it is. Otherwise, neither of us would be here now."

They approached the final heavy door that would lead them inside. Her gaze traveled up the face of the fortress nestled into the foot of the mountain.

It was no wonder the Barentians were an unconquered people.

She caught sight of a young Barentian with the same wild hair that Magnus had, peering down at them from a gap in the rock that she guessed was a balcony or large window of some kind.

His son?

Or just another curious youth, defying the rules?

Inside, the reception hall was cavernous, but they continued past it. Magnus led Ana down a stone-lined corridor to another room that showed the first hints of warmth.

It looked like a small clerks' office, with a large desk and a wall of fitted shelves supporting scrolls, books and other miscellany that Ana itched to explore. A lit fireplace provided heat.

Electric lighting suspended above the main desk and other work benches illuminated documents and manuscripts strewn across their surfaces.

A stout woman with graying auburn hair, carrying a heavy leather-bound book, approached from a doorway tucked into the back of the room. She stopped on the opposite side of the large desk, placing the open volume with care on its surface.

There were pens and pencils of varying types and inks. The woman ignored those in favor of a quill and inkwell that she withdrew from somewhere behind the desk. She set them near the book and adjusted her glasses.

"Registrar Maerie Gailensdotter," Magnus greeted her.

Peering over the top rim of her lenses at Magnus and Ana, nose twitching as she scented them, she spoke in English. "Prince Magnus Bjornson, I presume we are recording a union. Are there any offspring to account for?"

"Shouldn't the clan shaman be here to witness the record?"

"He will not be."

Magnus grunted. "I thought my father—the king," he corrected himself, "was determined to uphold all the values and traditions that Barentia has observed for centuries?"

"Millenia," the woman corrected. "It would seem our esteemed king is allowing some changes to our traditions."

"I'm standing here, a banished man, because he refused to change anything," Magnus ground through his teeth.

The woman's gaze flicked to the open door behind them before she removed her glasses, set them next to the open inkwell, and strode toward the door. With a quick peek into the hall, she closed it and returned to her post.

Retrieving the glasses, she tapped them against her palm, regarding Magnus across the desk, then turned her inspection on Ana, nose twitching again.

The woman's frustrated indecision rippled through Ana. A psychic wasn't needed to see the unspoken words in her expression.

Magnus had made it clear that he was banished and expected to be treated as a dead man. This ritual of their impending *marriage* was the only excuse that would grant them entry into the realm.

"You are not a bear, or a shifter." Her demeanor steeled when she turned her attention to Ana.

"I am not," Ana said.

To Magnus, the registrar said, "You were serious when you said Barentia should make alliances with outsiders."

Magnus nodded.

"The king seems to have changed his mind on the subject. Outsiders come and go as freely as Barentians these days." Her gaze flicked to the door again.

The woman's growing conflicted concern weighed on Ana's senses. She wanted to tell Magnus something.

But Magnus was a banished outcast. No one was supposed to be talking to him. Her sole role here was to record his impending marriage and any offspring.

After having observed the two for the last few minutes, Ana acted on instinct. Reaching for Magnus' hand, she looked up at him and thought of their night together. The memory of his tenderness and consideration radiated through her. She smiled, allowing her growing feelings toward this gentle man to show on her face and in the way she leaned into his arm. Her thumb stroked his.

"I'm honored to have the chance to be here, in Barentia. To see your childhood home, even if just a little bit." She laughed. "Perhaps if we have many children together, I may get to see a little more of it each time. Though it would be a shame that they might not know it as you do—did."

Magnus' fingers squeezed around hers affectionately as he looked down into her face.

She sensed his emotions flipping, but the corner of his lips lifted. "*Many* children," he repeated gruffly as his gaze turned heated.

Warmth bloomed in her cheeks, spread through her chest and down her belly, at the look in his eyes.

The registrar cleared her throat.

Her expression softened as she looked between the two, appreciating their affection for one another.

"You're only supposed to be here long enough to declare for the record, but if you like, I can give you a peek at the library where Magnus spent so much time as a boy," she said to Ana, tipping her head back toward the open door she'd come through with the book.

"Maerie's duties as registrar are just part of her role here in the stronghold. She's also the clan archivist and librarian."

"And clerk and secretary," she added, proud. She reached for the quill, dipping it into the inkpot. "Shall we?"

Magnus' fingers tightened on Ana's again. She glanced up into his face. Concern creased his brow as he stared down at the book. His apprehension was palpable.

She understood.

Returning her attention to the book, she considered the elegant script lining the pages of the thick tome.

Their names were to be inscribed in the clan's official register, tracking royal lineages.

Magnus was a prince. A shaman was supposed to witness this record. This act was part of the clan's long, long tradition and should not be treated lightly.

They were there under the guise of a pending marriage. A sham. A ruse.

A lie.

Ana's chest tightened as she looked up into Magnus' conflicted face under the weight of the moment.

When he turned his gaze to her, the feeling flowing from him took her breath away.

"Analiese, before we sign this register, if you have any doubts, we can turn back now. Leave the page blank."

They were already inside the stronghold at the heart of Barentia.

They didn't have to commit to the lie to fulfill their mission. They'd just needed access to the stronghold and territory. And they had it.

But, they still needed to confirm Barentian contact with the sigil to understand what happened to Aksel.

Here, now, can we still get that information without signing the book?

Studying the script, some part of her *wanted* to sign it.

"We can turn back now if that's what *you* want. I'll understand. The past hasn't been kind to either of us."

It hadn't.

Magnus' politically contracted wife had turned against him. Ulla had alienated him from his son, his father, and his clan.

Ana had been rejected by the man she'd thought was the love of her life. Although she and Antony had been together for many years, he'd never talked of their future together. They'd been little more than friends sharing a bed until she'd lost him to the ocean. Maybe he had always known his fate was with the sea.

After she'd lost her mother and Gran and then Antony, Ana had been alone, except for her growing family at the GPSA.

Magnus had also been alone, with the exception of those that worked for the Organization—the parent of the GPSA.

We understand each other.

When Magnus touched her, she wanted him to *always* be touching her.

She'd never experienced this level of connection with anyone before. Not even Antony.

Did Magnus feel it too? Or was she just becoming infatuated with the big, stoic polar bear shifter?

After all, how long had they known each other? A week? Less?

Does it matter?

She'd experienced so much in the last year, seen so much—too much.

When she looked into Magnus' eyes, she *knew* it was the same for him.

Could either of them ever truly have a 'normal' life? Even after they closed this case?

If they closed this case.

Ana didn't think she could. She didn't even know what a 'normal' life even meant anymore.

But she did know something. Now. She looked up into Magnus' eyes.

Her heart pounded in her chest, blood roaring through her. Tears sprang to her eyes as she realized, truly, that she wanted this man.

If they were to commit their names to that precious book on the Registrar's desk, she didn't want it to be a lie.

It shouldn't be.

She blinked away the threatening tears and tried to offer an encouraging smile that told him he didn't need to sign the book.

The registrar forgotten; Ana stood transfixed as Magnus' large hand reached for her cheek. Her eyes fell closed at the feel of his warm fingers caressing her jaw to cradle her nape. His lips brushed hers.

He kissed the corner of her mouth, her cheek and his warm breath tickled her ear as he whispered, "I would sign that book in a heartbeat, if it meant that your name was recorded next to mine for all of Barentian time."

Her breath hitched as she leaned her cheek into his palm, relishing the feel of his skin on hers.

The frantic pounding of her heart slowed to a steady thrum.

When she opened her eyes, he was still bent close, his gaze searching hers.

"I would take you as my mate, should you choose it."

Mate.

Intuition roared through Ana's being. "I choose you," she said, voice steady. She returned his kiss.

"I promised to keep you safe and warm," he murmured against her lips.

"So you did," she murmured back with a smile.

A promise.

Mate.

For all Barentian time.

Maerie cleared her throat. "My ink pot is drying out."

Ana and Magnus returned their attention to the woman with the wry smile and the task at hand.

Magnus reached for the quill and, with a few swipes, set his name to the register, then held the pen up for Ana.

She plucked it from his fingers and approached the handcrafted book. His signature was bold and elegant.

Magnus, son of Bjorn, son of Thorn. Prince of Barentia.

Analiese carefully set her name next to his.

Analiese Maria Marguerita Francesca Ortega.

SIXTEEN

MAGNUS SMILED AS HE stepped into the library. "This was one of my favorite places," he said to Ana.

His smile widened, noting her awe as she stared at the long room with its stacked concourses of floor to ceiling bookshelves.

Sometimes, when he was in Ireland, he'd visit the Trinity College library to soothe his homesickness. It was almost as magnificent as this one. He suspected that some rare, prestigious visitor had modeled it after the legend of the Great Library of Barentia, which was older than anyone could remember. He was sure he'd once seen cuneiform tablets stowed away in the special collections room.

He was pleased to see the oil lamps and wall sconces had been replaced with much safer electric lighting since he was last here.

If there was electricity in the stronghold, that meant there were infrastructural changes elsewhere in the territory.

I'll have to check for cell service once we're back outside.

Though he seriously doubted they would have gone so far as to erect a cell tower on the mountain. Then again, there was electricity in the place *now*.

He indulged in his appreciation of the large room's aesthetic while he observed Ana's reactions to his home.

His gaze fell to Maerie, who stood nearby, her attention on him.

"It may be blasphemous to allow you in here, and even more so to say it, but I am pleased to see you in your beloved home again, Magnus. I know what it meant to you as a boy," she said, no longer guarding herself against him.

She never had, here.

Few ever visited the beautiful repository.

After his mother's death, he'd sought sanctuary in the library when he missed her.

Maerie had recognized this in him, as she'd known it in his mother.

She was risking punishment by allowing his access to the stronghold to be prolonged longer than the signing of the register.

"He comes here too," she said, her voice quiet in the large space. *Elias.*

His father Bjorn never, ever, set foot in this wing that had been dominated by his mother's presence. Servants brought anything Bjorn wanted to his rooms.

Maerie had dared another risk, to speak of the family to a banished.

Frozen, he stared at her, wanting her to say more, yet not wanting to be tempted by what she could say. He glanced up into the stacks, lest someone should be watching, listening.

Registering his apprehension, Maerie stepped closer and kept her voice low. "He is so much like you—as you were at his age. And just as lonely."

Regret tore at his heart.

Magnus nodded, acknowledging the kindness of the insight she offered him about his son. Turning his attention to the stacks, his jaw worked as he considered the unexpected onslaught of emotion, touching the leather-bound spines to ground himself.

Back under control, he returned his gaze to her patient face.

Maerie had always been kind to him, even before his mother's death. There was no doubt she'd extend the same kindness to Elias.

"He is well?"

"As healthy as can be, despite his limited freedom."

"Limited?"

Maerie nodded. "Everyone is limited. Even the young prince—especially the young prince."

Magnus frowned. A prince should expect total freedom of the realm. How else was he to know his lands and people? "He doesn't leave the stronghold?"

She shook her head. "Nor does the king. He's rarely seen."

"He's ill?"

Maerie shrugged, but kept her voice low as she answered. "No one knows. Anyone that requests his presence is redirected to Mistress Ulla. Anyone that tries to circumvent her authority is met with the king's personal guard and either turned away or imprisoned, if they're too persistent."

"What is going on here?" The sharp demand drew everyone's attention to the open door between the library and the Registrar's office.

Magnus straightened when he sighted the guard.

Havard.

Magnus' cousin, boyhood friend, and head of security.

"The Registrar was just reminding me that I am forbidden to be in here, and demanded that I leave."

Havard nodded, eyes leveled on Magnus, expression unreadable.

There was no sense of their boyhood bond or fondness in the man as Magnus approached and passed through the door, then the registrar's office, and out into the open corridor.

Ana followed close behind. Maerie lingered at the threshold of her domain.

Several more guards waited.

They expect a confrontation.

Magnus decided it was time to push inward. "I demand to see my father."

Havard tilted his head up to meet Magnus' direct gaze. "You no longer have a father."

With his head up, Havard's beard was also lifted, exposing the black mark on his throat.

Magnus' gut tightened as he stepped forward, towering over him. The other guards tensed.

Were they all marked? The Barentian's propensity toward full beards obscured their throats.

He stared Havard in the face for a long moment. Ana hovered at his periphery with their backpacks in hand.

Although his stance was one of intimidation, he hesitated out of concern for Ana's safety.

"Doesn't he have a right to see his father once more?" Ana asked Havard.

"He is banished and has no rights at all," he spat.

"Blood is still blood," Magnus said.

Something flickered in Havard's eyes, but it was so brief, Magnus wasn't sure as they continued to stare at one another.

It was something Havard would often say to Magnus in their youth.

Havard scowled. To the men, he said, "Escort them out."

One of the men grabbed Ana's arm, shoving her toward the exit so hard she stumbled into the wall, dropping their bags.

"Don't touch her," Magnus snarled at the guard. He bent to help her to her feet and retrieve the packs. When he turned back to the guards, they'd all moved into defensive positions in the narrow space.

He stepped toward the men, ensuring Ana was behind him. He looked each man in the face then said, "if any of you touch my mate again, I will rip your fucking arms off."

"Looking for a fight, Magnus?" Havard smirked. "Come on, shift."

Magnus' growl reverberated off of the stone walls and floor of the corridor as he dipped into a loose crouch, both shielding Ana and preparing to launch himself forward should he need to.

The other Barentians growled back, gripping their weapons tighter.

The stink of their fear as they faced him stained his nostrils.

A figure appeared at the end of the hall behind the guards.

Magnus' heart stumbled.

"Stop!" A high voice cut across the deafening growls.

The others stopped immediately.

Magnus let his bass growl roll out, giving himself a few extra seconds to compose his reaction to the appearance of his son.

Still fully aware of Ana's rapid breathing behind him, he didn't ease his stance.

Elias strode forward.

The multiple guards surrounding Magnus hadn't phased his heart rate.

The approach of his son sent it into a wild staccato.

Ana's small hand slipped into his palm, soothing him.

By the time Elias stood just beyond the wall of Barentian guards, Magnus had eased his posture and controlled his emotions.

Despite her gesture to calm him, her fingers trembled within his grasp and her breath remained shallow.

Elias moved between the guards.

"Your Highness—" Havard stepped between Magnus and the boy.

No, not quite a boy, or not for much longer, anyway.

Elias' throat was unmarred.

With some relief, Magnus drank in his son's features.

Hair the same as his own. He stood at a level height with Havard. He would be as tall as Magnus, if not taller.

There was little of Ulla in Elias—physically, at least.

Gods, I hope he doesn't favor her in character. My heart would truly break.

The odds were much higher, with his absence.

After a long moment, Elias turned to Havard. "I would speak with my father in the library."

"Sire, it is forbidden—."

"I *will* speak to my father," Elias spoke over Havard, making his command clear.

Magnus struggled to maintain his impassive expression.

Did Elias remember him? He hadn't thought he would, since he was so young when Magnus left.

No, more likely that he'd heard Magnus had returned for the signing and was curious.

Elias strode through the Registrar's office, acknowledging her with a dip of his head. "Madam Gailensdotter."

Movement drew Magnus' attention to the far end of the hall that connected to a cross corridor where Elias had come from. Several figures hovered and ducked behind the corners.

Ignoring Havard, Magnus pressed Ana's fingers, pulling her ahead of himself to follow Elias back into the library.

As much as he'd dreamed of seeing Elias again, he never thought it would happen.

Magnus wasn't sure if he was ready for this.

He released her hand so that she wouldn't detect the tremble that shook his own hands now.

SHOCK, DELIGHT, AND FEAR swept through Ana on seeing Elias.

That was all layered on the instinctive terror that had ripped through her when the snarling echo-chamber had engulfed her senses.

She was so wide open, trying to read every little bit she could, anything that might help Magnus in some way.

The guards' fear of Magnus assaulted her.

Magnus' refusal to back down shored up her courage.

Even the librarian's distress over the confrontation was palpable.

And just like that, a single word cut through it all, allowing her a reprieve to draw breath against the powerful emotions stifling her.

Elias.

The tenor of the atmosphere changed so rapidly it jolted her off balance.

Sandwiched between the young prince and Magnus as they went back to the library, she struggled to control the flow of emotional energy surrounding her—against their conflicted emotions surging against one another like waves trapped in a pool.

In the library, Elias and Magnus took each other's measure.

Ana took theirs.

Elias: *You're here. You left me. You shouldn't be here. I can't believe you're here. We don't have much time. Take me with you.*

Magnus: *My boy. I miss you. You've grown. I never thought I'd see you again. We don't have much time. I need to get you away from here.*

"We don't have much time," Ana blurted, latching on to the most obvious. "Analiese Ortega," she said, shoving her hand toward the prince.

The corner of his lips quirked—like Magnus' did—before he accepted her proffered hand and shook it. "Elias Magnusson."

"Should I curtsy?" she whispered to Magnus.

Elias laughed, releasing some of the tension in his broad shoulders.

Ana glanced toward the door where the guards hovered, scowling.

The registrar remained at the threshold of the doorway, hands clasped so hard her knuckles were white.

"You don't have much time," Ana reminded them and moved away to give them a sense of privacy as she put her backpack on.

"No, we don't. The guards will have gone to fetch my mother," Elias said, scorn lacing his voice. "She forbade me from seeing you when the messenger announced your arrival at the village."

"Yet here you are," Magnus said.

Elias dipped his head, looking like the youth that he actually was.

Ana's heart swelled as their sense of longing overwhelmed her. Their desire to embrace for the first time in a decade.

Oh God, please hug each other before I crumble.

Before someone comes to pull you apart again.

It was all they wanted. That, and to leave Barentia.

She ground her teeth as they continued to face one another, neither reaching for the other.

Footsteps echoing in the stone corridor filtered in through the open door.

Damn it!

Just hug, damn it!

She desperately wanted to shove them together or blurt out what each was feeling to the other as they stubbornly remained silent.

The footsteps were louder now.

Her fingers dug into the straps of Magnus' pack gripped in her hands.

"I'm glad to see you again," Elias said to Magnus.

"As am I," Magnus smiled at his son, letting all his barriers melt away. A true, open smile.

The footsteps stopped. "Elias, I forbade you from coming here today," the woman's voice snapped through the room.

Elias stiffened.

Magnus' smile disappeared before he slowly turned around to face her.

"Ulla."

Ana looked from Magnus to Ulla's barely suppressed triumphant expression.

Her heart dropped.

This can't be good.

Her gaze met the apology in Magnus' eyes.

She slowly closed her eyes, resolved, and returned his gaze.

I trust you.

His face tightened, but he locked his feelings down before they gave him away.

Regret.

"Elias, you are to remain in your room until I decide your punishment," Ulla's hard voice made the boy flinch.

He said nothing to his mother.

His expression full of longing as he spared Magnus a last glance, he strode out of the library through the main door at the far end, rather than squeeze through everyone gathered here.

Poor kid.

Ulla ignored Ana, walking up to Magnus. "The banished are forbidden to speak to anyone in Barentia without official cause. Especially the royal family. I charge you with treason for attempting to influence the true heir of the realm."

Satisfaction roiled off of her like a heavy perfume.

Ana's fingers curled into a fist, as she wanted nothing more than to punch the woman in the face. Twice. No, twice wasn't even enough.

Ulla had used the prince to entrap Magnus.

Of course, Elias would defy her order to see his long-lost father. Possibly a once in a lifetime chance. What youth wouldn't rebel against an order like that?

They'd both expected it—Elias and Magnus. Both accepted the risks.

Did Elias understand the magnitude of the risk for Magnus?

Ana didn't think so.

"Lock these two up separately until I decide what to do with them," Ulla said to the guards and walked out.

Rage ripped through Ana. She shook with it. Struggled to control it.

It wasn't Magnus' feelings.

They were her own.

She'd never ever felt that about anyone in her life before.

How dare this piece of shit be so cavalier?

A guard reached for her.

Magnus snarled at the guard, then shoved him so hard he bounced off the stone wall with a crack. "Leave, Ana; take the plane and go home."

She was shaking her head before the words came. "No."

"Havard is marked. Like Aksel. Come back with Kane and the others."

Rooted to the stone floor, her gaze swept the scene before her. Magnus blocked the guards' access to her. She had a clear path out if she could remember the way.

"If you don't, they may kill both of us."

Would they?

Still, she remained frozen for what seemed minutes when, in reality, it was mere seconds.

She stepped toward Magnus and he roared in her face, allowing his features to morph into the fierce polar bear he was, sending shocks of terror through her nervous system.

She was running before she knew she was moving as she passed through the door to the first courtyard.

Kane.

She had to let Kane know they had confirmation that other Barentians were marked.

Kane would get Magnus out.

The Organization wouldn't abandon one of their own. Ana didn't know Aaron Connor very well, but she knew Raya Burns enough to know that she'd never leave Magnus to rot in a Barentian dungeon. And where Raya went, so went Ian, her formidable mate.

And Carson. She had no idea what his relationship to Magnus was, but Ana knew he'd help her, as would Lirikai.

She clung to the absolute knowledge that she wouldn't be alone. If she could get to the plane. A plane she didn't know how to fly, but that wouldn't stop her from trying.

Magnus, the banished, was still inside the stronghold. Everywhere outside of the stronghold remained deserted.

She passed through the curtain wall and across the last sheltered space toward the final exit, not daring to look back at how close any pursuers were. Her hammering heart, whooshing breath, the swish of her pumping arms and frantic boot falls made hearing anything other than herself impossible.

Belatedly, she realized she'd dropped Magnus' pack at some point, as her own bounced on her back. She ran harder, putting as much distance between herself and the stronghold as she could.

Her initial terror-fueled jump-start was fading as regular adrenaline rushed her veins.

It was a long, long way back to the village where they had docked their little seaplane.

As her muscles strained, she finally spared a glance over her shoulder. If anyone were pursuing her, surely they'd have caught her by now. They were shifters with far more strength and speed than any human.

The expanse of road between herself and the stronghold was empty.

Why hadn't they stopped her? Ulla had said to detain both of them.

Was she just not important enough to waste their time?

God, I hope so.

She never wanted to be so unimportant in her life.

Ana kept going as she considered her options, should someone try to stop her. She had her gun and her taser. Her pack held some few supplies, but not much.

SEVENTEEN

THE SUN WAS STILL below the horizon by the time the dark outlines of the fishing village came into sight in the dim light.

Her fatigued muscles threatened to drag her down into the snow.

How long had she been running?

The road declined sharply toward the village, forcing her to move with more care.

Would the villagers stop her? Had word somehow been sent that she'd escape the stronghold?

Magnus wasn't with her. Surely, they'd be suspicious, considering they were there to record their impending union. Banished, Magnus was forbidden to stay.

A distant sound drew her attention. Standing motionless, straining to determine what it was.

It was the whine of engines. Boats?

She hurried down through the village path.

This time, there was no one to witness her arrival. It was dark and silent. Eerily silent. Like the village was abandoned.

She rounded the downward bend, eyes searching the small harbor for their plane.

The dock was empty.

No! No, no, no!

She slipped the rest of the way down the path, desperately scanning the ocean in case maybe the tether had come untied and it drifted nearby.

The whine of engines grew louder, but there were no boats visible on the horizon.

The sound came from behind her.

Moments later, snowmobiles came into view.

Is there any other way off this island?

Even if there was somewhere to swim to, she'd freeze in the Barents Sea at this time of year—*any* time of year, if she were honest.

She considered drawing her gun. Instead, she ran back up the path, frantically tugging the doors to some houses.

All locked.

The snowmobiles were deafeningly close.

The temple. She darted toward the divine sanctuary. Locked.

She stared at it in disbelief.

Who locks temple doors?

Anyone trying to keep riffraff out.

Spinning around, she scanned the darkness, searching for somewhere to hide, then crouched, moving through the shadows.

Grunting against the strain in her exhausted muscles, she broke for the forest. Maybe there was some other way off the island.

There has to be a boat somewhere, right?

At the edge of the village, she gauged the distance between the cover of the buildings and the forest's edge above it. The snow cover was pristine, with little hint of how deep it was or how uneven the ground was beneath it.

She'd leave a glaring trail.

Her gut told her they weren't a surprise rescue crew sent by Kane. They would have identified themselves.

Run. Hide. Run. Hide.

Heart pounding, she ducked back as a black-clad snowmobiler sped past her hidden position.

They were circling, no doubt searching for her.

Unless, coincidentally, someone else was on the run from the Barentian authorities?

She huffed.

Where the hell is everyone?

Were they hiding inside, or had they all left?

"What are you going to do, Ana?" she muttered, watching for the next passing snowmobile.

Who are these people? Barentians?

Why aren't they just sniffing her out?

Because they aren't Barentian? They're probably the humans that the priestess mentioned.

The darkness.

Think Ana.

Another whizzed past her position.

She grit her teeth, trying to focus while hiding in an abandoned village from the deafening whine of snowmobile engines after running for what seemed an eternity.

Deep breath. Listen.

All she could hear was the incessant whining of the snowmobiles and the drum of her heart in her ears.

She crept along the wall to peer between the houses. The searchers were running their vehicles along the narrow paths.

She ducked back, flat against the wall.

You can keep trying to get into a building or make a run for the forest. Maybe there's another village along the coast with a boat.

Steal a snowmobile?

I'm trapped if I don't.

Ana, you don't know how to drive a snowmobile any more than you know how to fly a plane!

Hide. Run. Hijack.

Fan-freaking-tastic.

Reaching for her taser, her fingers closed around it.

Next one.

She crouched and scuttled closer to the edge of the building where she hid, waiting for the next pass.

With my luck, I'd tase one, Buddy would fly off and the damned thing would crash.

How to get one to stop?

Maybe let one see her?

God, I can't think straight!

She spared the open space toward the forest another glance. The snow was no longer pristine, as it was now marred with tracks from her pursuers.

A whining shadow raced toward her position.

The second it passed her, she launched forward, racing for the forest's edge. She dashed across the vehicle's tracks, and scrambled to climb the rocky incline to reach the darkness below the evergreens.

The noise behind her continued.

The trees were just yards away.

Pain pierced her back, instantly followed by the sharp snap of electricity jolting her body.

Fuck.

Rigid, she was dimly aware of falling back down the rock face toward a dark figure with an extended arm.

She wasn't the only one with a taser.

MAGNUS WOKE TO CHAINS dragging his wrists and ankles toward the stone floor.

Ana.

Was she safe? Did she make it to the plane?

Head pounding, he groaned as he struggled to sit upright, sliding his back along the rough wall.

The damp scents of barely frozen earth told him he was in the dungeon, while the shackles growled of an impossible escape.

Cracking an eye open, he confirmed his location with the sight of the banded oak door at the far end of the narrow cell, thanks to the illumination of an electric light affixed to the ceiling.

Fuck.

Escape would be impossible so long as he sported these chains. They made them to hold powerful shifters—like polar bear shifters. None had ever failed. Even against his bloodline. The biggest and strongest of Barentians. The reason they were the chosen kings in the days when they were under constant threat of warfare from neighboring territories.

At least he'd given Ana enough time to get out of the stronghold while he'd blocked anyone from immediately chasing her down.

With any luck, she'd be on the plane and on her way to meet with Kane.

He swallowed against the sudden dryness in his mouth.

Or, they caught her, and she's in the cell next door.

He had no way of knowing either.

If he'd ignored the temptation to speak to his son, Ana would be safe.

She trusted me to keep her safe.

They'd be on their way off this island together if he'd just adhered to the law.

She's an agent, Magnus. You were both here on a mission.

And what did they gain?

Confirmation that things weren't right here? Likely nothing to do with their mission, just clan politics.

That at least one other Barentian, on Barentian soil, bore a sigil.

Havard. Head of his father's guard.

Neither Elias nor Ulla were marked.

So, what does this mean?

He held his wrists up, shook his head, and dropped them again. The chain dragged and rattled against the flagstone floor with his movement.

"Well, Magnus, looks like you've got all the time in the world to figure it out now."

Was he down here to rot? Or simmer?

Ulla had charged him with treason. His father would have the final say on that, and his punishment.

They had already banished him.

That left life in prison or execution. They weren't likely to send him on his merry way.

He glanced up at the glaring light source.

His father had refused any type of infrastructural changes to the territory for decades.

Why now, in the time of Magnus' absence? After years of trying to convince him Barentia should modernize with the rest of the world?

Ulla.

Maybe his father had been right. The changes since he'd been gone didn't seem to benefit those few that he'd encountered since his arrival, despite the convenience of lighting up the dark spaces that traditionally were lit by oil lamps or torch.

There hadn't been any power lines or solar panels attached to the houses in the fishing village.

Were any of the island's other villages the same?

It would be out of character for his father to actually implement something on the island and not extend it to the benefit of the rest of Barentia.

Whereas, Ulla never gave a shit about anyone other than Ulla.

Not even Elias.

So, what is going on?

Magnus swallowed hard as a sudden wave of despair washed over him.

Surely my father isn't marked like Havard,

Impossible.

Bjorn Thornsson could be led by a pretty face, but he'd never be one's whelp. Never.

Doubt continued to scratch at Magnus' nape.

There was nothing he could do until someone opened the door.

ULLA MATOCHKIN PACED THE expanse of her private suite within the stronghold, chewing the edge of her left thumbnail.

Her right hand vibrated from the incoming message on her cell phone.

With a quick glance at the message, her lips stretched into a triumphant grin.

It had taken an awful lot of conniving to get satellite Internet in place to provide Wi-Fi to the archaic island. A *lot* of conniving, but it was already paying off.

"Gotcha."

Tucking the device into her pocket, she strode toward the door and made her way down to the dungeons.

I finally have Magnus by the balls.

Now it's time to twist.

Descending the stone steps with a light skip, Ulla ignored the baleful look of the lockmaster as she breezed toward him.

He unlocked the cell door and swung it open on silent hinges in time for her to step through without a break in her stride.

These Barentians are so well trained. Everyone in their place, fulfilling their roles to perfection.

She stepped into the cell.

Except Magnus.

He looked directly at her from his seated position on the stone floor, wrists and ankles encased in heavy Barentian manacles, expression guarded.

Many of her own people had fallen to the weight of those manacles in the long past.

Forearms resting on drawn-up knees, he laced his fingers together. The only signal of his agitation. "Ulla."

"Regent. You may call me Regent now."

That had him on his feet. "What's wrong with my father?"

"You have no father, *banished*."

His steel-gray eyes glinted as his jaw tightened. "He still has the final word on my fate, Ulla. Regent or not."

"Maybe," she said with a shrug. "If he's feeling up for it. If not, I will. As I do everything else these days."

"What do you want?"

"From you? Absolutely nothing more than to see you break."

Magnus snorted.

"What's so funny?" Every muscle in her body went rigid at his affront.

Gods I hate this man.

Her eyes flicked the length of him, head to toe, unable to resist assessing his attractive physical traits. She drew a deep breath. His scent invaded her senses, triggering memories. Images of their marriage bed tumbled through her mind, dragging her into their past—the best parts of it, for a few seconds.

"You're still as petty as ever."

"Regardless of what your skewed perception of me is, you're in prison and I have the power to save your life or end it."

"What do you want from me, Ulla?" he repeated, voice dropping in his displeasure.

"What I've always wanted, Magnus. Your cooperation. That's all."

"You don't want cooperation. You want everyone to kiss your ass."

"Same thing." She smiled.

"No, it isn't. Is that why you had Havard marked with a control sigil? Because he wouldn't kiss your ass? And Aksel too? Did he finally see how corrosive you truly are? How many others?"

The smile fell from her face. "Aksel? I would never—what are you talking about? Where is he?"

Her heart pounded harder with each second as his silence stretched.

Aksel had been on the ship that was seized, overseeing its journey to its distribution port.

Her ears rang as her head swam.

He escaped with the other crew members and just hadn't reported in yet.

Her fingers slid over the cellphone in her pocket. She drew a steadying breath. Any time now, he'd message her he was in the clear and returning soon.

But how could Magnus know Aksel had been on *that* ship? How much did he know about the sigils?

"Who are your new friends, Ulla? Who have you let into Barentia?"

He's fishing for the Organization.

Is that why he was really here?

What else does he know?

"When were you supposed to get married, Magnus? Or did you drag that useless human here for nothing?"

He glared at her.

"She didn't get far," Ulla smirked.

Magnus growled, rising to his feet. "Where is she?"

"Where is Aksel?"

"He's lying unconscious, under the care of GPSA medics. Where is Ana?"

"*Care?*" She stepped toward Magnus.

"Ana."

"Picked up by some friends of mine."

Magnus' eyes narrowed as he stepped toward Ulla, growling louder, despite the pull of the chains.

She stepped back toward the door, fear rippling throughout her body.

"Are these friends the same friends that marked Aksel with a sigil and beat him so badly he had to crawl into a control room panel to escape them?"

Pain bloomed in Ulla's chest as her lungs constricted.

Polar bear shifters never, ever crawled.

And certainly not Aksel...

Not Aksel.

"He wouldn't..." Wulker wouldn't. Nor would... Not to Aksel.

"Who wouldn't what?" Magnus pressed. "Who wouldn't what, Ulla? Your friend wouldn't do that to your little brother?"

"Shut up, Magnus," she snarled back, unable to think, her gut twisted so hard.

Ulla studied her ex-husband's stony face. He'd never been a liar.

But things change. He was an agent for the Organization.

Agents lie.

But how else could he know Aksel was on that ship, or about the sigils?

She met his eyes.

Her instinct told her he was being truthful.

Aksel was in trouble. Real trouble.

"Call your agency and have him brought to Barentia."

Magnus shook his head. "He specifically didn't want that."

"You said he's unconscious." She stepped forward, hands fisted.

"He is."

"You're making no sense."

"Ana communicated with him in the astral where he's trapped in bear form."

Ulla gasped, gaze dropping to the floor as her mind raced.

Magnus went on. "He's trapped in a sea of black ink or oil, or something."

She reached for the wall as her knees buckled.

Oh Gods, no.

"You and I—and Ana—can go to where Aksel is being safeguarded and you can see him for yourself."

Why? Why would Wulker do this to Aksel?

Aksel had to have challenged him. But *why?*

What was he thinking?

"It's too late for her—your human." Ulla squared her shoulders, lifting her chin as she glared back at Magnus. "That's on you, Magnus. You brought her here."

EIGHTEEN

ANA'S HEAD SPUN BEHIND her closed lids, brain pounding.

Magnus. I have to help Magnus.

Her body ached from the tasing.

God, I feel awful. I owe Raya a colossal apology.

The spinning in her head seemed to have gathered cotton in her ears, muffling any sound around her.

Stink crept up her nostrils.

Not brisk northern air.

Where am I?

She cracked her eyes open into more darkness, then let them close again.

Her hands grazed her waist, noting that her weapons were gone. Pulling her cell from her pocket, she confirmed there was no service before she tapped the flashlight function to illuminate her surroundings.

Oh no. No, no, no.

Above her was the familiar view of the interior roof of a cargo container.

They must have drugged her to keep her unconscious, to get her into one.

She groaned, trying to roll onto her side.

"I'd lie still for a while if I were you. It'll take some time for the drugs to wear off. We don't want you puking all over the place," someone said from nearby.

"Smells like someone already did," she groaned.

"Exactly. Don't need any more of that, along with everything else." The face to the voice loomed over her, squinting from the light. He held up a water bottle. "Drink this when the spinning stops."

"Are we on a ship?" With her head already spinning, she couldn't tell.

"Not yet."

A second face, creased with concern, loomed over her.

Ana's heart stopped. She blinked as she squeaked, "Antony?"

"Antony? No, I'm Emilio. You know Antony?" the first man said.

"You can see me?" Antony asked, astonished. "It's about god-dammned time, Ana!"

"What do you mean, it's about time?" she demanded. "I've been trying to reach you since you died."

"Uhm. Ma'am, maybe you should drink some water sooner rather than later." Emilio put the water on the floor next to her.

She pushed herself into a sitting position, balanced her phone on her knee, then swiped the bottle, uncapped and guzzled its contents as she glared up at Antony next to her.

"Thanks," she said to Emilio when she finished.

"Are you alright? You seemed to have hit your head. There's some blood," Emilio said, waving an index finger in a circle toward her.

She had some vague recollection of bouncing off rocks on her way down while she was being tased.

"Maybe that's why I can see you," she said to Antony.

Antony shrugged.

"Yeah, sure," Emilio said, stepping back.

Ana turned her attention to her surroundings. She swept the room with her light. She and Emilio and Antony weren't alone. A dozen other scattered people in the confines of the cargo container squinted at her with varying expressions of concern and annoyance. A few ignored her altogether.

"God, this is so bad."

"No kidding," Emilio said.

"Why are you here?" she said to Antony.

"Because you need to save them," he said, exasperated.

Emilio said, "because they picked us up after the confusion of the accident. Hey, you mentioned Antony and trying to reach him since he died. You're not Analiese, are you?"

Ana froze. "How do you know my name?" she grabbed the flashlight phone, aiming it at Emilio. He wore a dirty uniform. Shining the light back down the length of the room again, she noted several more men in uniforms. "Oh, my god," she whispered.

"Yeah, Ana. I told you to *save* them, not *join* them."

"You," she jabbed a finger in Antony's direction. "Your sarcasm isn't helping."

"I, uh..." Emilio said.

"You," she turned to Emilio. "You're one of Antony's crew mates, right? You were on his ship when the accident happened? How the hell are you *here*? And yes, I'm Antony's ... friend, Analiese."

"I should ask you that same question."

"Put the light out, will ya? You're blinding us. There's no cell service, so you might as well turn it off," one of the other captives said.

She switched it off, throwing the room back into darkness, and tucked the device into her pocket.

Ana sat in the darkness listening to her own breath and those of the other people trapped with her. Eventually, her eyes adjusted to the darkness and she could see the cracks of light outlining the door at the far end of the box.

This is real. This is real.

I'm trapped in a fucking cargo container.

I should have ignored Carson's call.

"Maybe, but that's not helping you right now," Antony said.

Jolted, she gaped.

Antony can hear my thoughts.

"Yeah. I can."

Just like Aksel in his Bear form.

"Who?"

Never mind. Where the hell have you been? All this time?

"Mostly bouncing between here, keeping an eye on my boys and trying to get your attention, Ana. So much for being a psychic if you can't even hear me when I'm yelling at you."

She drew her legs up, curled her arms around her shins and rested her pounding forehead on her knees.

You were in my nightmares.

"Nightmares? I was trying to show you what happened, Ana. And that my guys needed your help! Do you know how exhausting this is?"

Sorry. It's probably the guilt. It creates a barrier sometimes.

Tears stung her eyes.

Yeah, what kind of psychic am I when you needed me most?

"Hey, don't cry, Ana."

Don't cry? This is all my fault. And if they're still here after all this time, there's nothing I can do to save them.

"This is not your fault, sweetheart. It's because of you they're even alive."

She sniffled, dabbing her eyes on her sleeve.

What do you mean?

She had the sense he'd settled next to her. His energy felt closer, stronger as it mingled with hers.

"I-uh," he sighed. "Ana, I'm sorry I pushed you away when you tried to warn me something bad was going to happen at sea. Your ability kept these guys alive. Even though *I* died, I could save them because your warnings gave me the edge I needed to react in time to get them out."

The Navy is still investigating.

"Yeah, I've been watching that, too. They're doing their best, but you need to let them know what happened."

Ana snorted.

Right.

"No really. We're going to figure out how to get you out of here," Antony insisted.

Ana laughed. Someone shuffled further away.

Antony, they've been trapped for over a month If they—trained for conflict guys—haven't been able to escape, how do you think I can?

"You, sweetheart, have me. Now that you're listening."

She grit her teeth.

You haven't changed.

"Why should I?"

Aren't you supposed to be all-knowing and full of compassion and grace in the afterlife?

"Yeah, sure, but I got things to do first. Like save my guys, then I can go slap some wings on my back. Help me out here."

She rubbed her temples, praying the pounding would ease soon so that she could deal with this ... what the hell was this?

"Life, Ana. This is life," Antony said, dropping some of his bluster.

A cool prickling sensation drifted across her cheek.

If there had been more light in the room, she would have seen Antony's hand caressing her face.

She leaned into it.

I really miss you.

"Me too, sweetheart."

She had the impression he pressed a staticky kiss on her forehead.

"I have an idea. Do you know how to bi-locate, like that girl that you interviewed did?"

Just in theory. I'm not skilled enough in my ability yet. Any time Maeda tried to guide me through the process, I just snapped back into my body.

"Hmm. Okay, that won't work. We'll just keep it simple then. I'll guide you through an escape."

Ana thought of Raya's prison break—how she used her Ashray ability to guide Chuck Meduse out of the prison to freedom. The other inmates had thought he was psychic or delusional.

Her cargo mates would likely come to the same conclusions about her.

"Nah, I told them you're gifted."

Yeah, I don't know about that anymore.

"Stop feeling sorry for yourself and help me help you help them."

You could let me wallow for at least ten minutes, Antony. It's been a pretty crappy few hours and my head is still swimming.

"You're still alive, I'm dead. I'll give you five minutes before we start planning."

Ana sighed.

Nope, you haven't changed at all.

MAGNUS' NEED TO FIND and protect Ana warred with his desire to crush Ulla's throat with his teeth.

He'd never wasted his time hating anyone in his life, but right now, he had nothing but time to hate Ulla. His hands curled into fists.

When they banished him, he'd lost his world.

This disconnection, this powerlessness... that was nothing compared to this.

On his feet, he paced as far as the chains would allow, which wasn't far.

Knowing Ana was in danger while he remained trapped in this cell at Ulla's command, tore at him.

He didn't care that she was clearly distraught over Aksel's current position.

That's her problem—her fault.

There was no doubt in his mind all of this was her fault.

Barentia's downfall would be on her head.

He just couldn't decide if he'd seek her out and crush her before he went after Ana, or come back and do it then.

If he ever got out.

No.

When.

When he got out.

Ulla wanted to see him break?

Fuck her.

Rage tore through him. Pain stabbed his wrists and ankles, dropping him to his knees, forcing him to control his instinctive desire to shift into his bear.

Magnus, you can't afford broken wrists and ankles. Ana needs you.

He ground his teeth against the pain, forcing his animal to calm.

On his knees, panting, sweat slicking his forehead, he stared at his partially shifted hands, claws extended. The manacles bit into the flesh of his wrist as his body strained against the cuffs.

He willed calm and control throughout his body, removing the edge that allowed his body to return to full human form.

Save that for later.

Instinct later, thought now.

How to get out?

Once out, his way to freedom wouldn't be too complex—as long as there weren't many guards, or these chains, to contend with.

Remove chains, escape cell...

Three paces one way, three paces back.

The heavy lock clicked, drawing Magnus' attention to the cell door.

The lockmaster swung it open, flanked by half a dozen guards. "It's time."

Magnus' gaze flicked over their resolute faces. As far as he could tell, none were marked, but they were all prepared to carry out their orders. No matter what.

Magnus was no longer their prince. He was banished—a prisoner of the realm.

Now isn't the time to escape. Not yet.

He nodded.

... maybe I can take Elias with me...

He buried that thought as quickly as it came and waited while the lockmaster unfastened his chains from the wall.

Magnus' mind worked as they moved through the dungeon corridors, up the winding stone steps, twisting and turning down the too familiar halls of his former home.

My son's home. Elias.

He couldn't help block the thoughts of his son from his mind. He might see him again.

My boy.

No.

Ana. Ana needs my help. Ulla's partners have her. She isn't safe.

Magnus clenched his jaw, his instinct to protect both his son and his mate conflicting and overwhelming.

Every muscle in his body tensed as he passed through the open double doors into the ancient Great Hall. The sounds of his chains echoed through the vast room with each step toward his fate.

Two guards preceded him with two behind, and two on either side. More at key positions of the expansive room, as was expected when the king held court.

Escape wouldn't be easy from here. He considered his other options as he moved forward.

At the far end, his father occupied the throne. Elias stood to the right of the throne while Ulla stood to the left.

Where is the shaman?

His father, his son, his former wife—the three people he'd committed his life to, before his banishment.

He sucked in a breath as unexpected emotions slammed through him.

Betrayal. Regret. Disgust.

He focused on Elias as he approached his father's judgment.

No matter what, he'd imprint his son's face in his memory.

Even if he, too, hated him and turned his back on Magnus.

"Stop there," Ulla commanded.

Ignoring her, he turned his attention to his father, ten paces before him.

Sadness swallowed every other emotion.

Bjorn Thornsson, King of the Barentian Polar Bear Shifters, was no longer the physically robust ruler exuding power that he'd been when Magnus last laid eyes on him.

The arm of the throne supported his shrunken, sallow form. His once thick white and gray hair hung in limp strings to either side of his hollowed cheeks and bleary eyes.

Magnus sniffed. *Not right.* His father smelled of slow rot from the inside out.

Illness?

How?

Magnus searched for a mark denoting Ulla's influence on the elder man. His high collar encased his throat below his thinned beard.

Magnus turned on Ulla, ready to throw accusations at her.

She met his gaze, but there was no triumph or delight in her eyes. Fear?

Couldn't be. What is there for Ulla to fear? Here? Now? No.

He stayed his words.

"Magnus the Banished," his father rasped, still denying Magnus his paternal surname.

Still not Magnus Bjornson in Barentia's eyes.

He sucked in a breath at the resurgence of rejection, attempting to re-bury it.

He straightened his shoulders, staring at the sick old man, willing him to get on with his judgment.

The old man's jaw worked before he spoke. "I charge you with treason for attempting to influence the true heir of the realm," Bjorn repeated Ulla's words almost verbatim, panting against the energy those words cost him.

Magnus' keen hearing picked up the subtle movements of the guards surrounding him. Clenching fists on weapons, shuffling feet, deep breaths.

They were prepared for him to resist. To fight.

They expected it.

Gladly. But not yet.

Not yet.

Magnus kept his features neutral as he leveled his gaze at Elias' drawn expression.

"In consideration of your previous position as heir and member of the ruling family, I shall grant you mercy."

Tears glazed Elias' eyes.

Magnus nodded.

Execution then.

"By rights of the condemned, I claim my entitlement to a final interview with the clan shaman."

"You do not observe the clan ways," Ulla blurted.

"Hm," Magnus grunted, looking at his ex-wife. "Perhaps in my last moments, I'll make my final statements. One of which *may* indicate which facility Aksel is in, where they're working to keep him alive."

"You bast—."

"Tradition dictates that I have three days before the allotted execution date, doesn't it? Plenty of confinement time to consider my last words."

Ulla's fingers curled into fists as she struggled to control herself.

"Three days. The sooner you bring the shaman to me, the sooner I may relieve my conscience and set my soul right. So that I might not haunt my executioners."

Bjorn's glassy eyes found Magnus' face, frowning as he regarded him.

Magnus couldn't read him. He never could.

What happened to this family?

What has Ulla been filling his head with, all this time?

Before her arrival at Barentia, Magnus' relationship with his father wasn't exactly loving, but it was mutually respectful and healthy despite their differences of opinion on certain matters.

Ulla had always wanted control. She had it. In his absence, she'd gained control as regent, bridging the rulership between his still-living father and too-young son.

She was threatened by Magnus' appearance to sign the register, recording his impending union.

Insecure in her position?

"Summon the clan shaman," Bjorn wheezed, then waved Magnus away.

The guards' expressions were uncertain as they exchanged glances before they moved to fulfill their order.

Magnus looked at Elias one last time. "You will be a fine king someday."

He turned and left the Great Hall his ancestors had ruled for centuries. Probably for the last time.

Three days.

Magnus had three days to figure out an escape, or he'd fail Ana, Elias, and Barentia.

NINETEEN

CLANGING AND BANGING PRECEDED the opening of the cargo box door. Everyone squinted against the sudden splash of light filling the room.

"Breakfast," Antony said.

Two goons stood on either side of the door, holding automatic rifles, while two more distributed food.

Emilio shoved a bowl of gruel with a chunk of bread into Ana's hands. "Yummy," she muttered, staring at the gray slop.

The pounding and spinning in her head had gone away after a few hours of sleep, making it easier to focus and think.

Emilio and the other crew members settled around Ana before the doors closed, throwing them back into darkness.

She'd heard them whispering among themselves whenever she was awake, catching snippets here and there.

"What do you want to know?" she said, raising the spoon, hoping it was high enough to reach her mouth in the dark. After a few seconds, she lifted the bowl to her chin and just shoveled it in, gagged once, and powered on. She hadn't eaten since the snacks she and Magnus had consumed on their way to the stronghold.

"Antony."

"Okay."

"He said you're gifted. Like, woo-woo gifted."

Ana struggled against snorting the gruel out through her nose. "I guess you could call it that."

Did you seriously describe me as 'woo-woo' gifted to them, Antony?

"It was the only way to get them to understand what I was talking about when I tried to be polite about it."

"We figured he didn't make it after he got us out. He was, uhm... right in the middle of the, uhm... blast," Emilio said, then sucked in a breath.

"No. He didn't," she said, her voice soft. "The navy is going on the assumption none of you made it since they didn't recover you. Dead or alive."

"So they're not even looking for us," one of the other guys said.

"They're investigating. That's all I know," Ana said.

"No one in the world knows we're here," another said.

"No one knows any of us are here," a woman said from further away.

"No, but that doesn't mean no one's looking," Ana said. "It's what I do. I'm part of a team investigating this group that's stealing people, and selling them."

"That's fucking awesome," the woman said, laughing. "And you're in here with us."

"Yeah, thanks for pointing out the obvious. That's what Antony said, too."

"What? He's here with us? You weren't just crazed from that bump on your head?"

"Nah, I'm always crazed, bump or not. And yes, Antony is here. He's been here with you all this time and apparently trying to tell me about it. But I've had... communication issues."

Emilio grunted.

"My crew will come looking for us. We were so close. They'll find us," she said with more uplift in her voice than she felt in her gut.

"Yeah, how are they going to do that? We don't even know where the hell we are," the woman snapped.

"Well, they grabbed me from an island nation in the middle of the Barents Sea, so I expect we're still in that region or very close. My team knew where I was. And now that I've gone missing, they'll hone in."

"Lady, it takes a lot to find boats in vast areas like that."

"I'm aware. My crew is... special," she said, thinking of Carson's ability to shift into a water dragon. Ian too. Lirikai was also a fierce aquatic hunter. Raya was a hell of a fighter and could go anywhere there was a water source.

And Magnus. He'd be magnificent as his polar bear self. Her chest tightened, thinking of him. Had he broken free from the guards? Did Kane go in after him, guns blazing—or whatever it was she did?

"Like Navy Seals or SAS?"

"Yeah, something like that, but... more. A lot more."

"Bullshit," someone scoffed.

"Listen, Ana," Emilio spoke. "If Antony is here, can you tell him thank you for keeping us alive? Even if we got picked up by these pricks."

"Tell them they're all welcome and that wasn't part of the plan."

Emilio laughed when Ana relayed his words. "No shit, huh?"

"Have you all been together this whole time?"

"Our crew? Yeah, for the most part. We don't even know who these pricks are or what they want from us, but we've seen a lot of other folks coming and going. I think we're here because we're the troublemakers," he gave a short laugh.

"They're traffickers. Everything from drugs, weapons, animals, people—anything their clients want."

"Animals? Yeah, that makes sense. A while back, they had us in another crate and something happened that made the guards panic and all we could hear was roaring. Like a lion or something. Made all the hair on my body stand on end; kinda glad we were locked in here."

"It *was* a polar bear. Pretty freaky seeing it going wild like that before they brought it down with a tranq. I went to see what all the noise was when the roaring started," Antony said.

"A polar bear?" Ana asked. Aksel?

"Who knows?" Emilio said.

Antony said, "Yeah, big son of a bitch, too. It was weird. That girl you talked to that split?"

"Bi-located? Sascha?"

"Yeah, the one that gave you my message. She was there. I thought maybe the animal had tried to attack her or something because it went nuts when they pulled her out of the box. Emilio and the guys had stepped in and tried to protect her from some nasty shit they were doing to her a few days before. I thought they were going to feed her to it or something."

"Sascha? You've seen her?" the woman asked.

"Yes. My team seized the ship she was on. Everyone on board was rescued."

The woman sobbed. "Oh, thank God. Thank God. She's my student. I teach her English. They grabbed us together while on holiday. I'm so glad she made it out."

"Yeah, we were all worried the creepy guy got her," Emilio said.

"Creepy guy?"

"There's two of 'em in charge," Antony said.

"Who are they?" Ana asked.

"A guard mentioned Wulker," a crewman said.

"Adolf Wulker. Looks like an underfed accountant," Antony said. "There's another guy. Big guy. Doesn't say much. Clean-shaven blond guy that came around with a woman around a couple of times. A tall blonde. Nice to look at."

"Have you seen anyone with weird throat tattoos?"

"Yeah sure. Most of them don't get seen again, though. What is it? Like a brand or a tag for a gang or something?"

"More like a brand," Ana said, drawing a deep breath. "It's dangerous."

"The tattoo? Do they contaminate the ink with some contagion or something?" Emilio demanded.

"Ehm. Well. Sort of?"

"But?"

"Here's where the woo-woo comes in."

"Ah shit. Don't tell us. If we get tattooed, we're screwed?"

"Yeah, pretty much."

Clanging signaled the guards' return.

The doors squealed open, blinding everyone again as the bowls were collected.

A new figure appeared in the illuminated rectangle of the doorway.

"Shit, Ana, that's him. The Accountant."

Ana's breath caught as she squinted to make out details as her eyes tried to adjust to the light. The silhouette was smaller than the guards, his form outlined in a suit.

"That one," his accented, nasal voice commanded with a nod.

The two guards collecting the bowls moved toward Ana.

"Oh shit, no, Ana!" Antony yelled, swiping ineffectually at the guards to stop them.

"Hey!" Emilio and the crewmen shot to their feet. "Leave her alone."

One of the armed guards dropped the point of his rifle at Emilio. "Back off."

"Emilio. My team is coming. Be ready for them. They'll need all the help they can get from the inside when they get here," she whispered, raising her hands submissively as the guard grabbed her wrist. "Woo-woo or not, be ready."

The guard wrenched her wrist painfully, dragging her out of the box into the garish fluorescent lights of a massive warehouse.

Ana squeezed her eyes shut against the pain from the light stabbing her eyeballs, alternately squinting until they adjusted.

The nasal voiced man questioned another larger figure standing further away, who appeared to just nod.

"Analiese Ortega."

"Yes?" she blinked at the man who wasn't much taller than herself. "You are?"

Creepy Accountant seems about right.

"Here to collect my leverage." He grinned and turned on his heel.

Shoved by a guard, she had no choice but to follow him as the steel doors clanged shut again.

"Don't worry, Ana, I'm right here with you," Antony said as they passed the taller man that fit the description of the second man Emilio described. "I'm not going anywhere."

The man's eyes slid from Ana to Antony.

"Does he see me?"

The corner of the blond man's lips lifted.

"Shit," Antony said.

Ice slid through Ana's veins.

The armed guard shoved her forward again, forcing her to keep up with the Accountant.

JOEY KANE PACED BEHIND her desk as her team assembled in her office. Jack Maeda was on the line from his New York office.

"Please close the door," she said to Aaron Connor as soon as he jogged into the room.

With a nod, he did so and moved in.

Joey's gaze slid from team member to team member. Even the ones that usually masked their emotions exuded concern. Aaron Connor, Raya Burns, Carson Perenga, Lirikai of the Barra'kidai, Ian McLachlan. Everyone else associated with the case was still in the field.

Do I tell them about the Gate?

She bit her lip.

No, there will be time for that later. Focus on this *case right now.*

"We're all here, boss," Aaron prompted, fingers tapping against his thigh.

Right.

"Jack is on the line with us," she gestured toward the conference speaker phone on her desk.

"Ana and Magnus?" Carson leaned in.

They were all clearly impatient for a status report.

"Dark."

The team erupted, all speaking at once.

"Fuck," Raya said.

Carson said, "When are we going in after them?"

"They should have been back by now," Aaron picked up Joey's pacing across the back of the room.

"Yes," Joey nodded. "They should have. The seaplane they used to fly into Barentia hasn't been returned yet."

"What do we know?" Jack's voice came through the speaker-phone.

Joey hardened her voice. "First, we know they are both highly trained agents and that if they're in trouble, we need to give them time to resolve the situation. So we prepare in the event we will have to go in—and it looks like we may," she added before anyone could interject. "But we have to be careful."

"Fucking politics," Ian growled.

"Yes. Fucking politics," Joey repeated and reminded them of what they already knew. "While we have access to most waters, there are still some jurisdictions we are not free to enter without permission or a very good cause."

"And you know we can get in undetected," Carson said. "So, where is the problem?"

"Do any of you know much about the Barentians?"

Aaron and Raya were the only ones that nodded.

To the others, Joey briefly explained their history and relation-ship to outsiders.

"So grumpy, xenophobic polar bear shifters," Lirikai said.

"But why? The other polar bear communities don't go to the same extremes to keep outsiders away," Raya asked. "What are they hiding?"

"Everyone has their reasons to shut out the world," Ian said, casting Raya a grim look.

"What else do we know?" Aaron asked, bringing the meeting back to the point.

Jack filled in, "since Magnus identified Aksel Matochkin, our nearly dead shifter victim as his brother-in-law, we dug around into him. He and his sister Ulla are children of King Matochkin of the Novaya Zemlya polar bears. Their territory rides the line between the Kara Sea and the Barents Sea. Matochkin is notorious for his eccentricities and volatility."

"Seems an odd partnership for Thornsson to make," Aaron said.

"Magnus told me that his mother was from the Icelandic clan west of Barentia, while Ulla is from the southeast. Other ancestral matrons are from all over the arctic region, including northern Canada, Alaska and Russia," Joey said.

"Unions with each of the clans," Lirikai said. "Do you think Thornsson is planning something or expecting trouble?"

Joey hesitated, then blew out her breath. "Yes."

"Which is?"

How much do I tell them?

"Magnus' family has been the chosen guardians for an incredibly valuable artifact in the high north; only a handful of people in the world have some *hint* of its existence." She drew in a breath. "But our job is to focus on the human trafficking ring and rescue survivors in order to return them to their families. So, we'll focus on that."

Carson nodded, gaze locked on Joey's face. "You'll tell us about this artifact later?"

Joey resumed her pacing, ignoring the question. "Jack, what else do we know that can help us?"

"Matochkin is known to have worked closely with a company that provides renewable energy and satellite connectivity to remote areas like his. I sent you some files on that."

"Why is this of interest to us?" Joey reached for the device on her desk to switch on the monitor affixed to the wall, then the keyboard to retrieve the files Jack mentioned. On opening the file, several images cast to the screen, including the logo of an octopus with its arms enveloping a globe.

"Embraceable Energy. Embracing responsible technology to reach every part of the planet," Aaron said, reading the motto.

Jack continued, "I've had my tech team investigating to see if we could tap into this network. Most of the satellites in the north are government owned. Some allow us access, some don't. Barentia isn't covered because it's on a blackout list of protected areas."

"As per U.N. agreements with sovereign shifter nations. And?"

"And—."

"Look at the logo," Raya breathed.

Jack continued, "And the logo is suspiciously similar to the sigil tattoo."

Joey tapped a few keys to split the screen and bring up the images of the sigil. "Eight arms on the octopus. Eight bars on the sigil."

"Eight major shipping regions that we've seized human cargo from," Raya said.

"What do we know about the company's owner?" Carson asked, rubbing a hand over the back of his neck.

"Adolf Wulker. Shifter. Octopus," Jack said.

"Of course," Lirikai said, rolling her eyes.

Aaron resumed his pacing. "Why have we never heard of this guy before?"

"We're aware of him. We just didn't have cause to look into him before now," Joey said. "He's good at camouflaging himself and his activities."

"Slippery sucker," Lirikai said, crossing her arms.

Jack went on, "I've listened to all of Ana's interview recordings, including her trip into the astral realm with Aksel. She said the ocean was full of a black substance she wasn't sure was oil or ink. I think it was ink. Squid—Octopus ink."

"Meaning?" Carson glanced back to the enlarged image of the sigil.

"Meaning, I think Wulker is more than just a shifter. The sigils aren't just ownership brands."

"I'll have the medics analyze samples of Aksel's skin to see if they made the tattoo of squid ink and any other components," Joey said, following Jack's line of thought. "And if we can remove it."

"In the meantime, I'm going to have my tech department quietly poke around Wulker's infrastructure to see if they can find a way into his databases."

"Good," Joey said. "The rest of us are going to load the jet with gear and make our way to Norway. Whether Wulker has anything to do with the trafficking ring or not, we need to find out why Magnus and Analiese haven't contacted us via sat-phone. There could be a good reason they haven't reached out and I don't want to blow the mission if there is."

"And if not, we're ready to go in after them," Carson said, pulling Joey's attention.

He held her gaze.

She nodded, understanding that if she gave the order or not, he *would* go after Analiese.

"Dismissed." Everyone rose to clear out.

"I'll call in with an update as soon as we have something," Jack said.

"Prioritize this project above everything else."

"Understood." The line clicked off.

Joey turned, startled to see Carson waiting, hand on the door-knob. He closed the door, returning to speak to Joey eye to eye.

Carson's jaw tightened as he held her gaze, one fist enclosing the other as he considered his words.

Carson didn't look older than mid-thirties, like herself.

"We've both been on this earth for a long, long time."

Her lips quirked as she nodded toward the closed door. "Lirikai longer than you. I, a little longer than her."

His expression remained stern. "This artifact."

The two words stole away the budding smile.

"If this is what I think it is, Kane, it better not be the political road trap in our way of retrieving our agents. I don't care about that. Ana's life is worth more than that. And I'd have thought you'd feel the same about Magnus."

Joey's throat tightened. "I do. But, he also understands how important this is too, Carson. And yes, part of my hesitance *is* about the artifact. Magnus knows. He's always known. He will ride that line. That's why I'm giving him more time."

"If he lets Ana—."

"He won't," She cut him off. "He won't, Carson. I trust him as much as I trust you."

"If something happens to her..."

"I know. As I said at the top of this meeting, they're both trained agents. And I have to trust *them*. So do you. Now go and help Lirikai pack what you'll need. I can feel how close we are to shutting this case down."

Carson grunted, held her gaze a moment longer, then turned on his heel and left her office.

She watched him go, blowing out her pent breath, easing her hip against her desk. "Gods, please let this go the *right* way."

TWENTY

THERE WAS NO SENSE of time in the dungeon cell that they forced Magnus back into.

All he knew was that if he didn't find a way out, he'd die.

And that he stank.

When he wasn't plotting his escape, he was fantasizing about a hot shower with Ana. *His* Ana.

As soon as he ensured her safety. And he would, because he'd rip the world apart to find her. They *would* be reunited.

And when they were, he was going to take them both straight to the shower where they'd cleanse one another, and he'd worship her as he'd done the night before they flew out of Ireland for Barentia.

Only this time, he'd find all the little places he'd missed the first time.

Magnus never thought he'd find a mate. A true mate.

And a fragile human one, at that.

She fit so perfectly in his arms.

Their energies sparked similarly to how their bodies moved like they were made for each other.

Right from that first moment.

There was no way in all the frozen hells of the northern wastelands that he was going to find and then lose her.

First, he had to get out of here.

The metal tumblers in the lock clicked several times before dropping into place with a final clunk.

Magnus sighed and got to his feet, preparing for whatever came next.

The door didn't swing open like it had on previous occasions.

It drifted open, slow, tentative.

He grit his teeth, willing it to open faster.

What now?

A figure finally poked his head around the corner, expression uncertain.

"Elias?"

"Father." Elias pushed the door open the rest of the way, staring at Magnus, eyes flitting over the manacles and chains securing him to the wall.

The young man's eyes registered shock and sadness before quickly turning to fury.

"How dare they chain a member of the royal family?" his voice cracked as he surged forward.

"Which I no longer am, Elias," Magnus' own voice was calm and steady in the face of his son's outrage at his predicament. "Not as a banished one."

"Banished or not. You're still blood," he growled.

Magnus' heart soared with pride as he studied his son's face. His whiskers were starting. Patchy on the youth's smooth skin.

"Even if you are just here to spy on us."

Magnus' heart plummeted. "I came to sign the register."

"Why would you spy on us? For who? Mother says you can't be trusted."

"Since your mother is certain of these things, I'm sure she can answer your questions." Magnus glanced toward the door, half expecting her to come and send Elias away again.

"She isn't here. She left as soon as the guards confirmed you were chained and locked away."

Gone? Where would Ulla go? Why?

"And you've come down here. Why?" Magnus said, redirecting his thoughts to his son while he still had time to talk to him.

Elias shrugged. "I remember you. From before you left." He sighed, then cast Magnus a furtive glance. "I never could quite believe the things mother accused you of."

"I'm not surprised she spoke ill of me to you."

"She didn't. Not really. I, uhm, used to eavesdrop when she met with Grandfather. She would demand I stay in my room, but I never did."

"Like when you came to see me in the registrar's office."

Elias nodded.

"I see."

"She said you had spies sneaking around Barentia and that you would push Grandfather to give up the throne so you could have it. She said you were cold and calculating. That you were abusive during your marriage and would be again, should you be allowed to return."

"She said I was abusive?" Magnus gaped, then laughed.

"What's so funny?" Elias demanded. "There's nothing amusing about abusing your wife."

"No, Elias, there isn't. And I wasn't."

Elias glared at him imperiously. "Explain. I want the truth. I'm tired of everyone hiding everything from me. I'm not a child anymore."

Magnus considered this.

"No, you're not. And I saw that my fath—the king is very ill. You may ascend much sooner than I could have ever imagined."

"The truth. About mother."

"I never abused your mother. She would lose her temper and injure herself while striking me."

"You pushed her to it."

"No. I simply did not rise to her impulsive, unrealistic demands. I would not cooperate, and she would frustrate herself."

After a few moments considering this, Elias nodded.

He isn't blind. Thank the Gods.

Should I ask?

Magnus swallowed, chewing over the words.

"What happened to your grandfather? How long has he been ill?"

"I-I don't know. I don't know what's happening."

"Hasn't the shaman been able to do anything to help him?"

"The shaman is dead."

Magnus' heart skipped. "Dead? And no one has replaced him to ensure the king's strength?"

Elias shook his head. "Do you think Havard has something to do with it? Do you think he's betrayed us?"

"Why would you think so?" Magnus straightened his spine, mind racing.

The boy shrugged. "He's been... different. Different since Grandfather became ill."

"Do you know where your mother went?" Magnus said, bringing the conversation back to Ulla.

"No. Maybe."

"And she went with Havard and the other guards?"

"No, she went with Yvan."

"Yvan? Yvan Gorbinson, the stonemason?"

"No. Yvan Putinovski. Mother's human magician that she brought back from Grandfather Matochkin's court after you left—were banished."

"The king allowed a human magician in his stronghold?" Magnus gaped again.

"He's mother's trusted... friend. She was lonely, and he keeps her entertained with his tricks and illusions."

"Illusions?"

Awe slid across Elias' face. "Oh yes! He can create such wonderful images. Fill a room with beautiful colors, or make you believe you're in a place you're not. Even make himself seem invisible to the eyes."

"What else can this human magician do?"

"Oh, I have no idea, but he's very good at alleviating boredom. Or was, before mother had satellite television brought to the stronghold."

"What?" Magnus paced to the end of his chains, palms to face. "Forgive me, Elias. Did you say satellite television?"

"Yes, of course. Once the electricity was installed and proved to work, she arranged for other comforts."

Magnus glanced back at the light bulb. "What other *comforts* has your mother brought to Barentia?"

Elias smiled now. "We have internet from a satellite. The humans use snowmobiles to get around the island."

Humans plural? Snowmobiles?

"This doesn't make any sense. How long has all of this been going on?"

"Maybe a year or two? It took some time to have the work done to build the windmills and solar panels and run all the wiring through the stronghold."

"And your grandfather *allowed* all of this?"

"I *think* so?"

"This doesn't make any sense," Magnus said again as he resumed his short-strided pacing.

"He banished me for trying to encourage him to bring twenty-first century technology to Barentia."

"Mother has done a lot to negotiate with him *and* on his behalf. She arranged it all with this company that specialized in remote environmental access. They've done so much work, Grandfather gave them use of the smallest island at the northeast end of the archipelago."

"I see." But he didn't, really. Magnus' hands shook as he drew deep, steadying breaths. "Your mother arranged all of it?"

"Yes." Elias frowned. "She told him all about how this same company installed infrastructure all across Grandfather Matochkin's territory with brilliant success."

"And your grandfather didn't object to the idea of humans coming here?"

"Any outsiders that came into the stronghold were closely guarded by our men. Otherwise, they did most of the work outside."

"And they stay in Barentia?"

"Mostly at the base set up on the little island. But they periodically come onto the island proper, to train our people on how to do the maintenance."

Magnus snorted.

Un-fucking believable.

"What?"

Magnus just shook his head.

Bjorn Thornsson was so adamant that the island's borders remain closed—technological benefits or not — that he argued pretty damned hard with Magnus over it.

Having humans here—outsiders here — was what pushed him to banish Magnus. He was so paranoid about allowing anyone in. And now they were crawling with outsiders.

I guess he saw reason.

But not about me, apparently?

I'm still condemned to the mercy of execution.

Magnus dropped his head, shoulders bowed. The chains scraped on the stone floor.

He distrusts me so deeply, he would see me dead.

How did I fail him so badly?

He lifted his head, leveling his gaze at Elias.

Ulla has won. She has everything she could ever want or hope to have. She has my son. My father. The regency. The power to implement human comforts.

What's left?

Only direct rule.

Ice slid down his spine.

She wouldn't... would she?

No. She wouldn't. She at least had enough brains to understand that Barentians would rip her a part if she dared try to take it—even if something were to happen to Elias...

"What? Why are you staring at me like that?"

Magnus blinked.

He came here to find out how Aksel had ended up beaten to the edge of death, on a trafficker ship, with a tattooed sigil. And Havard, his father's personal guard.

Ulla had practically confessed to giving Ana over to them.

So this base that Elias mentioned had to be their center of operations. Hadn't it?

How far will she take this?

Does she want to rule Barentia herself, or destroy it?

"Father?"

"You shouldn't stay here."

"Mother doesn't know—."

"Barentia. You shouldn't stay in Barentia. You're not safe here."

Elias' gaze turned suspicious. "Are you insinuating that I can't trust Mother?"

Careful Magnus.

"You can't trust her friends."

"They're nothing. We're polar bears. They're powerless against us."

Sounds like something Ulla would say.

But Magnus had seen a lot in the decade since he left Barentia. Too much.

"They're not powerless, like you say. They did a lot of damage to your Uncle Aksel."

"Uncle Aksel? What do you mean? He's gone to visit Grandfather Matochkin for a few weeks."

"He's unconscious and under critical care."

"Wha—what do you mean?"

What do I tell him? Dear Gods, I never wanted to drag Elias into this madness.

He studied his son's face.

Not a child. Not anymore.

"Elias, I work for an organization that counter-acts human traffickers. I've been tracking them for years. These traffickers use a sigil to subdue and control some of their victims. When we found Aksel, he has a tattoo on his throat. Just like Havard."

"So, you *did* come here to spy on us," Elias' voice cracked as he paced back toward the door, hands curled into fists, cheeks flushed.

"Elias, these people—these friends of your mother's—have stolen a lot of people from their families. A *lot* of people. We've only rescued a fraction of those that were taken and sold around the world. These human *friends* are *not* powerless. They hurt Aksel. They've marked Havard, your grandfather's personal guard. What else have they done here?"

"Mother wouldn't let them—."

"She might not *let* them, but that doesn't mean they wouldn't try if she contradicted what they wanted. And those men set up on that little island you mentioned. I'm pretty damned sure that's what they're really doing. You're not safe here."

Elias stared at Magnus, chest rising and falling.

"You're just trying to trick me. Turn me against Mother and Grandfather."

"If my pack is still here and I think I saw Ana drop it before she ran, you'll find my satellite phone. Get yourself out into the clear, use it to call my team and they'll come and take you away to safety. Away from this group."

"You said they sell humans. So? What do I care?" Elias lifted his chin, eyes glittering.

"You don't mean that."

He shrugged, his face full of defiance.

"Leave me," Magnus said. "Just leave me alone."

"I have the right to be wherever I want and—."

"Get out," Magnus roared. He drew a breath, paused, then continued, voice so low it was barely a whisper. "Ulla gave my Ana to those traffickers. You refuse to listen to reason. I want to be alone in my last hours before I'm executed. Just leave."

Wide eyed, Elias backed out of Magnus' cell without another word.

Magnus doubted anyone had ever raised their voice to him, let alone roared in his face.

Right then, he was too heart-weary to care.

He slid down the wall and dropped his head in his palms.

He'd failed on all fronts of his mission. Lost everyone and every-thing—including his life.

TWENTY-ONE

"Keep it locked," Elias Magnusson barked at the lockmaster, who accepted his order with a nod.

Elias jogged back up through the winding corridors of the dungeons, up the stone staircases and through the back halls to the family's private living quarters. Where his father should stay, rather than in a dank cell, chained with meteor metal.

'Ulla gave my Ana to those traffickers.'

Would Mother do that?

Elias thought they just ignored the human world. It was of no consequence to Barentia. Except for entertainment. Yvan entertained his mother. Elias had satellite television to keep him entertained.

Entertained or distracted?

He'd noticed how easy it was to lose hours watching nonsense. Nonsense that his grandfather would never allow.

Grandfather.

Elias felt the sudden urge to visit the old man. Guilt panged in his chest, realizing he had not visited him much since he fell ill.

He immediately left his room, striding toward his grandfather's. As he approached, Havard stepped away from the wall, blocking Elias' access.

"Havard? Step aside, I'm here to visit with my grandfather."

"He rests. You may come back later." He said, toneless.

"I won't disturb him. I just want to sit with him for a little while."

"Come back later when he's awake."

"But I—."

"No, your highness. He is not to be disturbed."

Elias blinked at Havard's denial of his order, refusing to move out of his path.

Havard had never refused him access to his grandfather before. Ever.

He stared at Elias as though he were just another servant. He didn't lower his gaze to meet Elias', as he used to do. Instead, he stood so that his body blocked the path, chin lifted.

Elias noted the black marking partially obscured by Havard's beard. "What new tattoo is that, Havard?" He gestured toward his own throat.

Havard glanced down at Elias then. Uncertainty glimmered in his eyes. "All of my sigils are representations of my lineages, or for my position."

"Huh, I've never seen that particular one. What is it for? It's new since the shaman left us. Who did the ceremony for it?"

Havard frowned. "It is a mark of my unfailing duty to my king. The regent had her trusted servant perform the ritual."

"I see." Elias said, swallowing. His shoulders twitched against the sudden tightening in his muscles.

Sacrilegious. A human outsider performing shamanic rites?

"Havard, has my grandfather mentioned when a new shaman will be chosen from our priests?"

The older man jerked his head in the negative.

"Are you sure I can't just slip in and sit with him? I promise not to disturb his rest."

"No." The scowl deepened.

If Havard won't let me in, I'll just go around him.

He turned on his heels, walking back the way he'd come, rounding the corner. He passed two other guards, neither of whom, as far as he could tell, bore the same tattoo that Havard had.

Another right turn and a quick glance up and down the corridor to ensure he was alone as he approached his destination. He tried the handle.

Locked.

No matter. Elias was deft with locks. Before his mother brought the outside world to his room with television, Elias had spent his life inside this stronghold. Locked doors meant something interesting.

He pulled his familiar long metal needles from his deep pocket, inserting them into the lock. With a few deft twists, the lock released, and the latch gave way under his hand. He dropped the lock picks back into his pocket as he pushed the door open, stepped inside and quickly closed it again before someone saw him, slipping the lock back into place.

Turning, he gasped.

The shaman's normally pristine quarters appeared as though a wild animal had rampaged throughout the space. His carefully cataloged library of books and scrolls was nearly empty except for the odd discarded, unrolled sheet lying haphazardly. The shelves of neatly labeled ingredients were even more bare. Furniture stood askew, pulled away from walls, drawers open, contents spilling out. Ancient tapestries torn from the walls, strewn around and discarded in heaps.

Tears stung his eyes as he stared.

He swallowed the revulsion of the disrespectful violation of the shaman's private rooms.

Who would do this? This domain should have been preserved for the use of the next shaman.

Elias sucked in a breath and approached the wall of solid oak shelves. He ran his fingers over the carved scroll work of leafy vines. Once he located the exact etched leaf he wanted, he pressed. It gave under the pressure of his fingertip, sinking into the polished wood until it resisted with only a click. One entire unit of shelves slid into the wall behind it far enough to allow a person to slip into the space between the front of the shelf and the back of the room's wall, still supporting the other shelves.

Elias' grandfather and the shaman had begun grooming him for kingship. That all stopped when the shaman suddenly died in an accidental fall down the servants' stairs. Then his grandfather had become ill and retreated into his private rooms, which Elias was about to enter from the secret passage that not only connected these rooms, but many others in the stronghold.

He was mindful to close the secret door before opening the next. That was the rule.

"Don't leave a gaping trail after you." His grandfather had said, when the two elderly men were divulging their secrets to him, once the serious training had begun.

Elias recalled how excited he'd been to stand in the narrow, darkened path, itching to explore anew. He'd thought he knew every nook and cranny of the stronghold. He'd been wrong. Happily so.

Does father know of these secret passages too?

He faced the second secret door in the blackness, surrounded by the sounds of his own breathing, which he willed to slow so that he could hear if anyone waited on the other side. He didn't want to run into anyone by accident.

Elias remained still, listening. Scenting. The tang of stone and ancient wood mingled with a millennium of dust tickled his nose and coated his tongue. There were only the lingering scents of his grandfather and the shaman's presence.

As far as he could tell, no one else had accessed this passage. He waited another moment in silence to ensure no one moved inside his grandfather's room before his fingers found the switch in the dark and pressed. He stepped away as the shelf-laden wall slid back as its opposite had done, and Elias slipped into the gap.

The pungent scent of illness was a thick cloud in his grandfather's room. There were no electric lights here, and only the fireplace cast some light from its neglected embers.

Elias pressed the switch to close the secret door.

He approached the bed on silent feet. His Grandfather's diminished figure slept under the layers of quilts.

Elias swallowed a gasp, blinking away the sudden onslaught of tears blurring his vision as he stared at the sallow face. He had looked unwell in the great hall. He looked even worse now.

His chest barely moved under the covers.

True to what he'd told Havard, Elias had no desire to disturb his grandfather's rest. He didn't bother moving a chair closer to the bedside. Instead, he knelt, resisting the urge to reach out to touch the elderly man.

Bjorn Thornsson was not a warm man by nature, but Elias had never doubted his grandfather's fondness for him. He'd felt it in the way he'd looked at him, the change in his voice when he instructed him, and the pride in his expression when Elias succeeded at a task. Occasionally, Bjorn would lay a hand on Elias' shoulder and often, that was enough.

He wanted nothing more than to feel that solid presence. That reassurance of his grandfather's strength.

Bjorn's eyes cracked open, and he tilted his head toward Elias.

"Elias," the older man said on an exhale.

"Grandfather," Elias whispered, trying to control the emotions choking him. "I didn't know you were so ill."

Bjorn's throat worked as though he struggled to work words up to his mouth.

Elias shot to his feet, rushing toward a small table bearing a pitcher and cup, where he poured water for Bjorn.

"Here," he eased his arm under Bjorn's shoulders to raise him enough to drink.

He took several tentative sips and closed his eyes with a sigh.

Elias helped him lie back, then returned the cup to the table.

"Grandfather, what has happened? The shaman is gone, you're ill, and Havard is behaving oddly. He's so determined to keep me out, I had to use the secret way in."

Anger flared in the old man's eyes as he reached toward his throat. His fingers shook as he pulled at the collar of his sleep shirt. "Can't..." he puffed, panting as he struggled to find words.

Elias gasped.

"... speak," he finally managed.

"The sigil. Is it magic?"

Bjorn gave a weak nod.

"What does it do? Havard said mother gave it to him for his dedication."

"Heh," Bjorn laughed, his head rolled from side to side. "No."

"But who? Why?" Elias asked, voice rising.

"Hshhh," Bjorn cautioned, hand wavering out toward Elias with his eyes closed.

He's so exhausted.

"Ulla."

Elias' entire body turned more frigid than any arctic swimming he'd ever engaged in.

No.

His mind raced.

It's not true. There's no proof. None.

Except for the strange tattoos that the shaman had not etched, by Barentian tradition.

No.

"Magnus?"

"Chained in the dungeon, waiting for his execution." Elias couldn't hide the bitterness from his voice.

Pain clouded Bjorn's eyes before he closed them. "Let him go. When your mother is distracted. Use the tunnels." He drew a deep breath. "Tell him... I'm sorry."

"I can bring him here to see you, Grandfather."

Bjorn shook his head. "No time. Let him go and...and you hide until he comes back for you."

Elias stared in confusion, heart pounding. "I don't understand."

"Promise," Bjorn panted. "I don't have long, Elias. Promise!"

"Sire?" Havard queried through the door. The latch turned, and Elias threw himself under Bjorn's bed. Havard's boots appeared, inches from Elias' nose. "Rest, sire. Mistress Ulla will return to-morrow with more medicine to give you strength to oversee the execution."

The edge of the covers shifted as Havard adjusted them over his king before returning to his post outside.

As soon as the door closed, Elias slid out from under the bed.

"Go," Bjorn said with some of his usual steel returning to his voice, though he kept it low.

"I can't leave you like this, Grandfather."

"I command it."

There was no more room for argument as Elias held Bjorn's clear gaze.

Deep down, Elias feared he wouldn't see his grandfather alive again. Shoving his dark thoughts aside, he said, "I love you, Grand-father."

Bjorn's expression softened as he brought his hand to Elias' cheek. "And I, you, my boy. Now save your father, since I can't."

TWENTY-TWO

ANA SAT ON A comfortable high-back chair, arms crossed, hoping she exuded enough boredom and annoyance to mask her anxiety.

Her captors had marched her through their operations complex in a warehouse and out to a pier, where they pushed her into a boat for a brief ride across a narrow stretch of water. From there, they led her to a small cottage overlooking the Barents Sea.

On reaching the small house, Ana turned back to see how extensive the island base camp was. Two cargo ships waited, with goods being shuffled across the compact harbor between them. She noted the logo on several of the shipping containers.

Embraceable Energy? Where Have I seen that before?

"I've seen it too," Antony said.

There was no time to ruminate on the familiar image as they shoved her inside the cottage and into her current chair.

They were all speaking English, and she guessed it was to intimidate her.

Hence her determination to look bored and annoyed.

Never let a predator smell your fear.

"I don't care if you think she has abilities. I want you to get rid of her," Magnus' ex-wife, Ulla Matochkin, said, scowling in Ana's direction. "She has no use to any of us other than what you can get for her on the black market. *Sell* her."

"Ulla," the creepy accountant, Adolf Wulker's, voice was placating as he looked her way. "We can use her as leverage first."

"And I told you, whatever you think Magnus knows about this old thing Yvan is looking for doesn't matter. He's a stubborn bastard that won't tell you anything. I know him. He'll go to his execution in silence just to spite me."

Execution? Ana's hands fisted before she forced herself to unclench them.

"Oh, that doesn't sound good," Antony said. "Sounds like your rescue party hit a snag."

He's not my *rescue party. I'm* his.

Antony snorted. "You're going to rescue the big polar bear shifter from an island full of more polar bear shifters and whisk him away to safety? Right."

The big guy strolled into view from somewhere behind her chair, grinning down at her.

Fuck, I forgot about him.

"Me too, sorry Ana," Antony said, looking contrite.

He laughed, drawing Matochkin and Wulker's attention. "What's so funny, Yvan?"

"She thinks she's going to escape and rescue Bjornson," he said, in heavily accented English.

"Ridiculous, why would you say that?" Matochkin said, her expression incredulous.

"Her ghost friend said so."

The tall blond woman approached Ana, eyes narrowed. "Magnus said that you—." She glanced over her shoulder at her partners before turning her full attention to Ana. Her eyes glittered dangerously; color infused her cheeks as she dropped her voice. "Magnus said you can astral travel."

Ana hesitated, but nodded.

Matochkin straightened. "Leave us," she barked at the men.

They moved closer to the women, brows raised at Ulla's tone.

The three of them towered over Ana's chair.

"Ulla, darling. She's my property to do with as I please. You said you had no use for her when you gave her to me. Why the sudden change of mind?" the creepy accountant said, sliding a hand across Ulla's shoulders.

Ana almost leapt out of her chair at the sight of his hands shifting—separating into tentacles, massaging the woman's narrow shoulders and neck with intimate familiarity.

Oh gross!

She struggled to control her gagging revulsion.

"Ugh!" Antony echoed the sentiment.

"Besides, we have no secrets between us, right, my love?" Yvan said, caressing her face and kissing her mouth. "Whatever she has to say, we can know, too."

Ulla immediately relaxed her body. "Just five minutes. Female to female."

The men exchanged looks, released her, and moved toward the door.

Yvan stopped next to her chair, crouched so he could look her in the eyes and as he placed his large hand on her knee, he said, "If you say anything that upsets our Ulla, I will extinguish your ghost friend into oblivion and snap your neck so you may join him. I don't care how much money Adolf thinks he can get for you. I will do this." He gave her knee a single pat, rose, and left. The door closed with a soft click.

Ulla said, "You don't need to worry about Yvan. If you don't answer my questions, *I'll* snap your neck myself."

"Charming bunch," Antony snorted.

Quip all you want, it isn't your neck on the line, now is it?

"Nope, just oblivion, apparently."

"What do you want to know?" Ana said to Ulla, wondering if she could use this new situation to her benefit.

Ulla glanced at the door behind Ana. "Magnus said you spoke to Aksel in the astral realm."

Open desperation replaced the bitter scorn in Ulla's face. Her gaze flicked between Ana and the door.

Ana nodded.

"He's alive," Ulla said with guarded relief.

"He was then. That was days ago."

"And he had a mark on his throat? And don't lie to me or I'll—."

"Snap my neck, I know. And yes, he did. It prevented him from shifting, so he couldn't heal."

Ulla reached for the chair adjacent to Ana, sagging onto it. All the color drained from her face. "So it's true. He wasn't lying." She jumped to her feet, hands shaking as she paced the room.

"How can we remove it?" Ana forced as much calm into her question as she could.

"I don't know," Ulla said, her hand pressed to her forehead as she glanced at the door again. "I don't think it can be, not without a shaman, anyway." She drew a long breath, straightening her spine as her gaze searched the room, as though the answers were somewhere within it.

"Even if you decide to snap my neck, at least let Magnus go. Let him find a shaman that can help your brother. You *know* he would. Won't the king's shaman help him?"

"He's dead," Ulla said, resuming her pacing with a heavy sigh. "You know what? It's too late. It's too late for Aksel. I can't do anything to reverse it. I can't help him. It's too late."

"What's too late?" Adolf asked as he and Yvan entered the room.

"It's too late for her to *try* to bargain with me," Ulla said quickly, masking her emotions as she looked at Ana.

"Ah, well, did she tell you what you wanted to know at least?" Yvan asked, lacing his large fingers together as he moved into Ana's line of sight.

"No," she said, shrugging a shoulder. "I'm bored. We should find out what Magnus knows about this old artifact you want, so Adolf can sell her, and I can think about other things," she said to Yvan.

"Like becoming Queen." Yvan grinned, trailing a finger over her cheek.

She twitched away from his touch, seemed to catch herself, smiled, and placed a kiss on his finger. "Exactly."

"I like this idea," Yvan said, leaning in to nuzzle Ulla's neck.

Ana looked away, in a bid to control the returned revulsion churning in her gut.

I don't think I can take any more of this.

She glanced up to see Antony looking as ghostly green as she felt.

You should check on Emilio and the guys in case they decide to move them. If I survive this, I'll need to know where to direct my team.

Antony's hesitation was clear as he looked between her and the three lovers, pretending to have forgotten about her.

I'll be fine. And even if I'm not, you can't do anything about it, Antony. Don't get oblivated—if this guy isn't talking out of his ass.

Antony snort-laughed, then snapped his mouth shut when Yvan turned his attention on him. "Okay, stay alive," he said and blinked out of sight.

"Where's he gone, your ghost friend?" Yvan demanded.

"With the three of you heating things up in here, he didn't think he wanted to stick around if squid boy over there broke out the rest of his tentacles. So, he abandoned me to suffer alone."

Yvan backhanded Ana, snapping her head to the side with a crack. Her head rang as pain bloomed through it from the impact on her cheek.

"Don't damage my property!" Adolf shot forward, grabbing her face and looking at either side. "You're lucky you didn't break her. Now I'll have to wait till the bruising clears up before I can present her to the special clients I contacted. Damn your temper, Yvan. They don't like it when I tease them and delay presentations longer than necessary."

"I don't care about your vast network of clients. I promised the others we'd find the artifact and secure it. This is all I want, Adolf. Not money, like you."

"It's not just the money, Yvan." Adolf stepped closer to Yvan, snarling up at the taller man's face.

Ulla slid between the two, her bottom against Yvan's groin, her breasts to Adolf's chest, distracting both.

"We all want something, don't we? How about we head back to the stronghold and see if we can finish what we started? Yvan's right, we should bring the human woman, although I doubt the leverage idea will work. I have something else in mind for her." Ulla glanced Ana's way, leveling her glittering blue eyes at her.

Uh oh.

I DON'T CARE WHO comes in here next. I'll rip their head off if I have to, in order to escape and find Ana.

Thoughts of Ana being trapped on a ship like the ones they had seized over the last decade made the bile in his gut rise.

I have to get out of here.

But no matter what he tried, despite knowing better, he could not slip out of the manacles, nor break them. All he'd earned for his trouble were very sore wrists and ankles and a chipped tooth, with barely a scuff on the meteor metal.

He'd cursed his ancestors repeatedly for their exquisite skill in metal craft and shackle design and quality.

These are probably the original damned shackles from when the cell was built.

When he wasn't plotting his impossible escape, he calmed himself with fantasies of Ana and her sapphire blue panties, which turned out to be counter-productive and incited the urgency to escape all over again.

But then, there wasn't anything else to do. The chains were almost too short for push-ups.

Suddenly, the lock tumbled with a snap, and the door banged back against the stone.

Magnus was on his feet, ready to detach heads.

Elias stood, wide-eyed and panting. To the lockmaster he said, "tell them I stole the keys and knocked you out or something."

"But your highness—," the lockmaster protested.

Magnus eased back on the readiness to do violence. "Or go into hiding until this all blows over. You know they'll torture you for information if they catch you."

"Shouldn't I rally the guards to protect you?"

"They will follow their commander and they don't understand that he is compromised," Elias said, stepping into the cell. "I don't want the stronghold in an uproar when I'm trying to help my father escape quietly. Which key is it?"

The lockmaster freed Magnus in seconds.

"He's right. Hide yourself and your family. Once I get out, I will be back—and not alone."

"Yes sir. But I still think we should rally support. Not all Barentians agreed with the banishment and certainly many are not pleased about the scheduled execution."

"Nor am I, but please, take your family and go."

The lockmaster dropped his precious keys into Magnus' hand and disappeared.

His fist clenched around the ring of keys. Centuries old. He laughed.

Elias gave him a quizzical look from the door, his impatience to be away evident.

"Of all the plans I had to escape, not one of them included having the keys dropped in my hands and just being set free."

"Grandfather told me to take you through the tunnels to escape."

The tunnels! Dear Gods, I've forgotten about the damned tunnels!

"He did?" Magnus stood rooted in place.

Elias nodded, glancing up and down the corridor. "Yes, he ordered I set you free. So let's go, Father."

Magnus couldn't believe what he was hearing.

A second later, Elias' hand grabbed his wrist and yanked him toward the door.

Magnus had enough brain function to close and lock it before following his son down the stone corridor toward the hidden entrance of the tunnels. Neither spoke as they made their way, careful to avoid passing guards who were fulfilling their duties.

Only the royal Barentian family were aware of the secret tunnels beneath the stronghold that led through the mountain and out to a tiny inlet on the western side of the island. The path hadn't been needed in centuries because it had been that long since the stronghold had failed to keep invaders out.

Down the next corridor, the scent of alcohol signaled they were close to the tunnel entrance. Stacks of barrels crowded the narrow space. With a quick glance up and down the hall, Magnus shifted his hands, extracting his bear claws and drove them into the backs of some barrels, causing them to leak so that the pungent aroma would mask their personal scents.

Magnus led the way into the very back of the barrel cellar, squeezing between the largest ones with the thickest layers of dust. "Dwarven Ale," he murmured as he shimmied around behind it and along the wall to the dark corner. With no light source, he had to feel around for the correct stones. Magnus funneled his bear magic into his paw, extending the powerful claws in order to pry the stones loose, as he used to do in his youth.

He ignored the pang of nostalgia and focused on the genuine sense of urgency to move unseen and unheard.

"Got it," he grunted as the stone finally gave way, and then the next. With limited space, he only removed as many as was necessary for Elias and himself to crawl through, then pulled them back into place, using the meteor metal handles affixed to the backs of the stones for that purpose.

"Your pack is just up along here," Elias said, taking the lead through the tunnel. "I brought it down from the internal passages before going around to fetch the lockmaster."

"Thank you, Elias." Magnus blew out a breath, unable to see much in the dark. Both used their heightened sense of smell and hearing to navigate, guided by the changes in air drafts and echoes from the rooms above.

By the time they reached the pack, their eyes had adjusted enough to register slight variations in the dark.

Elias said, "After we last spoke, I went to see Grandfather. He's not well. I don't think he has long. He commanded I set you free, and to tell you he was sorry."

Emotions punched Magnus in both gut and chest, making it difficult to breathe. His father had never in his life apologized to anyone.

"He's dying?"

"Yes." Elias' voice sounded small in the confined space, reminding Magnus how young he was, despite his growing body. "And he's marked, like Havard. It was hard for him to speak. I wanted to take you to him, but he insisted you escape. He said you'd come back for me and that I was to hide until you did."

Magnus' heart pounded in his chest, torn between escaping to find Ana, getting Elias to safety, and seeing his father one last time.

One thing he never dreamed of was his father's death. He'd always thought of his father as eternal.

Foolish. Childish.

"Does your mother know about the tunnels?"

"No. Grandfather and the shaman expressly forbade me from sharing their existence with her or anyone else."

"Good."

"Can we take him with us, Father?"

Get Elias to safety and call Kane, or go back for his father? The sooner Kane and the team arrived, the much better chance they had of tracking Ana.

"Have you ever made the swim to Bear Island? It's a hard journey. Long."

"Twice. Grandfather said it was a tradition that every young bear makes the swim. I almost failed the first time, the second was much better. I made it there and back the same day."

Pride threatened to burst Magnus' chest at his son's words.

A strong swimmer. Good.

"Listen carefully, Elias, this is very important, and I want you to do exactly as I ask. Will you do that?"

"What do you want me to do?"

Magnus noted he didn't agree, but went on anyway. "I want you to run to the exit point. There should be a small boat stored in a safe place. Only after you ensure you are alone, row out to sea until you are clear of the island and use the satellite phone to contact my team."

"Okay."

"Identify yourself. Tell them Ana might be detained on a small island in the northeast sector of the archipelago."

"What about you?"

"Don't worry about me. As soon as you make the call, row the boat toward Bear Island, conserving your strength for as long as possible. Make sure no one sees you. This is vital, Elias. They *will* go after you."

"But I can help —."

"It doesn't matter that we're mighty polar bear shifters if there are so many humans, as you say. They will be armed with weapons that can kill us. I don't want any Barentians killed if I can do this discretely. Understand?"

"I understand," he said, but Magnus knew he didn't like it.

"When you're ready, shift into your bear and swim the rest of the way to Bear Island and wait. Just be a bear for a while. A few days if necessary. The local fisherman and environmental research crew won't bother you."

"That sounds lame. When do I come back?"

"You don't. You wait for me or one of my team members to come for you. The GPSA will keep you safe. No matter what, do not come back."

Magnus stared into his son's face, recognizing his own prideful stubbornness in his eyes. "Promise me."

Elias remained silent for an eternity before he finally answered. "Please save Grandfather if you can."

"I will try."

Elias suddenly gripped Magnus in a bear-hug, squeezing the air from his lungs. "Be safe, Father."

"Be safe, Son," he said, hugging his boy as tight as his boy hugged him.

Elias released him just as suddenly, grabbed Magnus' pack and ran down the tunnel. The run to the inlet would take many hours through the darkness.

Magnus had to trust his son would be safe. He listened until Elias' footfalls faded, then made his way along the tunnel back toward the junction that would give him access to the heart of the stronghold.

And to his father.

TWENTY-THREE

ANA HATED SNOW. AND she hated snowmobiles.

The one they'd forced her onto whined loudly and set her teeth on edge. Even more so now that it was no longer a source of potential escape, but one of further imprisonment.

She hated snow and cold. She hated the north and longed for her beachside home. The warm California sun, not this watery *sort of* light of the high north. Some people thought the high north was beautiful.

Beautiful?

Way up here in the wastelands of snow and ice and rock and nothing else?

They hit another bump, jarring her teeth as her helmeted head hit the guy's back in front of her.

She still wore the clothes she'd arrived in, the boots and jacket. At least she had that to fend off the cold, but didn't seem to be enough.

I've been cold since we disembarked from that damned seaplane. Where the hell is it, anyway? Had someone stolen it? Or maybe they just let it drift off to sea.

She almost laughed to herself, picturing some arctic wildlife riding the drifting craft around from sea mass to sea mass until it bumped up against an iceberg somewhere.

She thought of Aksel.

Her amusement died.

Would they do the same to her?

I couldn't bear to be locked inside my head like that. Especially not in a cold sea of icebergs.

Her worst nightmare, after the night terrors of Antony's accident.

Those had been horrendous. But at least now she understood he'd been trying to reach her. Show her what had happened.

But in the end, here she was. On a damned snowmobile, heading for what? Some sort of negotiation to force Magnus to tell them about some old antique thing before they killed them both?

No, they wouldn't kill them if they didn't have to. They'd subdue them and sell them to the highest bidder.

Like Emilio and the rest of Antony's crew would be sold off, eventually.

Unless Ana could get word to Carson and Kane and the others that it was all here. All this time. And they could end it all.

There hadn't been enough time, and she hadn't had enough energy to do an intentional reading of the place, but she was certain all the stolen victims had passed through this little island on their way to their buyers.

They hit another bump followed by a drop and Ana thanked God she didn't bite her tongue again or lose that little bit of gruel she'd had for breakfast.

That would be so gross inside this helmet.

Another sharp turn, another drop.

I'm gonna throat punch this guy as soon as he stops this goddammned thing.

The others rode identical vehicles behind her, fanned out so that if she'd tried to jump off, they'd either run her over or scoop her back up. And she didn't want to give Yvan the satisfaction of tying her to the damned thing.

They rounded another snowy bank of nearly black evergreens, and the stronghold came into view.

It was still impressive the second time, but now her foreboding intensified.

This time, the bad guys had her, and they were going to use her to force Magnus to give them information. They also had control over an entire clan of polar bear shifters that no longer owed allegiance to Magnus as a banished one, let alone one who, it seemed, was now on death row.

We're so screwed.

"Screwed, but not alone," Antony said, floating at warp speed beside her.

She almost jumped out of her skin, jerking the coat of the asshole driving the snowmobile so hard that he almost lost control.

He snarled at her with a few rude words.

You shouldn't be here! That Yvan guy said he can send you to oblivion. Go back and keep an eye on your crew.

"You don't believe that, do you? I think he's full of shit."

I don't know and don't want to risk it. Stay away from him!

Antony glanced back at the snowmobiles following behind. Concern crept into his expression despite his bluster.

"I'm going to check out this castle they're taking you to. Maybe I'll find you a way out."

He blinked out of sight, and Ana's snowmobile hit another bump.

ADOLF WULKER REMOVED THE helmet and dropped it on the seat of the snowmobile.

This is such a waste of time.

He was still fuming that Yvan had dared damage his property. Now he'd have to wait before presenting the little psychic to his favorite buyer.

A special buyer that would pay top dollar for her kind of novelty.

So now that he had to wait, he might as well indulge Ulla and Yvan in this little side project.

He signaled to Yvan that he wanted a few words once they went inside.

Adolf was worried about the subtle changes in Ulla since her brother had not contacted her. Her response to their touch, their usual means of keeping her happy, had cooled.

Does she know something?

Was she asking the psychic to use her ability to learn more about Aksel?

He threw his gloves down with a sigh.

She's going to be furious about what we've done to her brother.

Absolutely furious.

She would find out eventually. They just needed to keep her ignorant long enough for her to serve her purpose in their plans for *The Consortium* and, by extension, for themselves.

He followed the others inside the stronghold, ignoring the Barentian guards. So long as they were with Ulla, their regent, he and Yvan wouldn't be bothered by the dangerous shifters.

He tamped down his nerves under their disapproving glares.

The partners still needed her for a little while longer.

They'd already scavenged the shaman's grimoire collection, which had boosted his own ability beautifully and afforded them some level of safety, with both the king and the head guard under their control.

Still, Yvan was insistent they keep Ulla placated until he found the location of the artifact he was looking for.

Yvan fell in stride alongside Adolf. They slowed their pace until the others were out of earshot and no one else was close enough to overhear.

Adolf kept his voice low. "This device you're looking for. You're sure it's here?"

Yvan nodded, studying Adolf's face. "What are you worried about? We're very close, I can feel it."

It was some kind of access device or gate or key to another world. Adolf didn't know the details, he was too busy running his business.

He knew just enough to confirm that he wanted to be part of it. A prime opportunity for expansion. So he kept Ulla happy, Yvan happy, and *The Consortium* happy. Wins all around.

They continued walking toward the king's reception room next to the larger great hall, before ordering Ulla's ex-husband to be brought to them for questioning.

They wouldn't all fit in the dungeon cell.

"I'm concerned about the strength of my networks and my control over them as my venom thins," he spoke to Yvan, voice low so it wouldn't carry along the stone corridor to the shifters' sensitive ears.

Bringing energy solutions to the worlds' remotest areas had given him all the access he needed to thrive, both legitimately and illegitimately.

His network truly was global.

"With access to wherever this artifact connects to, you can expand. The opportunities are endless," Yvan reassured him.

Adolf loved the idea of endless opportunities.

"What kinds of merchandise will we find on the other side of this thing, do you think?" He imagined a whole new world of beings he could add to his catalog. "Yes, more novelty. More... unique acquisitions would do nicely."

"We've listened to Conrad brag endlessly about this powerful being he's controlled for centuries. Look at the power he has."

Conrad, a member of *The Consortium*, had manipulated a Djinn—if Adolf recalled correctly—into bestowing powers and longevity on him before he entrapped and siphoned her power for himself.

That's what Yvan wanted. He wanted to control powerful creatures like that for himself, boosting his own power.

"And you believe there are more like his creature, accessible through this gate?"

Adolf enjoyed a different kind of power. Power over the fates of the lesser and the powerful alike. Merchandise and buyers, there was little difference to Adolf.

A shiver rippled through him.

He provided services that fed his own sense of power.

They entered the room. Adolf watched the psychic as they settled in to wait for Ulla's ex-husband to arrive and tell them what they all wanted to know.

His gaze slid from the woman, returning to Ulla.

Her brother had been the last instance where he'd had to use his deeper ability to subdue a difficult situation.

He whispered to Yvan next to him, "The venom in my octopus ink is thinning."

"So you said before."

"My ability to overcome another's will is weakening. I've had to release some of my older connections in order to accommodate this last spell," he said, referring to Ulla's brother. "And the two before that. Shifter will is so much harder to control than human will."

Yvan scowled as his eyes flicked between Ulla and Adolf.

Neither Adolf nor Yvan were sure what had set off the polar bear shifter, but he'd gone on a rampage in the facility, screaming about one of Adolf's products. They subdued and spelled him, then put him on a ship. A ship which was eventually seized, and no one had heard from him since.

"Each time I used my venom to calm another, it drew on my strength, even with the spells you used to boost it. I'm stretched too far. My connections are thinning to fragile filaments; any more, and they may snap. I have no way of knowing what will happen. Could be some, could be all."

"Or drain you to a husk. I've seen it with other magic users that weren't strong enough to maintain their spells."

Adolf wasn't sure he liked the calculated look in Yvan's eye. "We're almost finished here. Once I have control of the artifact—on behalf of *The Consortium*, of course—it won't matter."

"If we can't control the king and his guard, we can't control the rest of the Barentians. If we can't control the Barentians, we sure as hell can't control the rest of the polar bear clans, who will no doubt want to overrun the territory for themselves. They won't stand by while humans take over."

"Once I have the power we're seeking, they'll do whatever we want them to."

"Are you so sure about that?" Adolph adjusted his posture on his seat, turning more fully toward Yvan as his agitation got the better of him. "Didn't one of *The Consortium* members say that we are ensuring control of the artifact for when it awakens? Meaning we won't have access to power right away?"

Yvan shrugged, scowling at Adolf's line of questioning. "Maybe. Maybe not. The shaman's books have histories and detailed spells to connect and use the thing. There just hasn't been enough time to read through them all yet. Ah, finally." He nodded toward the door.

Adolf turned his attention to the door as two guards appeared with grim expressions.

There was no chained Barentian polar bear shifter behind them.

"Where is he?" Ulla demanded, striding toward the guards.

"When we couldn't find the lockmaster to open the cell, we had to use the secondary key."

"And?"

"The cell is empty, mistress."

"Find the lockmaster," she roared as the guards rushed out, "Find Magnus!"

Adolf jumped to his feet when she charged toward Adolf's property, hand extended to grab her by the throat.

"Ulla!"

The woman, Ana, squeezed her eyes shut, stifling a whimper as she clutched the chair she sat on, head pressed into the back of it.

"Where is he?" Ulla demanded of the woman, shaking her.

"How the fuck should I know? I've been trapped with you assholes since you caught me at the fishing village," she forced the words out of her compressed windpipe.

Ulla shoved her as she released her, forcing the chair to rock backwards.

The woman clutched at her throat, gasping and coughing from the assault.

She'd have more bruises to add to her growing assortment.

More delays before Adolf could collect on her. His buyer liked his acquisitions pristine, unblemished.

"Will the two of you stop damaging my goods? *Please*," he shouted, no longer willing to conceal his exasperation. He sighed, running his fingers through his dark hair. "Control your tempers. Ulla, since your ex-husband appears to have escaped his inescapable prison and chains, where would he go? We're on an island. His choices are limited."

"He's banished. No one would dare defy the king's edict by helping him."

"Well, it appears the lockmaster has, or Magnus Bjornson overpowered him despite his predicament."

Ulla turned back toward Adolf's prisoner. "He knows his woman is bound for the black market. He'd go after her."

"So all we have to do is wave her around as bait to lure him to us," Yvan said.

Adolf said, "Ulla, you mentioned he had connections to the GPSA. If he brings them here, it would ruin everything I've—we've built. We're too close to lose it all now."

"Yes, so we have to find him as soon as possible," Yvan agreed.

Or I need to get out of here as soon as possible.

He glanced between his partners and his property seated across from him, weighing his options.

TWENTY-FOUR

"JESUS CHRIST, I HAD no idea the kind of shit Ana gets into in her line of work. No clue." Antony muttered as he drifted through the Barentian stronghold, seeking anything or anyone that could help him help Ana escape this crazy situation. "This isn't what normal people do."

All the time they'd lived together, when he was on shore leave, he'd always thought Ana was a ranked pencil-pusher at a government office in the town they lived in.

Boring, safe, easy.

"I thought *I* had the exciting life." He poked his head through a thick stone wall, expecting to find another bedroom. "Oh-ho! What's this?" he moved into the dark space between the rooms.

"Of course, an ancient castle has secret passages, on an island with people that turn into polar bears... and is aggressively occupied by a squid man that sells humans for money and a magician that can send me to oblivion. Of course." He threw his hands up in the air.

He followed the dark corridor to an intersection, where he saw movement. "I hope there aren't also giant-sized talking rats in this place. I don't think I could handle that." He drifted toward the movement, which turned out to be that of a large man.

Ana's large man.

Relief and jealousy ripped through Antony.

Relief because help was close by for Ana. Jealousy because her lover was close enough to rescue her while Antony couldn't.

Just because that guy had a body and Antony didn't. A very ripped body.

Yeah, he'd seen them in bed together. Accidentally. He wasn't a voyeur or anything. But it was enough to make him realize what he'd missed out on with the woman he'd never asked to marry him, and should have.

Instead, when she'd finally confided her secret ability to him, he freaked out like the coward he was and broke it off, convincing both of them that friendship was the best option.

Until she'd persistently tried to save his life with her warnings of the pending accident on his ship.

Such a coward.

"I never deserved her," he mumbled, following Magnus along the secret passages, hoping he was making his way to Ana to get her off this damned island so they could get back to the business of rescuing his men from the human traffickers.

His men. His crew were still alive because of her. And they would be rescued because of her, too.

"I know it. Just like I *know* you'll get her out of here," he said to Magnus' broad back, ignoring how much more muscle he had than Antony ever did.

Magnus paused, facing the wall, running his hands over the surface.

"You'd better be worthy of her, or I'll haunt the fuck out of you," Antony growled in his ear.

Magnus' head jerked toward the sound of Antony's voice. He stood still, listening, nose twitching as though he was scenting something.

"Did he hear me?" Antony waved a hand in Magnus' face.

Magnus turned back to the wall. After a moment, an audible click released the panel. He stepped aside as it backed into the space.

Antony passed through the wall ahead of Magnus.

An old man lay inert on a high bed, buried under several thick blankets which barely moved for the shallowness of his breathing.

The room was dark except for the few embers amongst the ash in the great fireplace at the foot of the bed.

Someone gasped.

Antony spun as the panel eased back into place, showing a wall lined with heavy bookshelves. His gaze flicked around the room to determine the source of the gasp.

A second old man with a tattooed face and wild hair emerged from a corner, gaping at Magnus in shock and relief.

Magnus ignored this man, his focus intent on the bed, where he dropped to his knees with a low sob. Carefully, he eased the man's beard and sleep shirt aside, exposing his throat— marred by a black ink tattoo. Retracting his hand, the fabric and beard fell back into place, obscuring the mark.

"Father." He reached for the sleeping man's hand. He didn't respond when Magnus touched him. Magnus' breath shuddered as he leaned his forehead on his father's arm.

Antony looked away from the other man's pain, clearing his throat to ease the dense emotion from his chest. "Yeah, I've been there buddy. It sucks."

"Who are you?" The second old man was suddenly in front of Antony, forcing him back a few paces.

"Wha—You—." Antony waved at the old man's finger extended toward Antony's face. Their hands passed through one another. "You're dead too?"

The lively, dead old man puffed up with indignation. "How dare you intrude in this room! You are not Barentian. You're not even a polar bear. You're..." he looked Antony up and down. "Human."

"Yeah, so? It's not like I want to be here. I've got a friend in trouble downstairs and half a dozen more in trouble on a ship bound for the continent. And only *that* guy can help any of them." He jabbed a finger in Magnus' direction. "And yeah, they're *all* human, well, mostly human. And all want nothing more than to go home." At least he thought they were all human. Psychics were human too, weren't they?

"What do you mean, mostly human? Not a shifter? An elemental? A Fae? Sprite? Please tell me not a vampire. Or *another* one of those sneaky magicians."

"Wha—No, none of those." Antony's head spun. "The only magician I know of is that big Yvan guy who's holding my friend hostage. She's a psychic. I don't know if that's human or not?"

The old man nodded, grumbling. "Yes, human. Naturally enhanced but still human."

"Ah. Well, she can see me, so can you tell me how to direct her out of here if I can get her away from that bear woman, the squid guy, and the magician?"

The old man growled. "Those three are abominations to all of paranormal society. They stole my sacred work and twisted it!"

The gnarled finger appeared inches from Antony's nose again before it whipped toward the bed. "They violated our king! I will not rest until he is restored or avenged."

Antony approached the bed, peering down at Magnus' father, who reminded him far too much of his own. The urge to help was overpowering, but Antony already had folks that needed his help.

"How do we wake him up?" Antony looked up at the old man. "If we wake him up, he can stop them, right? He can stop them from hurting Ana or selling her? I need her to help me save a shipload of people bound for the black market."

"Hmm, filth," the old man muttered, "Filthy matter. But we don't get involved in human affairs. We have far more important things to protect."

Antony grit his teeth in frustration.

"What's wrong with the king? What did they do to him?" He tried again, hoping to find some angle that would benefit his mission to free Ana. "Maybe Ana can help?"

Antony didn't know how, but given they were in the king's room and this guy knew the place, there had to be some way.

"What about you? Are you the king's manservant? Is there some secret I can relay to Ana, who can tell Magnus?" He knew he was grasping. Desperate. But there just hadn't been anyone else to communicate with and he didn't know how much time Ana had left.

"Manservant!" the old man thundered, reminding Antony distinctly of all the dramatic movie wizards he'd seen in his life. "I am the king's shaman!"

"Shaman! You're a magic worker too, then?" He glanced at the King. "What happened? Why didn't you help him?"

The old man deflated. "I was already dead by the time they got to him and cast their twisted spell. I couldn't protect him like this. Not enough to keep him safe. My energy is keeping him alive as he is."

"Spell? Is it something we—you can teach to Ana to break it?"

"She isn't a Barentian priest."

Antony wanted to scream, but maintained his calm. "But the magician that cast this spell isn't either."

The tattooed old man tilted his head up, looking down his nose imperiously at Antony. "They stole our spells. I will only share our sacred knowledge with another Barentian."

"Even if it means saving your King? If we can get Ana in here and it works, you can help him."

"Or she would have the power to kill him and enslave the rest, starting with Magnus."

Antony stared at the highly paranoid old man at a loss.

Magnus got to his feet, rubbing the grief clear of his face, and straightened himself to his full height as he looked around the room, whispering to himself or to his father. Antony couldn't tell which.

First, Magnus moved toward the nearly extinguished fireplace, knelt and carefully lifted the substantial hearth stone, revealing a deep gap beneath.

Antony couldn't believe how easily he moved the stone without any noise or effort.

"Christ, I'd have dropped the damned thing on my foot and alerted the whole castle."

The old shaman grunted in response.

Setting the stone aside, Magnus reached in and extracted a black rock with a leather thong dangling from it. It resembled a shiny piece of coal. He looped it over his head, dropping the rock behind his shirt, then replaced the stone.

"What is that?" Antony looked to the old man for an answer, but received only silence.

Next, Magnus rounded the enormous bed, reaching behind the solid oak headboard, and extracted what looked like a wall stone.

"Now what?" Antony gaped.

Magnus removed a wrapped object, then replaced that stone, too.

At the foot of the King's bed, Magnus lay his hand over the sick man's covered foot. "If I cannot save you, I will ensure Elias receives these."

The king still did not stir.

"We should never have banished Magnus. Our greatest mistake. Greatest," the old shaman said, voice heavy with sorrow. "He would have made a fine King of Barentia."

Magnus triggered the secret door.

Antony spared the Shaman a last look before following Magnus into the passage. As soon as the panel slid back into place, Magnus revealed another hidden cavity where he slipped the wrapped object and concealed it.

That done, his stride more purposeful, he made his way along the secret passages with Antony at his back until they passed through an area where voices echoed along the castle's arteries.

Magnus found a small panel, slid it aside, and peered into the room below. Antony pushed his head through the wall.

They'd found Ana.

Despite her bruised face and throat, she looked angry. Very angry.

Magnus growled, low and loud. The sound traveled throughout all the corridors, secret and public alike, reaching every wing in the mountain-based castle.

Antony's incorporeal form vibrated with it.

The king's banished son was back, and he was pissed.

"All right. Let's go get our Ana," Antony said, fisting his hands.

MAGNUS SLID THE PANEL aside, peering down into the meeting room.

Relief flooded his chest on seeing she was here and safe, rather than on a ship bound for Gods knew where to be sold.

Ana sat, spine erect, shoulders set, glaring at the room's three other occupants.

She turned to address Ulla, which allowed Magnus to see her entire beautiful face.

Her bruised face and throat.

Rage ripped through him, expressing itself in a roar that shook the ancient stones beneath his splayed palms and fingers.

He fought the instinct to shift as he ran down the passage seeking the next exit point.

Reason quickly returned, overriding his animal brain, reminding him that he was in a castle full of Barentian guards that believed he should be in a prison cell awaiting his execution.

And he'd just alerted all of them with his very loud announcement.

Why is Ana here?

Ulla had told him that she was with the traffickers.

Having reached the next exit point, he paused to think.

She's being held captive. Here. With a bruised face.

Was there any other purpose than to draw him out?

To make a show of his execution? It would settle things for the succession after his father died, which might not be long.

Gods protect Elias.

His hand drifted over his heart as he made the plea, fingers grazing the stone beneath his shirt. The key. He'd hidden the book in the passage's darkness.

Instinct had bid him remove the sacred objects from his father's room for safekeeping. They couldn't be taken by anyone that couldn't be trusted with them.

Only a king and his shaman had the right to these artifacts.

He would ensure that Elias received them, or that no one would.

He removed the object from his shirt, and likewise hid it as he had the book.

The sounds of guards running and shouting orders met his ears as he waited.

As soon as they saw him, they would converge on him.

When they do, I just have to make sure I'm nowhere near a passage access point so that they won't discover the tunnels.

The secret tunnels led to the sacred gate for which he'd just hidden the key and spell book. The gate that his family had been charged with protecting for millennia.

I can't let that end here.

Kane was convinced *The Consortium* wanted access to it. She was in a race to discover all the gates around the world to ensure their safety before *The Consortium* found them. Before the portals awakened from their slumber.

I can't worry about that right now.

Ana was being held captive, and they still had a mission to complete. People to save—if he hadn't blown it already.

Could he convince the Barentian guards the king was spelled, as was their trusted chief officer?

I have to try.

As soon as the exterior corridor was silent, he eased his way out of the secret passage. Ensuring it was closed and invisible to the eye, he silently made his way down the hall toward the meeting room. In the distance, the guards continued their search.

TWENTY-FIVE

ELIAS' MUSCLES STRAINED AT the oars as he propelled the small craft along the rolling ocean surface. He'd already made the call to Magnus' contact. Kane.

He recalled that name. Kane was the woman that had spun his life in a new direction when she visited Barentia all those years ago.

It was her fault that he'd lost his father, and all of this was happening now. He was sure of it.

Despite his overwhelming bitterness when she'd identified herself on the satellite phone, he'd relayed Magnus' message, then continued his journey.

The bitterness fueled his muscles as he rowed because he had promised his father he would continue on to Bear Island.

His pride screamed to go back. To help. To save his grandfather and people from the humans with weapons that could kill them.

Surely they could overcome them with their great bear warriors.

No. He'd seen the movies and the news on the television. Their warriors wouldn't even get near the humans to tear them apart with their claws and teeth. How could anyone fight against that?

But Magnus is going to.

He glanced at the pack, wondering if there was a gun in it. He hadn't explored its contents beyond extracting the needed phone.

He kept rowing, returning his attention to the rolling line of the horizon and the misty bump that was Barentia.

Dots fanned the surface.

He squinted, but even his enhanced senses couldn't make out their shapes yet.

Birds? Dolphin fins, maybe.

The weak sunlight caught the shape of a sail.

Boats.

'They will go after you.' Magnus had warned him.

They would mark him like they'd marked his grandfather and Havard.

Elias swore as he reached for his boots and shoved them into the pack, then pulled off the rest of his clothes, adding them to his boots. Yanking the zipper closed, he spared the growing dots one last glance, unable to determine how many pursued him.

He held his breath, leaped into the frigid Barents Sea and shifted.

His hands extended and widened into powerful paws with deadly claws. The pads of his palms thickened and turned black, while translucent fur sprouted from every pore of his body.

Power and strength surged through his muscles.

Still buoyant, the pack floated on the surface as he drew a breath. Grabbing it with his teeth, he began the long swim to the safety of Bear Island.

Or so he hoped.

ANA'S BREATH CAUGHT AT the sound of the great roar reverberating through the stronghold.

Magnus!

She glanced up in time to see Antony leaping through the upper portion of the high stone wall, looking like he was ready to fight.

Ulla's expression registered panic as the sound continued.

Yvan's gaze focused on Antony's dramatic entrance.

Adolf slipped out of the door, with no one but Ana noticing his departure.

The sound of thunder echoed between the thick rock of the mountain's base and the stronghold's stones. Growing steadily.

"Choppers!" Antony whooped gleefully.

Yvan and Ulla exchanged confused glances.

"Where's Adolf?" Yvan demanded, moving around the table toward the door.

"I don't know. Grab the human. Magnus is coming for her," Ulla shouted.

"Yeah," Antony said. "And he's pissed."

"You saw him?" Ana gasped.

"I was with him when he found his father. The King is dying, Ana. I think he's going to rip these two apart when he finds them." His eyes glittered as he looked straight at Yvan. "Especially him."

"Why?" Ana asked, looking between Antony and Yvan, who stared back at him, color flushing his pale face.

"Who's she talking to?" Ulla demanded.

"The dead human who can't do anything to help her, or stop us."

"Oh yeah? I know the shaman you killed is keeping the king alive, and he'd kick your ass himself for violating their sacred culture."

"They killed the shaman?" Ana's voice rose with her shock.

"Yvan, I told you to grab her; take her to the hall where we can display her when we catch Magnus," Ulla commanded.

Yvan grasped Ana's wrist, wrenching her forward.

"Ana, you have to escape. Bring a priest to the king's chambers so they can reverse the spell that's killing him before it's too—."

Yvan shouted several words in a language Ana couldn't understand, swiping his hand through the air in Antony's direction.

"Antony!" Ana screamed as he sailed through the air backwards, disappearing through the wall.

Yvan yanked on her arm. She resisted enough to draw back her free hand, and when he yanked again, she used the momentum to launch her fist into his face, cracking his nose.

Pain lanced through her knuckles and up her wrist, but she didn't stop striking the much larger man, despite his rock-like face breaking her hand.

Grunting, he grabbed her other arm, and she went at him with her feet like the little hellcat that Magnus had accused her of being.

"Subdue her, now!" Ulla shouted.

Yvan barked a few words as his clammy palm clamped on her forehead.

Ana collapsed as the world went white.

ADOLF DROVE THE SNOWMOBILE hard, pushing its engine as fast as it would go, as he raced back toward his compound at the northern edge of Barentia.

"No, no, no!" He screamed as a heavy transport helicopter buzzed overhead.

GPSA.

He cranked the engine harder, determined to get to his ships.

There's only one helicopter. I have an army of men with plenty of guns that will take care of those agents.

By the time he arrived at the water's edge, the helicopter hovered over his warehouse roof as black-clad agents dropped to the building below while taking fire.

Good. His men were doing their jobs.

Roaring drew his attention to the open landscape beyond the small marina, where an aurora of polar bears churned up snow and rock as they sped toward his facilities.

Panic rising, he glanced back toward his island compound across the water.

One ship had already left the small port. The other was gearing up its engine. It would keep going despite the raid, as instructed.

Adolf ran the snowmobile as close to the dock where his small watercraft awaited him. Jumping on board, he engaged the engine and steered it toward the departing ship. As he sped toward it, he sighted a second helicopter in the distance and assumed it was searching for the first ship.

Eyes on the sky as he sped toward the closer ship, he didn't notice the massive roll of ocean water until it was too late. Something large and gray barreled into his small boat, sending it flipping through the air.

Stunned, Adolf hit the water hard.

The shock of the cold water sent him to the surface, gasping for air. The large gray mass continued to circle him.

Not a shark or a whale.

He dropped below the waterline to see what blocked his path to escape.

He blinked. *What the fuck is that?*

He screamed ocean water as it turned and surged toward him, maw gaping, teeth extended.

He shifted instantly.

His slick body darted to the left, evading the jaws of the creature pursuing him. Extending one of his tentacles, he latched on to the back of the creature's neck with his suckers. Adolf ballooned the canopy of his body and enclosed his attacker's head so that it couldn't see. Wrapping the rest of his tentacles around its head and neck, he held on as it jerked left and right, trying to dislodge him.

Unable to, it swam toward the sound of the ship's motor, straight for the hull where a second creature similar in size but different in form appeared to push the ship's bow.

Fearing the creature would ram the ship head-first, which would crush Adolf, he let go.

The monster immediately twisted, though not before it impacted the ship, setting it to rocking.

By now, he understood these creatures were GPSA shifters intent on capturing his cargo.

Relieved that the ship didn't capsize, Adolf engaged his camouflage as he sank to the sea floor, creeping ever forward as fast as he dared, determined to catch the rudder and hide in a crevice. Even if they seized the ship, he could still escape.

A silver-scaled fish swam above him in the ship's wake. Adolf used it as cover until he made a dash for the gap between the rudder and the propeller and settled in the arch above the two, attaching every sucker, securing him to its surface.

The silver fish maintained its position, following the ship.

Suddenly, the propeller groaned to a stop. The ship continued to drift.

The distinct sounds of shouting and cheering echoed through the hull of the ship, amplified by the ocean surrounding it.

Adolf cursed that he'd lost another ship to the Global Paranormal Security Agency.

I can still escape.

A few moments later, a woman's voice traveled through the ocean water now that it was clear of the engine's vibrations.

"Okay Lirikai, track him, but don't eat him! Kane wants him alive."

Adolf did not know what that meant. He flattened himself against the rudder as much as his flexible body would allow.

The two larger creatures circled the ship in opposite rotations, capturing and rounding up Adolf's men as they jumped into the ocean to escape.

The silver-scaled fish drifted up to his level. From this angle, it was impossible to miss all of its razor-sharp teeth as it stared at him with hungry eyes.

His heart pounded as he considered his options, which were few. Very few.

A ghost-like figure drifted in next to the fish and grinned. "Gotcha. Go ahead, try to ink us, you little bastard, I dare you. She's hungry. *Really* hungry."

TWENTY-SIX

MAGNUS RAN INTO THE great hall, toward the door that opened to the meeting room, where Ana had been detained. A cluster of guards held fast, blocking the door with angled spears.

He stopped, spun around and moved further down the length of the great hall toward his father's throne.

As he'd expected, guards converged on his location and surrounded him in a semi-circle with the stone wall at his back.

I don't have time for this. They've already hurt Ana. Gods only know what else they'll do to her.

His mind slid away from thoughts of Ulla's partners marking Ana with a sigil too.

No, I won't allow that to happen.

But first, despite knowing his case was a lost cause, he had to reason with his kinsmen.

His father's castle guard spread out around him, every one of them grim-faced, fists tightening on spears, swords or other preferred dangerous weapons from ancient times.

"You don't have to do this." he said, loud and clear.

"Magnus, don't make this harder for us than it already is," Jan, Magnus' second cousin, said. "There is no joy in seeing you fallen so low, but our orders are clear. We must detain you by command of the king's edict, preceding your execution."

"Your king is under a spell and dying in his rooms at this moment." Magnus held his gaze, then looked into the eyes of the other men facing him.

"Ridiculous," someone to his right scoffed.

"Have you not noticed that your commander has a black sigil tattooed on his throat? That is not a Barentian rank symbol. It is a distorted emblem used to control him. My father—your King bears an identical one. As he fights its effects, it drains the life from him."

"Lies," another said, raising his weapon higher.

"You've all known me my entire life. Have you ever known me to lie?"

"Things have changed in the last decade, Magnus. As have you."

"I have," he conceded. "And you're right, things have changed a lot here. New humans roaming the island. Some sort of base set up on the farthest island of our archipelago, run by more humans, no doubt."

"The king allows it."

Magnus nodded. There was no denying that. "But why? And who among the Barentians have access to it? Any? I wager not."

"Mistress Ulla frequently visits the place."

"I'm sure she does." Magnus smirked.

"What are you saying, banished? Are you trying to sway us against your father and ex-wife? We understand your bitterness and jealousy in such a loss of pride. We understand your desire for revenge."

"That's not what this is," Magnus growled.

They were easing closer to him as they spoke, tightening the space.

Despite their weapons, he could take down about half of them in his polar bear form—if he acted fast.

Although determined to fulfill their duty, they didn't want to hurt him anymore than he wanted to injure them.

"Tell us then, Magnus. What is this? What do you hope to accomplish here?" Jan's voice was soft, leaning on their personal history as Magnus had hoped to do earlier.

Jaw clenched, he stepped back, heel striking stone.

The guards moved in closer. Their expressions didn't give away their nervousness, but he scented it.

He was bigger than they were and a fierce fighter. Men were going to get hurt if he resisted. They knew it. He knew it.

"I'm ensuring my son still has a Barentia to rule when my father is gone."

Some men registered surprise. They'd expected him to declare the throne for himself.

It was all he needed.

He shifted in a blink, swiped out with a great paw. Then the other, sending his kinsmen spinning in opposing directions before any reacted. Bracing a foot against the stone wall behind him, he launched himself forward, bowling some of the rest to the floor as he ran like a freight train over them, snapping bones as he went.

Several recovered from their shock, and abandoned their weapons to shift and give chase.

Magnus charged through the castle now. Alert guards, still in human form, moved along the narrow staircases and halls to intercept him on his way to his father's room.

As he ascended to a secondary landing, someone threw a spear. Its aim true, it embedded in his flank, causing him to stumble. He roared against the pain, dislodged it with a swipe and kept going. Blood flowed down through his fur, leaving splotching prints as he ran.

"Don't let him get anywhere near the king's chamber!" someone shouted.

Two bears blocked the hall. He knew them. He knew all of them. There wasn't a single bear on this island that he didn't.

He drew a deep breath, sprinted forward and lowered his head, aiming for the narrow space between them. The impact sent them crunching into the stone walls on either side. Pain wrenched Magnus' shoulder from the impact and the rending of flesh as one clawed at him to stop him. But they couldn't.

They wouldn't.

He knocked aside two more guards posted outside the antechamber to his father's quarters and slammed into the solid oak door. It gave way on the fourth hit, splintering inward, its pieces shattering against the interior walls. As the door gave, Ulla and Putinovski, with Ana draped across his arms, appeared from the opposite side of the antechamber, then ran into his father's room.

"Havard, defend your King with your life. Magnus is here to take the throne!" Ulla screamed before slamming the bedroom door closed.

The iron lock clicked into place as Magnus and Havard stared at one another. Magnus' sides heaved from the exertion of the run, the spear wound and damaged shoulder.

He already filled most of the small room. When Havard took his bear form, there wouldn't be enough space for two grappling bears.

Things were about to get messy.

And Ulla had just commanded him to fight to the death if necessary.

Given that she had just locked herself in his dying father's room with his vulnerable mate, Magnus was no longer sure he could afford the luxury of preserving Havard's life if he couldn't subdue him quickly.

Havard became his bear. Smaller than Magnus, but no less dangerous as he launched forward, jaws snapping at Magnus' face.

He jerked backward in time to avoid the sharp teeth, stumbling on the solid wood furniture tumbling under foot.

Under Havard's relentless offensive, Magnus swiped and batted away his face and claws again and again.

Tired and frustrated, Magnus rose on his hind legs and pounded Havard with his front paws, sending him flying into the opposite wall with a deafening crack.

Magnus roared at him to stay back.

Havard, dazed, stumbled to raise himself on all fours, shaking his head to clear it. He tottered for a moment, struggling to hold his balance.

Magnus dropped to plant his feet, preparing to either charge or divert Havard's attack when it came.

Both polar bears gripped their claws into the fine edges of the stone that made up the floor.

A roar from somewhere downstairs resounded throughout the castle, drawing Magnus' attention.

Elias!

No!

Magnus turned back in time to see Havard launch his entire body forward, jaw angled for his throat.

Pain shot through Magnus' neck muscles as Havard's teeth tore through the flesh and gripped him so hard, he inhibited his airflow.

Havard had him.

Havard tugged and slammed Magnus' head back against the stone wall.

Warm blood trickled down his back from the base of his skull to join the seeping gash across his shoulder. The blood flow from his haunch continued.

The roar resounded again, louder, closer.

Elias, putting himself in danger.

Ana could already be dead just beyond that door.

Deprived of air and weakened from loss of blood, his vision of the room narrowed, hazy and growing dark.

Magnus received the full force of Elias' third roar into Havard's face as he tightened his death grip on Magnus' throat.

The room went dark as Magnus sagged.

"Release him!" Elias' clear voice commanded. "Now!"

Havard growled, intent on fulfilling his duty.

"If my grandfather is dead, then I am your King. I command you to release your hold," he shouted, switching tactics.

Magnus' would have smiled if he could.

But he couldn't.

He drifted in the silence of the void.

I'M DEAD.

Nothing but blinding white light surrounded Analiese Maria Marguerita Francesca Ortega.

Her entire body tingled like she was wrapped in energized, raw cotton fluff.

"You're not dead. At least I don't think so," Antony's voice filled her head.

"Where are you?"

"I'm here, Ana, but you're encased in something… well, part of you is encased in something. Like Sascha was when she bilocated. Your body is unconscious and in the king's room."

She extended her hands. "I don't feel anything."

"I know you said you needed a priest, but Ana is the next best thing. If we can wake her up."

"Who are you talking to?"

"The shaman. He's not happy all these outsiders are invading the king's room."

"I'll bet," she murmured, turning in place, trying to discern something, anything that wasn't just more white space. Or cotton fluff. Or cloud haze—whatever *this* was. This certainly wasn't the same place Aksel was trapped in.

"The king is still alive, Ana, but just barely. The shaman is using his energy to keep him stable despite his resistance to the sigil."

"Is he in danger?" She peered in the distance, blinking. White on white movement. She drifted toward it.

"Not just yet. The bear woman and the magician are arguing over what to do while Magnus is fighting his way through the castle."

"Magnus?"

"Yeah, my god Ana, you picked a big bastard! I've never seen such an enormous bear in my life."

"Antony, you're a sailor. Have you ever seen *any* bears in your life?" she said, squinting into the light as the shape took form.

"That's besides the point. He's easily bigger than every other bear here. Anyway, we have to figure something out while this woman bear has her knickers in a panicked twist and is taking the other guy with her. Before they do something stupid."

"Okay," she murmured, full attention on the rounded figure that continued to move away.

"Okay? Listen to me. We can't break you out of this thing. It's hard as marble. You need to find a way out of it yourself."

"Oh, it's a bear!"

"What? Ana, are you listening to me?"

"Yeah, Antony, you can't break me out. There's a bear here. A white one. I feel like I should see where it goes."

She dimly registered a roar in the distance. But it wasn't coming from the white bear in her cotton fluff. It turned to look at her as she drew nearer. Its black eyes and nose were stark and glossy against the mass of white fur.

More roaring in the distance.

Ana was unconcerned.

Antony's insistent voice grew fainter as she followed the pristine polar bear away from all the noise.

A brush against her wrist drew her attention. Raising her hand, she stared at the garnet rosary her grandmother had insisted she keep. From it dangled both the crucifix and the carved polar bear the priestess had gifted her.

'When the light is blinding, the bear will guide you.' she'd said.

"Huh. Well, I'd say the light is blinding."

As she followed the bear, the quality of the light changed, allowing a bit of gray into the mass. Visible color striations pointed the way along a tunnel like structure.

Antony said I wasn't dead, and yet here I am going down a tunnel away *from the light.*

She studied the bear as they went, wondering if she could communicate with it as she had with Aksel in the astral.

Color drifted through the structure, mingling to form new colors, then drifted apart again. Threads of black also streaked through the mix of color and white and gray.

The bear stopped at a convergence in the tunnel where it branched off in several directions. The tingling she'd experienced in the white area intensified here, vibrating through her every particle, strongest along the center of her body from the crown of her head down to her pubic bone, reminding her of the Chakra diagram Jack had told her to memorize. Seven in all, with different functions and associated colors. Colors like those wisping through the mass surrounding her and the bear.

Ana turned toward the tunnel with more violet than any other color and stepped toward it.

The bear growled.

Ana blinked, returning her gaze to her guide. "Okay, not that way. Sorry." She turned her back on the attractive tunnel—and all the others drawing her attention—to focus on her designated direction.

The bear ambled down a greenish tunnel, which opened into a domed room. Not quite a dome, no... Ana squinted up into the ceiling. It was the roof of a cave covered in aurora borealis.

"So beautiful," she whispered, following the bear around a massive stalagmite. "But why am I here? What do I need to do?"

Beyond the stalagmite slumped a figure on the floor.

"Magnus!" Ana gasped, bringing her hands to her mouth.

Unconscious, he was naked and bleeding.

"Is he dying?" She rushed forward. She crouched, placing her hands on his face.

Next to her, the bear peered into his face, its expression so very sad.

"What do I do?"

The bear pressed its nose to Magnus' breastbone then poked Ana in the same place, shocking her by the gesture and the electric sensation. Her hand drifted to her chest.

Her heart.

Magnus' heart.

Her throat tightened. Instinct told her what the bear wanted her to do, but she couldn't form the words in her head.

Overhead, the lights shimmered green and blue.

Looking at the bear, she said, "I'm not sure I understand, but I'll try." The bear huffed and nudged her forward.

Ana straddled Magnus' thighs and sank to her knees.

Despite his weakened state, he radiated warmth.

With all her strength, she hooked her arms under his, leaning him toward her, chest to chest.

Heart to heart.

She closed her eyes. Listening to the beat of his heart and the beat of her heart.

In the magic of this place, it seemed to echo around them as they synced into a single beat.

Thoughts of one another had guided them together like a single pulsing polestar.

His hands slid around her waist and up her back as he nuzzled her shoulder. "Ana," his voice was hoarse as his arms crushed her to him. "I thought I'd lost you forever."

Enveloped in his embrace, she sank into him, eyes closed. "Not a chance, when you only just found me."

He pulled away just enough to look into her face.

It felt like a mile between them.

"What you said in the registrar's office?"

Mate.

"That I choose you?"

He nodded.

Emotion swelled her heart, making her throat constrict and her eyes tear up as her heart opened, responding to Magnus.

Love.

Acceptance.

That's all she'd ever wanted in her life, though she'd spent most of her time trying to bury that unrealistic longing.

In this place, somewhere outside of the reality they lived in, everything she felt was real. Everything that was in her heart, was real. It was all that mattered.

"For all time, Magnus." She took up his large hand and pressed his palm to her heart, and whispered. "For *all* time."

He pressed her palm first to his nose and lips, inhaling her scent, then to his heart, echoing her words. "I choose you for all time, Ana."

She brushed the tip of her nose across his.

He brushed his lips across hers.

They released each other's hands, and she reached for his face to deepen their kiss, while his arms wrapped around her waist and hips, pulling her impossibly close. He was naked beneath her, and his arousal was unmistakable.

She broke the kiss with a gasp, "Magnus, we're not alone—." Looking around the cave, the bear was gone.

They were indeed alone.

She looked into his eyes.

"Mate," she whispered. Instinct told her that this would be more binding than anything she'd ever committed to in her life.

"Do you want to finish this?"

"I want nothing more than to finish this," she said, quickly removing her clothes as a sense of impending urgency took over.

Undressing, here, was an act of deliberation in a place where they didn't actually have physical bodies.

They were all energy, co-mingling in this astral place—wherever it was.

All sensation and knowing and needing.

She resumed her place, straddling his thighs.

He slid an arm around her hips, pulling her close so that he could trail his lips over her heart.

She shuddered against the overwhelming sensation of emotion his tenderness elicited in her.

She slid her fiery core along his steely erection, then angled her hips so that his tip waited at her entrance.

Magnus claimed her lips, swiping his tongue along hers, teasing and enticing.

She moaned as need spiked through her. A need only Magnus could fulfill.

Ready, she drew him in, easing down his length.

Their breaths mingled as he filled her so that his tip rested against her sweet spot. Her toes curled against the intense pleasure.

Magnus grazed his teeth along the column of her throat, inhaling her scent and nibbling the tender skin until he reached the crook of her shoulder. With his forearm still encircling her hips, he pressed her down even further.

His breath hitched as he pulsed inside her.

She moaned his name as her hips tilted forward, then slid back.

Leaning against the support of his arm, she arched so that he had access to her breasts. As his mouth fastened on first one nipple and then the other, she rode him faster, harder still.

Magnus looked up into her face, reflecting her passion as they ascended.

He licked his lips. "You're sure, Ana? About the mating? It'll probably hurt."

As she looked into his eyes and saw her own vulnerability, she slowed her pace, rolling her hips.

She'd said forever, and that's what a mating was.

She'd spent enough time around shifters to understand that much, regardless of the mechanics.

"Yes," she breathed as her desire continued to ascend. "Yes, Magnus, I'm sure."

"Gods, I'll never get enough of you, Ana."

Tears gathered as her heart soared, opening to him. Those words sent her over the edge.

Too much.

"Magnus!" she warned; the colors in the room converged around them as she exploded. As her climax took her over, she gripped him, determined to take him with her.

Pain shot through the muscle at the crook of her shoulder. She dimly realized Magnus bit her as he joined her. It did nothing to detract from the rolling waves of ecstasy crashing through her.

TWENTY-SEVEN

"ANA! CAN YOU HEAR me, Ana?" Antony's voice boomed through Ana's consciousness.

"Yes, stop shouting." She groaned as energy continued to thrum through her while her shoulder throbbed with discomfort. She was back in the white space, the cave of coalescing colors nowhere to be seen.

This time, the texture to the place was different.

Internally, she felt different. The weight—no, the closedness—of her heart had lessened. Like her protective walls had crumbled away. It felt more open. Raw. Free.

"Ah thank God. I thought I'd lost you there for a minute."

"Only a minute?" She reached out, touching the film surrounding her.

I thought it was more like thirty...

"Yeah, you were talking about a bear, then just went quiet for a minute. I was freaking out here."

"Sorry," she murmured, fingers scratching at the film she'd been unable to see before, and pushed with her fingertip. It gave way like a dusty web coating an abandoned doorway.

Swiping at the clingy stuff, she cleared the way to step through into a room she'd never seen before, but instantly knew was the king's chamber.

And it was a busy place as she took in her new surroundings.

Antony stood to her immediate left, expression drawn in worry as he looked her over. At her feet lay her body, eyes closed and pale.

Across from her body, she faced another mirror aspect of herself, which sent a shiver through her.

This is too weird. I really need to wake up.

You can't wake up yet, she said. Her other *self* pointed to an old man standing by the king's bedside.

The shaman.

He needs you to break the spell before the king dies.

Shouting drew Ana's focus to the other side of the room, where Elias stood inside the doorway facing his mother and her companion. Magnus lay unconscious at their feet, a blanket draped over him.

"That human needs to be imprisoned," Ulla Matochkin said to the guards beyond the room as she pointed at Ana's inert body on the floor. "We stopped her from assassinating the king for Magnus."

Ana laughed at the ridiculous accusation, drawing Yvan's attention.

He opened his mouth to speak when the shaman suddenly appeared in front of him. "Filth! Despoiler!"

Yvan grinned at the old man.

"What is so funny?" Elias demanded of the magician. "My grandfather is nearly dead, and my home is in chaos."

"Nothing, your highness," Yvan said to the prince, checking himself.

It must be done now, before it's too late. Ana's other *self,* pleaded with her. *I will help bridge you.*

"Shaman," Ana said, drawing the old man's attention. "I think I can help you."

With a final scowl at Yvan, he blinked forward, peering into Ana's face. She had no idea what he saw, but after a moment he searched the room, his gaze stopping at her twin before he nodded.

"What's going on?" Antony asked her.

"Seems my other *self* over there insists we can help the Shaman."

"Other self?" his eyes widened, looking around the room.

"You can't see her? The shaman can."

Yvan, watching the exchange, blanched. Again, he opened his mouth, lifting his hand toward Ana's body. He shouted two words when he was interrupted.

"Stop!" Elias commanded; eyes narrowed on the man with disgust. "There will be no conjuring in this room."

Ana's other *self* stepped forward, reaching out her hands toward Ana and the Shaman.

The shaman placed his hand in hers. Ana hesitated, looked up into the old man's eyes, and touched the proffered hand.

So many things happened all at once and none of them eased the uncomfortable sensations roiling through her body.

Yes, her body. The hard floor was distinct below her, the painted ceiling above her was breathtakingly beautiful and Antony's face was far too close to hers. Her hand lifted, shoving him away, but she wasn't controlling it or the rest of her as she struggled to her feet, head swimming.

God, I feel like I'm going to puke.

She reached for her head, but the other force occupying her body forced it away as her feet stomped her toward the king's bed.

"What's happening? What's wrong with her?" Elias demanded, eyes wide.

"Silence, young man!" The shaman barked through Ana's vocal chords.

Ana cringed, almost dislodging herself from her body.

Don't! Her other *Self* warned, also from within. *You agreed to do this. If you retract your will, the shaman won't be able to save the king or break the sigils.*

From the other side of the room Magnus groaned as he regained consciousness.

"Father!" Elias said, crouching down beside him.

"What's happening?" he rasped, rubbing his throat where Havard had nearly strangled him to death.

"I'm not sure, but I think your Ana is channeling the shaman."

The sensation of the shaman's being occupying her body wigged her out. "Antony, this feels so weird," she said as he stepped into the space beside her. She continued to resist the urge to shake the old man out as their beings seemed to vie for space, slipping against one another while trying not to force the other out.

Relax.

She tried. Truly she tried.

While she focused on that, the shaman continued his work.

"You don't know what she's doing. Why would she be channeling your dead shaman? She could be trying to finish what she started to ensure the king's demise," Yvan protested.

Elias moved so that he faced Yvan, scowling up into his face. "I know my shaman's voice when I hear it. Do not interfere."

Magnus stumbled to his feet. "He's worried that Ana and the Shaman will break his spell, releasing the control he and Wulker have over their victims. Including Aksel." He directed the last words at Ulla.

"Don't listen to his lies, Ulla. We'd never—*I'd* never do such a thing."

Ulla moved next to her son, holding Yvan's gaze. "Wouldn't you?"

Ana couldn't maintain her focus on the exchange any longer. Whatever the shaman was doing, he pulled her into it.

The old man chanted a Barentian song, hands extended over the King's head and torso. His soul's force drew power up through the soles of her feet, along her legs and into her heart where it churned around and around, making her feel like she had awe-inspiring heartburn.

The power gathering, combining with the emotion in her physical body, made her shake and tremble with possibility.

She was an open conduit to the Shaman's will as he pulled what he needed from the surrounding earth to boost the king's soul energy and keep him alive.

Next, Ana felt as though the shaman jack-knifed the power, swinging an extended right arm in Yvan's direction.

Hold on! Ana's other *self*—her *Higher Self* yelled as her grasp on Ana's and the Shaman's spirits tightened.

Yvan lurched toward the Shaman, chest first, as though dragged closer.

The tenor of the words changed as the Shaman's left hand hovered an inch above the black ink sigil marring his king's throat.

Yvan struggled against the invisible grip, grunting and crying out as though the Shaman was clawing something out of him.

The inked sigil appeared to burn off in layers until it streamed away, soaking into the king's pillow, leaving his skin clear again.

Once the sigil was gone from beneath the shaman's right hand, he swung it too, in Yvan's direction, an inch from his throat now. Chest arched out, throat pressed in, he struggled on tiptoe against the shaman's power, gasping.

"No. No. No!"

"You wish to steal and defile our sacred magics?" The shaman growled at the human magician.

Now, the energy of the Shaman's bear surged forward, snapping at Yvan with vengeance.

Its energy threatened to overpower Ana. Had it not been for the hold her *Higher Self* maintained on her, rooting her in her body as the Shaman exacted justice, she would have been consumed by it.

Ana snarled in Yvan's face as her fingers curled into claws, as though she held his heart in one hand, his throat in the other. She felt the rapid beat of his heart against her palm, the gush of air through his windpipe at her fingertips.

From her left palm, energy, white and hot, seared the skin of Yvan's throat. By the time she was done—the shaman was done. It scarred him with the same sigil, without the ink.

Instead of the octopus shifter's venom fueling the curse, Yvan's own power looped back into it, binding his will, containing any magic he had within his own body.

Done. The Shaman released his hold.

Yvan dropped to the floor at Ana's feet.

The room was silent except for her panting.

"Havard!" a guard outside the room shouted at the sound of another body dropping to the floor.

The shaman turned toward his king, and seeing that the king's breath came steady and strong in his still-unconscious state, he nodded, released his hold on Ana and stepped outside of her.

She collapsed to the floor.

"Oh god, I'm going to puke for real this time." She gagged, hand to her mouth, trying to contain herself.

Having tied the blanket around his hips, Magnus pulled Ana to her feet, crushing her to him. "What the fuck just happened?"

She couldn't draw enough breath to answer with her face mashed into his chest. Her arms encircled his waist, drawing comfort from his nearness.

The king groaned, and everyone turned their wide-eyed stares in his direction.

"Mngsf." Ana's muffled plea earned her instant release as Magnus peered down into her face.

His thumbs traced the bruises as he scowled. "I should rip them apart for this."

"Your highness, there are some outsiders requesting an audience in the great hall." A guard said, glancing between Elias and the King.

The king struggled to sit up.

Ulla rushed forward, "You shouldn't strain yourself—."

"Get away from me!" the king roared. To the same guard, he said, "Take this woman and detain her in her quarters. No one in or out until I decide what to do with her. And send someone to tend to our guests while I prepare."

"Yes, sir," the guard said, clearly shocked, as he reached for Ulla.

"Don't touch me!" she ripped her arm out of his grasp and marched out of the room. Yvan moved to follow her.

"Take that one downstairs with guards. If he tries to run away, maim him."

Ana scanned the room. Only the king, Magnus and the prince remained. The shaman and Antony looked on.

The shaman's curious stare made her uncomfortable. With a quick glance, she noticed that not only was her other *self* not visible, but that she felt solid. Whole in a way she never had before.

The shaman's wrinkled, tattooed faces split in a grin. "Even *more* enhanced human now."

She blinked, not understanding what that meant.

Beside her, Antony laughed.

"I'm going to check on my guys, Ana. I'll find you again soon." He was gone before she could respond.

She whispered to Magnus. "Should I wait outside while you talk to your father and son?"

"I'm going to hazard a guess that our outsider visitors belong to you." The king said to Ana and Magnus. "Am I right?" He turned to Elias.

Elias nodded. "Kane's team is here for you."

"Wulker?"

"They have him," Elias confirmed.

Tears sprang to Ana's eyes.

Magnus gripped her to him. "Then it's done."

She pulled away, smiling up into his face. "It's done."

He bent to press his lips to hers. "I will join you soon. Unless I'm to return to my cell." He glanced at the king over Ana's head.

"We have things to discuss," the king said, dismissing Ana.

Magnus nibbled her lips one final time, whispering, "I had one hell of a dream while I was unconscious."

Ana slipped out of his grasp, her fingers lingering in his as she moved toward the door. She slid her hand over the shoulder he'd bitten. "That wasn't a dream."

His eyes widened as she exited the room, closing the door behind her.

TWENTY-EIGHT

MAGNUS AND ELIAS HELPED the king dress.

He was weak from his long trial under the effects of the dark sigil.

"My old friend was keeping me alive from the otherworld," he'd said, matter of fact.

"I've no doubt. That was some dramatic possession he did of Father's mate. I've never seen anything like it," Elias said, awed, handing some of his grandfather's clothing to Magnus to dress in.

"Nor have I, and I certainly have no desire to see it again if I can help it," Magnus said, pulling on the trousers and shirt, happy to do away with the blanket.

The three men spoke with a hesitancy alien to each of them.

Three generations of polar bear royalty considered one another with uncertainty.

Finally, the king said to Magnus, "We will discuss our family matters at a later time. I revoke your banishment effective immediately. In the meantime, we must decide the fate of our prisoners." He placed a gentle hand on Elias' shoulder. "We will handle your mother's judgment ourselves. As a citizen of the polar bear community in Barentian territory."

"Before we go downstairs, I want to return something. It will only take a few minutes," Magnus said. Triggering the secret door, he slipped into the dark passageway to retrieve the objects he'd hidden there for safe-keeping.

As the bookshelf slid back into place, he handed the stone and the wrapped book to Bjorn. "I would have ensured that Elias received these if anything had happened."

Bjorn nodded, staring at the objects in his hands. "I know you would have." He unwrapped the book, smoothing a palm over the etched leather surface, then rolled the chunk of jet between his fingers.

"What are they?" Elias asked.

"These are the reason for our being here, Elias," Bjorn said, looking at Magnus. "The keys to something precious and sacred, and so dangerous we must protect it with our lives. They should have gone to your father for safekeeping on my death, along with the crown. But I know his destiny is elsewhere."

Magnus nodded. "It is. Since I'm no longer banished and intended for execution, I will continue to do all I can to uphold our family's duty from outside of Barentia."

Bjorn sighed. "We should have done things differently, perhaps."

"Perhaps. Or perhaps things went exactly as they were meant to."

Elias looked perplexed by the exchange.

"No matter, we have guests to see to." Bjorn laughed as he and Magnus replaced the items in their hiding places. "We will discuss these artifacts later."

Magnus opened the door to the antechamber to find the head guard still at his post.

Despite the other guards' insistence that Havard go to the infirmary, he stubbornly remained outside the King's chamber.

Battered and bruised from his battle with Magnus, who looked equally so, he also looked at the king with haunted eyes. "Sire, I—."

"I know," Bjorn Thornsson said to his chief guardsman.

It seemed to be enough.

Havard nodded his head and stepped aside to allow the King to continue on his way.

As they entered the throne room, the king signaled that they should move into the meeting room.

Relief flooded Magnus on seeing his entire team present, hale and whole. Ana laced her fingers through his as he stepped next to her.

Bjorn leveled his stern gaze on Magnus' team leader. "Kane. What do we have?"

"We have the suspect we've been seeking for over a decade in GPSA custody, thanks to your grandson and your people."

Bjorn raised a thick gray brow. "Explain."

Elias recounted his escape by boat and the call that brought Kane to the island. One transport helicopter went straight for the archipelago compound, while the other met with Elias and the Barentian villagers who had followed him in their fishing boats to Bear Island to ensure his safety. "As she flew us back, we saw the roving gangs engaging with the humans on this side of the channel. She refused to allow me to join them and brought me back here instead."

"As is right," Bjorn said.

"We've detained two ships, both bearing human cargo bound for the interior. Seems some of them were ready for us. They struck up a riot on our arrival."

"I didn't have to do much persuading," Raya said, grinning at Magnus. "Usually, I have to convince them I'm not a delusion, but these guys were eager."

"Naval crewmen?" Ana asked.

"Yeah."

"Emilio and the guys. They were Antony's men. From his ship when the accident happened."

Kane nodded. "We will contact the Navy."

"I want to know more about these outsiders that my daughter-in-law brought to my court. Her deception was great and deeply damaging. I know anything she confesses to will be shaded with denials and lies. She said one was her pet illusionist from her father's court and the other a business connection, also through her father's court."

"As far as we've been able to discover, that is true. But I also believe both men were members of *The Consortium*."

Magnus flinched as his father growled, turning away.

The Consortium.

And the human trafficking ring.

The two topics that had sundered his family.

"Wulker used his corporation to mask and grow his trafficking business. Ulla Matochkin gave him the protected base of operations he needed to function outside of international law. In your sovereign territory."

Bjorn's jaw worked as he listened, eyes glinting. He didn't interrupt.

Kane continued. "As for Yvan Putinovski." She shrugged. "My Deputy Director, Jack Maeda, has been studying the nature of the sigils used. They used Wulker's venom to create the sigil. But until we interrogate him, I can only theorize that his motive was access to your gate."

Bjorn went rigid, his gaze darting to the faces of Magnus' team.

"They're all trustworthy," Kane assured him.

The king turned his focus to Magnus.

Magnus nodded. "We're all dedicated to opposing *The Consortium.* And protecting this gate, as well as the others."

"Others? You've found them?"

"Not yet," Kane said quickly. "We're close to discovering the location of one, but it's painstaking work." The weariness in her demeanor was obvious despite her centuries of dedication. "With your permission, King Bjorn Thornsson, on behalf of the Global Paranormal Security Agency, we will remove the ships, perpetrators and all of their assets from your islands."

"Hm," he grunted, pursing his lips. "We will handle Ulla Matochkin ourselves."

"Thank you. And our GPSA medics report that Aksel Matochkin is awake and free of the same sigil. We will remand him into your custody as soon as he is well enough to travel."

Bjorn's brows rose. "I see. Good."

They said their goodbyes to the Barentians and made their way out to the transport helicopter, waiting to fly them to the trafficking compound.

On arriving, Kane went inside the main building to meet with the lead of the forensics crew.

Magnus and Ana hung back, staring at the place. Carson, Lirikai, Aaron, Raya, and Ian joined them. Perpetrators were clustered in one area with their wrists bound behind them, while victims gathered in another as GPSA prepared to transport them out of Barentian territory for the next steps.

"We did it," Carson said, shoulders relaxed.

"Now we can enjoy that vacation that keeps getting interrupted," Lirikai said, slipping her arm around Carson's waist.

He squeezed her to him, then looked at the rest of his team. "Vacation at my place?"

"I've never seen your island. As long as it's some place warm, I'm happy to crash," Ana grinned, her excitement clear.

Fingers linked, Raya looked up at Ian's quirked smile and said, "We'd be happy to join you."

"Perfect. Bring your apron, Ian. You're making us all scones." Mischief glinted in Carson's eyes. "Aaron?"

"I have some family matters I need to attend to back in Toronto, but yeah, I'll join for a few days."

"Awesome. We'll sort out the details later. Back to work, folks!" Carson tilted his head toward the activity and strode toward it. The others followed.

Ana pulled Magnus' fingers, hanging back.

He looked down into her concerned face and brushed his fingers over her creased brow, then along the discolored skin of her cheek and throat.

"This case ended, as I knew it would. Just not how I expected it should."

The corner of her mouth lifted. "Same here. I expected to be in Iceland."

"Disappointed? We could go there if you wish—."

Her forefinger shot up, pressing his lips together. "Hush! I wish for no such thing. I've had more than enough snow and ice and sub-zero temperatures for a lifetime."

He frowned as his heart sank. "You won't come back to Barentia?"

She searched his face and smiled. "I will. I recall you said you wanted many children. If we are so blessed, we will have to register them, won't we?"

He nodded as his heart buoyed again. "We will."

"Come on, you two, we have work to do," Carson called, hands cupped around his mouth.

Ana sighed. "I love him, I do..."

"Do you now?" Magnus lifted a brow.

"I do but not as much as I love you, I think." She poked his chest.

He threw his head back and laughed at the sky as he squeezed her close. "She thinks."

Ana rose on tiptoe to kiss Magnus.

He met her smiling lips with unspoken promises of their future.

With a final nibble, she broke the kiss, squeezed his hand, and said, "Let's go. The man says we have work to do."

EPILOGUE

THE SUN BLAZED AND Analiese Ortega basked in it like a contented cat, eyes closed, face upturned, worshipping the heat.

Stretched out on a lounge chair on Carson Perenga's tropical island terrace, she enjoyed vacation time with her GPSA teammates.

Carson's voice carried across the open space. "News from Pia Jensen."

Ana turned her head toward the sound of his voice without opening her eyes.

"I called to give her the news that we closed the case, since she helped us out in Montreal, which she was incredibly pleased about and sends her congratulations along with an open invitation to her wedding next summer."

Ana smiled, pleased by the news. The panther shifter was an excellent agent and deserved happiness.

"So, she and Renni Diaz decided to make it official. Good for them," Ian said with a grin. "Silky soccer skills, that one."

"Yeah, he's a good guy," Carson said.

Ana turned her attention away from the direction of their conversation as they continued talking about Renni Diaz's soccer career and the signed jersey he sent to Ian at Carson's request.

She sighed and adjusted her posture under her beloved sunshine.

A shadow loomed over her, interrupting her sunbathing.

She cracked an eye open to find Magnus' head blocking her heat source. "You look like a sun god with all that glowing blond hair flowing around your shoulders," she murmured, accepting the sweating glass of iced tea he'd brought her.

"And you're my bronzed goddess." He leaned down to kiss her before claiming the adjacent lounge chair. "How's your shoulder?" He reached out, grazing his fingers over the healing wound he'd inflicted while in the astral realm.

"It's fine, for the hundredth time."

"I still can't believe that was real."

"Any regrets?"

He scowled at her. "You know there aren't." His lips compressed as he sighed.

It was obvious to her that he wanted to say or ask her something.

She sat up, worried. "I've never seen you so hesitant. What is it, Magnus?"

He reached toward her again, his fingers trailing along her bare shoulder next to her bikini halter strap, and cleared his throat. "It's Barentian tradition for a priest or priestess to perform ritual body art on a mating mark. In our case, a shaman would do it."

"Oh," she said, rubbing a hand over her bare shoulder. She caught his fingers and squeezed, seeing how important the matter was to him. She dropped her gaze to his collection of beautifully drawn tattoos adorning his body. "And you think that would be... acceptable? For me to have such an honor?"

"If you like the idea..." he hedged.

"I do."

"Then yes, I do think it's acceptable. And I'd be honored that you would consider doing this."

Ana stood from her lounge chair and slid onto Magnus' lap, running her fingers through his loose hair. "Aside from the fact I'd do anything for you, I think it's a beautiful honor and look forward to having my first piece of body art created by a Barentian priest. How much more meaningful could that be?"

He cupped her face and claimed her mouth, expressing how important her acceptance of the matter was to him.

"We should go to our room," she murmured against his lips.

"We should." His muscles tensed to stand.

"We got a hit!" Joey Kane said from somewhere behind Ana, excitement in her voice.

Magnus rested his forehead against Ana's with a sigh, remaining as they were, but turned to give Kane their attention.

With her phone held aloft, Kane strode across the terrace, her swimsuit cover-up flowing around her slim legs.

"We've got a lead on a location for another gate!" she said again, eyes sparkling.

Ana smiled at her intense excitement. "That's great news, Joey."

"I've never seen her so animated," Magnus whispered. "And I've known Joey for a very long time."

Kane beamed. "Aaron called me with the information. I'm leaving in the morning to meet with him. When your time off is done, we'll convene and plan the next steps."

Ana breathed a sigh of relief and laughed. "I was worried you were going to send us all back this afternoon."

"Don't tempt me, Ortega," Kane said with a wink as she maintained her energetic stride and skipped back up the steps toward Carson's house, where Lirikai joined her.

"Let's go before anyone else has an announcement." Magnus set Ana on her feet, grabbed her hand, and tugged her toward the house.

Ana giggled, practically running to keep up with Magnus' long strides.

"Ana!" Raya called. "Ian's making scones soon if you want to join?"

"Not now!" Magnus growled, heading straight for their room.

"Maybe later," Ana called, laughing as she flew down the hall in Magnus' wake.

Pulling her into the room, he slammed the door shut and reached for Ana, intent on claiming her lips.

Magnus swooped her up into his arms, carried her to the bed, and lay her down without breaking the kiss. He pressed his body into hers and she wriggled beneath him, aligning his erection to her hot center.

Ana wrapped her legs around his clothed hips, drawing him closer.

His palm smoothed down her chest, over a breast, and continued on down her flat stomach. As his fingers hooked and tugged the band of her bikini bottom, his mouth slid along the same path, before finding her bellybutton.

"I'm going to worship you, Ana. Every inch." He nibbled the tender flesh just above her bikini band.

"If you insist," she moaned as his lips traveled lower, causing her to arch against him. "If you insist."

Please consider leaving a review of The Aquatic Investigations trilogy on your favorite platform.

Read more GPSA...

PROWLER

Relationships seem impossible when your secrets can cost you everything.

As an undercover GPSA agent, love and lust are high stakes risks that Pia Jensen prefers to avoid. But once Pia catches Renni's irresistible scent, her lonely inner kitty goes on the prowl.

Superstar Renni Diaz is at the pinnacle of his career when a hot little traffic cop pulls him over for speeding. Unable to keep her out of his mind, he knows that he's scored his heart's desire... even when she moves the goal posts on him.

After their first inevitable kiss, their 'no strings attached' relationship has a sizzling, fast-paced start.

When Pia's secret, and Renni's past, collide, they spiral down a path that compels them to choose between their growing love and the lives they had.

Carson & Lirikal   Ian & Raya   Magnus & Ana   Renni & Pia

The Global Paranormal Security Agency

Read on for Chapter One of *Prowler*, a Global Paranormal Security Agency story...

PROWLER
CHAPTER ONE

Pia Jensen grunted as she thumbed past another text and tossed her phone on the passenger seat beside her.

Erin had just bailed on her, again.

Pia's squad lead, Tamara Cole, at the Global Paranormal Security Agency had encouraged her to integrate further with the Montreal police department she was embedded with, but she was only here for a couple more months, then she would be reassigned.

Mingle. Socialize. People.

The last year had been hard, and 'peopling' was very low on her list of priorities.

She missed her team. A team of kick-ass women GPSA agents. It was the one place where she'd finally felt like she belonged. And here, in Montreal, she was alone and still working solo. *Mostly* alone.

Her old friend and sometimes lover, Erin lived here but...she was busy with the chaos of running her club.

Pia sighed, swallowed some coffee from her favorite travel mug to lessen the sting, and acknowledged that this placement had been at her request.

For her dad.

She gulped more coffee, this time to bury the sharp rise of grief.

Her sensitive hearing picked up the growl of an expensive engine, gearing up. The speed radar triggered as a black sports car blew past her concealed location.

Time to go.

With a cursory glance for oncoming traffic, she threw the cruiser into drive, hit the gas, siren, and lights, speeding off in pursuit.

First thing in the morning, too.

These assholes in their tailored cars seemed to think speed limits were vague suggestions—simply inapplicable to them.

Probably another weasely twenty-seven-year-old living off Mummy and Daddy's millions.

Following the car as it rolled to a stop on the hard shoulder, she killed the siren, then called in the license plate. She left the cruiser lights in their loop as she exited the car.

Pia sighed, putting her bitch face on, mentally prepared for some bullshit as she strode alongside the F-Type Jaguar, resisting the urge to trail a finger along its sleek fender.

The window eased down and a darkly tanned hand with long fingers extended identification details. The arm was encased in a crisp gray suit sleeve with working buttons. The cuff obscured the edges of black ink on the man's skin. An Aikon glinted in the sunlight. Bergamot and black pepper tickled her sensitive nose as his aftershave, mingled with the undertone of his personal scent, drifted toward her on the morning breeze.

Human.

Her inner kitty's attention was piqued.

"Good morning, sir." Fingertips resting on her hips, she took the last step up to the window, ignoring the proffered identification. "Are you aware we have speed limits in this city?"

"Yes. I'm late for work." Shadows obscured the driver's profile, with his face turned away as he scrolled through messages on his phone.

She didn't miss the Spanish accent.

Pia's teeth ground. Arrogant prick wasn't even deigning to pay attention to her.

"Late for work or not, you were driving thirty kilometers over the limit for this zone. There are kids and seniors that have places to go, too," she said, doubting her point would have any affect.

He put his phone down and turned to look up at her.

Had she stopped breathing? Damn... *Damn*! She knew that face. It adorned a thirty-foot banner next to the front doors outside the local soccer stadium.

Renni 'The Pitch Prowler' Diaz.

Her stomach quivered.

The tickets in her locker at the station were for the derby that night. Both of Montreal's professional soccer teams would be going head-to-head. He was expected to appear on the starting line-up. The growing rivalry between the teams promised excitement on the field. She'd been looking forward to this game, all week.

And he was so *damned* hot.

She steeled herself against the fan girl excitement gathering in her stomach, threatening to erupt in a juvenile giggle.

Her eyes drank in the view for a moment. That mouth. She'd fantasized about those lips, many nights.

"Yeah, listen, I really am in a hurry after a meeting that ran late this morning. Can we just call it a warning and I'll be on my way? I promise to be mindful in the future," he said, tossing her a grin.

Pia straightened. "I see." Disappointment steamrolled her as she pulled her pen and pad from its place on her vest, taking her time. Plucking the cards from his still-extended hand, she began to fill out the speeding ticket.

"Do you like sports?" He turned his wrist, glancing at his watch. "I can get you tickets to tonight's soccer match. Bring a friend?"

Her eyes flicked up from her pad, just having written his name. Renni Diaz. His address told her he'd been coming from home, heading for the training facility. After being embedded with local law enforcement for the last year, she was getting to know the city districts well enough.

"Already going," she grunted.

"Ah wonderful. Perhaps we'll see each other later tonight." He let his gaze sweep her from head to hip, before resting on her face, brow quirking.

Was he seriously trying to flirt his way out of a ticket?

It wasn't like he couldn't afford to pay it...

Image.

Speeding tickets didn't look good on a high-profile personality's image.

She shrugged. Not her problem.

She finished writing up the ticket, handing it to him. "Good luck tonight." She turned, stepping toward her cruiser.

His fingers ghosted hers as he accepted the slip of paper. "Will I see you after the game..." He glanced at the ticket. "Constable Jensen?"

Glancing back, she quirked a brow, ignoring the shiver caused by his touch. "I will be joining some friends for drinks downtown."

If Erin didn't bail on that too.

He squinted at her, considering. "L'Auberge, Dominion or Chatton Noir?"

That was a pretty specific short list. "Chatton Noir," she said, surprised.

"I have friends on the force, too." He grinned again.

"Have a good day." She dismissed him, again turning toward her cruiser.

"I'll see you tonight," he said as he pulled away from the curb, resuming his drive. At the stop sign, he gunned the engine a couple of times, pulling her attention to see if he was going to speed away.

He didn't.

Instead, he waved and turned the corner.

Weird.

She dropped back into the driver's seat of her cruiser with a snort.

She couldn't help pondering the image he'd conjured of meeting her at the bar later.

Bullshit.

Too bad; it dulled the shine of her fantasy of him a little.

Except for how hot he was. So much better in person. And he smelled amazing.

A guy like that wasn't going to just show up at a pub looking for her.

With a grunt, she dismissed that train of thought and put her cruiser into gear.

Back to work.

READ MORE OF *PROWLER* AT:
https://jodikendrick.com/book/prowler/

Thank You!

Dear Reader,

Thank you so much for taking the time to read the Aquatic Investigations Trilogy. I hope you enjoyed it and are interested in reading more of my work.

Awakened and *Surfacing* were originally part of the **Aquaterrestrial Task Force** Series of Milly Taiden's *Federal Paranormal Unit* shared world published by MT Worlds Press.

Other Authors in this ATTF series are:

- Mandy Rosko: *GET KRAKEN*

- Renee Hewett: *THE WILL'OW RESCUE*

- TB Mann: *BULL PROTECTORS*

- Alexa Gregory: *THE KELPIE'S REDEMPTION*

I encourage you to read Milly's original FPU works as well as these awesome *Canadian* authors.

-Jodi

Jodi Kendrick

Jodi Kendrick lives in Eastern Ontario Canada with her *Favourite Person* and chompy furbaby, while their adult children explore the wider world.

As a romance author, she writes in paranormal, fantasy, steampunk & gaslamp subgenres, and sometimes delves into urban fantasy and paranormal women's fiction. Her characters are often quirky, sometimes cranky, but they all woman-up and get the job done while their partners ensure they survive with all their bits and bobs attached.

A history enthusiast and word dabbler most of her life, she enjoys exploring 'beyond-the-everyday' and the 'time-before-now', discovering relationship threads weaving individuals through time and place. She's rarely seen without flashy notebooks and colourful pens.

Follow Jodi on Social Media:

Dragon Island

Dragon Heat

Enchanted Ardor

Wish

EveL Worlds : FUCN'A

Tough Nut
Diamond in the Ruff
Honeyed Nut
Gorilla in the Hiss
FUCN'A Collection One
Pedigree Collection

Finely Aged

Dragon Steel

Global Paranormal Security Agency

Awakened
Surfacing
Polestar
Prowler

The Kindred Chronicles

Healer
Mercenary

The Soaring Dragon Chronicles

Return Flight
Changeling

www.ingramcontent.com/pod-product-compliance
Lightning Source LLC
Chambersburg PA
CBHW020822030726
47496CB00001B/53